I0621875

"Perception is reality... and reality be damned!"

Free
Enterprise

By the author of *Silent Option* and *Broken Seals*.

Opium Lysergic Acid Diethyl amide *Heroin* $C_{21} H_{23} NO_5$

Amphetamine

Marijuana

Designer Drugs
Hashish MPPP

Mescaline

MPTP

Peyote DMT

Psilocybin

Morphine **PCP**

$C_{17}H_{19}NO_3$ THC **LSD**

Aculllcu DET

Quaalude

Methadone

Cocaine **Bazuko**

$C_{21}H_{21}NO_4$

Larry Simmons
Former Commander of Seal Team Five

THIS BOOK IS A WORK OF FICTION

Neither the action events nor the characters described in this novel reflect any actual incidents or portray any real persons. The names of some public figures have been used in passing to fix the time and locale of the story, but they are not characters in the novel.

Simmons International Consulting Group
Copyright © 2013 by Larry Simmons

ISBN-13: 978-0983875666
ISBN-10: 0983875669
First printing: Amazon-Createspace
Printed in the U.S.A.

Larry Simmons

The *Red Menace* is no more. Today, a *White Menace* infects us like a plague, leaving behind a manmade disaster of shattered lives, street gang violence, and crack addicted babies. Men fight and die in heroic effort to stop this scourge. Billions of dollars have been committed to the cause. But remember this the next time a slick-talking politician tells you we are winning the *war on drugs*. In the early 1980's cocaine sold for as much as $50,000 a kilo. Since then the price has dropped to as low as $8,000, proof that despite our best efforts the supply of cocaine has increased. ***Demand* powers Cocaine Inc. and Heroin Incorporated. The real drug kingpins are drug users.**

"Commander, you cannot imagine the misery this drug will cause if this formula is made available to the streets," the caller pleaded, appealing to Evans's sense of patriotism. "It will literally change mankind as we know it."

"You know something, whoever-you-are?" Evans growled.

"What?"

"I don't like this secret squirrel bullshit."

"We invaded this country and arrested people?" Masure asked, incredulously.

"Yeap. It made a blip on the international news, but not much. Operation Blast Furnace was designed to strike a mortal blow at Bolivia's drug traffickers. But you know the deal. Conceived by DEA bureaucrats. Planned by Pentagon bureaucrats. Executed by an army dominated SPECOPS community."

"Let me guess. It amounted to swatting mosquitoes with a sledgehammer and the skeeters weren't at home?"

"You broke the code," Evans said.

"*Manos arriba!*"

The two drunken youths jumped out of the paste pit like frightened jackrabbits and bolted for the jungle. The first one to make it to the bushes ran face first into a rifle butt. The force of the blow knocked him to the ground. He rolled around in the dirt, half-conscious, moaning in pain. The second dancer threw up his hands and began begging for his life. "Don't kill me! Please, don't kill me!"

The soldiers dragged them back to camp like a pair of scruffy dogs.

"Leopards, please don't kill us!" the old man begged. "Please don't kill us. We are just poor campesinos trying to make an honest living."

"Making coca paste is against the law, *viejo*," Miamani replied. "That's not honest. You know that."

"But we have to eat," the old woman cried.

----- About the Author -----

Larry Simmons entered the naval service in 1966 and rose through the ranks of the US Navy Seals from seaman to commander. The Seals are a special operations force whose missions include counterterrorism and other high-risk operations. Larry deployed to Vietnam as a member of Seal Team TWO and served in operational billets from Vietnam to commanding officer of Seal Team FIVE in Coronado in 1993. A graduate of Ohio State University, he has a Master of Science in Operations Research from the Naval Postgraduate School in Monterey, California and a Master of Science in Education from National University in San Diego, California. Commander Simmons is a Master Training Specialist and is still teaching men to move, shoot, and communicate. After retiring from the service he served in Saudi Arabia training a maritime special operations force, in Mexico as Regional Director to an organization specializing in kidnap recovery for fortune five hundred companies and in the Middle East, as Project Manager for KBR and as Country Manager of Falcon Security, the largest nationally owned private security company in Iraq. In 2010, Larry spent a year with the SWAT team in Abu Dhabi. In 2012, working out of Dubai he worked government projects in Afghanistan. He is currently working as a consultant on projects in West Africa and South America. He is the author of several action adventure novels.

To those who answer the call to shoot, move and communicate.

Foreword

Carlos Lehder Rivas, the Colombian narcoterrorist who established the Bahamian cocaine pipeline once said, *"Cocaine is a Latin-American atom bomb aimed at the United States and I am the generalisimo in the fight against U.S. imperialism."* Carlos Lehder wasn't a general in a paramilitary army. He wasn't even a good businessman. He was little more than a middleman that saw an opportunity to make millions trafficking cocaine for his associates in Medellin, Colombia. Men with a mind for business like Pablo Escobar Gaviria made billions.

This novel is about the international drug trade. It is about money, power, and corruption, and the belief in a free market world economy where commodities move across international borders unimpeded by government regulations. If the latter sounds faintly familiar, it should. We are the champions of free enterprise. The economic system of the United States is commonly characterized as "capitalism," or "free enterprise." By definition, free enterprise is an economic system characterized by private ownership of the means of production and distribution, and their operation for profit under competitive market conditions. The structure of free enterprise is built upon the traditions of private property, self-interest, economic individualism, and competition in the marketplace.

But do we really have a free market economy? The phrase has an appealing ring to it, like life, liberty, and the pursuit of happiness. Newspapers publish editorials lauding the benefits of a free market. Politicians espouse the evils of government intervention in free market economies. But how many of those who preach the theory would endure the practice. There would be, for a start, no labor unions. In an ideal free market, each worker would receive a wage determined by the impersonal inter-play of supply and demand. There would be no price supports for farmers. Each farmer would have to decide how much to grow and what to grow? Corn, wheat, beans, tomatoes, cannabis, poppy, coca? There is tremendous demand for the latter three and in an ideal free market system, the law of supply and demand would rule.

Pablo Escobar, the infamous narcoterrorist of Colombia, saw a vast untapped market for refined coca and he capitalized on the insatiable, self-generating demand. He saw himself as a free market entrepreneur in the likeness of Joseph Kennedy who purportedly made a fortune for the Kennedy clan smuggling booze during the Prohibition Years. At the height of his power Pablo Escobar was making more than two million dollars a day and he was not the only one cashing in. He was just one of several hundred cunning entrepreneurs who saw the huge profits to be made in the illicit trade in narcotics. It has been estimated that more than a million Colombians are involved in the cocaine industry. Then there are the Venezuelans, the Ecuadorians, the Peruvians, the Bolivians, the Chileans, and anyone else with the brass to challenge the United States. Escobar is dead, but not the international network he created, not his cronies, nor his clones, and certainly not the force of supply and demand. And why not? Answer. The product is astonishingly inexpensive to produce, profits are astronomically high, and the demand is self-generating.

In the Andean culture of South America, coca has been cultivated for millennia. They chew the leaves of the scrawny little bush to ward off hunger, cold, and the effects of high altitude. It is as much a part of their culture as smoking tobacco or drinking alcohol is in the U.S. and it has been so since before recorded history. The drug lords simply turned coca, the cultural crop, into coca, the cash crop, creating a class of economically dependent people who have no other source of income. Moreover, demand is insatiable. The desire for mankind to escape his reality, whatever it may be, has existed since the first dream. Drugs are a pernicious means of altering reality, a way of chemically entering the dream world.

The United States is the number one champion of capitalist philosophy and the drug lords argue that the U.S. has grown filthy rich by raping the third world with its brand of capitalism. They see this struggle quite differently from us. From their perspective, free market restrictions on the sale of their products is hypocrisy. This is, after all, a moral and ideological issue, not a rational one. Rationally, restrictions on the sale of their products defy the most basic law of free market capitalism -- people supply goods if there is a market for them.

The new international gangsters that sit astride the criminal equivalent of multinational corporations see themselves as champions of *free enterprise*. They are more business-like than Pablo Escobar and Carlos Lehder. They are careful to sterilize their trails, careful not to draw attention to their cover enterprises of legal commodities. Their estimated annual profits from illegal activities exceed a trillion dollars, almost the size of the U.S. federal budget. That kind of money is raw power that corrupts nations.

Because of the destructive nature of drugs we have declared war, in spirit, on the entrepreneurs who seek to exploit the free market demand for narcotics. We have even coined a terms for it; the *war on drugs*. This is an extremely dangerous metaphor that began as a figure of speech that slowly took on the form of reality as money, men, and material were committed to the cause. The word *war* creates the notion that the way to win is through the barrel of a gun and it connotes the idea of an eventual victory. In war there is no substitute for victory. But the fight against drug use and the drug trade is not war. It is a social problem like venereal disease or driving under the influence. *And it cannot be defeated like an external enemy of state!* The best we can hope to do is to manage the problem, control it, reduce it and treat it. For me the war metaphor conjures up painful memories of Vietnam, a dirty little war, inglorious, futile, and seemingly unfinished.

Enjoy this trip into the world of the smuggler and those who would stop them. Jack Duran, a young SEAL Lieutenant assigned to train a secret Colombian search unit, the *Bloque de Busqueda*, runs head first into reality and finds out that perception is reality..., and that reality can be damned. Like many men involved in the *war on drugs*, the SEALs are sent off to the struggle not really knowing the nature of the problem. They stumble into it like a troop of soldiers in a field of cow pies. The nature of the problem is human nature in all its ugly facets: Greed, corruption, the desire for power, the drive to survive amidst grinding poverty, and the desire to escape reality if only for the moment. The means of smuggling are real. Anything goes, anything conceivable from submarines to honey coated plastic containers swallowed and excreted by international travelers. The naiveté and deceit are real. Only the story is fiction.

Free Enterprise

Bolivian Rock Song

I'm off to Sinajota, a shabby little town
Where they sell merchandise to make the country fall apart.
I'm off in my old banger to a cardboard town,
Of narcos from Sacata, others from El Bolson.
I grow my little coca bushes and stomp them on the road,
So that narcos and little soldiers can stuff their wallets.
They call me an ant, because I carry bundles of coca leaves,
Merchandise for junkies and señores.
At the far end of Sinajota, where the vultures perch,
They sell merchandise like sweets, like sweets.

Larry Simmons

Prologue

"Fox Two, this is Fox One. You copy?"

"Good copy, Flight Leader. I'm on your six. Three hundred yards."

"Roger, out."

The two Black Hawks circled the east end of Tindell Field and went *feet wet* over the Gulf of Mexico. They paralleled the coastline at fifteen hundred feet until they reached Apalachicola, then preceded to station at five thousand feet five miles offshore. In the distance Highway 98 looked like a string of Christmas lights strung along the panhandle of Florida marking the boundary between land and sea. The lights on shore didn't resolve into a grid but lay scattered like jewel spilled on black velvet. A few veins of light crisscrossed the scatter but too few to impart any sense of a road network. Beyond the coastline, Apalachicola National Forest loomed like a black abyss devoid of human activity. No lights dotted the immense park. It was home to snake and gator, and the occasional poacher.

"Fox Two, this is Fox One, over."

"I copy."

"There he is. Right on sked," the Flight Leader said.

"I see 'em."

"Then, let's get some."

"Roger that, boss. Right behind ya."

"Tally ho."

Like birds of prey the two helicopters swooped out of the night sky. They flanked a slow moving seaplane, taking station above and behind the smuggler so that the men inside couldn't see them. The agents began filming with infrared cameras.

"How do you reckon the suits knew the exact course and time this doper would go *feet dry*?" asked the co-pilot in Fox One.

"Hard intel," the pilot replied.

"They gotta have somebody on the inside. We've been batting a thousand the last three times out."

Through the FLIR the scene below took on a surreal appearance. The image was in black and gray, like an x-ray negative in motion. Luminous pools of heat streaked back from the plane's engine. The aircraft was skimming just above the waves and just below the Aerostat radar coverage in the northern part of the Gulf of Mexico. The bird was so close to the water that on radar it would appear to be a boat.

With the Black Hawks shadowing, the smuggler flew up Apalachicola Bay, popped up just high enough to clear the causeway then began tossing out bundles of narcotics.

"He knows we're here. Let's get on 'em," radioed Fox Two.

"How the hell does he know we're here?" the flight leader grumbled. "Any boats down there?"

'Negative," his co-pilot replied. "Whoa! Belay that. He's got company. A cigar just appeared from beneath the bridge. He's heading for the merchandise."

"Fox Two."

"Roger, One."

"Take the boat and vector in the cavalry. I'm gonna give that son-of-a-bitch a haircut."

"You got it, boss. I'm on 'em like a big dog wantin' to hump," the pilot in Fox Two replied.

Fox One swooped down on the seaplane like a falcon on a pigeon. He blew by at seventy knots and circled back to take station just above the left wing of the smugglers. With his external speaker and a spotlight he hailed the slow mover.

"This is the DEA. Nobody out here but you and me, fool. Land her on the bay or I'll shoot you down!"

The smuggler waved his wing, gained a little altitude, and circled back toward land as if to comply with the order.

"That was too easy. He ain't buyin' it, boss," the co-pilot commented. "He's makin' for the swamp."

"Let's give him something to think about," the pilot said.

The experience DEA pilots dogged the seaplane with close encounters all the way across the bay and up the mouth of the Apalachicola River.

"He's makin' a run for the swamp," the co-pilot reported on his headset. "If he has friends waiting the posse will never catch him."

Apalachicola National Park is a vast swamp of huge cypress trees and tangled waterways. It was a perfect location to disappear.

"Yeah. But he ain't a goin' get there," the pilot growled. "Hold on to your peck, number two."

"Let's do it," the co-pilot agreed.

The Black Hawk backed off then closed at a hundred and twenty knots. At the very last second, the pilot yanked back on the cyclic and blasted the infiltrator with rotor wash causing the awkward floatplane to pitch and toss like a sparrow in a hurricane. When the smuggler regained control he landed the plane on the river and ran it up onto the bank. With prop still turning, two men jumped out and ran for cover. The agents laughed as they watched the thugs scurry from bush to bush like rats being chased by a broom. They gained altitude and tracked them from a distance with infrared. Against the cool background of earth and vegetation, the modern day bootleggers stood out like buoy lights in the Gulf of Mexico. The helo maintained station at five thousand feet and when ground elements arrived they directed the lawmen into the bush. With amusement they watched as half a dozen cops surround the felons.

"I don't see 'em," the RTO's in the ground unit complained.

"That's because you are standing on top of 'em, numb nuts," the co-pilot replied. "If you take a piss you will give one of 'em a shower."

The cop shined his flashlight into a thicket of palmetto palms and illuminated one of the goons hiding behind a clump of fronds. Four agents pounced on the thug before he could give up.

"Perfect op, man! Miller time!" the co-pilot exclaimed, as he watched the troops below cuff the second felon.

But it wasn't a perfect operation. The DEA's pigeon was a sacrifice, a slight of hand set up by mastermind of chicanery. Three hundred miles west another smuggling operation was going down at the mouth of the Big Muddy and it would have deadly consequences.

Chapter 1

The old contractor checked his bearings at the confluence with the Mississippi and brought the boat to all-stop.

"She's all yours Boomer," he said, to the burly man standing over the radarscope.

The *Flash*, as her designers affectionately called her, was a marvel of modern technology. She sported two thousand-horsepower engines pushing an aerodynamic stealth design. Idling like a racecar at the starting line, she shuddered with each revolution of her powerful engines.

"There's a lot of traffic out tonight, Mr. Stenson," Master Chief Ronald Savarese complained.

"Can't be helped, Boomer. You the folks what been hollering fer delivery," the old man replied, shifting his position so Savarese could take the helm. "We're just meetin' our contractual obligations," he continued in his deep southern drawl.

"And makin' a mint too," Savarese croaked, with a hint of envy.

"That be business, boy," Stenson relied. "Say, you' retirin' soon. Why don't you come to work for me?"

It wasn't the first time Savarese had heard the offer.

"Nah. I'm headed for South America."

"Why the hell you wanna do dat fer, boy? I'll pay ya top dollar to be my test pilot. You know dat D. C. project manager would be happier than an junebug in heat if you'd come to work fer me."

The *Flash* required a test pilot rather than a coxswain. She could do more than ninety knots in good weather and turn about in her own length of eighty feet. Constructed of composite materials like a stealth bomber, she was contorted in to radar reflective angles that looked odd in the light of day. But she wasn't made for the light of day or for the elegant beaches of Florida's Gold Coast. Outfitted with state-of-the-art electronics, the *Flash* was soon to be America's newest weapon in the war on drugs.

"Can't do it, Mr. Stenson. As soon as I deliver this fast-mover to the zone, I'm going to work for my old boss." Zone was Savarese's short talk for the Panama Canal Zone.

"Doin' what?" the old man asked.

"Teachin' bone-heads to move, shoot, and communicate."

"Ain't cha had enough of gettin' shot at, Master Chief?"

"It's me that does the shootin', Mr. Stenson."

13

"What's he paying ya?" Stenson demanded.

"Dog shit," Savarese chucked.

"I'm missin' somethin', boy. From what ya tell me yer damn near broke and yer pension's too small to pay all your alimony. I can fix that little problem fer ya, boy. I'll tell ya dat. You come to work fer me and I'll pay ya a hell of lot more than Uncle Sam can afford."

"That's a mighty fine offer, Mr. Stenson. But it's the chase that *tweaks-my-twigger*," Savarese said, mispronouncing trigger like a sissy.

"Suit yer self, boy. But if you don't pay dat alimony you'll be the one gettin' chased. I'll tell ya dat. Old john law will damn sure tweak your *twigger*."

"Thanks, but no thanks, Mr. Stenson. It's South America for me."

"Suit yer self." Stenson put his face in the rubber cowling that covered the radarscope. "Now would be a good time to ease her out into the channel."

They had plotted what amounted to a flight plan before leaving the boatyard. The purpose of the plan was to minimize exposure of the craft to prying eyes. But traffic was seldom light at the mouth of the Big Muddy and the old contractor didn't have the luxury of waiting for a better night unless he was willing to pay a penalty. Pressure was on. The boat was scheduled for delivery to the Navy in less than a week. Savarese was the Navy's technical representative sent to evaluate the boat's final test and acceptance. His last official duty before retiring from the SEALs was to deliver the *Flash* to the Panama Canal Zone for duty in the war on drugs.

Savarese peered in to the darkness of the Mississippi and muttered a curse under his breath. He didn't want to get out of the Navy but he had reached high year tenure. With all the cuts in manpower no one was allowed to stay over thirty years. The thought of an eight-to-five working in a boat factory just to pay his alimony sent a shiver down his spine. He knew the old man wasn't about to incur a late penalty for security reasons; a fact that told him Stenson was a tight wad. That was how he had become so rich he ran southern Louisiana. The Navy was paying twice too much for the black program that produced the *Flash* and similar boats like her, a fact directly attributable to Stenson's political connections and pork barrel politicking.

Savarese was impressed by two things; the high price of the vessel and her incredible performance. She was closer to an aircraft than a boat, and he was one of the few men who knew how to handle her tactically. It was a skill that put him in a position to make a nice chunk of change after retirement. But none of the carrots the old man offered him was enough to persuade him to give up a life of adventure. SOC Inc. a private security company headed by his previous commanding officer, promised a life of sex and danger, and like the military,

14

bottom-dollar for his best efforts. He was determined to work for Commander Derek Evans, even if it was for room and board. The habits of a warrior were hard to break. Savarese was thinking of swilling beer with his cronies in every stinking bar from Cartagena to Bogotá when the old man broke his train of thought.

"There's nothing to speak of between us and the Gulf," Stenson said, with his face still planted inside the rubber cowling covering the radarscope.

"Roger," Savarese replied. "Let's see what she'll do."

"You can take her up to ninety, Boomer. But my kidneys can't take a poundin' anymore. When we come on to the ocean swells put her up on the planes if you don't mind," Stenson ordered, referring to the hydrofoils, which hydraulically extended from the hull. They allowed the *Flash* to ride above the waves at high speed.

"Sure thing, Mr. Stenson. My pleasure"

The burly SEAL eased the throttles forward a couple of inches and the engines rumbled to life in their sound attenuating compartments. In seconds she rose up on step like a cheetah ready to pounce on an antelope. In the main channel he eased the throttle forward to 'all ahead one-half' and blasted down the Mississippi toward the Gulf of Mexico at fifty knots. Stenson saw the small fishing boat in the radarscope as they zipped by but he didn't bother to report it to Savarese. He knew they were just local boys out passing a good time.

* * *

"Eugene!"

"Yeah Swamp-Cabbage," replied the man seated at the stern of the small wooden boat anchored near the bank.

"There goes one," Charlie hollered, pointing out toward the main channel.

It was too dark to see anything without lights and the *Flash* was cruising at darken-ship.

"One what?" Eugene asked.

"One of them boats what almost swamped us last month, Gator-Breath," Charlie said, slurring his words.

Eugene strained to see the phantom. All he saw was a glimpse of a rooster tail shooting twenty feet behind the fast moving boat. As quickly as it appeared, it was gone.

"Eugene?"

"Yeah, Swamp-Cabbage."

"You think they smugglers or government boys?" Charlie asked from the front of the fourteen-foot run-about. He spit out a mouthful of tobacco juice and wiped his chin with the back of his sleeve.

"From what I hear, I reckon they're G-men of some variety," Eugene answered.

"Well, I sure hope they have more luck at catchin' what they's after than we are," Charlie complained. "Let's go up to that old wharf just south of Belle Chasse. I guarantee we'll catch some big 'uns up there."

"That's what you said about this spot, Charlie. We come all the way down here cause you said this was the best fishin' hole in South Louisiana." Eugene swung wildly at the swarm of mosquitoes hovering about his body.

"Fish are like women, Eugene. They always movin' just to be movin'. Just when you think you've got 'em figured out, they up and make a galldurn fool out of you."

"You're damn sure right about dat. I'm fer haulin' buggy. There ain't nothing around here but a swarm of nasty skeeters."

"Chunk me a brew and quit complaining. You startin' to belly ache like a damn Yankee."

"Whoa now Charlie. Them's fightin' words," Eugene snarled.

"Hell, if you was at home your old lady would be bitchin' at you fer watchin' TV."

"You're damn sure right about dat. I'd much rather be sittin' out here in this damn dingy with the likes of you *pond-a-fy-kating* on the similar nature of fish and women."

Eugene pronounced *pontificating* with a Cajun drawl.

"Now yer startin' to talk like a damn Yankee. What the-hell does *pond-a-kating* mean?" Charlie asked.

Eugene ignored the question because he wasn't sure what the word meant. He fished around in the ice in the bottom of a Styrofoam cooler and pulled out two ice-cold cans of beer.

"Comin' at ya, Swamp-Cabbage," he said.

"Chunk it hera," Charlie replied impatiently. The half-drunk southerner caught the beer and immediately popped the top. He drained half the can and belched loudly. "Man dat gooood!" he said, smacking his lips.

"Hell. We gettin' mighty low on fuel," Eugene complained, referring to the beer. "The way you guzzling 'em down, Greedy-gut, we'll be out 'afore morning."

"Start the boat and quit your damn Yankee bitchin', Hog-Breath," Charlie snapped. "We been drinkin' one fer one ever since we left the house. But hell, who's countin'. I'll buy another six-pack when we get back to the landing."

"We ain't goin' back to the landing, Greedy-gut. We gonna catch some fish or we goin' to the fish market. You know I'll catch hell if'n I come home half drunk with nothing to show but bait fish."

"Wouldn't be the first time. Stop flappin' your jowls and skedaddle 'afore the fish move some where's else," Charlie ordered.

Eugene yanked on the outboard several times to start the engine. It coughed and smoked and sputtered and finally came to life with a clatter. "I hope you brought the paddles. This thing sounds like Bill Clinton not inhaling," Eugene chuckled.

"No. No paddles, Gator-Breath, just bait and beer. That's all we've ever needed. Bait and beer."

"I hera ya. And the bait never got us nothing either. Good thing the fish market's open all night," Eugene snickered.

"Bessy's been up and down this here river a hundred time," Charlie argued, "and she ain't never failed us."

"Yeap," Eugene agreed. "I'm back here prayin' fer number one hundred and one."

He spit out his chaw of tobacco and took a big swallow of beer before pulling the lever that kicked the propeller into drive. "Haul in the anchor," he ordered like a sea-going skipper of a big ocean going freighter. Charlie complied in an alcoholic fog.

Twenty-five miles north, the lights of New Orleans reflected off the cloud cover creating a natural navigation aid. Caught between heaven and earth, moonlight bounced back and forth between Lake Pontchartrain and the white cumulus clouds billowing off the Gulf of Mexico. Eugene headed into the current toward New Orleans.

The men enjoyed their nights on the river. Their grousing was half the fun. Drinking beer was the other half. Fishing was just an excuse to get out of the house. They puttered along drinking beer and verbally arm wrestling, indifferent to the commerce plying the busy river. Factories, warehouses, wharves, and refineries, new and old, cluttered the banks of the main channel and the fingers of turbid water that jutted off in every direction. The Mississippi Delta was a vast swamp of tangled waterways, marked and lighted haphazardly like the winding streets of a third-world city. To the untrained eye it was total confusion. To the *Flash* it was simply an electronic map with waypoints to be navigated. To Charlie and Eugene it was home.

Few locals knew it, but less than ten miles from Belle Chasse the U.S. Navy contracted for the construction of the most sophisticated special operations craft in the world. It was an excellent location for secret projects. Boat building and repair was a way of life, and hundreds of old piers and warehouses cluttered the area, providing perfect cover for Stenson's Boat Building and Repair.

The *Flash* wasn't the first of her kind. Naval Special Warfare possessed a variety of classes of boats, each designed for specific missions. The troops called them sock boats, short-talk for special operations craft. On occasion, one would emerge from its secret haven and rocket into the Gulf of Mexico for a test run. Charlie and Eugene had seen them before and they had heard stories from some of the men who worked in the boatyard. There was a thin cover story developed by Naval Intelligence. Smugglers. But the locals knew differently. They pretty much kept the information to themselves. It was good for business. Besides, boats like the *Flash* were sorely needed to counter the sleek cigarette boats used by drug smugglers. Local news reports were full of chase scenes and shoot-outs between smugglers and the law.

Charlie and Eugene were watchful as they approached the tributary that led up to the contractor's boatyard. A fast moving sock boat had almost swamped them one night as it raced home to beat the morning light.

"It's all clear, Eugene," Charlie hollered from the bow of the boat.

"I can hear you, Swamp-Cabbage. Besides, they don't come out when there's ships in the channel," Eugene said, referring to a freighter that had just passed them on its way up river.

"I know that, Gator-Breath," Charlie replied cantankerously, warmed by the alcohol.

Just in case, Eugene motored across the hundred yards at the mouth of the tributary as fast as the boat could travel and headed for an old wood-gray wharf that was collapsing under its own weight. He was a hundred yards from Charlie's second favorite fishing hole doing five knots when he ran aground fifty yards offshore.

"What the hell," Charlie yelled, as the boat scraped bottom on something metallic.

It rocked to one side as if high and dry on land. Eugene grabbed his flashlight and shined it to one side and then the other. A few feet from Charlie, his light swept passed a periscope sticking up two feet out of the water. He shined the light up and down the small mast not believing his eyes.

"A submarine?" he muttered.

Both of them stared at the strange contraption. The top of the mast slowly rotated around to face Charlie. He took a big gulp of beer and held up the can like posing for a camera. Then he made a face and stuck out his tongue. The periscope rotated around again then turned back toward the shore. A few seconds later the current kicked up ten yards behind them and the submarine, boat and all, began moving toward a large hangar on the bank of the river.

"Must be some sort of secret military contraption," Eugene said. "Water's too shallow for a real submarine." He shined his flashlight to the side. "*Look Charlie!* It's as wide as a damn barge. This thing is huge."

"Damn if that don't beat all. We catch the biggest galldurn fish in the Mississippi and it belongs to Bill Clinton," Charlie chuckled. He stood up for a better look, staggered and fell down in the center of the boat laughing. "Goddamnit," he complained, "who put that thing there," he said, referring to a cross transom in the middle of the boat.

"Let's get out of here," Eugene suggested. "I ain't for joinin' the military under no circumstances."

"How we gonna do dat, Gator-Breath? We high and dry," Charlie said, slurring his words from the bottom of the boat.

"Get out and shove us off," Eugene ordered.

"No way. I ain't gettin' outta dis boat. You think I'm crazy?"

"No. Just drunk."

With the two fishermen arguing, the vessel closed the shore. They fell silent when the hangar doors opened on a large boathouse. As the sub deftly maneuvered inside they strained their eyes to make out several figures lining the berth. Then the doors closed and the lights came on, momentarily blinding them. When they regained their vision the seriousness of their situation hit home. Heavily armed men surrounded them.

"Oh shit," Charlie mumbled.

"What the hell have we got ourselves in to?" Eugene whispered

"We in deep shit, man," Charlie whispered.

Charlie gulped down his last swallow of beer and dropped the can in the bottom of the boat. Just as it clattered underfoot the submarine shuddered and belched. Momentarily it ascended to a height of two feet above the river. With mouths and eyes wide-open Charlie and Eugene stood in their small boat gawking at the gunmen glaring down at them.

"*Venga aqui - come here*," a man on the pier growled.

He motioned at them with the barrel of an Ingram MAC-10 slung from his shoulder by a leather strap. The Military Armament Corporation Model 10 was a favorite of criminals because of its small size and firepower. Charlie and Eugene had seen them on TV. They knew the weapon wasn't standard military or law enforcement issue.

"Eugene," Charlie whispered. "Those are New Orleans choppers, man," he said, referring to the MAC-10s. "These folks ain't military."

"You got dat right," Eugene hushed. "They smugglers, man."

Shocked by the sight of so many gunmen, the two half-drunk fishermen stood frozen with fear in their small fishing boat. Two gunmen jumped down on the submarine and dragged them up on the dock.

"*Ve a buscar a Gato. Immediatamente!*" ordered a pocked faced man who looked as if he was in charge. He had a large purple birthmark on one side of his face that looked like a squashed spider.

"*Sí, Carlos,*" the youngest of the gunmen replied. He ran off toward the back of the hangar.

"What did he say? What'd he say?" Charlie stuttered.

"Hell, I don't know," Eugene. "I think he sent him to fetch someone."

"*Pablo,*" the thug with the birthmark snapped.

Pablo glared at his older brother. *"Tranquilo, hermano. Tranquilo."*

He gestured defiantly with an upward movement of his chin, then climbed down on the submarine and rapped on the hull several times with the butt of his pistol. Momentarily the hatch opened and two men emerged. They climbed up on the pier and eyed the two fishermen with astonishment.

"*Idiotas - idiots,*" the skipper of the sub said. He stretched and yawned. "*No los ví - I didn't see them,*" he said, shaking his head and gesturing with both hands.

Carlos, the gunman with the portwine stain, said nothing. He used the barrel of his machine pistol like a pointer to order several underlings into action. Two men hustled down inside the sub and began unloading plastic covered bundles the size of small cement blocks. When several hundred pounds of cocaine had accumulated on each side of the vessel, the doors at the back of the boathouse opened revealing a commercial van parked at the loading dock.

"We in deep shit, man," Charlie whispered.

"You got dat right," Eugene mumbled.

Chapter 2

Dr. Carolina Quintero Galán picked up her remaining sample of C_{31} and examined it like a jeweler eyeing the facets of a diamond. Through the plastic vial it looked like a fractured macadamia nut, creamy smooth in texture and lustrous like a pearl. In her mind's eye she visualized a lattice of atoms held together by an as yet unidentified chemical bond.

It has to be a neurotransmitter of some type, she thought.

She knew that shape was the key to its power but she hadn't been able to duplicate the shape of the molecule in the lab. Like heroin and cocaine, it was mostly carbon, hydrogen, nitrogen, and oxygen but it was different in affect. It didn't stimulate or depress the senses like cocaine and heroin. It merged them.

She placed the sample back on her desk and typed a few strokes on her computer keyboard. A three dimensional molecular diagram appeared on the screen with carbon atoms in black, hydrogen in blue, nitrogen in green, and oxygen in red. For a few moments she studied the shape of the hypothetical molecule like a biologist admiring the double helical structure of deoxyribonucleic acid. Using a mouse pen she rotated it about its axis to get a better look at different profiles. Satisfied with a facet, she hit a function key to reduce the size of the molecule to one quarter of the screen. A molecular diagram of cocaine, heroin, and nicotine appeared in the other three quadrants.

This configuration is close in size to cocaine, she ruminated in the silence of her office. *Perhaps it's a neurostimulant that suppresses the release of dopamine.*

In her work for the government she had identified a dozen chemical keys that mimicked the body's natural neuro-transmitters and more than two dozen that influenced communications between neurons. Excitatory molecules like cocaine and inhibitory molecules like heroin possessed a rare ability to cross the brain-blood barrier and reap havoc with the machinery of synaptic junctions of the brain. C_{31} fascinated her because it appeared to both excite and inhibit synaptic function.

Maybe I should move the base carbon atom a little closer to the center, she thought.

Using a mouse pen she drew another molecular diagram depicting the possible atomic bonds that might shape the molecule into the powerful chemical key she had in the plastic vial. The computer automatically adjusted the diagram to accommodate the new shape and listed the number and type of atoms below the image. She reduced the size of the molecule and compared it to the other drugs. Molecules like cocaine and heroin are similar in substance and structure. In the language of the chemist, cocaine is written as $C_{21}H_{21}NO_4$, heroin as $C_{21}H_{23}NO_3$. Cocaine comes from the coca bush and heroin from the poppy flower. The atomic difference between the two molecules is just two atoms of hydrogen and one atom of oxygen. It is the shape of a molecule that determines which chemical lock it fits in the human brain, not the number of atoms.

C_{31} was the most psychoactive substance she had ever encountered. It was so soluble that her lab technicians had become slightly euphoric from handling it in the normal course of lab work. Even she had experienced its enchantment on several occasions. Some of those experiments were deliberate exposures, a fact she attributed to scientific curiosity. In her journal she recorded her feelings as exhilarating, frightening, and wonderful, as sight turned to sound and sound turned to taste.

She picked up the vial containing her only remaining sample of the drug and eyed it intensely. Desire flooded her brain, a powerful desire from a deep hunger that ached inside her. It took all of her willpower to resist taking the pebble-like lump of matter out of the vial. Alarmed by the emotions, she put the sample down and forced her thoughts to scientific matters.

For an hour she worked on several possible molecular configurations and was about to join a discuss group on the Internet when a piercing scream startled her. She jumped up from the desk, heart pounding, and peered through a small window separating her office from the lab. Inside she saw several policemen manhandling her lab assistants. As her eyes focused a gun discharged. But there was no sound. A pink mist appeared at the back of Byron Richmond's head. In what seemed like slow motion he fell to the floor, mouth agape in death as if not believing the fate that had befallen him.

It happened in the blink of an eye as if time was distorted in a nightmare. Then the sound of her lab assistant screaming registered in her brain. The killer backhanded her with his pistol, knocking her into the lab bench like a rag doll. Before the woman regained her senses, he grabbed her by the hair and jammed the pistol in her stomach. Carol couldn't understand the words, but she could see the back of the killer's head bob with each demanding grunt. The terrified technician pointed at the lab bench. In what seemed like slow motion the brute turned and for the first time Carol Galán saw his face. Her heart skipped a beat. She couldn't believe her eyes. The man's nose was mangled and parts of his lips were missing, exposing his teeth in a permanent maniacal grin. Saliva was running down his chin. Frozen with fear, she stared at the gruesome scene, unable to move, unable to scream.

I'm hallucinating, she thought. *Some of the substance must have been on the outside of the vial.*

Petrified with fear and indecision she watched as the policemen plundered the laboratory, grabbing files, lab books, and samples. Like watching a horror movie in slow motion she held her breath as the killer pistol whipped Laura Shula to the floor and shot her twice in the head. The body quivered in spasm with each gunshot. But there was no sound from the pistol.

This is a bad dream, she thought.

In seconds two people were dead while she stood at the lab window staring, frozen with fear, waiting for the drug induced nightmare to end. Then the killer glanced in her direction and their eyes met in a moment of uncertainty. His mutilated face contorted with astonishment. In a heartbeat Carol Galán realized by the look in the man's eyes that he was after her. She flipped the lock on the heavy metal door, grabbed her purse and the sample of C_{31} off the desk, and ran for her life.

In sheer panic she raced through the empty corridors of Syntec Pharmaceuticals looking for the security guard, for anyone to help. But it was late and the building was empty. As she dashed into the lobby and around the reception desk, she stumbled over the body of the contract security guard. A pool of blood issued from his head. On her knees, she screamed as a jolt of adrenaline slammed into her brain. Out of instinct she jumped to her feet and scrambled outside. Seeing no one on the street, she ran to the parking lot. She was in an utter state of panic and completely out of breath when she reached her car.

"Oh, my God! Oh, my God!" she cried, over and over as she fumbled with her keys. She dropped them on the ground twice before she was able to unlock the car.

As she climbed inside the killer closed the distance between them like a charging bull. Frightened out of her wits she had trouble inserting the key into the ignition. When the engine finally rumbled to life the killer was on top of her. He yanked the door open a split second before she hit the button on the power locks. With the crazed eyes of a madman he stared down at her, panting for breath, foaming at the mouth through his exposed teeth.

In slow motion Carol watched the pistol slip out of his shoulder holster and sweep toward her. Death was so close she could feel her heart pounding in her chest. Her temples throbbed and her eyes bugged out in horror. Her mind was racing, completely out of control with adrenaline overload, screaming for her to flee, but her body wouldn't move. As the barrel of the pistol came around toward her, instinct took over. She slammed the car in gear and jammed her foot on the accelerator. The impact of a bullet smacked into the dashboard just before the door slammed shut. Speeding away from the killer, she hit one of his goons as the man dashed across the parking lot in front of her. His body bounced off the fender and rolled on the macadam behind her. Carol yanked the steering wheel, floored the accelerator and squealed out into the street, smoke boiling from her right rear tire. Shaking in uncontrollable fits she kept repeating the same words over and over.

"Oh, my God! Oh, my God! This can't be happening! I'm hallucinating! I'm hallucinating!"

Carol sped the short distance to the freeway and headed south on Interstate 805. Weaving in and out of traffic at ninety miles per hour, she watched her rearview mirror to see if the men were following her. Near Highway 163, she came down from her adrenaline rush enough to think clearly.

I'll take one sixty-three downtown to the police station," she thought.

She pulled over into the exit lane and reduced her speed to sixty-five. Glancing in her rearview mirror, she took several deep breaths to calm her jittery nerves.

"This is a nightmare," she mumbled out loud. *In the morning I'll wake up and this will be a bad dream,* she thought.

But she knew it was real. The look in the man's eyes had told her she was the object of his pursuit. It was Laura Shula's misfortune to be working late. And there in front of her was a hole in her dashboard from a nine-millimeter bullet. She reached out and touched it to assure herself of reality.

Carol glanced in her side mirror and saw the headlights of a car barreling up behind her at high speed. For a few seconds she was frozen by indecision, unsure if it was the killer, a cop, or just another crazy California driver. She gasped as the car swerved into the exit lane and slammed into her bumper causing her to slide sideways. Noise and smoke shrieked from her tires as the Lexus nearly over turned. A man on the passenger side of the car aimed a pistol in her direction. Out of instinct she whipped the steering wheel to the right to correct for the slide, then she jammed on the accelerator and at the very last second swerved to the left as sharply as she could. The expensive luxury sedan responded like a nimble little sports car, bounded across the exit median and back on to Interstate 805, barely missing the barrier split. She heard the screeching of tires and glanced back to her right. Smoke was boiling off the tires of the late model gray Oldsmobile as the killer tried to recover. But it was too late. He was committed to Highway 163 and she was cruising down Interstate 805 at high speed. Carol put the accelerator to the floor and roared down the freeway hoping a cop would stop her.

"Never a cop around when you need one," she grumbled, watching her rearview mirror like a car thief on his way to the border.

She crossed over Interstate 8 at Mission Valley at a hundred and thirty miles per hour. When she reached Highway 94, she reduced her speed and took the downtown exit. She was only two blocks from the police station when she spotted the gray Oldsmobile cruising the street several vehicles ahead of her. She could see the men inside searching all directions like radar. Panic seized her, complete and utter terror. In automatic she hooked a quick left, went around the block, and headed for Highway 94 in a stream of late evening traffic.

When the freeway turned into a two-lane macadam road and began meandering through the foothills, she relaxed the death grip she had on the steering wheel. Mentally exhausted, she cruised down the road nervously watching her rearview mirror like a coyote running illegal aliens. Satisfied she had lost them, she stopped at the Dulzura Cafe. It was a little place near the rifle and pistol range where her instructor had taught her to shoot before going to South America on a plant gathering expedition.

I'll call Evans. He'll know what to do. The arrogant bastard always knows what to do, she thought.

Inside, she ordered a Coke and used the phone. She connected with Evans's answering machine.

"You have reached Special Operations Consultants, Incorporated. Please leave your name and number and someone will return your call."

"No. No! I hate answering machines," she muttered. "Oh my, God, what am I going to do?"

"May I help you ma'am?" the owner asked. She was a small woman with bright intelligent eyes.

"No. No," Carrol babbled, lost in thought. "No, thank you."

She hung up the phone without leaving a message and returned to her table.

I'll call Rita, she thought. *She'll help me. But, not from here. From Mexico. The Tecate border crossing is just down the road a few miles. But first I have to calm down. Get a grip on yourself, Carol.*

"I can't," she muttered. "I can't think."

Another idea seized control. She glanced down at her handbag. It was inside. Waiting. Carol opened her purse and pretended to rifle its contents. With both hands out of view she opened the plastic vial and stroked the smooth surface of the substance just a few times, just enough for a thin film of molecules to cover the tip of her finger. She snapped the top back on the vial and rubbed her finger into the palm of her hand.

Fear is a human emotion to be controlled, she thought. *Fear is the essence of survival*, she repeated to herself in a quivering inner voice, while rubbing the tip of her finger in the palm of her hand. *Those we call courageous, like Commander stuck-on-himself, know-it-all Derek Evans knows how to smother fear with calming thoughts. I can do it.*

She took a deep breath and focused her mind as the drug took affect. She saw the earthiness of the Dulzura Cafe for the first time. Then she heard the music and the chatter about her as if someone had just flipped a switch. It had been there all the time. She just hadn't listened. She could almost see the sound and taste the colors. Real America. Self-reliant, rugged, individualistic. A border patrol agent tipped his hat at the proprietor as he walked to exit. "See ya later, Kitty," he said.

The proprietor gave Carol a concerned look as she served her a frosty glass of Coca-Cola.

"Will there be anything else?" she asked.

"No. No thank you," Carol stammered.

My God, she thought, returning a fake smile she didn't feel. *I must look like a frightened child.* Carol took a sip of her Coke and began planning a drug induced great escape.

Chapter 3

With growing anxiety the two inebriated fishermen watched as more than five tons of cocaine passed before their eyes. Truck after truck rumbled off into the night with hundreds of pounds of drugs concealed beneath raw coffee beans.

Fear gnawed at their stomachs when a distinguished looking man dressed in an expensive business suit walked down the wharf toward them. He was thin, in his forties, and he moved like a cat, with careful light steps. His eyes darted from side to side furtively like an animal exquisitely tuned to its surroundings. It was apparent by the way the others stepped out of his way that he commanded great station in life. Immaculately dressed, he sported jet-black Indian-hair tied tightly back tango-dancer style in a small, tight ponytail.

Charlie swallowed hard as the man's cold brown eyes sized up the situation in two heartbeats. He held up his hand like a priest and the pock-faced man yelled.

"*Silencio! - silence!*"

Every thug in the building stopped what he was doing.

"*Digame, Menendez,*" he demanded of the skipper of the sub. His voice was so muffled and soft-spoken his words were nearly inaudible.

"*Gato. Son solamente pescadores,*" the captain pleaded, explaining that the interlopers were only fishermen. "*No los ví cuando entre.*"

Gato's eyes cut deeply in to the skipper's without blinking. They seemed to pierce the man's soul. In a low, calm voice he asked, "*Estas seguro, Menendez? - are you sure, Menendez?*"

"*Sí, Gato,*" the skipper replied nervously. "*Estoy seguro.*"

The captain's legs began to tremble and he looked down at the wharf.

"*Carlos?*" *Gato* snarled, at the pock-faced man with the purple birthmark.

"*Es verdad, Gato. Son dos pescadores,*" confirmed the gunman.

"*Bueno. Matalos. Tiralos en el submarino,*" he ordered quietly. "*Desasemos de los cuerpos en Colombia.*"

The men on the pier were shocked by the orders. They gawked at him like looking at the Pope. Charlie couldn't speak Spanish but he correctly understood that the gist of the words mean, *Kill them and put them in the submarine.* He seized the opportunity and dashed down the wharf, trying to get to the muddy water behind the vessel. Like a cheetah *Gato* deftly removed a pistol from beneath his suit coat and squeezed off one round that struck Charlie in the base of the skull. The Southerner fell to the wooden planking with a thud. Eugene's mouth was

27

agape, frozen in fear, when he turned to face the Colombian.

Gato raised one eyebrow in mock pity and shrugged his shoulders. "This is a brutal business, *amigo*," he said in English.

The words were so softly spoken the fisherman had to strain to hear them. The look in the Colombian's eyes caused a chill to run down his spine. The world appeared to stop turning. He couldn't breathe and he couldn't move. Numbed by alcohol and petrified with fear he watched the pistol rise slowly to eye level and fire directly at his face. The last thing he saw was the huge hole down the barrel of the 1911 Colt .45. The image didn't have time to register before the bullet ripped through his skull exploding the backside of his head like a melon.

With the body quivering at his feet, *Gato* Gaviria turned his cold gaze on the sub skipper.

"You have failed in your duties, *Capitán Menendez*. This is the third time," he said, raising his voice slightly.

"*Por favor - please, Gato. It wasn't my fault! They came up from behind me! I didn't see them!*" the skipper pleaded in blistering Spanish.

The pistol appeared and Menendez's eyes grew in size. When he realized his fate his whole body began to tremble.

"You are *not* paid to make mistakes, Menendez," *Gato* grunted, his lips barely moving.

The weapon discharged and the submariner fell to the pier twitching in a death spasm beside the American. *Gato* tossed his head back like a defiant bullfighter and glared at the remaining pilot.

"Diaz," he snarled.

"*Sí, Señor Gaviria!*" Diaz blurted with a nervous gush of fear.

"Don't fuck up or I will have Pablo carve out your liver."

One of *Gato's* gunmen sneered, showing a rack of ragged gray teeth stained by heavy tobacco use. He smirked at the new captain and whipped out a switchblade knife. The blade clicked into place and he felt the edge with a greasy smile.

"*Sí, Señor Gaviria. Sí Señor. Comprendo. Comprendo,*" the nervous new skipper stammered.

Gaviria turned to face the others. "*A trabajar! -- to work!*" he snapped, like an army general on a battlefield.

A dozen men scrambled to offload the submarine.

"Leave nothing behind. *Nothing*," Gaviria commanded, shaking his finger at his three cousins.

Satisfied the situation was under control he turned about and walked down the landing toward the back of the hanger. There was other business to attend to. He wanted to personally see the latest in boat technology to size up the opposition.

Carlos Cataño, the oldest of the three gunmen began issuing orders, directing men to break the fishing boat into pieces small enough to fit through the hatch of the submarine. After *Gato* left the building, Pablo turned his attention to the bodies.

"*Coyote*, look at this shit, meng," he snickered, like an excited teenager.

He pushed Eugene's head to the side with his shoe. The .45 caliber bullet had exploded the backside of the skull exposing the brain.

"This Yankee has a fouckin' headache, meng," he chuckled.

He stepped down on the fractured skull case causing some of the brain matter to squeeze out onto the dock.

"*Jesso Christo*, Pablo," Juan blurted. "Don't get that shit all over the dock, meng. *Gato* said not to leave anything behind."

One of the underlings stepped up with a hose and began spraying the blood and matter off the dock.

"*Wait a minute! Wait a minute, maricon,*" Pablo yelled, pushing the man back. Pablo's knife appeared and the blade clicked into place. "I want this fouckin' Yankee's ears, meng," he snarled.

"*No!*" Carlos yelled. The purple birthmark on his face had turned a darker shade. "Stop screwing around, Pablo. *You!*" he yelled, pointing at several thugs, "put the bodies on the submarine. Wash off the dock," he ordered the man with the hose.

"*Coyote*," Pablo snickered. "*Araña*'s got a sissy stomach, meng," he grinned.

In South America, paid gunmen are called *sicarios*. They live a macho life of bravado and danger. All of them take on nicknames that fit their deeds or disposition. Carlos Cataño's handle was *La Araña* - The Spider - because the portwine stain on his cheek resembled an arachnid. Juan was called *El Coyote* because he was wiry and shifty like a canine. Pablo's pet name was *El Alacrán* - The Scorpion - because he enjoyed using a knife to kill his victims. He liked to flick and jab it like a scorpion's stinger.

Pablo eyed his older brother and yielded to his authority.

"No problem, *essay*. I'll cut their fouckin' ears off later, meng. Fouckin' Yankee bastard," he cursed. He spit on the corpse and stomped down on the skull with his heel causing blood and brain matter to gush out on the dock.

"*Jesso Christo*, Pablo," Juan complained, with a sour expression on his face. He crossed himself in the Catholic style. "You should not desecrate the dead, meng."

Pablo chuckled. As low-level goons hosed off the mess, he walked down the dock to examine Charlie's ears.

Several men carried the bodies to the deck of the submarine and laid them out like cadavers in a morgue. Loading the corpses and the shatter fishing boat would have to wait until another six tons of cocaine were removed from the sub.

La violencia was the Spanish term the Colombians used to describe such incidents. The stark savagery of Cocaine Inc., was a way of life born of necessity. A marijuana deal could be done with a handshake. A cocaine deal had to be done with a gun.

Carlos Lehder Rivas, the Colombian drug smuggler who established the Bahamas pipeline in the early 1980s, once bragged, *Cocaine is a Latin-American atom bomb aimed at the United States and I am the generalisimo in the fight against U.S. imperialism.* But Lehder was no general. In fact, he was little more than an opportunist who encountered a lucrative opportunity. He was just a middleman and the product of failure on the part of the United States government to recognize the changing tide of America's drug habit.

Gato, the Cat, Canrado Cataño Gaviria was a real general who commanded a paramilitary force with an annual budget of more than a billion dollars. He controlled an army of thugs, an air force of mercenaries, and a navy of boats that included flat barge-shaped submarines designed to lock on to the bottom of ocean going freighters. Six days after passing the two unlucky fishermen on its way up the Mississippi River, the Ballesteros ship, the *Don Blás*, would rendezvous with the submarine and transport it back to Barranquilla, Colombia. There, she would take on board another load of premium Colombian coffee and fifteen tons of cocaine for the submarine fastened to her belly. Ironically, special boats designed to stop *Gato* Gaviria's navy were constructed less than ten miles from the cartel's warehouse south of Belle Chasse, Louisiana.

The Ballesteros, the Gavirias, and the Cataños were *paisas*, a name the people of Medellin, Colombia called themselves. It was an ancient word taken from the mythical Antioquian people who populated the area of the Magdalena River Valley of Colombia long before the Spanish Conquistadors arrived.

Understanding Medellin, and the people who call themselves *paisas*, is crucial to understanding the commerce of cocaine. Tourist brochures call Medellin the "City of Eternal Spring," and the "Orchid City." It is a mile-high mountain metropolis of two million living in a high river valley amid the forests of north central Colombia. The *paisas* are outwardly modest, aggressive, and ambitious people who are hard working when it comes to money and social position. Anyone, rich or poor can earn prestige if he has enough guts, brains, and vision to succeed. In Medellin the ends justify the means, no questions asked. The objective is to get filthy rich.

In colonial times the town was isolated, squalid, and short on social graces. The *paisas* were considered to be in-bred, pale-faced loquacious louts by *the*

Bogotaños who graced the capital. But by the middle of the twentieth century the joke was on the rest of Colombia. The *paisas* had turned Medellin into a thriving center of free enterprise. Creative businessmen, high-risk takers had traveled extensively seeking out opportunity. To mining, they added cattle, coffee, cut flowers, and smuggling. Throughout Colombia, Medellin earned a reputation as a smuggler's lair, earned by *paisa* peddlers who sold notions to rural housewives all over the country. Highly respected men, and many of ill repute, made fortunes bootlegging liquor and cigarettes, and airlifting TVs, stereos, and radios from the duty free ports in Panama. Trafficking in illegal goods was culturally excused long before cocaine wreaked havoc in the United States.

To this cultural stew came the opportunity to make billions smuggling a white substance the consistency of powdered sugar. The leaves of the coca bush from which it was made had been chewed in the Andes for centuries. The product itself was dirt cheap to produce, the demand was insatiable, and the smuggler's know-how was ingrained in the culture. The *paisas* simply commercialized it. For years they quietly provided the drug to a demand market.

In the 1970s cocaine became the drug of fashion for the glitterati. It dusted the swank parties of movie stars and infiltrated the thrill seeking habits of middle class yuppies. Then, the rock rolled into the ghettos, addicting the poor and spreading misery to the most miserable corners of American society. They called it snow, white lady, charlie, toot, happy dust, flake, nose candy, C, blow, crack, rock, or simply coke. Whatever name it took, it became America's favorite drug and it swept the country like a white blizzard, leaving a trail of shattered lives, crack-babies, and street gang violence.

Before anyone in power realized what was happening, a handful of Medellin *paisas* had climbed to the top of the smuggler's ladder, fighting rival mafia like vicious packs of wolves to establish dominance in a deadly game of free enterprise. Some of them achieved infamy and precipitated the birth of a new word. *Narcoterrorism.* By the mid 1980s Medellin cartels were smuggling as much as 50 metric tons of cocaine annually into the United States. *Gato* Gaviria could achieve the same quota in a month.

Pablo Escobar Gaviria reached the top of the smuggler's ladder and was called *El Padrino, the Godfather*, in fashion of the Sicilian mafia. He was *Gato* Gaviria's first cousin and mentor. From his modestly successful career as a hired gun, kidnapper, and car thief, he built a vast criminal empire and made billions smuggling cocaine. At his death at age forty-four Pablo Escobar Gaviria was worth fifteen billion dollars.

Carlos Lehder's big mouth and Pablo Escobar's brutality precipitated the *war on drugs* and brought the magnitude of the cocaine trade to the light of public scrutiny. The *paisas* won the first skirmish in the *War on Drugs*. The causalities were relatively low from their point of view. Lehder was jailed for life and Escobar was gunned down like a common thug. But that was a small price to pay for the billions of dollars flowing into Medellin. The formidable federal posse that brought the tip of the iceberg to the surface drove the smartest and most cunning *paisas* to deeper cover, downsizing and streamlining their organizations like multinational corporations. Those like *Gato* Cataño Gaviria, who survived the first skirmish, were career criminals, tough, smart, deadly, and battle hardened. They had been tested by fire, by police, and by rival traffickers throughout South America, even by governments. And they had survived.

Gato Cataño Gaviria was *generalisimo,* the general of the most successful, the richest, and the deadliest criminal enterprise on Earth, a new, more business-like *Medellin-corporación.* His boss, Alajandro Cataño Ballesteros, controlled production, smuggling, marketing, and money laundering networks throughout the world, the criminal equivalent of a multinational corporation with an annual profit of five billion dollars. Charlie and Eugene were loose ends. They were just simple men who were in the wrong place at the wrong time. They joined the ranks of *los desaparecidos -- the disappeared.* South American soil is full of *desaparecidos.*

Gaviria watched from the bank as the *Flash* entered the tributary and began idling toward them. One of his men began snapping pictures with an infrared camera. In the illicit drug business good intelligence was often a function of money. *Gato* had money to burn, enough to fund the entire black program that produced the *Flash* and have enough left over to buy every politician in Bolivia. If he couldn't buy one like her, he could buy a copy of the plans and produce a boat in North Korea for a tenth of the price the U.S. Navy was paying.

Vessels like the *Flash* could chase down anything on the high seas. For that reason the Ballesteros Combine had taken to the depths to avoid detection. Their newest modus operandi was to give the Yankees two or three cigarette boats to chase, an airplane or two to shadow, and infiltrate the bulk of the product right under the Yankees's noses in a submarine. Gaviria had succeeded in electronically bugging most of his major competitors so it was their boats and aircraft he offered up as sacrifices to the DEA, anonymously of course.

Gato wasn't really troubled by the existence of the *Flash.* He was just curious. His spied on U.S. Government black programs to stay one step ahead of the DEA. But there was a new, more deadly enemy threatening the Combine, a changing tide of technology. A synthetic drug that was easy to produce in a junkie's kitchen could put the Ballesteros Combine out of business the way synthetic rubber had ruined the natural rubber market. That was something he couldn't let happen. It was his job to prevent such mishaps.

Cocaine Inc., was a brutal business. In a few hours he planned to fly to Miami to buy the Cali cartel's spymaster, Gilberto Mora Mesa. Mesa was an expert at electronic espionage. He had succeeded in bugging the highest levels of the DEA and the Justice Department, as well as the whole of the Colombian government. Between Mesa and his own spies, Gaviria planned to acquire all the information the DEA had on Dr. Galán and Syntec Pharmaceuticals. When his target folder was complete, he intended to go to San Diego and eliminate the threat. Fortunately for Dr. Carol Galán less sophisticated narcoterrorists were two days ahead of him or she would have joined the ranks of *los desaparecidos.*

As Gaviria watched the *Flash* slowly maneuver up current toward the boatyard, his thoughts boiled over.

How many times do I have to tell Don Ballesteros that the key to our survival is intelligence. The advantage doesn't go to the most creative, the most inventive or the most efficient. It goes to those with the best vision, to those who have the best information. Espionage and deceit ruled in Colombia.

Gaviria would have flown into a rage if he had known the Savajés had been tipped off to his plans to kidnap Dr. Galán. He was spending enormous sums of money to maintain his intelligence network. An army of thugs and electronic bugs constantly watched his rivals. But they had missed the Galán operation.

Ramón Savajé understands. If it weren't for me the crazy bastard would have a nuclear weapon to bargain behind.

Gaviria had informed the U.S. Government about his rival's attempts to acquire a weapon of mass destruction from the Russians. To foil the Savajés' grab for power, he had provided the crucial intelligence necessary to seizing the weapon and ten tons of cocaine. A reciprocal relationship had subsequently developed between the Ballesteros Cattle and Coffee Consortium and the CIA.

Perhaps it is time for Don Ballesteros to step down. Maybe he should run for President. That would suit his Excellency and get him out of my hair. The direction he is taking the Combine will eventually lead to our ruin. Sooner or later Ramón will get wind of the submarines. Or the Yankees will discover them. Evans is close. Perhaps he is Roth's backstop. Yankees always cross-reference their intel. Then he thought, *The next time Ramón makes a deal with the Russians, I'll grab the weapon and I'll have the power of a blinding white flash to use as I please.*

Gato, Canrado Cataño Gaviria was one of the few men in the narcotics smuggling business who truly understood the importance of intelligence. In his mind's eye he quoted Sun Tzu. *What enables the wise sovereign and the good general to strike and conquer, and achieve things beyond the reach of ordinary men, is foreknowledge. I'll bug Roth, then his boss, Dr. Alysin Harris. To hell with Alajandro. I'll bug them all.*

His intelligence expenditures had recently raised concerns within the cartel when he had proposed an operation designed to penetrate the Central Intelligence Agency. It was the only arm of the U.S. Government no cartel had been able to penetrate. He was seething with thoughts when the *Flash* idled by. The men verbally grousing on board the special boat momentarily distracted his musings. In his worst nightmare he could not have imagined that one of the men onboard the stealth boat would soon threaten the existence of the Ballesteros Coffee and Cattle Consortium.

"Boy, you sure know how to pass a good time," Stenson said, taking the helm to pilot the boat back into its hangar.

"You ain't seen nothin' yet, cap'n," Savarese boomed. His voice carried across the water to the drug lord's lair. "Wait till I put her through her paces with a minigun blazin'."

"Sure you won't come to work for me? I'll pay ya top damn dollar, boy. I guarantee."

"Nah. I'm headed south. Deep south. Why don't you come along, Mr. Stenson. The women down there are most accommodating."

"You one crazy fool, Boomer Savarese. One mule-assed crazy fool."

"Damn, Mr. Stenson, you've finally figured me out."

Chapter 4

Derek Evans picked up the telephone on the second ring. "Sock ink," he grunted, using the corporate short name for Special Operations Consultants, Incorporated.

"Commander Evans?" a deep male voice on the other end of the line asked.

"Retired," Evans corrected, referring to his military status.

"I have a contract for you, sir."

"Who is this?" Evans asked, mindful of the word contract.

"My name is not important, Commander."

"Okay. What's this all about?" Evans asked, picking up a pencil.

"Drugs, money, and murder."

"You've got the wrong guy, pal," Evans said, putting the pencil down.

"No I don't, Commander," argued the smoky deep voice. The tone of confidence gave Evans pause. He waited for the caller to continue. "Have you heard of the case of the frozen addicts?"

"No," Evans replied, just as something inside his head went click: *Santa Cruz.*

"It happened several years ago up in Central California. A bunch of junkies got hold of a batch of synthetic heroin."

"Ah, I vaguely remember the incident," Evans admitted.

"You can bet the junkies will never forget. You see, this amateur chemist was trying to cook up a batch of synthetic heroin, a designer drug known as MPPP. He screwed up the recipe and produced a caustic chemical known as MPTP. The dope destroyed a critical part of junkie's brains, a thumb size glop of gray matter called the substantia nigra."

"I remember," Evans said. "I saw a program on PBS called the Frozen Addicts."

"That's the case. The junkies froze like cadavers. They could breathe but they couldn't move. Some couldn't even blink their eyes."

"What's this got to do with me?" Evans complained.

"I'm getting to that," the caller said tastily, annoyed by the interruption. He paused for a few heartbeats before continuing his story. "As you know, San Diego is home to several companies that are on the cutting edge of biotechnology. One of those companies is the world leader in synthetic drug manufacturing, and it turns out that the most brilliant scientist in that company was a consultant on the case of the frozen addicts."

"So?"

"So her experience with the frozen addicts and with synthetic drugs gave her a marvelous idea. Why not design drugs which seek out and bind with narcotic agents thereby rendering them non psychoactive."

"Listen, whoever-you-are. I don't know squat about drugs, legal or illegal. What the hell does this have to do with me?"

"You know the woman, Evans," the caller grumbled.

An image popped into Evans's head. Dr. Carol Galán. She was the smartest woman he had ever known, and the most unpredictable. Dr. Galán lived in a world of chemical equations and naive academic solutions. SOC Inc. had provided physical security for her company, Syntec Pharmaceuticals, during several plant-gathering expeditions into the rain forests of Bolivia. It had been a real challenge to protect her. Just keeping her from plummeting off a cliff had taken major effort. Evans couldn't help but picture her in knee length khaki shorts and a Rammar-of-the-Jungle pit helmet trudging excitedly from plant to plant without any sense of the world beyond her immediate objective. The image of combat boots and long slender legs momentarily blocked out the image of an eccentric, mercurial genius of chemistry.

Drugs, money, and murder? he thought, *and who the hell is this secret squirrel?*

"Okay. Who is this mystery person, secret agent man?" Evans demanded.

The caller ignored the question. If Evans couldn't figure out whom he was talking about, he was the wrong man for the job.

"If I may continue, Commander, I'll try to explain."

"Please do," Evans insisted, picking up his pencil.

"Her inspirational idea led to the creation of a black program call Project Mandrake, after the magical plant mentioned in Genesis."

Evans swallowed hard as the caller continued his briefing. Black programs were secret government projects so sensitive that funding was hidden from Congress to prevent leaks.

"It consisted of developing drugs designed to inactivate the psychotropic effects of narcotic compounds in the human body. Put simply, Syntec Pharmaceuticals was supposed to produce drugs that negate the effects of dope in humans, the magic pill to cure addiction, so to speak. They were working on the development of an anti-cocaine compound when they made a critical mistake. Like the kitchen chemist, we think someone screwed up the recipe. Instead of binding with, and canceling the effects of cocaine, the drug they cooked up turned out to be more addictive than heroin. The crap is so psychoactive they got high from just touching it."

The hollow in the pit of Evans's stomach grew as he pictured Carol Galán as the head of a sensitive black program. He was one of a handful of men who knew how desperate the U.S. Government was for a solution to America's drug habit. Laboratories all over the country were quietly researching herbicides and plant eating insects that could destroy the coca, poppy, and marijuana fields of South America and South East Asia. One program was aptly called bugs-for-drugs because it consisted of developing plant-eating moths. There were even programs to produce plants that lacked the enzymes to produce narcotic compounds. The intent of the program was to introduce altered genes by viral infection spread by means of aerial spraying like Agent Orange and Spike. Chemical and biological warfare had been secretly declared on drug traffickers and the peasants who grew the crops. Evans was one of the few men who understood the dimensions of the problem.

The thought of the tall, dark-haired beauty with high cheekbones as the head of a black program didn't set well with Evans. His sexist military background compelled him to see her in bed and not in the boardroom as the leader of one of the nation's most sensitive projects. It was just such a character flaw that had led to friction between himself and Galán and ultimately to a falling-out between SOC Inc. and Syntec Pharmaceuticals.

"Okay, Okay. I got the picture. Now cut to the chase," Evans demanded, like talking to a disobedient seaman.

He knew the answer. One of the agencies was looking for assistance. SOC Inc. had been used and abused and he was in no mood to be jerked around by a persistent agent looking for a free ride. Besides, he didn't need anymore business. He was hard pressed to execute the contracts he already had.

"I was told that you're a difficult and impatient man."

"Oh yeah. By whom?"

"My source was correct," the caller complained.

"Well I'll cut to the chase, pal," Evans snarled. "If you don't make your point in the next sentence, I'm off the net. You got that?"

"A million bucks, pal!" the angry caller blurted out. "A million dollars if you come up with this old broad, and no questions asked how you do it."

"She's not old, *pal!*" Evans shot back. "And she's certainly not a broad."

The caller waited until the heat of the exchange cooled off. "So you know who I'm taking about? Evans, our objective is to get the Doctor before the bad guys get her."

"Your objective is to keep her formula off the streets at all cost," Evans said loudly, guessing the man's mission.

"Does a million bucks get your undivided attention, Evans?"

"That it does my friend. We are now speaking the same language. Continue,"

Evans ordered.

"What we have here, Commander, is a symbiotic relationship."

"That remains to be seen. You said drugs, money, and murder. Continue," Evans insisted in a commanding voice.

"Two of the scientists involved with Project Mandrake have been murdered. A third is in a private hospital for drug addiction. And the fourth, well, your guess is as good as ours."

"I haven't read anything about this in the news?" Evans probed.

"It's a black program, Evans," the caller sighed.

There was silence for what seemed minutes before he continued. Evans waited patiently, knowing that the man was under orders to recruit him or he would have hung up a long time ago.

"Our objective is to protect the public and we'll do whatever it takes to do that. Obviously, SOC Inc. is not the only organization we're calling."

"I can understand that, whoever-you-are," Evans said. "But let me tell you something. I am tired of being used by mysterious assholes who lack faces and names."

The caller ignored the comment.

"The South American players want the Doctor dead or alive. Right? They don't want competition from kitchen chemists," Evans asserted. "Crystal meth has already cut their profits by twenty-five percent."

"You're probably right, Evans. If this drug becomes generally available like methamphetamine, they're out of business," the caller agreed.

"Interesting. Continue," Evans grumbled.

"Your organization has been providing advanced security training for a Colombian firm of, how shall I say this, of questionable ethics."

"The only contracts I've taken in South American have been at the insistence of faceless, nameless assholes like you!"

"Be that as it may, Commander, we believe you are in a most advantageous position to make some real money."

"How so?"

"You know the woman, Evans. You know what she looks like, how she thinks, her habits and weaknesses. You know whom she knows in South America and whom she's likely to contact for assistance. Maybe she'll even contact you."

Evans recalled the garbled message someone had left on his answering machine.

So that was Carol, he thought. "Oh. I don't think so," he said. "Dr. Galán thinks I'm a rude, sexist pig."

"I dare say she's at least got the rude part right," dared the caller.

Evans ignored the cut. "Obviously, you think she's in South America or you wouldn't be calling me, secret squirrel. She could easily pass herself off as European, you know. She speaks several languages."

Galán was a Hispanic American by heritage and spoke fluent Spanish. But she also spoke several other Romance languages. The caller ignored Evans's statement.

"Second, you know the most powerful Colombian players, the ones with extensive intelligence connections."

"How do you know the Ballesteros are players?" Evans asked.

"I never said the Ballesteros were players," griped the caller and I never said that we are looking for Dr. Galán. "Let's just say we have very sharp eyes and very big ears and your lady friend is in deep trouble."

"Then you're certainly not, DEA or BATF, are you?" Evans said, referring to the Drug Enforcement Administration and the Bureau of Alcohol, Tobacco, and Firearms.

Evans had a great dislike for the BATF, and their cowboy attitude, and he wasn't impressed by some of the marshmallows the DEA was sending to South America.

"Who I work for is not important. I assure you, the Ballesteros organization is relatively clean. Like most big corporations they have trouble once in a while with a shipment of product," volunteered the caller trying to establish his bona fides, "but we think it's just low level employees using the combine to make a quick buck."

"And, of course, the Ballesteros provide your company with juicy little bits of information that are not available from any other source. Why have I been maneuvered in to a contract with a known cartel?" Evans demanded.

"I just said, *we don't believe the Ballesteros are dirty.* Besides, that's not my department, Commander."

"I'm a cut-out. Someone you guys can use like toilet paper," Evans growled. "*For free!* Let the dopers pay my bills, huh? What's the plan, to roast the Ballesteros's coffee beans when the intel dries up?"

"It's not my department." The caller's tone told Evans he was dealing with a government employee of similar rank to a commander and one that had been ordered to recruit him at all costs. "Our current problem is quite different," continued the husky voice.

"And simple," Evans interrupted. "The FBI can't find her in the U.S. They think she's flown the coop. Your company fired most of its field agents and your slick electronic gizmos can't locate her, can they? You don't know where she is but you think she might be in South America, in the middle of a damn jungle, right?"

"Commander, you cannot imagine the misery this drug will cause if the formula is made available to the streets," the caller pleaded, trying to appeal to Evans's sense of patriotism. "It will literally change mankind as we know it."

"You know something, whoever-you-are?"

"What?"

"I don't like this secret squirrel bullshit! Not one damn bit. I don't like being used like shit paper because you guys leak like a sieve. And I don't like you!"

"I may be able to fund your efforts on a pay as you go basis, Evans" the caller volunteered.

"Kiss my ass. That's real nice, whoever-you-are. No Doc, no money. And of course, I'll need a government travel voucher filled out in triplicate to justify my expenses. And if I, or any of my men, get killed snooping around Cocaine Inc., well that's our tough luck. Huh? Pure irony, pure unadulterated goddamned irony. This has to be the first time the Agency, the DEA, State Department, Pentagon and the traffickers all have the same objective."

The caller took a deep breath and exhaled with a gush.

"Let's have a PM," he suggested, using spy talk to refer to a personal face-to-face meeting. He knew he wasn't going to recruit Evans the way he had several other adventurers.

"In Socal pal," Evans agreed, referring to Southern California.

"I'll get back to you with a time and place in your area."

"And then you'll have a face, whoever-you-are. One I can rip off if I get hung out to dry. Think about it before you head west."

"Commander, I assure you, you'll have our full support."

"Sure I will. Just like I do with the Ballesteros Combine, huh?" The caller didn't respond. "One more thing, whoever-you-are," Evans said, with a degree of intensity.

"Yeah?" the caller replied indignantly.

"Tell your boss I'm not in to parasitic relationships. From now on, I'm in to free enterprise. You got that?"

"What?"

"Bring your checkbook, dickhead!" Evans shouted.

"I'll be in touch."

"You do that!" The dial tone assaulted Evans's ear.

"Goddamned man-eater," he mumbled, referring to the man's boss.

He hung up the phone and slumped back into his office chair. An image of an emerald green rain forest shimmering in sweltering jungle heat momentarily flooded his mind. He saw the earth-toned peaks of the snowcapped Andes towering above the jungle in misty white clouds.

Isolated, humid, remote, the *Chaparé* region of Bolivia was a huge natural greenhouse brimming with exotic forms of life, many of which were unknown to science. It was the most perfect place on Earth to grow coca bushes. Cocaine Inc., had turned the *Chaparé* into a giant plantation, the leaves of the coca bush into a cash crop, and the Indians and mestizos of the forest into *zepes*, ants. There were no roads in the *Chaparé*, only foot trails cut by brigades of machete wielding Indians and mestizos. Like leaf-cutter ants, a huge army of *zepes* transported thousands of hundred-pound bags called *la carga* along jungle trails to clandestine processing laboratories hidden in the jungle. It was a lawless frontier beyond the authority of the corrupt Bolivian government.

Evans eased his mind into an alpha state, wondering if Carol Galán was with one of the families they had met during their expeditions.

It's the only way she could survive down there, he thought.

In his mind's eye he saw her traipsing around the jungle. Then a helicopter lifted off angrily from the combined Bolivian-DEA base camp at *Chimoré*, a barbed wire encircled encampment in a vast sea of green. It *whooped* off in shimmering waves of steamy jungle heat toward the Red Zone, *la zona roja*, ferrying a combined troop of agents on another futile bust.

"Time to put another *lavaperro or zepe* in jail," he mumbled.

The narcos called their underlings dogwasher and ant. In his mind Evans pictured the military base at *Chimoré*, nestled up against the *Chaparé* rain forest. Surrounded by hundreds of square miles of lush green jungle, the strew of barracks, bunkers, and sandbag fortifications looked like an oozing cancer on the face of a beautiful child. Bolivian Leopards in spotted camouflage fatigues milled about the compound not really mixing with immaculately groomed Special Forces soldiers dressed in BDUs. Scruffy cowboy-minded DEA agents dressed in mismatched uniforms stood out like hippies in the Queen's Guard. Their lives were separate. Their huts were segregated. Their foods were different. Their thoughts were disconnected. Their objectives were dissimilar. Their pay was disparate.

Evans's mind roamed the make-ship encampment he had taught at in the early 1990's. He remembered the sign over the door of one of the huts. It read, *Welcome to the Chaparé Safari*. Inside, neat rows of mosquito-netted bunks lined walls plastered with photographs of lovers and nude pinup girls. He could almost smell the sweat, the urine, and the gun oil, over the odor of aviation fuel and *melange,* the gristly Bolivian stew devoured by the Leopards. Shades of Vietnam haunted Evans. Operation Snowcap had shades of Vietnam.

She must be in Bolivia, he thought. *They think she is or they wouldn't call me. The Agency has more assets than a mangy dog has fleas, but not in narco infested primeval jungle. They think she's in the Chaparé and they're right. I can feel it. She discovered something there. I saw it in her eyes in the Sopocachi. Maybe it was a plant or an insect, or a new part of herself. Whatever it was, it's called her back.*

Evans mused over the thought of Carol Galán tromping around the *Chaparé* alone. The heart of South America was the last great frontier on planet Earth. Evans knew the country well. He had operated there while on active duty with the SEALs and he had made numerous trips as a private consultant, including several with Dr. Galán. The jungle wasn't Carol Galán's element. It was wild, untamed, rugged, and lawless.

She has to be with one of the families we met during the expeditions. But which one?" he mused. "Maybe she's hiding out with Rita Contreras in La Paz? Nah. They would have checked her out before calling me. But with Rita's help she could be hold up in the Chaparé, or the Beni.

Evans was staggered by the task. The *Chaparé* was a lush tropical highland jungle located on the rain drenched eastern slopes of the Andes. It was strategically located between Santa Cruz, the drug capital of Bolivia, and the *Beni*, a wild savanna transition zone between the steamy Brazilian Amazon to the north and east, and the cold windswept Andes to the south and west. The *Beni* alone was large enough to accommodate the whole of Great Britain.

She could be anywhere in South America, he thought. Anywhere. But, I'll bet she heads for the jungle, to one of the mestizo families that helped us find plants. Okay. While the FBI beat the streets of San Francisco and New York, and the CIA listens to distant voices bouncing back from geosynchronous satellites, I get to slap mosquitoes in the Chaparé, on a pay as you go basis. All right. But the jokes on you, assholes, you faceless, nameless, usurious, assholes. Because I love this kind of shit.

Evans picked up the phone and dialed a long distance number in the Louisiana exchange. It rang twice before a man with a loud booming voice answered.

"Savarese, here."

"Boomer."

"Yeah, Boss."

"You know that gig I told you about down in Colombia?"

"Yeah."

"Forget about it," Evans ordered.

"But, Boss. I was countin' on a little action. I'm bored shitless," Savarese begged.

"I want you to meet Fred Swan in La Paz in three weeks. Can you make it?"

"La Paz? As in Bolivia?"

"Yeah."

"You bet I can!" Savarese boomed, so excited he hurt Evans's ear. "I have to put the Flash through her paces and then I'm out of here."

"Three weeks. Check in to the Sopocachi Hotel and wait for Fred."

"The Sopo-what?"

"Sopocachi. I spell, S-O-P-O-C-A-C-H-I."

"Roger that. Tell Popeye I'll have a couple of little *señoritas* and a cold one waitin' for him," Savarese roared excitedly.

"Whatever tweaks your trigger, Boomer. I'll fax you a gear list. *Luego*," Evans growled. He hung up the phone and leaned back in his chair to think. "Goddamned man-eater," he mumbled.

Chapter 5

The storm grew in intensity until sheet lightning spread across the night sky illuminating the jungle in flickers and flashes. Then a massive thunderhead reared up like an angry thoroughbred and bolted out of the east unleashing its full fury on the jungle. Lieutenant Duran halted the patrol with a whisper to the man on each side of him. There was no shelter and no place to take cover. As the rain forest exploded in violence the sixteen-man patrol hunkered down under thin ponchos to wait out the storm.

Bolts of lightning broke in front of them, and then closer to the right and left, ten thousand volts zipping along ionized trails at one hundred and eighty-six thousand miles per second sending down counter surges in a split second. The troops saw them as singular flashes of light followed by claps of thunder like artillery shells booming all around. The wind freshened and the rain came. At first it seeped through the triple canopy jungle like coins through the fingers of a hungry man. Then, it turned from scattered splashing drops driven by gusts of wind to torrential waves that lashed the jungle with abandon. For fifteen minutes the rain forest cracked and rumbled and crashed as a deluge of water and giant tree limbs plummeted to the forest floor. A huge horizontal branch covered by a dense carpet of orchids, bromeliads, and rain soaked humus, plunged one hundred and sixty feet to the leaf litter below barely missing the men huddling in the darkness. They couldn't see it. But they felt the ground shake and knew death was close.

Then, as quickly as it came, it stopped and the sound of raindrops blended with the call of leptodactylid frogs. They struck up a loud and monotonous tone delighting in the fresh shower. The jungle came alive with animals on the move, hunting, searching, digging in the rain-softened earth. Like amphibians, the SEALs too came to life. They packed away their ponchos in silence and headed down the trail, maneuvering slowly through the dense jungle like a long green snake slithering through wet grass.

The world underneath the canopy was humid, wet, and perpetually dark. But it teemed with life on the move. Ninety-nine percent of the animals made their way by chemical trails, imperceptible little puffs of odor that marked the way in total darkness. For men, dependent upon a weak visual sense, it was an experience in sensory deprivation, black and dank like the inside of a huge cave. Without night vision devices the men of Alpha Platoon, SEAL Team TWO would have been blind.

As he felt his way step by step down the trail Lieutenant Jack Duran watched the green-dark figures patrolling ahead of him. He flipped up his NVGs and used a thermal imager to scan the trail ahead. Unlike his night vision goggles, which amplified ambient light, the imager detected heat. Thirty yards in front of the patrol he spotted a jungle cat. A reddish-orange smear of body heat filled his eyepiece as the animal scurried into the bushes intimidated by aliens in its realm. Duran flipped his NVGs back down and surveyed the formation again. The interval was too close for comfort but necessary for the circumstance.

They are good troops, he thought, *the best in Colombia.* Then, he looked at the officer walking directly in front of him. Awkward. Gangly. Out of his element. *All but their leader.*

Duran's sixteen-man platoon was divided into two squads, each with eight Colombian trainees from the *Bloque de Busqueda*, a secret counter narcotics unit. Half of his men, mixed with another squad of Colombians, were somewhere ahead and he had lost communications with them.

For several hours the platoon hiked down trail toward a river that cut through the center of the valley. Just after first light Master Chief *Stick* Masure held up a clenched fist and halted the patrol from the front of the formation. The signal passed silently down the file to the rear security man who took up a defensive position behind a tree. Masure looked back from his position behind the Colombian point man searching the deep green foliage for Duran. They locked eyes in the dim green light filtering down through a tangle of branches. Masure signaled with a half salute.

Duran strained his eyes to see the reason for the stop. With exception of the pause for the storm they had been on the move since last light. He pushed the button on his inter-squad radio and whispered. The faint sound of his voice vibrated the throat mike strapped around his neck. Masure heard the question through a tiny earpiece the size of a hearing aid.

"What's up, Master?" he whispered.

Like the other men in the patrol, Masure was camouflaged in face paint. He had drawn a black tree branch across his left cheek that ran up to the right side of his forehead. It distorted the image of a face by breaking up the light green he had used as a base color. Sweat and rain had washed off some of the paint and had blended the colors naturally like the jungle. All Duran could see was the whites of Masure's eyes underneath an Australian bush hat. A bird called loudly overhead welcoming a new day.

"I got a bad feeling, L.T. Something just crawled over my grave," Masure whispered.

He cupped his fingers over his face like a catcher in a baseball game. It was the hand and arm signal that indicated enemy ahead.

"For Christ's sake, Stick. This is just a damn training op," Duran whispered, with a hint of annoyance in his voice. "Cut the histrionics."

Stick was Masure's nickname. It was derived from a measuring stick and related to his other nickname, Tripod, an allusion to his extraordinarily large male appendage that saw a great deal more action than his M-16. Masure's appearance was deceiving. He was too handsome for a warrior. Six feet two with bedroom-green eyes, he was a lady-killer on the prowl. But his muscular frame and boyish good looks hid the soul of a warrior. Senior officers often questioned his E9 rank when he wore his khaki uniform, because he didn't look old enough for the highest enlisted rank in the Navy. Masure always countered such investigation with a disarming smile and a question. *May I see your ID card, sir? You look a might too old to be in a fighting service.* He would grin until the questioning officer smiled. Tough as nails and as hard as a rock, Stick Masure was one of the best fighting men in the U.S. Navy SEALs.

"Let's take a break and palaver, L.T." he suggested, exerting his experience.

L.T. was SEAL short-talk for lieutenant. Masure had operated in every theater of the world and had seen combat action in several undeclared wars. He knew the handsome young officer would agree to just about anything he suggested as long as he was never proven wrong. After two years working together he was still batting a thousand.

"Roger. Come on back," Duran ordered.

Duran gave a hand and arm signal that traveled like a wave to each end of the formation. It was a silent order to get off the trail. The troops quietly faded into the foliage, covering their tracks behind them. Before Masure could work his way back to the Lieutenant's position the fourteen men accompanying them were invisible.

"I got a bad feeling, Boss," Masure said, whispering in Duran's ear.

"You said that on the radio," Duran complained.

Duran raised his canteen and took a swallow of tepid water that tasted of iodine. It failed to quench his thirst. He grimaced, wiped his mouth with a wet sleeve, and offered the canteen to Masure who declined with a shake of his head.

"What'd you say I have the men lock and load?" Masure asked.

"No fuckin' way, Tripod."

Duran often called Masure, Tripod, when he disliked his suggestions. He was a Yale graduate and sailor-talk didn't fit him the way it did most sailors.

"Half of Alpha Platoon is out there," he frowned, pointing down the trail. "If we walk into them loaded up, bad shit could happen."

"This op sucks, sir." Op was SEAL slang for a military operation. "You know I don't like separating the men, for any reason. And I don't like integrating BB's into our formations."

"Master, we've been workin' these guys for three months. It's their country. Lieutenant Rodriguez is in charge of this op," Duran argued.

BB was short talk for *Bloque de Busqueda,* a secret unit of elite Colombian troops especially trained for counter narcotics operations. The CIA and DEA had hand picked and carefully screened each man. Alpha Platoon was assigned to train them in small unit tactics, close quarters battle, and shipboarding. After three months on the job Duran was confident in their abilities to move, shoot, and communicate. Up until the present mission he had been sure that they were ready for assignment to the operational units working the hot areas around Medellin, Cali, and the jungles of the Amazon Basin. But two hours after insertion his confidence had been shattered. The radioman had lost HF communications and his inter-squad radio lacked the legs to reach his assistant officer in the other platoon. Duran was worried the two groups would stumble into each other and someone would open up. Half his men were out there closing in on a mock target in a pincer operation designed to simulate two units simultaneously hitting a drug lab and he needed HF radio communications to coordinate the final assault on the target. Masure was worried about the mission too but he was more concerned about narco-terrorists, powerful men who could buy and sell small countries and have money left over. Commander Evans had put the fear of caution in his soul.

"Boss, have I ever been wrong?"

"No," Duran replied, solemnly.

"I'm telling you, sir, the shit is going to hit the fan. I can smell it," Masure insisted.

"Do you realize the chance you're asking me to take?" Duran asked.

"Proper previous planning prevents piss poor performance," Masure whispered. "An empty weapon is like a car without gas, worthless as tits on a bull. Hell, we might as well be carrying around baseball bats."

He emphasized the point by holding up his M-16 and shaking it.

"Master Chief, this is a national park," Duran argued without conviction. "We've worked this area for months. This op has been cleared for days."

"And that's what's buggin' me, sir," Masure complained, too loudly. "Too many people know we're out here. The BBs are gettin' a reputation. The Medellin unit cut Pablo Escobar down like a cheap thug. The man was a multibillionaire, sir." Masure's eyes grew in size. "He commanded a small army. Paybacks are hell, LT."

"We've been over this ground, Master Chief," Duran argued.

Duran knew Masure had a sixth sense for danger. Like an animal he could see and feel things that others couldn't. Masure was famous in the ranks of the SEALs for his exploits in secret little wars, and in dirty little bars. Duran didn't want to walk around the jungle naked without loaded weapons, but he was fearful of getting into a firefight with his own men. He was afraid the Colombians would get rattled if he ordered them to load their weapons and that one of them might spook and open up on the other platoon if they bumped into each other.

"Sooner or later they're going to get popped and I don't want to be in the frag zone with an empty weapon. They lost comm, didn't they? First time in three months. How many times did you tell him, sir? You got one, you got none. You got two, you might have one. He brought one and now he's got none," Masure said, referring to HF radios. "I don't like it, LT. I smell shit and I don't like it."

"It's the first time they've dropped comm since we've been workin' 'em."

"How do we know someone isn't set 'em up. Or settin' us up. We got thirty-two men out here running around out here with unloaded weapons. This is a war zone, Lieutenant," Masure complained.

Although they were speaking in his whispers his voice carried to the men crouching in the bushes around them.

"This is *not* a war zone, Master Chief," Duran argued, bring the tone of the conversation back to a hushed whisper. "This is a national park."

"Tell that to the trainees that got ambushed last month. Eight KIA in thirty seconds." KIA was short-talk for killed in action.

"This is bad-guy country, sir, and they ain't packin' blanks."

Masure pushed the button on the side of his M-16 and let the empty magazine slide out into his left hand. He stuck it in his pocket and pulled out a magazine loaded with full metal jacket. He eyeballed Duran with determination and conviction. They locked eyes for several seconds before Duran nodded his head in agreement.

"Okay," he conceded. "Be cool. The Colonel may have some Green Beanies out here spying on us."

Green Beanie was SEAL slang for Green Beret, U.S. Army Special Forces soldiers. The traditional rivalry seen at army-navy football games at the Academies extended to the services. The Army colonel in charge of the overall training mission in Colombia always gave preference to the Green Beret. He used the SF to evaluate the SEALs even though man for man they were much more highly trained. The Colombian trainees that had been killed the preceding month were students of the SF.

"I don't shoot friendlies, LT. And I don't walk into an ambush unarmed," Masure said, with a deadly serious growl.

He slipped the magazine into his assault rifle and quietly eased it home. Only Duran heard the distinctive *click* of a full magazine sliding home. Masure eased back on the bolt and chambered a round. He watched Duran with hard eyes as he loaded a thirty round magazine in his own rifle. It was an act that told him how much faith the young officer had in his sixth sense.

Masure possessed the luck of the Irish as well as animal instincts. The hair on the back of his neck was standing and he didn't know why. He loaded a 40mm flechette into the M203 grenade launcher attached to the barrel of his M-16 and eased the breach closed with a *click*.

"What about the men?" he pressed.

"No way. What if,"

Masure interrupted him. "What if we run into a bunch of booger-eaters bent on paybacks, sir?"

"And what if we run into our own men?" Duran countered, "and one of our trainees smokes someone? That's not an option."

"Okay. Okay. Then, how about Simons? He knows the sound of incoming. He saw a lot of action with Commander Evans before he retired."

Duran shook his head no, then reluctantly gave in. "Okay. But tell him not to engage unless he's one hundred percent sure of his target. And don't let any of the men see him swap mags."

Duran took another swallow of the tepid water in his canteen then glared at Masure. "Goddamnit, Tripod. Now you've got me spooked."

Masure grinned showing perfect white teeth behind his mask of green face paint. He knew he had the Lieutenant under his thumb.

"Have I ever been wrong, sir? I can smell trouble like I can smell pussy."

Duran smiled. "Listen. This is what I want you to do," he continued as he pulled out his map and a red lens flashlight. "Hang a left at the bug shack and head back down to the river. It's about two clicks due south."

"I know where it is, LT." Masure cut. "I got this damn jungle memorized. We're aborting?"

"For the moment."

"What about Lieutenant ready-for-action Rodriguez. I thought he was in charge?" Masure chided, referring to the Colombian officer hiding in the bushes next to them.

Rodriguez had been watching the conversation but he had made no effort to join in the discussion.

"Hang a left at the bug shack. We'll hail down one of the support boats and pick up another radio. When we make comm we'll set up a new time on target."

"And if we don't?"

"Then we'll abort."

"We should've packed a SATCOM. Hell, I would've carried it myself,"

Masure reproved, referring to the satellite radios preferred by the SEALs. The Colombians didn't possess the sophisticated equipment or the satellite links necessary to use them.

"Now you're startin' to piss me off, Tripod. Leave the politics to me," Duran scolded.

"My pleasure, as long as it doesn't cost us our heads," Masure countered.

"You know Colonel Tulley put a lot of heat on me to let Rodriguez go it alone," Duran whispered.

Rodriguez heard his name and stood up from his crouch in the foliage as if called by a superior officer.

"Yeah. And I can see where he's at," Masure said, cutting the Colombian a glare.

Masure had fought tooth and nail against combined squad operations. He didn't like integrating foreigners into SEAL formations, even for training. Moreover, working two combined platoons against the same target was his worst nightmare. He had almost been killed in Indonesia by a team of Russian Spetznaz while involved in a similar training mission. Duran had protested too, but Colonel Tulley, the U.S. Army colonel in charge of the MAAG mission, had insisted on integrated squads. He had also insisted that Lieutenant Rodriguez plan and lead the mission. During the planning and briefing stage at TOC headquarters the Colombian officer had performed well. It was a pattern the SEALs had come to know in the three months they had been training the *Bloque de Busqueda*. At headquarters Rodriguez stepped up to the plate. In the jungle, he became one of the boys waiting for Duran to make the command decisions.

Colonel Tulley's words echoed inside Duran's head.

As you were Lieutenant Duran! Tulley had yelled, gruffly cutting off Duran's protest. *You boys are down here to train these men, not baby sit 'em. All of them, goddamnit!* he had snapped in a deep southern accent. *I want to see the same success out of you SEALs that I've seen out of my A-Team.*

Masure had been standing outside the doorway with several others and had commented loud enough for the Colonel to hear. *Yeah, eight friendly KIA.*

Tulley had ignored the anonymous wisecrack. He thought SEALs were a bunch of ill disciplined swabs that got too much media attention.

Lieutenant Duran, if you do everything for Rodriguez, he'll never learn shit. Dump it on him! he had shouted. *Step back out of the way and let the man have the goddamn ball.*

Sure thing, Colonel. I'll pass it. But he's not much of a receiver.

Colonel Tulley was a tanker with no experience in special operations. He didn't understand SOF or the men assigned to him. The *Bloque de Busqueda* was actually the best fighting unit in Colombia. It wasn't the men who were in question but rather the leadership. In South America privilege and money often acquired military rank and position. Lieutenant Rodriguez was a good man from a wealthy *Bogotañeo* family. He was an excellent shot and a polished leader at HQ. In the field he turned into a frightened schoolboy.

Rodriguez crept over to Duran and whispered. "*Que pasa?*"

"*Nada. Vamos a rio por un otra radio,*" Duran reported, telling him of his decision to go down to the river for another radio.

"*Bueno,*" Rodriguez agreed. A bird screeched overhead and Rodriguez's eyes grew in size. He nervously searched the jungle all around.

"You know we're not that far from target. The main shack is about a half click down the trail," Masure said, pointing to Duran's map.

"I know," Duran snarled, watching Rodriguez hunker down in the bushes waiting for him to give the order to proceed. "I know this jungle too," he frowned.

"It's higher ground," Masure continued, ignoring Duran's annoyance. "Maybe we can reach Lieutenant Spear with an inter-squad radio," he suggested, referring to the junior officer leading the other combined platoon.

SEAL platoons were composed of two officers and fourteen enlisted men. They often worked as separate squads of one officer and seven enlisted. Lieutenant junior grade Chuck Spear was an independent thinker and an outstanding leader who adapted to problems readily. If he had communications with the TOC, he was aware Alpha had lost HF contact. He would be listening for them on his inter-squad radio. Duran was hoping to make contact so Spear could serve as a communications link with the TOC. Masure was hoping they could make comm so they could compare positions and load up with live ammunition.

"I'm switching channels," Duran said. "If I don't make contact by the time we get to the bug shack, take the trail down to the river."

"Roger, Boss. Good decision."

As Masure made his way back to the point a shiver ran down his spine. Somehow he just knew something bad was going to happen.

Chapter 6

It was one hundred degrees at ninety-nine percent humidity when Carol Galán reached the steamy jungles of the Bolivian Amazon. She entered the poverty-racked country by river through the back door from Peru. As her ferry neared port she reached over the rail and threw a coin in the *Madre de Diós*. With it went her best wishes and her emotions. The river was so murky the coin disappeared instantly in the mocha colored water. Watching it, it seemed to watch her, watching it. Drowning in a stream of emotions it pulled her thoughts down into murkiness.

I can't dream that dream anymore. It haunts my nights, and now my days, she thought, seeing the killer's permanently disfigured face in the swirling river. His crazed eyes stared at her as he panted for breath, foaming at the mouth about his exposed teeth. And the other men. They were dressed as policemen.

I keep running and running and I can't get those images out of my mind. What am I doing here?

Looking over the rail, she tried to cast the horrible thoughts into the water.

I've traveled so far and I don't have a plan.

For an instant she saw Derek Evans's handsome face. Then she saw him sneaking out of Rita Contrares's hotel room. Anger coursed through her veins, then loneliness, then fear, then despair, until depression overwhelmed her like a noxious gas.

In my life there's been so much heartache and pain, most of it my own doing.

She had taken an instant like to the handsome SEAL. The physical attraction had gradually grown into a deep emotion and a strong desire that manifested itself as intellectual challenge. The three of them, Evans, Contrares, and herself, had argued for hours about politics, religion, and the nature of mankind. She had hidden her affection and desire behind spirited verbal fencing matches.

It's not his fault, and it's not Rita's. I never told him how I felt about him. Nor Rita. All I ever did was bash him in the face with a contrary idea. I've always hidden my feelings from others and I've always reached too high. That's the tragic side to my life. Blind ambition. I've let my work drive my life and I've ignored my emotions for so long I've forgotten how to be a woman. Now there's a little white lie that surrounds me and I can't see clearly without it.

Using her given name, Carol had made her way from Rodriguez airport in Tijuana to Mexico City where she had friends who had helped her acquire a fake passport in the name of Maria Sanchez. With a new identity as a Mexican citizen, she had flown to Caracas, Venezuela, traveled by bus to Cartagena, Colombia, and caught a flight to Cuzco, Peru. There she had contacted Rita Contreras by calling a professor in an office down the hall from Rita's. They had arranged a meeting in the small Bolivian town of Riberalta. It was Rita's hometown, a nice little country village she had visited during one of the Syntec plant gathering expeditions.

From Cuzco, high in the Peruvian Andes, she had taken a bus down to the jungle town of Puerto Maldonado and caught a ferry down the *Madre de Diós* to Bolivia. As the ferry churned the water pier side, rivulets of sweat poured down her body underneath her blouse. She cocked her tattered straw hat back on her head and surveyed Puerto Heath with a cautious eye. It sweltered under billowing cumulus clouds in stifling tropical heat. A brief squall during the night had added to the humidity and the muddy conditions ashore. It was still the dry season but by the look of the sky she knew the rains would come soon and with them misery.

The decrepit port of entry consisted of several discolored wooden docks and a slough of board shacks and mud-brick hovels. The shanties were set up muddy alleyways that branched off one unpaved main street that paralleled the river. As the crow flies she was only two hundred miles up river from Riberalta. But there were falls down river at Esperanza that limited river traffic to small native boats. The next leg of her journey would have to be by bus.

It looks like rain, she thought. *Dark clouds fill my skies and paralyze my mind. But I know the sun is going to shine. In life a little rain must fall. So let it rain.*

For a second her thoughts flashed back to the horror she had witnessed in her lab in San Diego. The images haunted her day and night surging up like tsunamis of fear that overwhelmed all other emotions. She questioned why she had fled the country, why she hadn't gone to the FBI for help. In her heart of hearts she knew the reason but she wasn't willing to admit consciously that the drug was influencing her decisions, coloring her thoughts. Emotions were flooding her mind in waves that varied from elation to utter despair.

The ferry nudged up against the pier and the crew dropped the gangway with a clank. Momentarily the gates opened and a throng of people rushed to the gangway to be the first in line to clear customs.

Life is a door that opens wide. Each person must step inside and search for answers that give life meaning. Go forth, Carol, she thought, *and seek those answers with finesse.*

With resolution she shouldered her backpack and followed the crowd off the ferry.

What is done is done, she thought, as she walked down the gangway.

She looked around and saw the poverty that was Bolivia.

Poverty, disease, greed, despair, weapons of mass destruction, drugs.

Intractable human problems embroil this dog eat dog world. Why do I feel the emptiness? Do I have a hole in my soul? Then she thought, *Time has a way of making one see how life's pressures take their toll.*

Up the pier a group of men in uniform were directing passengers with harsh unfriendly orders. When she saw the soldiers fear surged through her entire body, almost paralyzing her muscles.

Oh God, I don't want to do this, she thought, stopping on the wharf. *What am I doing here?*

She wanted to run, to find a phone to call Evans, to beg him to come and rescue her. But there were no phones in the Bolivian Amazon. There was no place to run. She took a deep breath to calm her nerve then joined the queue.

All along the wharf scruffy looking guards dressed in dirty uniforms were inspecting barges overloaded with goods. The sound of merchants arguing with corrupt officials in rapid-fire Spanish mixed with the noise of saucy Latin music blaring from nearby billiard parlors. One of the guards eyed her suspiciously as she walked up the wharf. To thwart his interest she asked a rancher she had met on the ferry an innocuous question about immigration, making it appear as though she was traveling with him. She walked close beside the man to the customs house.

The immigration building was a decayed, whitewashed, mud-and-wattle shack set just off the docks. It was an old turn-of-the-century rubber warehouse that had been converted to government use. Inside, Bolivian officials, clad in dirty drab-olive fatigues walked among bags and crates of Peruvian merchandise, scribbling notes on their clipboards.

Shortly after entering she was greeted by a customs-immigration officer, a fat moon-faced man who wore dark sunglasses to hide his greedy eyes. She handed him her passport without speaking.

"Do you work for the Mexican government, *Señora*?" he asked with a suspicious eye.

"No. And I am not married, *Señor*," she said pleasantly.

"*Sí, señorita.*"

As soon as she had spoken the words she realized she had made a mistake. He eyed her up and down like a prize heifer then examined her passport thoroughly. He had never seen a Mexican passport before so he turned it around from every angle waiting for his bribe.

Run your stubby fat tobacco-stained fingers over the pages again, Paco, she thought. *Do it a fourth time, fatso. Now check the printer's marks, the cut of the paper, the photo, the face, the numbers. Yeah the numbers. Now look up the numbers up in your registry of stolen passports. Oh, you don't have one do you, Paco? Too far out in the jungle, eh? So what are you waiting for, fat man?*

Money?

"Why do you visit Bolivia?" he asked.

"I have friends in Riberalta and I am on my way to visit them," she replied.

"We don't see many Northerners in this town, *Señorita*. Why did you not go through La Paz, like other visitors to my country?" he asked, showing a set of gray-brown teeth stained by heavy tobacco use. He watched her eyes carefully for clues.

"I am a teacher and I was visiting a schoolhouse in Peru where I once taught. It was easier to travel down river than to go back to Cuzco and fly to La Paz," she explained.

The answer appeared to satisfy him. But she was beginning to get nervous and the customs officer sensed it. With a suspicious eye, he set her passport aside and ordered one of his men to search her backpack. Carol watched the man closely, and from time to time the other agents as they rifled the bags and crates of nearby passengers. Then it dawned on her. From the amount of money passing from hand to hand without documents, she realized that virtually all transactions were contraband approved by bribes. She surreptitiously slipped the rotund immigration agent the equivalent of ten dollars and he immediately stamped her passport. His surliness evaporated and he cheerfully offered to buy her foreign currency. Carol declined his offer, gathered up her belongings, and left the building as quickly as she could.

Outside, a young boy, barely twelve years old, offered to change money for her. He was barefoot, as skinny as a starved dog, and dirty. Taking pity on him, she agreed to his terms. She smiled when he counted out the notes like a machine. With a toothy grin he handed her a huge wad of near worthless Bolivian currency.

"*Soy una millionaires* -- I am a millionaire," she joked, as she exchanged a twenty dollar bill for a stack of Bolivian bills the size of a brick.

She asked the boy where she could find a hotel and he offered to show her to the best one in town. As they walked down the muddy street, people eyed her like hungry dogs looking for a meal. Music blared from open-air bars and billiard parlors, and people argued in the street. On one corner three men were practicing with their trumpets, playing their music slightly off key the way Bolivian peasants like it. Several scruffy young men on motorbikes gathered about her, putting along on their bikes as she walked along behind the boy. They pestered her the entire length of the town, offering taxi services to nowhere. She ignored the persistent entrepreneurs and followed the boy without question.

He led her to a bare-board hotel built on stilts out over the river. It was a single story structure that looked more like an old plank warehouse than a hotel. The boy barged through the open door as if he owned the place. She followed. Inside, it smelled of tobacco and sweat, and greasy *melange*. The proprietor eyed her up and down lustfully, then tried to gouge her for twice the rate. But the boy protested and yelled something to a woman working out back. Threatening the kid with a backhand, the manager grudgingly accepted the going rate and showed Carol to a room. It was dank and dark, and the bed was filthy, but from experience she knew it was the best in town. To thank the boy she offered to buy him dinner.

He led her next door to a small shack where dockworkers ate and ordered for the both of them as if he were her husband. Over the best meal Victor Fernandez had eaten in two months, she hired him to stand guard over her room while she slept. Exhausted after eating she returned to her room and collapsed with Victor standing guard outside her locked door. It turned out to be money well spent. During the night she had two visitors, first the proprietor then the corpulent customs agent. Victor made so much noise both men went away to avoid the hassle. At first light she thanked Victor, paid him well, and caught the first bus into the Bolivian interior.

The road into the *Beni* was narrow and rutted, and full of muddy wallows that cause the ancient Mercedes to groan and wheeze like an old hog seeking relief against a fence post. There had been a brief squall during the night adding to the discomfort of the humidity and the poor conditions of the dirt road. As the bus bumped along, sometimes at a mule's pace, Carol thought about her upcoming meeting with Contrares.

I'll get Rita to retain a peke-peke to transport supplies into the jungle, she thought. *Maybe she can hire those two guys we used last year. What were their names? Slimy and Slippery. How could I ever forget those characters? I couldn't have gotten along without them. I'll set up a hide-site several miles from Rodrigo's farm, somewhere down near the last navigable part of the river where they can drop off supplies. The only person who knows I'm in Bolivia is Rita and even she doesn't know about Rodrigo.*

A surge of fear slammed through her body for no apparent reason.

Oh God. Why are you here, Carol? she questioned. *You should have gone to the police. But those men were wearing uniforms,* she remembered, seeing in hallucinatory detail a gang of thugs plundering her lab.

She worried and planned mile after bumpy mile. The bus was loaded with campesinos carrying chickens and produce and crying children. At each stop more seemed to get on than get off. She settled into her seat for the long bumpy ride and mused about the future.

I hope the equipment I left at Rodrigo's is still working. I only have a small amount of the sample left. Without it I don't have a prayer of figuring out the molecular structure. Then she thought, *there must have been something special about that last batch of coca leaves Rodrigo gave me. Perhaps they were from a different species of plant? Perhaps...*

A puzzling sensation overcame her, a mescaline like intensification of sight that rendered colors so palpable they seemed to come off on her hand when she touched them. Up ahead the muddy red clay road became a palette of swirling ochres and raw umbers flanked by the brilliant emerald and olive greens of the jungle on each side of the road. The sky above turned to a mixture of glowing crimson, salmon, and vermilion, mixed with baby blue and purple. She could almost taste the colors, and smell them. For several minutes she delighted in the beauty around her until the man seated next to her spoke.

"Are you okay, Señora?" he asked, concerned by the blank stare on her face.

Then fear consumed her.

"Yes. Thanks," she answered in excellent Bolivian Spanish. "I must have dozed off."

To avoid his eyes, she turned and looked out the window.

I can't allow myself to be exposed to the substance again, she thought. *It's beginning to affect my sight, and my reasoning. Don't do it again, Carol. You need every molecule for analysis.*

After a brief bizarre episode in Cuzco, she had promised herself she wouldn't touch the substance again. But deep down inside she knew it was a promise she couldn't keep. Just after the bus departed Puerto Heath, she had reached inside her bag and stroked the magic substance with the tip of her finger. C_{31} was slowly and insidiously affecting her brain chemistry and she knew it. She just didn't want to admit it. She felt the need to take it out of her backpack and rotate it in the palm of her hand. It was a deep longing more intense than any hunger she had ever known

No. No. I won't do it again, she repeated inside her head, mile after bumpy mile. *I won't.*

The hallucination wore off before she reached Riberalta. Her ten thousand-mile-journey ended with the dying shudder of a bus engine. In silence she remained seated to absorb the sensations of motionlessness, of not feeling chased. In a few days she would take a boat up the *Rio Mamoré* and hike into the *Chaparé* to Rodrigo's farm. He was an old Mestizo she had befriended when his son, the family's only means of support, had disappeared. Rodrigo, like most inhabitants of the *Chaparé* was a poor coca farmer but she didn't hold that against him. It was a way of life endemic to the region. In fact she respected Rodrigo. He was a wise old medicine man who possessed a tremendous wealth of knowledge about medicinal plants. She was so comfortable around him she had set up a small lab near his remote farm to study the plants he used to treat people who came from miles around to seek his help.

When the bus stopped the other passengers immediately crowded toward the exit and piled off, but not Carol. She just sat there in the dark until the driver asked her if she needed help.

"*No Señor. Soy completemente consado* -- I'm just tired," she answered with a flawless accent. "Very, very tired."

He again offered to help her but she declined. Wearily she got up and staggered out of the bus. Riberalta only had one hotel. She ambled the short distance down the dark clay road and checked in for the night. To ensure a good night's sleep, she stroked the magic substance just once before going to bed. It was enough to absorb a few million molecules of C_{31}.

Chapter 7

The noise overhead increased in volume with the growing intensity of morning light. Birds and monkeys began playing in the canopy searching for food. The sounds comforted Master Chief Masure because they were natural. He led the patrol down a mountain trail and maneuvered across the valley toward a field lab used by scientists who studied the rain forest. With light the interval widened until the sixteen men in the platoon were spread out for over a hundred yards. Lieutenant Duran was more than thirty yards behind him when the point man reached the outskirts of the clearing containing the field lab.

Masure halted the patrol and sniffed the air. He noticed that there were no animal sounds. The silence troubled him but he assumed that jungle creatures avoided the area to avoid pesky scientists. He carefully surveyed the building with binoculars to ensure it wasn't being used, then looked back at Duran for guidance. The Lieutenant shook his head and pointed in the direction of the river, indicating that he had not made contact with the other platoon. Masure nodded acknowledgement and sent the point man across the clearing to the trail that meandered down to the river. It was on the opposite side of the grounds from the footpath they had planned to use to hike up to a second field shack that was serving as a mock drug lab. He waited for the point man to seek cover then crossed the corner of the clearing on the double.

Any location where men are exposed to enemy fire, SEALs designate as a danger area. Alpha Platoon had developed set procedures called standing operating procedures or SOPs to minimize exposure. One at a time, covering each other, the men scurried across the danger area. A third of the men were across when a shot rang out. The sound reverberated off the jungle like a firecracker. Then automatic weapons opened up from the tree line on the opposite side of the clearing. A fusillade off hot lead lanced out at the Colombian soldiers around Masure and Simons. One of them screamed and fell to the ground clutching his chest as if a swarm of angry hornets had cut into his body. He wriggled on the ground and died with a horrible groan.

With the crack of the first shot Masure dropped to the ground and slithered to the base of a tree. He knew instantly that he wasn't in a kill zone. He aimed his M-16 and cut loose with a burst on full automatic. Simons joined him and their weapons began hammering back at their unknown assailants in chattering bursts that seemed to alternate.

On hearing the crack of the rifle, Duran stepped behind the cover of a tree trunk. Startled, he studied the direction of incoming fire, trying to fathom who was shooting at them. When the sound of an AK registered in his brain, he yelled at the top of his lungs.

"*Ambush right!*"

He cut loose with thirty rounds on full automatic. The M-16 chattered away spraying the tree line with lethal fire. Next to him, Lieutenant Rodriguez slithered on his belly for a few yards, jumped to his feet and bolted back up the trail like a buckshot coyote. He ran by the SEAL rear security and disappeared into the jungle. Several BBs near the end of the patrol started to follow him but the U.S. SEAL blocked their way. He ordered them to change magazines then led them down the trail to join the firefight. The troops near the open ground fired back out of instinct, but their blank ammunition only succeeded in making noise. It was Duran, Masure, and Simons who held the tide until the others exchanged magazines and joined the fight.

Duran changed the channel on his inter-squad radio, then fired off another thirty rounds, placing single shots up the mouth of the northern trail.

"*Stick!*" he spoke, loudly into his throat mike.

"*Yeah, Boss!*"

"They're set up along the northern trail."

"*Roger the fuck out of that!*"

Masure knew by the accuracy and variety of weapons firing at them that it wasn't a professional army doing the shooting. When he spotted men running from the cover of field shack he recognized them as rag-tag guerrillas. The U.S. SEALs opened up on the exposed insurgents, some on automatic, others with two and three round bursts. They cut down a half dozen men before they could reach the cover of the jungle. Then the SEALs began lobbing 40 mike-mike grenades into the tree line. Explosions punctuated the rattle of machine guns as a shower of hot metal fragments rained down from airbursts that cut the jungle foliage and the men below to shreds.

After several seconds of intense fire without a round in return Duran yelled, "*Cease fire!*"

Silence reigned as if someone had switched off a radio. Then the sound of men moaning in pain cut through the silence. From Masure's position came the cry, "*Corpsman!*"

Then Duran's earpiece vibrated to life.

"*Alpha, Alpha, this is Bravo, Bravo, over?*"

"*Roger, Chuck. Go,*" Duran said excitedly.

"*What's happening, Jack?* the voice on the radio asked.

"Ambush at the main field station. I got several men down."

"Roger, Jack. Good copy. I'm about a half a click from your pos," Spear reported.

"They ran up the northern trail toward the second field station. I couldn't tell how many but there's a bunch of them."

"I'll set an ambush. Spear, out," the junior officer said, signing off.

Duran yelled across the clearing. *"Stick! Coming at you!"*

"Roger. Got you covered."

Duran motioned for his men to follow then ran toward Masure.

"Count off!" he ordered, taking cover behind a tree.

The men counted off in English and then in Spanish. From the numbers that were missing he knew who was down hard. He was checking a wounded Colombian when he heard assault rifles rattling to the north. From the intensity of the fire, he could tell Chuck Spear had caught the assailants in an ambush. For two minutes the jungle roared with the sound of weapons reverberating through the forest. Then silence.

"Alpha, this is Bravo, over?" came Spear's voice in his earpiece. He was excited.

"Go."

"I caught about twenty-five gomers running up the trail. Ten, maybe twelve are KIA. The rest scattered into the jungle."

"Do you have any loses?" Duran asked.

"No."

"Roger. Work your way to me. Hustle it. I've got several wounded and some dead. Have you got comm with TOC?"

"Roger," Spear said already on the move. He was breathing heavily.

"Have the boats meet us at the landing at the head of the southern trail. Request medevac."

"Roger. Good Copy. Spear out."

"Listen up!" Duran yelled to the men in Alpha platoon. "Bravo will be coming in for link up in about five mikes. Hold your fire."

He repeated the order in Spanish and turned to the corpsman for a report on injuries. The news was bad.

After link up, the two platoons moved quickly down to the river carrying the wounded and the dead. When they reached the landing Spear called in the SOC boats. The troops bounded aboard in record time still high on adrenaline. Racing against the clock, the coxswains rocketed off full throttle for the TOC and medical help. When the boats reached step, Masure relaxed the death grip he had on his M-16 and eased over to where Duran was crouched on the transom.

"What happen to Rodriguez?" he asked, over the sound of thundering engines.

"Hell, I don't know," Duran grunted. "He ran like a yellow bellied coward."

"Doesn't surprise me."

"Me either."

"You know something," Masure said.

"What?" Duran asked, expecting Masure to say something derogatory about the Colombian.

"There were bullets raining all around me and Simons. Nothing touched us."

"You got the luck of the Irish, man."

"I don't think so. They shot the guy on each side of me. Simons was in the open when they cut loose. Not a scratch."

"What are saying, Tripod?" Duran asked, with a furrowed brow.

The wind was whipping the handsome Master Chief's hair around. As was his trademark it was too long for a military cut. He brushed it back just as the boat took a nasty bounce over the wake of its sister craft. Both men grabbed the transom and held on tight.

"I'm saying they were trying to kill the Colombians, not us," he said, shaking his head.

"I don't buy it. We're all painted green, man."

"They're wearing arm bands, Boss. We're not."

An expression of doubt crossed Duran's face. "Why kill them and not us? It doesn't make sense."

"Maybe whoever's behind this shit doesn't want to stir up any more stink with Uncle Sam," offered Masure, reiterating a thought Derek Evans had planted in his brain.

"I don't buy it. No way," Duran objected.

"Did you see the way they ran back across that clearing when we started cuttin' 'em down. Looked to me like they were expecting blanks. I think they had in mind to kill the BB's and maybe capture some of us."

"A leak?" Duran suggested.

"I'd say so. In fact, I'd bet on it. They were set up on our route. If we hadn't of dropped comm, we'd walked right in to 'em. Coincidence?" Masure shook his head. "I don't think so."

"Who then?"

"Could be anybody. Staff. Training unit. Operational units. You can bet Rodriguez got wind of it. He probably fixed it so the comm would go down. Probably ordered it. The opposition's got money to burn, Boss. Big money. Did you know Pablo Escobar was making four million dollars a day when the BB's greased his ass?"

"No. I didn't."

"That kind of money corrupts."

"You're beginning to spook me, Tripod."

"Think about it. Escobar was the head of a multibillion-dollar enterprise. Someone took his place. You heard what his son told reporters, didn't you?"

"No."

"He said, *I'm going to kill those sons-of-bitches.*"

"Who told you all this?" Duran asked. He put his hand over his forehead to shield his eyes from the wind and stared into Master Chief's eyes.

"Commander Evans," Masure replied. "He said there are a bunch of narco-terrorist organizations down here, some better than Escobar's. He said they are linked internationally and when they aren't cutting each other's throats, they help each other out."

"Where did you see Commander Evans?" Duran asked, surprised by the revelation.

Evans was retired, but he always seemed to turn up in hot spots like Colombia and Lebanon. He had put them both through SEAL training and Duran idolized him as the kind of leader he hoped to be when he gained rank.

"In Bogotá. When you were boning your woman down in Cartagena last month. He gave me an insider's brief on the problems down here. Did you know that the estimated annual profit from organized crime is more than one trillion dollars a year?"

"No. No, I didn't."

"That's almost the size of the federal budget," Masure continued, repeating the information Evans had told him.

"What's the Commander doing down here, Master Chief?"

"Your guess is as good as mine. He said he's doing security work for some big corporation."

"I'll bet," Duran said, cynically.

"I heard several of the broken SEALs are in the AO but I haven't seen any of them."

Broken SEALs was a term they used to describe ex-SEALs that had been hurt in the line of duty.

From mid deck the corpsman yelled at Duran to get his attention. "Lieutenant."

He had been working frantically over one of the wounded Colombian soldiers. Duran looked at him and he shook his head.

"*Damn!*" he cursed. "Four KIA on a simple training mission."

"And one MIA," Masure added, reminding him about Rodriguez. "Some fuckin' training mission, huh?"

"Stick, after the debriefing, stand Alpha down for the next two weeks."

"You going to Bogotá?" Masure asked.

"You damn straight I am. And you're going with me."

"What about Colonel Tulley?"

"*Fuck him!*"

"He's not going to like you going over his head, Boss."

"Too bad. He should have listened to me. I told him this op was too spread out. You know I tried like hell to talk him out of it."

"The general won't listen to a word you say without the Colonel present. You know that. That's the way it works, LT." Masure said in a fatherly voice.

"So you're suggesting I do nothing? You just told me you believe we were set up."

Masure shrugged his shoulders.

"We both argued until we were blue in the face," Duran continued. "What the hell do you think I should do?" he asked, with an angry expression.

"Get laid," Masure said with a smile. "It'll do you good. It'll relieve the frustration and clear your head."

Duran stared at him in disbelief. "What? My head's clear, *goddamnit!*"

"No, it's not, sir."

Duran knew the salty master chief was right. If he bucked the chain of command every SEAL in Colombia would pay the price for his brashness, perhaps even those in Peru and Bolivia too. Then he thought about Maria Christina. She was the one good thing about his assignment to Colombia.

"Okay. Stand the platoon down," Duran ordered. "We'll wait until they call us."

"I wouldn't do that, sir, at least not just yet. Rodriguez is well connected. They'll have every man in Colombia looking for his scrawny yellow ass. We gotta help."

Duran stared at Masure and shook his head, realizing he was right. "Of course."

"When Rodriguez turns up, they'll have to stand down the BB's to rebuild this unit. Between now and then, act like none of this shit bothers you. Four KIA and a VIP MIA will get the General's attention. Tulley won't be able to fend him off. He'll ask to speak with you, personally, and when you get your chance, unload on him. Probably won't do any good though."

"Stick. You piss me off," Duran scowled.

"How?" Masure asked, perplexed by the statement.

"Cause you're always right."

"Just trying to do my job, sir."

64

"What's that? Provide adult leadership to the entire wardroom of SEAL Team TWO?" Duran sighed.

"I'm not going to touch that with a big stick," Masure replied.

The coxswain backed off on the throttle and let the boat fall off step just short of the pier. As he maneuvered the boat alongside, Duran spotted Colonel Tulley among the people standing on the landing. The look on his face said everything. In a panic he ordered a medic to do a line handler's job. Then, he stared down at Duran with hard eyes that seemed to accuse him of causing the disaster.

He pointed an accusatory finger and yelled at Duran. *"What the hell happened out there, Lieutenant? I told you to maintain radio contact!"*

Duran stared back at him with unblinking eyes in a bitter contemptuous gaze Tulley recognized.

"LT. back off," Masure whispered, reading Duran's face. "Remember, he's the boss."

Tulley looked away first.

"Yeah," Duran growled as he climbed out of the boat behind a stretcher.

His first emotion was loathing. His second was to stomp the crap out of the over weight tanker right on the pier in front of God and everybody. But he knew that would only result in a court-martial. He shouldered his weapon and walked to the TOC, mentally preparing himself for a meaningless debriefing with a man who thought he knew everything about special operations but didn't know squat.

Chapter 8

Tom Roth followed Highway 94 out of downtown San Diego and drove toward the mountains of Southern California. When the four-lane highway turned into a two-lane macadam road and began meandering among the foothills he began to worry about his navigation.

I must have made a wrong turn, he thought.

When he reached Jamul, the backcountry crossroads where Evans lived, he pulled over to check his map.

"Crap," he muttered, under his breath.

He was already off the folded sheet of paper the rental car agency had provided as a map and he was only twenty-five miles from downtown San Diego. He picked up the folder lying on the passenger seat and glanced at the notes he had taken during his brief conversation with Evans. *Stay on Highway 94 until Dulzura,* were the words he had scribbled down on his note pad.

Okay. So were the hell is Dulzura? he asked himself.

He looked around and saw a grocery store, a hardware store, and a liquor store.

No church? he thought. *Got to be a couple of churches.*

"Where the hell is Jamul?" he cursed out loud, looking for the center of town.

The highland valley of Jamul was above the city of San Diego more than a thousand feet and it wasn't a town like Roth expected to see. It was just a collection of country stores set beside a road that snaked into the mountains. Many of the houses surrounding the valley had views of the Pacific Ocean. Roth knew one of them belonged to Evans, but he didn't know which one. He scanned the hills out of curiosity.

If his personality is consistent with his service record, he owns one up on high ground where he can take a bead on anyone coming up through the valley, he thought.

Roth's supposition was correct. Evans's ranch was up on a hill above the valley and he did have an arsenal capable of reaching out and touching someone down below. Roth wanted to know more about the man than just the information available in his the sterile military service record. He had Evans's address in his briefcase and for a moment he considered driving by his house.

A man's car and home says a lot about his personality, he thought, thinking like an Agency spook.

He glanced at his watch and thought better of the idea. In twenty minutes he was supposed to meet the enigmatic Commander Derek Evans, a man whom according to his boss, Dr. Alysin Harris, had single handedly saved South East Asia from destruction.

"Stay on Highway 94," he said out loud. "Okay, Commander Asshole, I'll stay on Highway Ninety-four."

Roth fixed his tie and groomed his hair with his fingers before pulling out onto the road. The Agency had recruited Tom Roth right out of college and he had been with them for almost fifteen years. His GS rank was equivalent to a full commander and he was determined not to let Evans take the lead, a character trait Alysin Harris had warned him about.

Evans is a take charge kind of guy, Tom, she had warned. *He doesn't take no for an answer. Think of him as a bulldozer that once set in motion can't be stopped without a nuke. He's arrogant, pig-headed, honest, patriotic and absolutely ruthless. Strange combination. Do your homework before you meet him. And Tom*, she had said with a serious expression, *make damn sure he goes looking for Dr. Galán.*

How much can I offer him? he had asked.

We can't go paying privateers to tromp around the jungle. Offer the reward and nothing more.

Harris had smiled deviously. Something in her eyes had told Tom Roth that there was more going on than she would confide in him.

Roth's primary assignment was to identify and analyze South American cartels marketing illegal drugs in Eastern Europe and Russia. Dr. Harris's mission was to stop the trade in weapons of mass destruction and she knew that the narcotics trade was linked to illegal arms transactions. Much to his dismay she had assigned him a collateral mission of recruiting mercenaries to search for Dr. Galán.

Roth had chosen a nice restaurant on the waterfront to meet with Evans, but the wily SEAL had cut him off at the knees. Roth bristled at the thought. When he had called Evans to give him the time and place for their PM, Evans had ordered him around like a common seaman.

Meet me at the Dulzura Cafe in two hours, and don't be late, or I won't be there, Evans had warned.

The other mercenaries had been easy to recruit. A few intriguing hints, an offer of a handsome reward, and they were off to the races at their own expense. But not Evans. If Dr. Harris hadn't countermanded his decision, Roth would have scratched Evans off the list immediately after their first conversation. Somewhat peeved and dressed in a suit and tie, Roth headed into the foothills of Southern California to meet the only man of the ten he was responsible for handling who had insisted upon a personal face-to-face meeting.

Roth cruised up the curving mountain road wondering what the connection was between Dr. Alysin Harris and an old retired sailor. In his wildest imagination he could not have envisioned that they had once been lovers. Evans was retired. Dr. Harris was young, vibrant and married to a renowned professor. Moreover, she was the head of the most important new function in the Central Intelligence Agency, a new Desk, dedicated to the problems of proliferation of weapons of mass destruction. Roth was one of the old hands that had been passed over for the job and he had a great dislike for women with power. Harris rubbed him wrong. Her insistence on recruiting Evans further angered him. He didn't think much of military personnel to begin with. To Roth, military officers were a dumb lot incapable of grasping the world problems the CIA had to grapple with.

About fifteen minutes from Jamul the highway began to snake back and forth sharply, climbing higher and higher. He came out of a series of curves that climbed nearly five hundred feet and almost passed the town of Dulzura before he realized it. Roth stepped down hard on the brakes and whipped the rental car into the dirt parking lot outside a small cafe. It was just a little place set right next to the road. From the car he checked the surroundings. The town consisted of a post office, a few houses, and a rustic backcountry restaurant that had once served the likes of the Wells Fargo Stagecoach line. He expected to see horses and cowboys with six shooters strapped to their hips, not Border Patrol agents and ranchers.

Evans's kind of place, he thought. *Everyone knows everyone and I'm the outsider. The man is just like Harris. They are both goddamned control freaks.*

In its heyday, Highway 94 had been the only way through the mountains to the interior of the Southwest. The Dulzura Cafe had quenched many a thirst. It was still dressed in that rustic western style that made the West famous. At the entrance Roth noticed a rough stone mortared to the steps outside the door. At first he wondered why anyone would place such an obstacle on the steps, then he realized it was there so cowboys could clean the mud, or other foul smelling substances, off their boots before entering the building. He looked at the aged walls and rough cut timber.

"Genuine. What's this man trying to tell me?"

In Roth's world everything was a signal or a symbol. He assumed Evans's choice of a meeting place was a conscious decision meant to send a message. It wasn't. The Dulzura Cafe was near Evans's favorite shooting range.

Roth opened the batwing doors and stepped inside on to the rough-cut board floor that had felt the heels of a million boots. It was dark inside, compared to the bright sunlight outside, and it took a few seconds for his eyes and prescription tinted glasses to adjust. The first things that caught his attention were stuffed animal heads on the walls. Bear, deer, cougar and some critters he didn't recognize.

If I'm not careful, Evans will have my head mounted on a wall, he thought. *One word to Harris and I'll get reassigned to Rwanda. I'm already on her shit list enlisting mercenaries to do the DEA's dirty work.*

It was common knowledge in Washington D.C. that drug traffickers had infiltrated the DEA and the Border Patrol. Both agencies had to rely on the CIA to compartmentalize important projects.

When his eyes adjusted Roth noticed the old licenses plates tacked to the walls. Some were from the early thirties. Then he felt the eyes of everyone in the establishment. Dressed in a suit and tie he was out of place among people dressed in pointed toe boots and cowboy hats. He quickly cased the place looking for Evans. He had a picture of the Commander in uniform but it was out of date. Failing to catch anyone's eye, he walked up to the lady behind the counter.

"Hi. May I help you?" she asked pleasantly.

"Yes. I'm looking for ah, Derek Evans."

She was pouring a cup of coffee for one of the old geezers seated at the bar.

"Thank ya, Kitty," he croaked in a Western drawl.

"Who's asking?" She eyeballed him without blinking.

"Ah, a friend."

"Right over there," she said, pointing to a man seated near the jukebox. Roth glanced at the man. He looked as if he was in his mid thirties, athletic and clean cut.

"The gent I am supposed to meet is retired, late forties."

"Derek Evans, you said?" Kitty queried.

"Yes."

"That's him," she insisted, pointing directly at a man seated near the jukebox.

Seeing Kitty point in his direction, Evans motioned the case officer over with his finger as if calling a child. Roth was off his guard again. The man seated at the table looked younger than he did. He was square-jawed and muscular, a sort of Robert Conrad knock off. Roth glanced up at the boar's head on the wall behind Kitty, momentarily indecisive. He was expecting to meet a grumpy old man who had fought a war in some far off place called Vietnam. The man seated at the table didn't look old enough to have gone to war in Southeast Asia.

Evans is playing some kind of friggin' mind game, he thought.

When he looked back at the waitress, she handed him two open bottles of beer.

"If you want to get on his good side, take him a beer. With strangers he's got a hard edge about him sometimes," she warned.

"Sometimes?" croaked the old timer seated at the counter. "He's as cantankerous as an old rattle snake. A mighty hard feller to get to know, but if you make a friend of him boy, there ain't none better."

Roth furrowed his brow.

"It's on the house," she said.

Roth took the beers and walked over to Evans's table.

"Evans?" he asked, handing him a bottle. He had the momentary feeling he had just been reduced to a common waiter. "The lady at the bar said this was on the house."

Evans recognized Roth's voice from the telephone. "Have a seat, secret agent man," he ordered, grabbing the beer. He took a big pull on the bottle and gave Kitty a grin and a mock salute.

Roth extended his hand. It was a gesture he soon regretted. Evans gripped down so hard it nearly brought tears to his eyes.

"I'm pleased to meet you, Commander. I've heard a lot about you," Roth said, taking the chair opposite Evans.

"*Bullshit!* Cut the crap and don't call me Commander. We're about the same rank, I reckon. Huh?"

"Yes. But you have a bit more experience."

"That's correct. I reckon." Evans eyed Roth like he was a criminal about to make a move. "So what's the deal?" he asked, before the agent could adjust his chair and his thoughts.

"Like I told you on the phone, sir, there is a sizable reward if you can find the lady in question," the case officer answered.

As soon as he had said the word *sir* he realized he had made another mistake. There was something about Evans's disposition that made him ill at ease and it wasn't just his boss's interest in the man. It was something in his penetrating, unblinking gaze. His green eyes seemed to probe Roth's brain. Evans was in control and Roth knew it. He had forced the meeting, the location, turned him in to a common waiter, gripped his hand until it hurt, and sat him down on his butt like a seaman reporting to his commanding officer. Roth was displeased and it showed on his face. He glanced around the restaurant gathering his thoughts.

From now on I'm taking the offensive, he thought, remembering the tricks he had learned in his case officer's course.

He looked Evans in the eye. "The deal is simple, Evans. Like I told you on the phone, a million dollars if you come up with the lady first. Take it or leave it," he said, in the deepest masculine voice he could muster.

He continued staring at Evans, determined to hold his gaze until Evans looked away. But he couldn't. The Commander's eyes seemed to accuse him with words like, *I don't like you, agency boy, and you need a hair cut, boy, and I'll kick your ass all over this place if you don't look down at the table, boy.* Evans's cheek quivered and then he sat absolutely motionless until Roth looked down at the table.

Annoyed by the engagement, Evans went off like a loaded gun. "Tell me something I don't know, Roth," he demanded, with a sarcastic edge.

"She called a friend in La Paz ---"

"I know that. I've got her phone records," Evans said, cutting him off.

"Well, then you know she called the University of ---"

"I said, I have her phone records," Evans snapped. His eyes bored into Roth's skull.

"Commander."

"Don't call me Commander," Evans ordered. "Now tell me something I don't know, boy."

"Like what?" Roth bristled, completely off balanced by Evans's abusive manner. The word *boy* had tripped his trigger.

"Like why the hell did she bolt in the first place? If a bunch of goons hit her lab, why didn't she go to the cops?"

"Ah, ah, we don't know. But ah, we suspect that her aberrant behavior is related to her exposure to the drug," Roth stammered.

"*Bullshit!* I ain't buyin' that, not for one damn second. The woman is a genius. Her mind is like a steel trap, too powerful to let any substance control her behavior."

Evans stared at Roth until he was uncomfortable.

"We don't know why she left the country, plain and simple," he countered, with a degree of bravado.

"I like it plain and simple, buddy. Keep it coming. So how do you know she left the country?" he demanded.

"Well, we don't know for sure that she did. We believe she..."

Evans interrupted him again like volcanic explosion.

"She crossed the border into Mexico right down the road from here at Tecate, secret agent man," Evans snarled. "She called my office from that phone," he growled, pointing at the pay phone on the wall next to them. "Drank a Coke at this table." Evans slammed his fist on the table and glared at the agent. "You know, you people should really start communicating with other agencies. You could learn a lot. She caught a plane in Tijuana for Mexico City. Her car was abandoned at Rodrigues Airport. It's in the impound lot in Tijuana. From Mexico I believe she flew to Caracas under an assumed name. I don't know where the hell she is but I suspect she's making her way to Bolivia."

"Commander, you are light years ahead of us, ahead of everyone," Roth stammered, impressed beyond his ability to describe in word.

"I know that. Tell me something I don't know."

Evans gave Roth a hard look so Roth took out his cigarettes. "Do you mind?" he asked, referring to his need to smoke.

"*Yes I do,*" Evans replied, staring him down. "I hate cigarette smoke."

Roth put his cigarettes back in his pocket. Then Evans asked a question that hit him in the face like a cold glass of beer.

"Your branch is primarily concerned with weapons of mass destruction," he asserted. "What's your connection to Cocaine Inc. in general, and the Ballesteros, in particular, and why have I been maneuvered into a relationship with a known cartel?"

There was a fire in Evans's eyes that disturbed Tom Roth. He was shocked by his abrasive manner and by the penetrating nature of the question. His mouth fell open and he cleared his throat several times.

"Ah, hum, aaahhh, sir?"

"We're the same rank, remember?" Evans growled. "Drop the sir."

"Ah, ahum." Roth cleared his throat again. "Evans, I can't discuss such matters like that in a public place."

"Why? This is real America, pal. Gut center. No left wing liberals or communist bastards in here."

For five seconds Evans studied Roth's face probing for details, waiting for him to answer. When he didn't, Evans unloaded on him like a machine gun.

"Very well. Since you're so worried about the security forms you've signed, let me see if I've got the big picture." Evans leveled his gaze on the case officer like sighting down the barrel of a gun. "Organized crime is accelerating beyond the ability of our current institutions to deal with the problems, *right?*"

"Well. That's not exactly what…"

"Don't answer that. Remember you signed a stack of security forms not to divulge all that super sensitive secret shit. One breach and you go to jail with your buddy Aldridge Ames."

"*Evans,* I resent that…."

Evans cut him off again and shook his finger in the agent's face.

"Let's see. We have cocaine, heroin, hashish, raw opium, marijuana, money laundering, counterfeiting, and a brisk trade in illegal arms, not to mention illegal aliens and slavery. Have I left anything out? Oh yeah, terrorism and a growing trade in materials of weapons of mass destruction. That's your specialty isn't it? Yours and Doctor Harris's. Now, let's see if I've got the exchange system down? In 1991, Czech authorities found two hundred and twenty pounds of cocaine in a shipment of beans from South America. They tipped off the Poles who found another two hundred and forty pounds of cocaine near Gdansk. *Right?*"

Roth nodded his head.

"Then there was a ton of cocaine last year, seized in Saint Petersburg, shipped out of Finland if I'm not mistaken. As I recall it was linked to a group of Russian thugs. And that's just the tip of the proverbial iceberg, just the shit that went public. Such quantities titillate the imagination. I smell Colombian involvement, don't you?"

Roth was stunned. He just nodded his head in agreement. Evans took a swallow of his beer, leaned back in his chair and continued his briefing.

"Shipments of that size require friends in high places. Now, what do our new friends in the Eastern Block have to trade? Money? No," Evans said, shaking his finger. "I don't think so. But they do have nasty little germs, thermonuclear bombs, and other hideous little toys that the Arabs are interested in, eh? Yeah, I think I got it," Evans exclaimed in mock surprise. "Harris is worried about the exchange. The Arabs have the money, the Russians have the weapons, and the South Americans have the dope. What is it that bothers you guys, the transfer of arms or the lives destroyed by dope? Oh! Maybe it's the squeaky-clean dollars conveniently laundered and transferred to South America. Legal money. Money is power, secret agent man. Is some rich narco son-of-bitch planning to overthrow the Colombian government, Venezuela, Ecuador, Peru, Bolivia?"

As Evans recited the countries that ring the Amazon Basin, he watched Roth's eyes carefully. They were confused. The agent had come to recruit the commander and Evans was briefing him on the very problems facing Dr. Harris.

"Could there be some sort of coup brewing that I should know about? Maybe something your boss got wind of?"

"So you understand the nature of the problem," Roth replied.

"I understand the basics of the problem, secret agent man. Human nature. It's greed, corruption, the desire for power, the drive to survive amidst grinding poverty, and the desire to escape reality if only for a few brief chemically induced minutes. But what I don't understand is why I've been sucked into this vortex. Tell me something I don't know."

"Simple, Commander. You know the woman."

"*Bullshit!* I was maneuvered into a contract with the Ballesteros long before Carol Galán took a hike."

Roth wet his lips and swallowed hard. He took a sip of beer and looked around the cafe before meeting Evans's eyes.

"Commander, murder is a growth industry in Colombia. Conversely, so too is protection. There are a lot of guys like you working the business. I don't personally know one cartel from another," he lied with a furrowed brow.

Doctor Harris's Desk was deeply concerned about the possibility of drugs for money, money for weapons, weapons for power. Roth was just one of several field agents she had working the issue. Evans saw the agent's pupil constrict and knew the man had just lied to him. He sat back in his chair and glared contemptuously. Roth took a drink and swallowed hard as Evans rubbed his chin.

"Colombia has suffered greatly from the violence associated with the drug trade. Peru has made some advances but in the scheme of things they are largely symbolic. The goat pens they call jails down there are overflowing with retched people who made a devil's bargain and lost. Bolivia is constantly on the edge of collapse. The coca crop is the only thing between its dirt-poor farmers and starvation. Let me tell you something, buddy. We're going about this all wrong. It's demand that drives the flow of narcotics."

"I'm not into that sort of business, Commander," the agent replied in a subdued voice.

"I roger that. Your job is to investigate the possibility of whether or not an organized criminal group operating out of South America could get their hands on a nuclear weapon, or something worse. Well, let me cut the chase short for you, pal. The answer is yes. The black market in Russian arms is completely out of control and anyone with enough money can play the game."

Roth felt Evans's eyes probing his thoughts like radar. He looked down at the table uncomfortable under the interrogation. Evans studied the agent's face for a moment.

"Do you know what a man turns to when he has his own fleet of aircraft, his own zoo, his own stash of gold bullion, and any woman in the world he wants?"

"Ahhh, no. No, I don't," replied the agent sincerely. "And I don't see the point of this conversation."

"Politics. Politics is the pursuit of the filthy rich. It's true here in the U.S. and it's true in South America. Escobar was headed for the presidency of Colombia. Suarez was headed for the presidency of Bolivia. Am I right?"

The agent nodded his head in agreement.

"Only circumstances got in their way. *Us!* Don Ballesteros has a pretty good shot at it, don't you think?" Evans pressed.

The color drained out of Roth's face. Evans had correctly articulated the gist of the problem. Huge sums of money were flowing out of the Middle East to South America and large quantities of narcotics were being shipped into Eastern Europe and Russia. The logical conclusion was that there was a third leg to the triad and the only commodity of exchange the Russians had was weaponry. The politics of the matter was a dimension he hadn't thought of. Evans read the expression on the agent's face. He exhaled heavily, leaned further back in his chair, and studied him like a bug for a few seconds before draining his bottle of beer.

"I think I understand what's happening," he said. "Intelligence organizations like the Agency are refocusing their operations from spies to terrorists and criminals, and for good reason. Organized crime is moving about a trillion dollars a year through the underground economy of the world. With that kind of money changing hands it's only a matter of time until a criminal, a crazy, or a fanatic gets his hands on a nuke or something worse. That's power. Real power. Can you imagine Ramón Savajé with a nuke?" Evans asked.

Roth was lost for words. He didn't know why the Agency was interested in Dr. Galán. As far as he knew she was just a scientist working on a black program call Project Mandrake. He didn't know the specifics, just that it involved anti-drug compounds. There were hundreds of black programs ranging from secret stealth aircraft and boats to laser weaponry. As far as he knew the Agency was just helping out the DEA because the DEA was concerned about leaks. Evans assertion that the Agency was redirecting assets at international criminal organization was one hundred percent accurate. In Washington, the name of the game was the *battle of the budgets.* Every government organization from the BATF to the CIA was scrambling for scarce taxpayer dollars. Significant contributions to the war on drugs were seen as relevancy and high ground in the budget battle, even if it was beyond the charter of the organization.

"Commander, Doctor Galán is being pursued by every major cartel in South America, for good reason. She is trying to put them out of business. She openly discussed her research on the Internet and she briefed her findings in open forum at several scientific conventions. I offer you the same reward I've offered several other consultants, one million dollars if you deliver her to us unharmed."

"Okay, mystery man. Either you won't or can't tell me why I've been maneuvered into my current contract with the Ballesteros. So, how much money do I have to work with?"

"I'm not prepared to offer an advance, Commander," Roth answered.

"*What?*" Evans exploded. "*Damn your eyes!* You're wasting my time, *secret agent man.* I told you to bring your checkbook." Evans's piercing eyes bore holes in Roth's skull. He shook his finger in Roth's face as he said, "You go back and tell Harris I want fifty-kay for travel and expense. *Up front!* Not a penny less."

"We're not authorized to pay any of our consultants an advance, Commander."

"Oh. It's not an advance. I don't work for free anymore. And as for the Ballesteros, you tell Harris the information I've been providing just dried up."

"Ah,"

"Don't interrupt me. I was about to say that if I get hung out to dry and you don't personally inform me of my predicament, I will come and find you."

"Are you threatening me, Evans?" Roth bristled, like a cur dog.

Evans smiled. "Yes I am," he growled. "If I get hung out to dry on this one I will come and find you if I have to ring your identity out of Harris's scrawny neck. Is that clear?" he said, as he slammed his fist down on the table.

"I'm not in charge of this operation. She is," Roth sniveled, alarmed by the look in Evans's eyes.

"I don't care who's in charge. You are the one making promises to me and you're the one I will hold personally accountable. That's the deal. Take it or leave it. And fifty-kay up front."

Roth stared at Evans and swallowed hard. He felt a hollow in the pit of his stomach under the glare of Evans's penetrating eyes. In all his years with the CIA he had never been involved in an act of violence. Across the table sat a man who had been involved in every low intensity conflict since Vietnam and he was not the type of man to make idle threats.

"But,"

"No *buts.* No excuses. If you hire me, you support me, or you pay the price. Now before you trot off to the Watch Center like a whipped dog to tell Alysin Harris what an asshole I am, here's my account number just in case you need it."

Evans handed Roth a folded sheet of paper. Roth accepted it and stuck it in his suit pocket.

"And get me a satellite link and an access code so I can get in touch with Harris, or you, if I need hard intel. I've got the radios to make the connection."

Roth nodded.

"That's all, Roth," Evans said, dismissing him like a seaman after Captain's Mast. It was the first time Evans had used his real name. His eyes widened surprised the Commander knew his identity.

"I'll talk to her," he said, getting up from the table. "But I can't promise anything."

Evans frowned. "You do that."

Roth walked through the batwing doors and didn't look back until he got to his rental car. As he opened the door he cursed Evans and Harris.

Chapter 9

The Mamoré River averages two miles in width and runs north for more than six hundred miles from its sources in the Andes to its confluence with the Madeira River at the Brazilian border. Carol Galán looked across the filthy open-air cargo bay at the muddy water ahead. River traffic had decreased significantly since leaving Trinidad but there were still occasional passenger ferries and a few cabin cruisers. The cruisers were notorious for transporting contraband. And then there were the ubiquitous *peke-pekes*, the fishermen's dugout pirogues named for the puttering sound of their long-shafted propellers. They were numerous. One such boat was loaded on the stern of the barge. It belonged to two boatmen Carol had used during her previous expedition to the rain forest. Rita Contreras had hired them in Trinidad and, along with Carol, they had board the sixty-foot barge at La Loma for the long trip up the Mamoré.

She was cruising on a sixty-foot barge-boat powered by an ancient, smoky diesel and it was packed with breeding cattle headed up river to a remote ranch in the *Beni*. The cows were hoof-deep in excrement and she was downwind. From the moment she had climbed aboard the trip had been miserable. Rain, humidity, mosquitoes and biting flies added to her discomfort. She was two days south of Trinidad and making way upstream at barely five knots.

Resbaloso approached her with a bowel of watery beef stew and a plate of mashed overripe bananas mixed with corn, rice, and peppers. It looked so unappetizing at first glance she took it for cow dung.

"*Señorita*, here is some food for you," he said kindly. His nickname, *Resbaloso* was Spanish for slippery.

He smiled at her with his dark-skinned Inca face and extended the bowel with both hands, like a servant offering food to a royal princess. Contreras had offered the pair a special bonus, to be paid at an unspecified date in the future, to keep the secret of Galán's presence in Bolivia, a sum that amounted to more than two years wages for just keeping their mouths shut. To *Resbaloso* and *Viscoso*, Carol Galán was a goddess. In addition to the bonus, they were going to get paid well for delivering supplies that were not contraband. Their first mission was to take her into the jungle and establish a cache site to drop off her supplies on future trips.

Downwind from the animals and the smoky diesel, Carol was in no mood for Bolivian victuals. She declined the offer with a forced smile.

"Gracias, *Resbaloso*. But I'm not hungry," she explained in flawless Spanish.

"*Sí, señorita*. I will save some for you," he smiled.

She had brought along some fresh fruit, a few tins of tuna fish, and some mineral water for the long trip south but the odor of cattle feces had spoiled her appetite. *Resbaloso* took the food back to cook. He had prepared the meal on the open deck in front of the wheelhouse just a few feet from the cattle. *Resbaloso* barked a few words at the cook in rapid-fire Spanish and the man returned the food to the cooking pots. She listened to the staccato prattling of the pilot yakking at the cook about the meal. He was a dirty unshaven, heavyset man with black teeth who spent more time reading comic books than steering the boat. The cook, wearing a tattered straw hat, spat out a few curses, then threw a crust of bread at the pilot.

Carol watched the crew and other passengers eat the muddle with relish. The sight of them gulping down the mush caused her stomach to turn over. There were no cabins on the barge so she climbed in her hammock and searched the river for comfort. Basking on a sandbar at the river's edge, she spotted a few caiman -- South American alligators. Egrets clung to the trees like huge white blossoms. Then she saw a pink dolphin diving in and out of the wake.

How did you get so far from the Atlantic, my friend? she thought. *Are you lost like me?*

Dolphins had swum up the Amazon River millennia ago and had adapted to the fresh water. By air, the *Rio Mamoré* dolphins were more than fifteen hundred miles from the Atlantic. By river, they were more than three thousand miles from their ancestral home.

No. This is your home now, isn't it? I'm the one that is homeless.

The tropical sun seemed to radiate off the light brown water like heat off an electric toaster. Soon it would set in a flaming fiery ball and then the tedium would return, and so would the mosquitoes. Carol hated mosquitoes with a passion. To her they were disease-carrying bloodsuckers without redeeming value. Bent like a crescent in her hammock she would find herself at their mercy throughout the night.

The boredom was almost unbearable with the chugging diesel, the smoke and the odor of cattle manure. Carol thought of the mysterious drug in her bag and almost succumbed to its temptation.

No. No, she thought. *In a few days I'll be at Rodrigo's. Then I'll solve this mystery.*

She leaned her head back in the hammock and sighed. Staring at a cluster of thatched roof houses set high up on stilts, she wondered what her life would have been like if she had been born there on the bank of the Mamoré. The pilot had steered a course near the western bank so she had an excellent view of life ashore. The river was so wide she could bare make out details with binoculars on the opposite bank.

The *Beni*, a vast region of dusty tropical plains, meandering rivers, and caiman infested swamps, was the center of Cocaine Inc. Stretching from the Andes to the Brazilian border, it covered 214,000 square kilometers, an area the size of Kansas. In laboratories hidden under thick jungle canopy, the third step in the cocaine manufacturing process was carried out in secret, the transformation of coca paste into cocaine sulphate, or base. Unlike the primitive *pozo* pits of the *Chaparé*, *Beni* labs were relatively sophisticated. Sites were strategically chosen outside the range of the Huey helicopters used by Bolivian and U.S. law enforcement agents stationed at Trinidad. Hidden under trees, the labs were invisible from the air. But they were usually located only a few hundred yards from a dirt airstrip or a river.

A gunshot reverberated down the densely jungled bank. Startled, everyone on the barge stood and looked toward shore. A lookout in a stilt house on the bank had spotted the Leopards before anyone on the barge knew they were speeding up behind them. A walkie-talkie operator in one of the houses up river was almost certainly passing the word to clear some nearby paste processing lab. The boats sped by and beached in plain sight up river. Scrawny Leopards in spotted uniforms scrambled ashore. Some plunged in waist deep and clumsily hauled themselves up the bank. Others jumped ashore. They forged into the jungle like a troop of army ants. Some turned and ran along the bank. Others ran into the jungle.

Through her binoculars Carol could clearly see the action ashore. The first Leopard to climb up to a stilt house kicked in the door. Others rushed in behind him to search it. Momentarily, they dragged out a young man with dark curly hair and began smacking him around. He was barefoot, wearing only pants and a tee shirt. Realizing he was doomed he stared sullenly down at the bare-board deck of the porch like a man about to be beheaded. One of the Leopards shook a small hand held radio in front of his face and yelled words that Carol couldn't hear. Another kicked the boy in the back of the head sending him face first into the planks of the porch. As the barge motored up river, the others on board went about their business as if what they had just witnessed was an everyday occurrence. Carol was shocked by the violence. But she knew it was civilized behavior compared to the horror meted out by the traffickers. She had witnessed the horror personally in San Diego.

A hundred meters upstream from the assault, she saw two dogs copulating on the bank, undisturbed by the nearby violence. She absorbed the image without prurience.

A rey muerto, rey puesto -- for every dead king, a new king appears, she thought.

Then it dawned on her in the last moments of partial sanity, that she had become a victim of something inside her own skull, an infiltrator possessed her.

The infiltrator had to be hunted down, exposed, and killed before it destroyed her. But how to smoke him out?

"Understanding," she muttered. "Knowledge."

Watching the dogs, still hooked together on the riverbank, she thought, *I'll solve this puzzle and create a molecule that sucks up C-thirty-one like a sponge. Then I'll find a vacuum for heroin and one for cocaine. I'll kill the drug monsters and I'll do it from the jungles of Bolivia.*

Then a puzzling sensation overwhelmed her, a deep desire to take the magic substance out of the Ziploc bag where she was hiding it and rub it into the palm of her hand like a worry stone. She knew she was progressively blinding herself to all parts of the world that didn't conform to her delusional systems of thought.

"Life goes on no matter what happens," she mumbled, staring at the dogs.

Poverty, deprivation, and despair force peasants to grow coca. Hopelessness compels the inhabitants of inner city ghettoes to consume it. Solving these problems is the key to eradicating the drug menace, not Project Mandrake. Then she thought, *those problems are not going to be solved. They've existed since the beginning of time. Ultimately, the problem and the solution lie within us. I cannot create drug magnets that cleanse the body of the desire to escape retched conditions. And it's not just poverty. The desire to escape reality is deeply imbedded in all cultures, in all of us.*

Mile after dreary mile Carol pondered the depths of the world's drug habit, all the while fighting a craving that gnawed at her guts. Through sheer willpower she resisted temptation. For two weeks she had avoided touching the drug. Rita Contrares had been waiting for her in Riberalta and upon hearing Carol's account of the murders in San Diego, she had taken charge. Bolivia was her country and she knew the ropes. She took Carol to her parent's home in the country and nursed her back to health while making arrangement for the trip into the jungle. By bus, the two of them had travel from Riberalta to Trinidad to meet the barge for the long trip up river. Rita was Carol's last window to the world and she had sworn an oath to keep it shut.

On the third day of the journey near sunset, rain lashed the barge in a torrential downpour that lasted twenty minutes. The roof of the bridge sprouted a dozen leaks and forced her to climb into the dreaded hammock at the stern of the vessel. There, alone with her thoughts in the middle of a storm, she succumbed to her craving for the drug. She touched the substance with the tip of her finger. It was only a slight touch but it was enough to coat her finger with millions of molecules. As she rubbed them into the palm of her hand a great sense of calm possessed her and she relaxed for the first time in two weeks.

Driftwood cluttering the river soon forced the pilot ashore. At dusk he tied up near a tiny village to let the cattle graze and water along the bank overnight. Tied up to the bank the night soon engulfed her and she fell into a deep restful sleep that lasted until dawn. At first light she was awakened by the sound of cattle being herded back into the barge. Along with the other passengers, she quickly took care of her bodily needs in the bushes ashore and they pressed on up river. All morning a deep calm possessed her. She even ate Bolivian mush and joked with *Viscoso* and *Resbaloso*.

After lunch, when she saw the boatmen staging supplies on the deck near their *peke-peke*, fear surged through her veins. Soon they would take her into the rain forest and she would be utterly alone.

I'm beginning to see a pattern, she thought. *Calm, a deep soothing calm followed by clarity of thought, followed by overwhelming fear. But it's not an addictive feeling,* she tried to convince herself. *I don't need to touch it. It's just that I've been under so much stress lately. It helps me relieve the pressure and think more clearly.*

Chapter 10

Master Chief Masure put Lieutenant Duran in a taxicab in front of the *Nueva Granada* Hotel in downtown Bogotá and saw him off to the airport for the short flight to Cartagena. It is safer to fly in Colombia, despite the perils of third world maintenance. Flying avoids guerrillas and criminals who come down from the hills and out of the jungles to rob travelers, like *banditos* in the Old West. When the cab disappeared down the street he bought a copy of *El Espectador,* the leading Bogotá newspaper and pretended to read the headlines. He walked down the sidewalk, paper under his arm, looking for *La Fonda Antioqueña*. It took him a few minutes to locate the restaurant. He was early so he cased the entire block.

Evans was seated strategically with his back to the wall so he could observe the entrance as well as the street scene outside. It was a natural survival instinct that had served him well. He spotted Masure sauntering down the street.

He looks like a damn tourist, he thought.

Then he spotted two pickpockets following Masure at a cautious distance.

If they lift his wallet, they better not get caught. He'll chase 'em down and beat 'em to death.

He slowly sipped his drink and waited patiently for the handsome young Master Chief to return. In the parlance of the spy Evans had agreed to a personal meeting or PM, complete with a recognition signal, *El Espectador.* But the modus operandi had gone over the Master Chief's head. Evans had wisely left out the sign and counter-sign, knowing there was plenty of time to teach Masure the fine art of tradecraft.

Evans had spent years in special operations, retiring with the rank of commander, and he knew all the tricks of the trade from clandestine methods of operations to field expedient homemade explosives. He made eye contact with Masure as he entered the restaurant and waved him over to his table. At first Masure was unsure. Evans looked different from the last time he had seen him. His athletic physique was perfectly concealed beneath local clothing.

"Hi, Boss. How's your hammer hanging?" Masure asked, taking the chair opposite Evans.

"Don't call me boss."

"That's gonna be a hard habit to break, Commander."

"And don't call me commander. Call me Derek, for Pete's sake."

"Hell. Is that your name?" Masure said in a joking manner. "I've known you most of my life and I've never called you anything but sir, or commander, or."

Masure stopped in mid sentence.

"Go on," Evans urged, with a stern expression. "I'm humored," he grunted.

"I'd rather not," Masure said, cutting off the line of conversation.

"Well, I'll finish for you. How about Commander Asshole? I've heard it a few times, but not to my face, mind you."

Masure smiled, "Well, don't forget Commander Double Tap and Commander Donkey-Dick," he chuckled.

Evans wasn't amused by the latter reputation and it showed. His handsome Robert-Conrad-face gnarled from a smile to a scowl. "Okay. Okay. Enough of this bullshit," Evans warned gruffly. "What do you want?" he asked, referring to the purpose of the meeting.

Masure had called his office in San Diego, California several times requesting a meeting.

"Whatever you're having, Boss," Masure replied, pointing to Evans's drink.

"*Jesus Christ!*" Evans exclaimed, shaking his head. "*Mozo!*" he called to the waiter. "*Una otra aguardiente,*" he said gestured at Masure.

A neatly dressed waiter rushed over and poured Stick a shot of the licorice-flavored liquid popular among the campesinos of the Andes.

"Now that we've fixed that little problem, I'll repeat myself," Evans muttered, in a disagreeable tone. "What the hell do you want this time?"

Masure's expression turned deadly serious. "We almost got popped last week, Boss, four Colombians KIA. They were chopped down all around me."

Evans eyeballed him, carefully studying his face. He had put the younger warrior through SEAL training and had groomed him for leadership. Masure had even deployed with him on several overseas assignments. He had watched him grow from a skinhead trainee into the finest warrior in the SEAL Teams. The thought of Masure and the other young SEAL getting killed in an undeclared war disturbed him. Special operations on foreign soil were always dangerous. He accepted that. It was part of the business. Men on the front line accept danger as a way of life. But they are not suicidal, and they always stick together no matter the service or country.

"What exactly is your mission, Stick?"

"You know I can't tell you that, Commander" Masure replied.

He eyed Masure meanly for a few seconds.

"Is this place bugged?" Masure whispered.

"No. I checked."

Evans opened the bag he had placed on the table just far enough for Masure to see inside. It contained a handful of bugs, a pocket scanner, and a monitoring system.

"Well let me guess," Evans said. "You're down here to teach some dumb son of bitch how to shoot some other dumb son of bitch in the most efficient manner. Does that about sum up your mission, Patrick Masure?" Evans grumbled half under his breath.

Masure grinned. "As usual, Boss, you have a way of cutting through the bullshit. I guess that about sums it up." Masure focused hard on Evans's eyes and whispered. "What are you doing down here, sir?"

"I work on this damn planet," Evans said, noncommittally. He continued to give Masure a hard look until the Master Chief looked away. "I told you the last time we met. I'm a private consultant. I do private consultant kind of things."

"Well, that makes a lot of sense to me, I think," Masure replied.

Evans had a way of making people nervous. He did it on purpose to pry between the lines. To cover his uneasiness Masure smiled a boyish Brad-Pitt-smile that disarmed Evans and forced him to recall his youth in the SEALs. Masure knew how to handle the Commander even though he out-ranked him in years and experience. But for a twist in the road Evans would have been a Master Chief. He had changed ladders from the enlisted rank to the officer rank after Vietnam, changing the path of his life irrevocably. Evans would have still been on active duty if he had stayed an enlisted man. As an officer he had promoted himself out of an operational job in the SEALs. The last real non-staff SEAL job was the commanding officer of a SEAL team and Evans had retired as Commanding Officer of SEAL Team Five, the best commando team in the Pacific Theater. Warm thoughts of young SEALs training on the Silver Strand in Coronado, California tugged at Evans mind as he scanned a face that trusted and admired him. He was wondering how many of the men in Alpha platoon he had put through SEAL training when Masure interrupted his thoughts.

"Truth is, Boss, you're right on. It's the same old shit. We're just teaching men to move, shoot, and communicate," Masure said breaking the silence.

"The *Bloque de Busqueda?*" Evans pressed.

"Ah, yes, sir," Masure stammered, surprised that Evans knew the name of the secret Colombian unit he was training.

"I saw you and Lieutenant Duran visit DAS, today." DAS was the Colombian Department of Administrative Security, equivalent to the FBI. "You also paid a call on F-2." F-2 was the police intelligence section. "They didn't tell you shit, did they?"

"You do get around. Have you been dogging my trail ever since I hit Bogotá?"

"Somebody's got to cover your six. Half the women in Bogotá are eyeing you after your little samba performance last night at the *Nueva Granada*. But they just want to jump your bones. The pickpockets are closing in on your Rolex. The thugs are trying to figure out how to remove that bulge from your back pocket and the queers just want to play with the one that's hangin' between your legs. You look like a damn tourist."

"I thought I was being casual, Commander," Masure argued, taken aback by the attack.

"You are, Southern California casual in Bogotá, Colombia. Get yourself a get-up like this," Evans gestured, indicating his clothing. "Get rid of that damn expensive watch. You know the deal, big watch, little dick. Get some piece of shit that looks like this," Evans continued, pointing to his watch. "There ain't a petty thug in Bogotá that would pick this *piece of shit* up off the street. Buy yourself a sombrero like this one," he said, picking up a nondescript hat out of the extra chair. Stomp on it a few times to make it look lived in."

Evans stopped the lecture. He was beginning to sound like he was on active duty and he didn't like the approach he had taken. Masure was one of Evans's favorite SEALs.

"You don't have the foggiest notion what you guys are in to, do you?" he asked gently.

"No, sir. Just what you told me the last time we met, and what we were briefed in Norfolk by Naval Intelligence."

"You might as well have been briefed by a bunch of high school students, Master Chief. F-2 and DAS, are not going to tell a gringo like you shit. They only respond to thousand dollar bribes and that's just for tidbits. This country is awash in drug money, enough to buy just about anybody or anything. I told you all this the first time you asked for a PM," Evans complained. He paused for breath after the mild scolding. "Did you get anything from the Embassy?"

Both the CIA and the DEA had offices in the Embassy compound and the SEALs had access. Masure was embarrassed to tell Evans the general was too busy to see them for five minutes. He had canceled Lieutenant Duran's meeting at the last minute, a cancellation Masure suspected was orchestrated by Colonel Tulley to isolate Duran.

"No. Same old shit about the FARC and M-19 extorting money from businessmen," Masure answered.

The *Fuerza Armada Revolucionaria de Colombia* and the *Movimiento 19 de Abril* were guerrilla groups whose political ideologies and opposition to the Colombian government had led them into shaky alliances with the traffickers. The common denominator was money and the drug barons had plenty. FARC and M-19 were the most notorious and dangerous groups in Colombia, with exception of the *sicarios. Sicarios* were paid gunmen who did the trafficker's dirty work. Their modus operandi was a fusillade of lead fired from the back of a moving motorcycle.

"They had some info on a new group trained by some Israeli merc."

Merc was Masure's short-talk for mercenary.

"Morena?"

"Yeah. That's the one."

"The merc is my competition. He's training a private army of men employed to protect a group of cattlemen. They are really traffickers, of course. Listen. Just do your job, keep your men on a tight string, and get the hell out of here as soon as your mission is over. That simple."

"Easier said than done, Boss. The boys get tired of liberty on the base. Even the Lieutenant is banging a little Colombian *verraca.*"

Verraca was a local term for hot number.

Evans nodded. "And you?"

"Well, you know how it is, sir," Masure replied sheepishly.

"Yeah. *La verraca* has a sister. Maybe a half dozen."

Masure smiled confirming what Evans already knew.

"You're following your dick around, Stick, and if you're not careful some *sicario* will cut it off."

"Come on, Boss. I've done exactly what you told me to do. We only hang out in high-dollar nightspots and when we go, we always travel in numbers. *Just like you told me!*"

"I'm not your boss. I'm not even in the damn military."

"I know that. But you're in the know. You're always in the know."

"Stick. I told you what's going down in South America, drugs, money, and corruption, unbelievable amounts of money, sums that stagger the imagination of a drunken SEAL. And corruption that extends to the highest levels of government. I've been studying this so called *war on drugs* and I don't believe we can win at this point in history."

"You know what my problem is, Commander? I don't know what the fuckin' *problem* is. And I'm getting shot at in somebody else's jungle. We could've lost half the platoon if I hadn't of talked the lieutenant into loading up. Twenty minutes before the shit hit the fan, we were packin' blanks."

Evans stared at him with a lost expression. Thoughts of Indonesia flooded his mind. He had been the lieutenant in change of a SEAL platoon that had been ambushed by Russian Spetznaz in the jungles of Java. He had lost a man in bloody hand-to-hand combat in the melee. Masure had been one of the young shooters in his platoon.

"Intell briefed us on the FARC and M-19, the cartels, and the Andean Strategy, and poisonous snakes, and piranhas, and all that sort of *bullshit!* So why do I feel like a damn mushroom, kept in the dark and fed a ton of shit? Nothing they've told me will help me keep my people alive. Since I've been in Colombia, all I've seen is a bunch of thugs stomping around the countryside beating the shit out of campesinos. Hell, when they catch one of the hated enemy, the bastard looks just like the friendlies."

Deja vu shook Evans with a torrent of memories. He saw himself back in Vietnam with an unknown enemy all round. They were on the streets, in the jungles, in the rice paddies, working on the military bases. They were everywhere, all around him. Vietnam was a dirty little war that wasn't a war, inglorious, futile and unfinished. It had robbed Evans of his youth. He had killed a man before he was old enough to vote. Several men.

Colombia was different, but the game was the same for the young SEALs walking the jungle trails. They, like their counterparts, were just minor players in a game of political chess. They had been sent into harm's way to take the battle to the enemy. And like the soldiers sent to Vietnam, they were told only what they needed to know to get by. But who was the enemy? The *cocaleros* who barely survived on a handful of rice and beans provided by the narcos who bartered for coca leaves? The traffickers who built fortunes conforming to an American entrepreneurial spirit in keeping with the law of supply and demand? The users hopelessly addicted to a false reality? The SEALs were the pointy-end of the national sword along with the DEA, the CIA, and the State Department personnel who were working the Andean Strategy. Unfortunately, the U.S. government often worked at cross purposes at the front line in a war that wasn't a war, while the rear security forces, customs, police and border patrol agents, battled MAC-10s and Uzis with six-shot revolvers. There was a strategy to the *war on drugs* but it wasn't transparent and it was doomed to failure as surely as the Vietnam strategy. To Evans, it was as clear as mud, politically saleable but fatally flawed.

Evans was a math major and he saw four equations to the solution; repression at home, repression abroad, prevention at home, and prevention abroad. Repression at home was a non-starter. Americans are not partial to compulsory drug testing, searches and seizures, and long prison terms at hard labor. Mandatory drug testing had cleaned up the problems in the U.S. military, but the cost was a loss of a degree of personal freedom. Most Americans found it abhorrent to have another person watch them urinate in a bottle. The military could not say no to such tests and with zero tolerance for drug use, the military was cleaned up in short order. Astute politicians knew that the American public wasn't ready for the repression they had forced on the U.S. military, even if the bitter medicine had cured the disease. The long-term plan was to allow mandatory drug testing to slowly migrate from the military to the society at large. Until then the war had to be fought on foreign soil.

Prevention at home came in the form of *Just Say No*, and similar programs like *DARE*. But a generation was already infected, their minds diseased with drugs. Moreover, America's role models, those who achieved a degree of fame and notoriety were not on board. Cocaine is one of the most powerful stimulants known to humankind. Unlike heroin, which is a depressant, cocaine stimulates the body's natural responses to pleasure, creating a feeling of euphoria and power, and it doesn't discriminate between the glitterati and the ghetto dweller. From the likes of Marion Berry and Darryl Strawberry to famous actors and musicians like John Beluchi, River Phoenix, Jerry Garcia and Mick Jagger, echoed a corrosive message. Eric Clapton preached the message in his rock song, *"She's all right, she's all right, she's all right, cocaine."*

Evans wasn't about to waste his breath trying to verbally explain the issues to Master Chief Masure. The best way was to see them up close and personal. One had to see the human side of the equation to really understand it. Repression and prevention abroad was the name of the game. The Andean Strategy, the operations that the SEALs were an insignificant part of was a two thousand five hundred million-dollar program designed to interdict and disrupt the flow of narcotics traffic into the U.S. The high profile part of the strategy was the seizure of drugs and the arrest of traffickers. The low profile effort amounted to seizing the precursor chemicals necessary to process drugs and wiping out the crops that produced the products.

State Department and Justice Department personnel were working overtime to arrest and jail the kingpins who bought and sold narcotics. Their major obstacles were national laws. Thousands of men like Boomer Savarese and Alex Gomez risked their lives to interdict narcotics traffic. Their major obstacles were lead bullets.

Evans had studied the efforts to eradicate crops and the programs that helped farmers break their economic dependence on coca, poppy, and marijuana. He was convinced they were futile. It was during his study of the Andean Strategy that he had first met Dr. Galán. She was an academician, a scientist disconnected from the real world. Even her experience in the jungles of the *Chaparé* had not convinced her that there wasn't an easy solution to America's drug habit, one that came from a pill or a syringe. They had argued the issues for hours.

Galán's project wasn't the only black program Evans had been exposed to. There were several programs like Project Mandrake. Some rushed to develop herbicides like 2-4D and Tebuthiuron, known in the Andes as *Spike*. There was even a secret program to develop *bugs for drugs*. The plan was to unleash swarms of tiny white coca-eating moths called *malumbia* to wipe out the coca fields. U.S.

government science laboratories were working day and night to genetically engineer a coca plant that couldn't produce cocaine. The diabolical plan called for introducing the altered gene into the coca fields by means of a virus disseminated by aerial spray. It was biological warfare in the jet age and Evans was convinced it was all for naught.

The SEAL part of the strategy was insignificant in the over all scheme of things. Their job was to teach commandos to operate efficiently which in SEAL-talk was to teach men to move, shoot, and communicate. Masure didn't tell Evans that the second half of his mission was to teach close quarters battle or CQB. It amounted to entering manmade structures to arrest bad guys, and survive the assault without killing innocent people. The SEALs developed the tactics used by the FBI Hostage Rescue Team and other major law enforcement organizations in the U.S. They had developed the tactics out of concern that terrorists would seize a vessel on the high seas and hold nations hostage with huge quantities of natural gas or oil supertankers converted in to massive bombs or environmental weapons. The SEALs were the best in the U.S. military at teaching CQB tactics. Their specialty was ship seizure and hostage rescue from underway ships. Duran's final objective was to teach the *Bloque* night underway shipboarding, the most difficult of all special operations missions.

Evans already knew what Lieutenant Duran's basic mission was. It was common sense; teach men to move, shoot, and communicate. He had done it a hundred times in thirty different countries and with no great feat of intellect he correctly guessed the ultimate objective of Alpha platoon's mission. Since the Green Beret could do everything the SEALs could do except underway shipboarding, and they were the force of choice in the army dominated U.S. SPECOPS community, he correctly surmised the SEALs were in Colombia to teach underway shipboarding. It also explained the reason why they were hanging out in Barranquilla and Cartagena, Colombian, naval seaports located on the Caribbean coast. Evans chose not to press the issue.

"I don't know how much I can help you, Stick. I've already told you the score; U.S. a few kilos of cocaine and a few traffickers; dopers, billions of unwashed dollars and the power to corrupt nations. The best I can do is to give you an education." Evans focused on Masure's eyes. "How much time do you have before you start the next phase of your training?"

"About two weeks. The group we've been training is being regrouped. They took four KIAs and a couple of WIAs. Hell, we even had an MIA for a while."

"Captain Rodriguez?"

"*Jeez, Boss!* Is there anything you don't know?"

"Yeah. I don't know who the enemy is," Evans replied, solemnly.

"Start with Rodriguez. He crawled out of the jungle without a scratch."

"Nah. Rodriguez is just well connected. Someone told someone who told someone else. You know the deal. He's just trying to stay alive. When do you start CQB training?" Evans asked.

CQB was short talk for close quarters battle and was a necessary step before teaching shipboarding.

"In about four weeks we'll begin training in the kill house," Masure answered, with a look of concern. "I'm hoping we have a new OIC to work with by then."

OIC was SEAL-speak for officer in charge.

"Why? Rodriguez is connected, man. He's in the know. Use him like an alarm bell. If he gets jittery, put your antenna up and get *real* cautious."

A devious smile crossed Masure's face. "Of course. Why didn't I think of that?"

"You got your passport with you?" Evans asked.

"You bet. I never leave home without it," Masure said.

"Okay. We'll catch an evening flight to La Paz. I'll show you what's happening at the root of the problem. Order me some *frijoles rojos, aijiaco y arepa.* I'll be back in a minute. I have to relay a couple of messages through San Diego to set things up."

Masure's eyes brightened. It was show and tell time. He knew Evans wasn't in South America for a vacation. Word was out in the SEAL community that several retirees were working for SOC Inc. in Colombia. Even Evans's choice of a restaurant was deliberate. It specialized in ethnic food from the Antioquia Province of north central Colombia. Medellin was the major city of the region, a fact that didn't get by Masure's attention. He wasn't the youngest Master Chief in the United States Navy for nothing. From Evans's familiarity with the waiters he knew the Commander frequented the place, probably because it was filled with patrons from Colombia's drug capital.

The stewed chicken and corn cakes arrived just as the Commander returned to the table. The waiter had timed their arrival to his return.

Before they finished their meals a distinguished looking gentleman in his forties entered the restaurant. The staff immediately began fawning over him as if he was a movie star. They gave him the best table in the establishment and rushed to decant his favorite drink. Masure caught Evans studying the man out of the corner of his eye. Then the gentleman looked their way and waved at Evans. Evans returned the greeting with a mock salute and a fake smile Masure recognized.

"Who is that dude?" Masure asked under his breath.

"That, my friend, is Canrado Cataño Gaviria, otherwise known as, the Cat. He is the most famous *vaquero* in all of South America. In his rodeo days there wasn't a horse in Colombia that could buck him off. That's how he got his nickname. He always lands on his feet. Today, he's head of security for the largest coffee and cattle consortiums in South America. He owns this place."

"No wonder they're all over him like a cheap suit," Masure commented. "So what's your interest in him?"

"Who says I have an interest?"

"I just assumed you had…"

Evans cut him off. "Assumption is the motherhood of fuck up, Master Chief."

"Maybe so," Masure exclaimed, holding his own. "But I know you chose this restaurant for a reason, *Commander Asshole*. And even from here I can see the man has stone cold killer eyes."

A wave of pride crossed Evans's face.

"There's hope for you after all, Buck-O." He studied Masure's face for reaction as he said, "I have a small contract to train his men in VIP security." He wanted to know if Masure knew the objective of his effort was Lieutenant Duran's *verraca*, Maria Christina Ballesteros. Training her bodyguards was like training hooded cobras to spit accurately. "It pay's top dollar," he said.

Masure's eyes gave no sign of recognition. "So that's what Popeye and the boys are up to," Masure said, referring to the retired SEALs who worked for Evans.

"Among other things, partner," Evans replied, noncommittally.

* * *

On the way back to the *Nueva Granada* to collect their bags, Evans spotted Tom Roth leaving the hotel. He quickly pulled Masure aside.

"What's up, Boss?" Masure asked, reading the look in Evans's eyes.

"See that guy?"

"The turd in the suit?"

"Yeah. CIA. I can spot 'em in the dark. He's on foot. Let's tail him."

Masure smiled. "You got it."

They followed Roth for several minutes as he window shopped, using the reflection to see the street scene behind him. They deftly avoided detection and followed him back to the restaurant. Near *La Fonda Antioqueña* Roth pretended to window shop at the store next door until he saw Gaviria exit. Using the chance encounter he casually walked up and asked him for a light. Evans chuckled.

"What's going down?" Masure asked.

"The classic Humphrey Bogart brush pass straight out of the tradecraft training manual."

As Gaviria handed Roth his cigarette lighter he also passed him a small scrap of paper with a message dropping the dime on the Savajé cartel's next big drug shipment.   Roth thanked the Colombian for the light and strolled on down the street.

"Let's get out of here," Evans said.   "Enough of amateur hour."

Chapter 11

Maria Christina down shifted the 911 Porsche Carrera and took a sharp curve at maximum speed. She needed space, privacy, and freedom to think for herself, by herself. She needed a moment alone before joining her father for lunch. The men following her in the late model Ford Explorer were bodyguards. They followed her every movement like a shadow. That was their job and she accepted the need for protection. But sometimes it smothered her. She felt like a gilded bird in a golden cage and she needed to escape if only for a few moments. She glanced in her rearview mirror. The Explorer was losing ground fast. She entered another set of curves at warp speed. Down shifting to second gear, she pressed the accelerator to the floor the way her driving coach from SOC Inc. had taught her.

Her bodyguards were a tough bunch to lose, even with a high performance sports car on a curving mountain road. Gato had blood kin seeing to her safety and he had spared no expense in their training. All of them attended a special driving school once a year to practice emergency driving. SOC Inc. even sent a team of experts from San Diego, California several times a year to train them in martial arts, weaponry, and counter surveillance techniques. Such precautions were the norm in Colombia. It was the price the rich and famous paid for being rich and famous. Both M-19 and FARC had kidnapped children from prominent families. Her father, Don Alajandro Cataño Ballesteros, spared no expense for her protection.

Carlos Cataño, the Spider, was an excellent driver but it took two vehicles to stay with Maria Christina and her Carrera, one in front and one behind. The second vehicle, driven by Juan, the Coyote Cataño was already at Kevin's restaurant where she was planning to have lunch with her father.

The souped-up Explorer was no match for the Porsche on a winding mountain road. A few miles south of Kevin's, she checked her rearview mirror then powered into a tight set of s-curves. Halfway through the slalom she hit the brakes hard. Like a springbok the nimble little sports car responded without a screech. She whipped it into a scenic lookout and switched off the engine. A few moments later the Explorer labored by like an overloaded rocket. It had become a game between her and the men. And they would pay hell if they lost her.

If Carlos is smart he'll drive the road a couple of times before he reports to Gato, she thought.

On his second pass she planned to take pity on him. She intended to slip up behind the Explorer like a bat out of hell and blow by it at warp six. It was exercise, like a little bird fledging its wings before taking flight from the nest.

Maria rolled down the window and took a deep breath of fresh mountain air. It felt good to be free if only for a few minutes. Then bad thoughts crossed her mind. It was only a matter of time before *Gato* told her father about Jack.

I have to tell him, she thought. *Gato knows. I saw it in his eyes, his all-knowing eyes. He knows.*

She opened her purse and flipped through the pictures in her wallet without seeing them. The outrage she had seen in Gaviria's eyes blocked out the image of the handsome young *Norte Americano* she had met in Cartagena.

I wonder if he knows I slept with him? she worried.

Maria focused on one of the pictures until the image burned through the anxiety. She felt a flutter in her abdomen, a longing, a deep need she didn't understand. Her first man and he was a Yankee sailor. Gazing out over the city of Medellin in the valley below made her recall the first time she had seen him. It was from the balcony of the family penthouse on Boca Grande on the shores of the Caribbean. From the twelfth floor she, and her best friend Juanita, had spotted a group of young men frolicking around the swimming pool of one of the four star hotels on *El Lagiuito*. They were diving and swimming, drinking and dancing, and putting the moves on all the rich young women lying around in string bikinis. There were more than a dozen of them, young, tan, and well muscled. From a distance they all appeared the same, like they had been cut out of the same bolt of cloth. With binoculars the two girls had inspected the troop like eyeing a group of thoroughbred racehorses at the track.

Maria smiled remembering their skimpy red swimming trunks. They had all worn the same scanty Speedos that barely covered their privates. The swimming trunks had attracted women like magnets. Their lean hard bodies had done the rest.

As Juanita joked and giggled, Maria's eye caught on one of the young men. He was lying on a chase lounge soaking up the Caribbean sun and paying no attention to the women hovering about the man seated at the table next to him. Tall and slender, he sported short wavy black hair and a pencil thin mustache like Zorro. No matter how hard she tried to keep the binoculars away they seemed to focus back on him and each time they did she felt a little butterfly in her stomach. Juanita had talked her in to going down to the pool in their bikinis and had urged her in to making eye contact. When she did, it was love at first sight.

How can I tell my fossil of a father I'm in love? In love with a Yankee. He'll go crazy. He'll never understand. All he dreams about is work and money. Cattle, coffee, flowers. They drive him to exhaustion. It's the paisa-dream. No. The paisa-curse, she lamented.

She knew he wouldn't understand, but she had to tell him. She was practicing her confession when the Explorer roared back down the road. She heard tires squeal and gears grind as Carlos slammed on the brakes and threw the truck into reverse. Momentarily he pulled into the turn off and parked behind her at a distance as if to give her space to breathe. Carlos was getting wise to her ways. She looked in her rearview mirror and saw Pablo Cataño grinning at her from the passenger seat.

Disgusting man, she thought.

She hated the way Pablo looked at her. She had asked *Gato* to fire him but he had refused. Carlos, Pablo and Juan Cataño were blood kin, cousins, so he couldn't fire them without a very important reason. Maria waited until Carlos switched off the engine before firing up the little Porsche and peeling out.

With the Explorer hot on her trail, she wheeled into the parking lot determined to tell her father she was going to get married. She left the Carrera amid a score of luxury vehicles and hurried into the restaurant with the grit of determination. The concierge jumped to hold the door for her. He greeted her with a bright smile reserved for the aristocracy of Medellin. As she walked by he stared lustily at her long legs and perfect posterior. Then he felt angry eyes boring holes through his skull and looked up to see *Gato Gaviria* eyeing him from the bar up above. Like rat he scurried to the cover of the kitchen.

The waiter in the restaurant greeted her with bow. "*Buenos dias, Señorita Maria Christina Ballesteros.* Your father is still in his meeting. May I bring you something to drink while you wait, *Señorita*?"

"Please, Ricardo. A glass of iced tea."

"*Por supuesto, Señorita*," he said, showing her to the best table in the house.

He helped her with the chair and disappeared like one of the Queen's royal servants.

Maria gazed at the spectacular view of the valley and lost herself in thought until she felt eyes on the back of her neck, *Gato's* all-knowing, all-seeing eyes. Her marvelous table was in direct view of the bar on the second floor.

She couldn't help but watch as Carlos entered the restaurant, climbed the stairs and reported to Gaviria. His purple birthmark always seemed to darken when he was anxious. From his table Gaviria commanded a view of the dining area, the parking lot, and the large meeting rooms used for conferences like the one her father was chairing. Don Ballesteros was brokering a meeting for all the coffee growers in the area and security was tight. Brokering gave the smaller growers an opportunity to pool their crops with the larger growers for shipment to the U.S. and thus receive a better price for their labor. It was a service the Ballesteros were popular for providing. As usual Gaviria had security men stationed all over the area. From time to time one would report to him with a nod or a mock salute as he walked his beat.

Gaviria slowly sipped at his coffee as Carlos told him about her little excursion at the scenic lookout. Maria smiled proudly as Carlos left the bar and walked back down to the parking lot. She chuckled when she remembered how easy it had been for Jack and his friend to fool them.

The two SEALs had taken a service elevator to the roof of the penthouse and climbed down the outside of the building using a bed sheet. Juanita had almost fainted when they had swung onto the twelfth floor balcony like bats out of the night sky.

That first night had been so exciting. They had turned the lights down low, drank champagne, and talked all night to the sound of steamy salsa music. Juanita had taken the handsome SEAL called Stick Masure to the guest bedroom on the very first night. Her pleasure-moans from behind the closed door had been a bit embarrassing for Maria but exciting nonetheless. I was the slow dancing she remembered best. She felt her face flush and her lips get hot as she thought of slow dancing in a Caribbean breeze with Lieutenant Jack Duran, United States Navy. Her thoughts were interrupted by one of Gaviria's gunmen reporting from the conference room. When he resumed his post, Gaviria got up and walked down to her table.

"*Buenos dias, Bonita*," he said pleasantly, like a father talking to his own daughter.

Gaviria had seen to her safety while she was still in the womb. In some ways he knew her better than her father.

"*Buenos dias, Gato*. My father is busy, no?" she asked, knowing the answer.

"*Sí, Bonita*. He sends his regrets," he said, his attention momentarily attracted by a big black Mercedes screeching into the parking lot like a tank on maneuvers.

Several men piled out of the car and walked briskly toward the entrance. He nodded to his guards and they relaxed their vigil slightly from the alert posture they had assumed. Ramón Savajé walked directly to the conference room door and tossed his head back arrogantly like a bullfighter challenging a bull. Gaviria nodded his head and the guards at the door allowed him to enter without a body search.

There were several important families in Medellin capable of putting together huge shipments of coffee, thereby commanding better prices from the Yankees. Smaller growers were invited to piggyback with the large growers for leverage. Brokers like Maria's father always called meetings at swank Medellin restaurants like Kevin's or to fancy hotels like the Intercontinental. Everyone who wanted to contribute to the shipment was invited. The meetings were flashy, uniquely South American affairs that took on the ambience of a party. Local DEA agents knew that illicit commodities were also handled during brokerages so they sometimes staked out the meetings to gather intelligence.

Like Gaviria, Maria couldn't help but take note of the last participant to enter the conference room. He was a well-known narcotics trafficker who covered his illegal activities poorly with cattle and coffee. Ramón Savajé was not welcome at the Ballesteros brokerage and his presence meant trouble. Recently he had become an *extraditable*, a person sought for extradition to the United States for drug smuggling. He was also a brutal killer no one wanted to cross.

Gaviria eyed Risitos Savajé who had stationed himself near the entrance to the restaurant. His eyes were like radar, scanning the entire area, but they always returned to the burly killer at the door. He was missing his lips, a deformity caused by a letter bomb sent to Ramón by a rival trafficker. It left Risitos with a hideous permanent grin that lent him his nickname, giggles. Ramón had killed the rival trafficker's entire family for the grudge before Risitos was out of the hospital.

"*Bonita*, I'm afraid your father is going to be busy all afternoon. He is brokering a very large shipment and some of the growers are late," he said politely. "Perhaps it would be best if you took lunch at home," he suggested, not taking his eyes off Risitos Savajé.

"Very well then. Would you please tell my father I'll be spending the weekend at the beach," she said angrily. "Arrange for the plane to take me to Cartagena," she ordered with a pout.

Gaviria's eyes hardened as he turned to look at her. "The plane is already scheduled to go Tingo Maria and Trinidad. There is much business to attend to this weekend, *Bonita*."

Tingo Maria was a small town in Peru. Trinidad was in Bolivia where the Ballesteros owned huge herds of cattle. Both towns were centers of gravity for the drug trade.

"Then arrange for commercial transportation please," Maria bristled, ordering Gaviria around like a common servant.

He was half listening to her while watching Risitos put his hand to his nose and snort.

"Pardon me, *Bonita*. What did you say?" he asked, still staring at Risitos.

"I said, *arrange for commercial transportation please!*" she snapped.

"As you wish, Maria," he said, not really paying attention to her.

But his all-knowing eyes seemed to accuse her of something dirty. It was her unconscious mind working overtime. Gaviria was angry because Risitos Savajé was snorting cocaine in plain view. He would have killed the Savajés long ago if he could have done it without arousing public anger. The Savajés gave a great deal of money to the poor and Ramón owned the local soccer team. He was thinking of creating an accident along the mountain road that led back to Medellin when Maria verbally assaulted him.

"You don't approve, do you?" she demanded.

Gota's eyes focused on her like a pit bull. "Your father would be most disappointed, *Bonita*," he muttered, barely moving his thin lips.

"Then you haven't told him?" Maria fretted, like a frightened little child.

Her big brown eyes softened slightly and her lips pursed into a little pout that always soften Gaviria's heart. Her full lips quivered slightly as if she wanted to cry. Maria Christina Ballesteros was a beautiful woman. Her friends all told her she looked exactly like her idle, the American *tejano* singer, Selena. Even Gaviria's stone cold killer heart was melted by her little moods. He had been her family's protector for more than twenty-five years.

"I have told him only what he needs to know, *Bonita*. This gringo is no good for you," he said, staring at her with unblinking eyes. "It will break your father's heart if you become seriously involved with a Yankee."

Maria swallowed hard. *He doesn't know I slept with Jack*, she thought.

"Gato. Jesus Christo! I'm twenty-three years old. What I do is my business," she snapped back.

"What you do affects the whole family, Maria. We all love you. I don't want to see you make a mistake that you will regret all of your life. I encourage you not to see this Yankee again."

Gaviria's lips barely moved as he spoke. Sometimes even Maria had difficulty understanding him. Cold and calculating, yet protective like the family dog, he was her knight without the shining armor. *Gato* Gaviria had saved her family from death on numerous occasions and for that she was thankful, and respectful.

"But *Gato*. I love him," she confessed, as she had planned to do to her father.

"No Maria. You do not love him. You love your father. You love your mother. You are simply attracted to this gringo."

"No. It is different this time."

"Perhaps I will encourage him to leave Colombia," he suggested, with a far away expression.

"If he leaves, I'm going with him," Maria threatened, with fire in her eyes.

Gaviria had already tried to encourage Jack Duran and his whole platoon to leave Colombia. He had hired a group of *sicarios* to ambush and kill their counterparts. He had paid them well to kidnap one of Duran's men and demand the U.S. withdraw its soldiers from Colombian territory in exchange for his safe release. But the *idiotas* had botched the mission. He had also paid a large sum of money to a contact in Bogotá to have the SEALs quietly withdrawn. This too had failed.

98

The last thing Gaviria wanted was a dead Yankee soldier on Colombian soil. Such attention was bad for business. He knew Maria Christina. He had watched her grow to womanhood. Maria Christina Ballesteros was a beautiful, spoiled, rich *paisa* that possessed a defiant nature and if he, or her father, forbade her to do something, that that was exactly what she would do to spite them. He knew her nature and he knew not to push her. He would have killed Jack Duran after their first date if he had known her infatuation was serious. He had no idea she had slept with the gringo. If he had, Jack Duran and his whole platoon would have been eliminated.

"Maria, please consider your father and mother before you make rash decisions. Soon this man will be recalled to his country. He is a Yankee warrior and the Yankees meddle in the affairs of all nations. Sooner or later they will send him to another country to cause problems there. Maria," counseled Gaviria, shaking his finger, "you cannot go with him to mess up the affairs of other nations. I strongly encourage you not see this man. He is no good for you."

"*What I do is my business!*" Maria bristled.

"Very well, *Bonita.* That is true," he exclaimed with exasperation. "I will make arrangements for your flight."

He tipped his head back like a *Bogotañeo* gentleman and resolved to rid Colombia of Jack Duran by whatever means necessary.

Time for more creative measures, he thought. "Please excuse me, Maria. I have business I must attend to."

Gaviria walked to the entrance of the restaurant and shook his finger in Risitos's face like an angry father scolding a child. The man's permanent grin seemed to increase in size and he braced his body for an attack. One hand reached inside his suit coat. Instantly, five of *Gato's* thugs appeared, MAC-10 submachine pistols slung low from their shoulders. Facing an army, Risitos slowly removed an empty hand. He shrugged and his disfigured face contorted into a snarl. He flipped up a defiant palm ten inches in front of Gaviria's face to show his hand was empty.

"What is your problem, *amigo*," he growled, tossing his head back arrogantly, like a bullfighter.

"You," Gaviria hissed, his lips barely moving. "This is a coffee brokerage, not a party for *traficantes* high on cocaine. If you want to fry your brains, *sicario*, keep it out of sight."

"*Por supuesto, Señor Gato Gaviria, jefe de putas -- chief of whores,*" Risitos replied, contemptuously. He eyed the men stationed around him without fear.

Armed men didn't frighten Risitos Savajé. He had eaten a bomb and survived. He had killed dozens of men, just to watch them squirm in the moment of death. He had even cut the tongue out of an informant's mouth and threw it into the backyard of the local DEA agent. The only thing that frightened Risitos Savajé was running out of the White Lady.

Gaviria locked eyes with him in a death stare. He mumbled something Risitos didn't understand. The chemical fire in Risitos's brain was waning. He needed another fix. For that reason and that reason only, he retreated. Standing at the entrance of the restaurant, he couldn't get a large enough dose by pinching the crystals between his thumb and forefinger. Mucous was running out his smashed nose and saliva was dribbling down his chin through his exposed teeth. Grinning his permanent grin, he tossed his head further back. Without taking his eyes off Gaviria, he bumped his shoulder as he passed him. He smirked at the thugs standing around and walked back to the parking lot.

Maria watched the whole exchange. She saw the burly man retreat to the big black car, but she had no concept of the world inside Risitos's twisted head or what he was about to do in the backseat of the big Mercedes. But Gaviria knew. Many of the traffickers became addicted to their own product. It was the biggest mistake in the business.

Risitos slid into the Mercedes and slumped back into the plush leather seat. He glared out through the dark tinted windows at gunmen who couldn't see him. Anger contorted his gruesome face.

"You can't tell me what to do, *puta*. Only Ramón, *mi hermano,* gives me orders, you son-of-a-whore."

He flipped them the bird like a gringo sailor spoiling for a fight. But he knew they couldn't see the gesture of disrespect.

The Savajé cartel had crushed several families that had refused to cooperate with them and the Ballesteros were next on the list. Ramón had crashed the brokerage to make a point. The Ballesteros were next.

The Ballesteros cover their merchandize with flowers and coffee to give la pinchicata a good smell, he thought. *But they are just pompous self-righteous paisas assholes that are afraid to fight like men.*

"*Gato es un maricon!*" he yelled, spitting saliva through his exposed teeth. It sprayed the window of the sedan. "*Jefe de putas!*" he shouted to no one.

There was strength in numbers and Ramón Savajé knew it. He was forming a larger *corporación*, one with the monetary, political, and force of arms to rule Colombia. He was tired of being an *extraditable* and he was tired of hiding from Yankee imperialists who wanted to kidnap him and his brother for trial in the U.S. He wanted the support of the Ballesteros in a bid to overthrow the government and repealing the ridiculous laws that allowed Yankees to extradite Colombian citizens to U.S. courts. If the Ballesteros didn't cooperate, there would be war.

"*Foouck dee gringos and the horses they ride on,*" Risitos yelled. "*And foouck *dee Ballesteros!*" he raged, saliva running down his chin. *"Hijos de putas! Foouck dem all!"*

Risitos felt the pistol underneath his expensive white Italian suit as he pulled the small glass bottle out of his inside coat pocket. Fuming with anger, he continued to fish his pocket until he found the small straw he needed. With deftness born of repetition, he removed the cap and let it fall into his lap. With his right hand he inserted the straw deep into his right nostril. With his left, he clutched the bottle with his fingers and simultaneously pressed his thumb against his left nostril. Inhaling forcefully through the straw, he vacuumed up the magic white crystals like a Dust buster on high.

Deep in his lungs the chemical worked its magic. He slumped deeper into the leather seat, exhaling slowly, letting his thoughts run wild. His brain sizzled with a chemical fire, imagining a razor sharp knife cutting deep into human flesh. He could see the blade slice through the jugular. He could see blood gush out, painting Gaviria's chest with sticky red ooze. He could see the pupil in *Gato's* eye change at the very moment of death, like the eye of an animal when life leaves the body. He had seen it before, dozens of times. The moment of death fascinated Risitos Savajé. His mind flashed back to the lab in San Diego and his hand instinctively gripped his pistol. He had been so close to Carol Galán he could smell her perfume. Two days ahead of Gaviria's plans to kidnap her, thanks to a *sicario* informant who worked for the Ballesteros.

Where is that bitch? he thought.

"That foucking Carlos Cataño had better not double crossing us," he mumbled out loud, "or I will cut off his dick and shove it down his cock-sucking throat."

Risitos paid Carlos big money to keep him informed. He expected a return on his investment. His over stimulated mind flashed back to Gaviria.

"*Jefe de putas*, does not know we own *La Araña*. It's just money, *maricon!*" he laughed. "He thinks we only merchandize to the Yankees. *The stupid bastard!*" *We make more money from the fouckem Russians than we do from the fouckem Yankees and when we get the bomb, maricon, no one can touch us.*

"Ramón is a genius, you asshole," he mumbled out loud. "And Carlos Cataño, is our fouckem Judas goat, *jefe de putas,*" he shouted.

Not two feet from Risitos Savajé, an electronic eavesdropping device picked up some of his ranting. Even loud salsa music from the car's expensive stereo failed to mask all the words. He would have gone crazy with anger if he had known Carlos Cataño had planted the device at Gaviria's orders. His rambling thoughts turned from hate to murder. In his mind's eye he saw himself standing over Gaviria's body. He took out his penis and urinated in *Gato's* lifeless face.

"*Fenomeno,*" he mumbled, as he visualized the desecration.

He laughed out loud and pet his pistol like a cat.

"Sí, Señor Gato Gaviria, jefe de putas. Plata o plomo, maricon?" he repeated over and over, boiling with anger inflamed by the chemical fire of cocaine. Silver or lead.

Chapter 12

Colombia's strategic location at the top of South America is perfect for drug smugglers who want to market their products in the United States and Europe. It is within relatively easy flying distance of the U.S. and it has a culture that looks the other way if not outright condones smuggling. n many ways the story of Pablo Escobar Gaviria exemplifies the story of America's addiction to cocaine. From a lowly drug courier and petty car thief, Escobar rose up the smuggler's ladder to become a multibillionaire in just a few years. His drug wealth bought him a mansion in Miami, multimillion-dollar ranches in Colombia, a professional soccer team, and even his own zoo stocked with camels, giraffes, and a kangaroo. He owned a fleet of airplanes and politicians by the score and was even elected to the Colombian National Congress.

In 1982, when President Reagan declared war on drugs, he declared war on Pablo Escobar and those like him. Shortly thereafter the drug lord was photographed red-handed, along with high-level Nicaraguan government officials, loading a DEA informant's airplane with cocaine. For betraying him, Escobar had the informant, a man named Barry Seals, murdered in Louisiana by a Colombian death squad. This only resulted in a tightening of the noose around Escobar's neck.

What traffickers like Escobar feared the most was the U.S. Justice system and prisons where guards couldn't be bribed and judges intimidated. To prevent the passage of extradition laws they bribed Colombian politicians by the hundreds. *Better a grave in Colombia than a cell in the U.S.A.* was the motto of the time. When pressure by the United States eventually led to the passage of an extradition law that allowed drug traffickers to be tried and jailed in the U.S., open warfare ensued.

Using their huge drug profits traffickers financed an attack on the Palace of Justice on the very day the Supreme Court of Colombia was scheduled to rule on the extradition law. Nearly one hundred people were killed and all of the extradition files were destroyed. Still the Colombian government refused to deal, in part because of the slaughter at the Palace of Justice. In the struggle that followed, *sicarios* killed fifty-seven judges, twenty-five journalist, and more than five hundred members of the Patriotic Union. Even Colombia's leading newspaper, *El Espectador*, was car bombed killing sixty-three people and wounding six hundred. Bodies floated down the Magdalena River by the hundreds. Judges resigned in droves under death threats. The bullet-ridden

Colombian justice system almost collapsed. When the drug barons threatened to kill ten judges for every trafficker extradited to the United States, President Gaviria repealed the Extradition Law and *La Violencia* cooled to a bubbling simmer. Round one was over.

To help the under gunned Colombian military, the U.S. quietly sent arms, aircraft, helicopters, and advisors. Uncle Sam also quietly encouraged dozens of men like Commander Derek Evans, U.S. Navy SEAL retired, to get involved in the region. At the urging of one of Harris's agents, Evans had reluctantly taken a contract to train the security forces of the Ballesteros Cattle and Coffee Consortium. Dr. Harris knew that, as a retired member of the United States Armed Forces, Evans was honor bound to provide key information he deemed to be of intelligence value.

There were several large consortiums working the Magdalena River Valley. The most notorious was the Savajé Coffee Consortium. It was moving large amounts of cocaine into Mexico, Europe, and Russia. Harris knew the Savajé cartel wasn't the only criminal organization shopping for weapons of mass destruction. There were several hundred organizations on her target list. But she excluded the Ballesteros Consortium from close scrutiny because she had struck up a marriage of convenience with Don Alajandro; information for top notch security training, with Evans providing the training. The Ballesteros were moving huge quantities of coffee, beef, and flowers, and they were prime targets for kidnappers and extortionists. Occasionally small amounts of drugs turned up in their shipments, a fact Harris attributed to enterprising employees. Helping Don Ballesteros, who had his eyes on the presidency, was a small price to pay for the highly reliable information the Agency was receiving from his organization. *Gato* Gaviria had provided Tom Roth with intelligence that had resulted in several cartels being completely wiped out.

* * *

Before returning to Colombia, Tom Roth had briefed his boss, Dr. Alysin Harris, on his meeting with Derek Evans. Throughout the briefing she had smiled like a Cheshire cat. Again he recommended dropping Evans from the list. But she would hear none of it. She wanted the man on the trail and she was a heavy hitter within the Agency. Harris was responsible for the newest and most difficult challenge facing the nation, keeping nuclear, biological, and chemical weapons of mass destruction out of the hands of criminals, crazies, and fanatics, and off the streets of the United States of America. One word from her to the Director and Roth would find himself re-assigned to some meaningless job in Central Africa. Reluctantly, she had agreed to the fifty thousand-dollar advance payment that

Evans had demanded but hadn't agreed upon a method of payment. She simply listened to Roth's briefing, issued a list of succinct orders, and dispatched him back to Colombia by the first available flight. As he stood duty at the Embassy in Bogotá he ruminated over the relationship between Evans and Harris.

He's right, he thought. *The arrogant asshole is right on. But he's guessing. He doesn't know about the bust.*

Recently, the counter-proliferation force under Dr. Harris had seized three nuclear weapons on the high seas. They were hidden in special lead lined containers in the bowels of Russian fishing trawlers. Two of the bombs were confiscated in the Black Sea. The third was seized off the Pacific Coast of Colombia. All three were disguised as common suitcases and designed for terrorist operations. Through spies in Russian, the Agency had learned that two of the weapons were being shipped to a Middle Eastern terrorist organization. The third buyer was Ramón Savajé.

Another thought struck Roth.

Harris is cagy bitch. She's feeding Commander Asshole jobs for a reason. He could be the fuse that ignites an explosion between the Savajés and the Ballesteros. If they kill each other off, problem solved. What was it he said? 'Harris is worried about the exchange. The Arabs have the money. The Slavs have the bombs. The South Americans have the dope.' Sounds like Dr. Harris and Commander Asshole have had a few PMs, maybe of an intimate kind.

Then he thought about the nuclear weapons that the Agency had confiscated from the Russian trawler.

Surely she wouldn't tell him about the nukes. What would she tell him? Just enough to use him like shit paper. And that's why he's pissed. But what was all that bullshit about politics? I don't get it. Everyone knows Don Ballesteros is positioning himself for a run at the presidency. So what? Evans is a damned mushroom being fed a load of crap by a friggin' pit viper. Then he thought, *He thinks Ballesteros is shopping for a nuke.*

The climate of violence that revolved around the cocaine trade attracted scores of private security consultants, counterinsurgency experts, and adventurers from all over the world, many of whom were veterans like Evans. In Colombia rich children didn't brag about their father's car. They bragged about the number of bodyguards he had. Roth was right about one fact. Harris had been instrumental in Evans securing a contract from Don Alajandro Ballesteros but she didn't want him in between two powerful South American organizations.

So what's the relationship between Harris and Evans? He's just the kind of guy she would go for, and the very type that would be turned off by a powerful aggressive woman. He must have been her squeeze before she married Tom

Harris.

Roth couldn't have imaged that Harris had fallen head over heels in love with Evans while on a mission to recover several nuclear weapons in Southeast Asia. She had slept with him on several occasions and she would have left her husband if Evans had given her the least bit of encouragement.

Maybe the asshole dumped her and she can't get over the rejection, he thought. *For whatever reason she wants him in the middle of this mess. One thing is for sure. He's going get his arrogant ass snuffed out if he's not careful. It would serve the jerk right.*

The telephone on the desk rang, causing Roth to jump.

"Damn," he cursed.

He grabbed it and answered in his most masculine voice.

"Roth here."

"I'm going to stand down the men," reported the voice on the other end of the line. "Big party tonight at the disco. They picked up a couple of bitches and have settled in for the night."

"Okay," Roth agreed. "Maintain A.V." he said cryptically, referring to audio-visual surveillance.

"Music's too loud," reported the agent.

"Do it anyway," Roth ordered.

"Roger. Out here."

Roth's Tactical Analysis Team monitored the Savajés around the clock with all the assets available to the Agency. The men on duty tried to listen to the conversation going on inside Ramón's huge house but the music was too loud. Inside Ramón and Risitos were making the biggest mistake in the business. They were using their own product.

"How old are you?" Ramón asked, of the young girl he had picked up at a swank discotheque.

"Seventeen, *Señor Savajé*," she lied.

She was only fifteen. Her slim body was sinuous and child-like, and hadn't taken on the squat-bodied look of a mature mestizo woman. She was still lovely and innocent looking. Ramón leered at her lustfully and walked over to his dresser. He picked up a joint and lit it. As he returned to his huge heart-shaped bed, the sweet acrid smell of marijuana followed him. He held it out to her and she took a deep drag.

"Champaign?" he asked.

"*Sí, Señor,*" she said eagerly.

He filled her glass to the rim. She was already stoned out of her mind. She took another toke from the reefer and coughed.

106

"This is good grass," she giggled, as she passed the joint back to him.

He grinned and put the weed in an ashtray beside the bed. Then he opened her blouse and exposed her apple-sized breasts. He cupped one in the palm of his hand and squeezed the nipple until pain flashed across her face. He quickly undressed her and pushed her down so she was seated on the edge of the bed. She was young, but she knew what she had to do to earn a big payday. Everyone knew Ramón Savajé was filthy rich and that he was most generous with the whores who pleased him.

She unbuckled his trouser. Ramón wore nothing underneath his pants and when his short stubby little penis faced her, erect and throbbing, she almost giggled when she saw its pitiful length. Ramón was short and stocky and his phallus reflected his general appearance.

He pushed her away, "Beg," he said, with a brutal expression.

She looked up at him, her naked body glowing in the dim light of his narco rich bedroom. "Please," she whispered. "You know how much I want you, Ramón. Please."

He relaxed the grip he had on her shoulders and let her take him into her mouth. As she worked on him he took a small vial off his nightstand. It had a tiny gold spoon attached with a slender gold chain. Expertly, he took a spoonful of the white powder and snorted it up each of his nostrils. Then he looked down at her.

"Your turn," he said.

She stopped working long enough to answer.

"*No Señor Savajé*. I never do that before," she replied, while softly stoking his penis.

He jerked her hair viciously, snapping her head back and lifting her to her feet. For a few seconds he glared at her then filled the spoon and held it under her nose.

"Do as I say, girl," he commanded.

She sniffed and the powder lifted up from the spoon. Numbness traveled up her nostril and exploded in her brain. She felt butterflies in her genitals. Then her knees buckled and she fell back on the bed.

"*Madre de Diós!*" gasped the young whore. "*Maravillso!*"

Ramón laughed. He climbed on the bed and she laughed with him. She had never felt so good. Holding her down, he licked her nipples until they were hard and wet from his tongue. Then he sprinkled a little of the magic powder on each of them and slowly teased her with lips and tongue. She had never felt her breasts grow so hard, as if they were going to burst with pleasure.

Moaning and writhing, she begged, "Please. Please, Ramón. Fuck me. Fuck me now."

Her legs spread wide to accept him. But he didn't mount her. Instead he sprinkled coke all over her clitoris and like a dog after a bitch in heat, licked it off. His flicking tongue drove her to gushes of pleasure. She found herself screaming and shivering in orgasms she had never dreamed possible, each one higher and higher. Then she found herself staring at his stubby little penis, her brain sizzling in a chemical fire. Grabbing his buttock, she pulled herself around so she could take it in her mouth. Greedily she sucked at him. She wanted to swallow him alive. For a few minutes she worked on him until he pushed her away and turned her around on the bed. He held her legs apart and forced himself inside her violently. As he pounded up and down she heard herself screaming as orgasm after orgasm rippled through her young body like waves on a beach. Just as he exploded inside her the door to his bedroom burst open. Risitos stood over them, naked, penis erect. Ramón looked up at his mangled pathetic brother and yelled, "Go away, Risitos, you perverted bastard. You got your own woman, meng!"

"You fuck her, Ramón. The fouckem bitch laughed at me, bro," Risitos said, slurring his words.

Risitos was so high he was staggering at the foot of the bed.

"You been watchin' me, meng?" Ramón complained, withdrawing from the girl. Risitos laughed.

"Ahhhh! You have the bitch," Ramón snarled.

He got up out of bed dripping with juices. He glared at Risitos and staggered off. When Risitos looked down the girl was staring at him in horror. His appearance unnerved her. She had stared at his disfigured face at the discotheque and it had angered him. Now, with her brain in a drug-induced firestorm, her eyes expanded in horror, giving away the repugnance she felt inside.

"Fouck you, *puta*," Risitos bellowed, recognizing the look of revulsion written on her face.

Compared to his brother Risitos was heavyset and muscular. He grabbed the girl's arm and spun her around like a top so that the half-moons of her young buttocks were shinning up at him. Kneeling behind her he placed his erect penis at the opening to her anus and savagely pulled her back on her hips. With one powerful thrust he forced his way inside. The young girl froze for a moment and then screamed in agony. She tried to escape his grasp but he grabbed her by the hair and snapped her head back. Smothering her screams, he held her face in an iron grip. With the girl writhing in agony, he grunted and humped like a rhinoceros in heat. As he reached orgasm he twisted her chin around with such force the bones in her neck snap like twigs. When his penis stopped throbbing he released her and let her fall face forward on the bed, lifeless.

From the other room Ramón yell, *"Risitos, you dumb fuck. You killed this bitch, meng! I want my fouckem woman back!"*

Risitos sucked the saliva up between his exposed teeth.
"You can have her, Ramón. This whore is just dying for you, bro," he laughed.

Chapter 13

Evans and Masure cleared customs at El Alto Airport near La Paz and took a taxicab down the cold cobbled, high altitude streets of the capital of Bolivia. Armed soldiers in worn out fatigues milled around the major intersections like an army of occupation. In the bleak light of evening the sight of so many troops was disquieting to an unarmed warrior like Stick Masure. He eyed the soldiers apprehensively and unconsciously felt for a pistol that wasn't there. Evans saw the hand movement and read the look on his face.

"There have been more than one hundred and eighty coups in Bolivia in its one hundred and fifty year existence," he commented.

"Pleasant thought. Are they due for one now?" Masure asked.

"Who knows? When Scotty was stationed down here," he said, referring to a retired SEAL they both knew, "Arnell used to offer the soldiers coffee and donuts between firefights. Don't sweat it. No one wants trouble with Uncle Sam."

"That's what I thought," Masure replied, "until I had a dead Colombian port and starboard."

Evans acknowledged the comment with a raised eyebrow and turned to study the street scene passing by outside the cab. The driver had taken *La Avenida 16 de Julio*, the main street of La Paz, and the roadside market stalls lining the boulevard were closing for the day. The locals called it *El Prado*, the meadow. Modern hotels, restaurants and theaters lined the avenue like a veneer of expensive mahogany covering a reality of particle-board poverty. In La Paz the rich live in town and the poor live in the suburbs.

In the plazas Indian merchants wearing brightly stripped *sarapes*, bowler hats, and multilayered skirts known as *polleras*, packed up their merchandise for the long trek up to the barrios that encircled the city. The sight of llama trains snorting along with overburdened loads of maize, potatoes, *quiñoa*, and woolen goods, contrasted sharply with modern buildings and Spanish styled cathedrals. Masure was mesmerized.

Founded by the Spanish in 1548, La Paz, the Spanish word for peace, reflected the desire of the time to encourage trade along the route between the old Inca capital at Cuzco and the silver mines of Potosi in the high Andes above the city. It is the highest government seat in the world, lying more than eleven thousand feet above sea level in a deep gorge cut in the Altiplano, a high plateau between the Cordilleras Oriental and Occidental. Above the city loomed Nevada Illimani. At more than twenty-one thousand feet it was permanently capped in snow.

Near Plaza Roma they passed the University of San Andres. The driver turned off the main road and meandered up a secondary street for half a mile to an ancient cobbled trail better suited to llamas and alpacas. The old Ford coughed and sputtered in the thin mountain air, struggling up the narrow lane to an ancient place that deserved a name like Tiahuanaco or Titicaca. The sign over the door spelled, Sopocachi.

Masure shivered in the cold mountain air as he waited for the cabby to retrieve his bag from the trunk of the beat up Ford. They weren't far from the equator. In the jungle down below the Altiplano it was sweltering hot. But in the cold wintry air of the capital he blew smoke rings with his breath while waiting for Evans to pay the taxi driver.

An old Andean peasant sitting on the hotel steps eyed them both like a hungry dog. He was dressed in a woolen hat common to the Aymaran Indians and clad in a shaggy woolen coat that was threadbare and dirty. Black and gray toenails protruded from his grubby leather sandals. Tough and unaffected by the cold, his reptilian skin was calloused and furrowed like an old piece of rawhide. As he eyed Masure with suspicion, he wet the tip of a stick in his mouth and stuck it in a small gourd that he clutched to his side like a box of precious jewels. When the stick reappeared it was coated with a white powder. Masure's eyes grew in size, wondering if *cocaine on a stick* was the latest Bolivian drug craze.

Evans read his facial expression. "That's not what you think it is, Stick," he said, retrieving his bag from the cabby. "That's lime. The quid in his mouth is coca."

"Oh," Masure grunted, staring at the Indian in disbelief. "I knew that," he said facetiously.

The old man stuck the stick in his mouth and sucked off the powdered lime. He struggled to his feet, all the while staring glassy-eyed at the aliens on his sidewalk, then staggered toward them. As Evans paid the cab driver, he held out a calloused, sun baked hand, begging for a few bolivianos.

"*Buenos dias, Señor,*" Evans said, placing a few coins in the Indian's dirty palm.

He smiled through a mat of facial hair, showing several purple gray teeth stained by years of *acullicu,* the chewing of coca leaves.

"*Muchas gracias, Caballero. Muchisimas gracias,*" he said, fingering the coins in disbelief.

"*De nada, Viejo,*" Evans replied, as he headed up the steps.

The staff of the Sopocachi Hotel welcomed Evans like a long lost friend and helped him with his small bag despite his insistence to the contrary.

They put their bags in their rooms and rendezvoused in the hotel bar. It was a warm little pub complete with a guitarist playing Spanish music in front of a roaring fire. Constructed of dark hardwood as old as the Inca Empire, it was appropriately named Sinchi's, after a legendary warrior from the days before the Spanish conquest. The walls were adorned with Indian relics. Beside their table hung a large round golden metal mask that looked like the man in the moon, Inca style, with a cud of coca distorting one cheek.

Sinchi's served Peceña beer and imported liquor to Bolivians who made a modest living. Though below North American standards, it was well beyond the means of the average Bolivian. Masure quickly surmised that it was the favorite watering hole for the university crowd. A few academics had already gathered to chat and argue politics. Evans ordered two beers and listened to the guitarist for a few minutes. Masure read his facial expression and let him be with his thoughts.

Evans had first stayed at the hotel during a tour of duty at *Chimoré*, a Bolivian base near Sinajota on the edge of the *Chaparé* rain forest. He had gone to La Paz for rest and relaxation to get away from the corruption that was driving him mad. At breakfast one morning, he had the good fortune of meeting an honest cattle rancher who lived in the *Beni* Province of Northern Bolivia. Evans had recharged his batteries at the Sopocachi and had made a lifelong friendship with the Blackthornes.

Since the hotel had brought him good luck, Evans had used it as a base of operations on two subsequent projects. The first time was when he had written a critical analysis of the Andean Strategy for Rand Corporation. The second occasion was for Syntec Pharmaceuticals. All the major pharmaceutical companies were interested in the exotic plants of the rain forest and in their haste to collect promising specimens several people had been kidnapped. To avoid such problems Carol Galán had hired SOC Inc. for security.

Evans knew Carol Galán's habits, and most importantly, her South American friends. They had spent weeks together tromping around the jungle and hours discussing politics at the very table where he was seated. He suspected she was somewhere in La Paz or with one of the campesino families they had befriended in the *Chaparé*. He was musing over the possibilities when he noticed Masure grimace and squeeze his temples between his finger and thumb.

"Headache?"

"Yeah," Masure answered, squinting.

"Me too. It's the altitude. The day after tomorrow we'll catch a plane down to the lowlands." Evans motioned to the bartender. "*Maté, por favor*," he ordered, holding up two fingers.

"*Sí señor, Evans. Enseguida cuenta*," replied the waiter.

In moments he served up two steaming cups of hot liquid and a plastic bottle of honey. He had remembered that Evans liked a sweet taste to his *maté*.

Masure smelled the yellowish liquid and took a sip. "What is this shit?"

"Tea."

"Hummm. Taste's funny to me. Sort of like spinach."

"It should. It's coca tea."

"*Cocaine!* Great. Just great. Can I still pass a piss test? I can't retire yet, you know."

"Sure you can," Evans chuckled. "The Pope drank *maté* to alleviate his headache when he visited La Paz a few years ago. There's not much business in it. Just enough to fix your headache."

Masure took another sip. "The Pope doesn't have to golden flow or have an occasional black box." Black box was the SEAL slang for lie detector.

"Listen. I'm going to show you something that few Americans have ever seen."

"Like what?" Masure asked.

"Like a thousand square mile greenhouse filled with coca bushes and impoverished Indians living on the edge of starvation. Their children pluck coca leaves like tea. When they become teenagers they get juiced up on *chica* and *buzuko* and dance in a fetid mixture of coca leaves and kerosene." He paused for thought before continuing. "But first you need a formal education and I need some information."

Masure looked at him curiously.

"Tomorrow night we're going to meet a couple of local gals for drinks," he explained.

Masure looked at him completely perplexed.

Evans explained. "I arranged it from Bogotá with a call to the office in San Diego."

"Oh."

"Have you ever heard of Trinidad?" Evans asked, studying Masure's face for reaction.

"Yes, sir. I have. It's a Snowcap base up in the Amazon."

He had heard tall tales from SEALs who had operated out of the Snowcap base and he envisioned it as some sort of military installation surrounded by barbed wire fences and guard dogs. Actually, agents lived in the Ganadero Hotel and used the local airport for air operations

"Not exactly. Trinidad is a town in a province called the *Beni*. It's a land of cows and coca. The *Beni* raises cattle and cows are perfect cover for cocaine smugglers. The Colombians have access to the precursor chemicals necessary to refine paste into cocaine hydrochloride. So the big cartels process coca leaves in the *Beni*, refine it into powder up north in Colombia, and sell it at huge profits in the U.S. and Europe. Trinidad is one of the most remote places on Earth. The only way to get there is by air or boat. In a few days we're going to visit an old friend who owns a cattle ranch in the *Beni*. He's one of the few honest men in this country."

"Why are we going up there?" Masure asked.

"I've got some men poking around in the edge of the jungle."

"Keith and Swan?"

"No. Swan and Savarese. Keith is in Trinidad. Decker is right here in La Paz. He would have met us at the airport but I don't want to blow his cover. Tomorrow we'll service his dead drops."

"Jeeze, Boss! You damn near got a platoon down here," Masure exclaimed.

"Better than that," Evans replied. "I got the best men the U.S. Military ever mustered out of the service. Have you ever heard of Operation Blast Furnace?"

"No, sir. Doesn't ring a bell," Masure answered, locked onto Evans's every word.

"On the fourteenth of July, nineteen eighty-six, residents of Santa Cruz awoke to the sound of a C-five and several C-One-Thirties rumbling down their sleepy little jungle runway. Nearly two hundred Special Forces soldiers and a bunch of DEA agents scrambled off those birds."

"A US Op.?" Masure asked, surprised by the revelation.

"Combined. They rush about the runway like pissed off fire ants spoiling for a fight. Santa Cruz is strategically located at the base of the Andes near the coca fields of the *Chaparé* region and paste processing labs of the *Beni*. And it just happens to be on the old rail line that links Bolivia with Sao Paulo and Rio de Janeiro on the Atlantic Coast. That's why it's home to biggest drug traffickers in Bolivia."

"We invaded this country and arrested people?" Masure asked, incredulously.

"Yeap. It made a blip on the international news, but not much. Operation Blast Furnace was designed to strike a mortal blow at Bolivia's drug traffickers. But you know the deal. Conceived by DEA bureaucrats. Planned by Pentagon bureaucrats. Executed by an army dominated SPECOPS community."

"Let me guess. It amounted to swatting mosquitoes with a sledgehammer and the skeeters weren't at home?"

"You broke the code," Evans said. "You, my friend, are a very small part of the Andean Strategy. Blast Furnace was a combined op executed by Special Forces in concert with DEA and the Bolivian Police. The last link blew the cover."

"The dopers were tipped off, huh?"

"Traffickers own this country, partner," Evans continued.

"So what happened?"

"Snowcap, partner. Snowcap. They invaded like a pack of hungry wolves

114

ready to devour a gut shot mule deer. They off loaded a few helos, built them up, and flew off into the *Beni*. At Trinidad, which is about two hundred and fifty miles north of Santa Cruz, they established an FOB so they could strike the processing labs ID-ed from satellite imagery. But guess what?"

"The traffickers weren't home and the labs were empty," Masure answered.

"Too bad our politicians don't have your common sense," Evans smiled. "On the surface, Operations Blast Furnace was a raving success. The helos swooped down on the coca labs like eagles on snakes. The price of coca leaf dropped to an all time low. But arrests and seizures were dog crap. What the DEA got was what the traffickers wanted to them to get, a few *zepes*."

"*Zepes*? As in Ants?"

"You got it. The narcos call the small fry, ants or dog washers."

"I must have been overseas. I don't remember this shit," Masure exclaimed.

"Operation Dope, as critics called it, was a complete failure. But it played well in Washington. While U.S. troops were ferrying Bolivian police around the jungle, the suits in D.C. were arguing about what had gone wrong. The first lesson was crystal clear. If interdiction was ever going to work, it had to be all American. Operation Blast Furnace gave birth to Operation Snowcap."

"The pieces are starting to come together," Masure whispered, shaking his head in the affirmative. "Now I understand."

"No public announcement was ever made, and no one knows the amount of money Uncle Sam threw at the Andean Strategy but literally hundreds of men were sent to Colombia, Peru, and Bolivia. Billions of dollars were poured into the effort, perhaps trillions. You my friend, are a very small part of the Andean Strategy."

Evans spared Masure the statistics. The initial goal of Operation Snowcap was to reduce the amount of cocaine entering the U.S. by one half over a three-year period. It was sold to Congress as the answer to America's drug problem. Like body count in Vietnam, the measurements of success were tangible; the number of kilos of cocaine confiscated, the number of airstrips blown up, the number of acres of coca bushes destroyed, the price of coca leaf, etcetera, and etcetera. It mattered naught that holes in the airstrips could be patched in hours or that the capability to produce a kilo of cocaine far exceeded the capability of seizing the product.

Several sensational drug busts made international headlines and were used as proof that America was winning the war on drugs. But behind the headlines was reality. Snowcap fell far short of slashing the supply of cocaine on America's streets. On the street, the supply increased. Three years after Operations Blast Furnace, the goal of Snowcap was revised; reduce the amount of cocaine entering the U.S. by one half over a ten-year period. But despite all efforts the metric tonnage of cocaine hydrochloride increased every year following Blast Furnace, driving down the price of a kilo of cocaine to new lows. By the time Evans conducted his study of the Andean Strategy, Colombian drug lords had amassed a fortune and their biggest problem was laundering huge quantities of used greenbacks. They had created the largest criminal enterprise on Earth, created a cash crop where one hadn't existed, and succeeded in making the Andean culture dependent upon them for survival. Moreover, they had succeeded in creating an insatiable demand in user countries that was self-generating.

"We'll be staying several miles south of Trinidad, way up the *Rio Mamoré* near the jungle. But before we go up there, I have some business with an old friend down near Cochabamba. He's one of the few honest Leopards in Bolivia."

Bolivia's anti-narcotics police, officially known as UMOPAR for *Unidad Mobil de Partullaje Rural*, are nicknamed Leopards because of their spotted fatigues. Evans assumed Masure was aware of the term. He wasn't, but he didn't want to appear ignorant so he asked a related question.

"Cochabamba is down where the Andes meets the jungle?" he asked, pretending to know more about the terrain than he did.

"Close, partner, but no cigar. Cochabamba is still high country, but not this high. On the map Bolivia looks small. But it's about the size of France, Germany, and Italy combined. In the west there are two huge mountain ranges with a high plateau in the middle called the Altiplano. That's where we are, and that's where most of the people live. About eighty percent of Bolivians live up here in the western two-fifths of the country. The east and the northeast are jungle. Cochabamba is down on the eastern slope of the Cordillera Oriental. Below that lies the Amazon Basin."

"When I think of the Amazon, I think of Brazil," Masure said.

"Most people do and most of the Amazon Basin is Brazilian. But Bolivia, Peru, Ecuador, Colombia, and Venezuela claim part of the Basin. Not many people live down there though. The insects are pesky, tropical diseases are rampant, and the soil is so rain-washed it's not very good for growing traditional crops."

"And it's beyond government control," Masure volunteered.

"You bet it is. Coca grows all over the Andes, but it grows best on the rain soaked eastern slopes that feed the Amazon. And that's where we're going."

Masure smiled. "I like it wild."

"This kind of wild can kill you. What I want you to see is the culture of coca and that begins right out there on the steps of the Sopocachi. Once you understand it, you'll see the futility of Trinidad, the nonsense of the *Bloque de Busqueda,* and for that matter, the ineffectiveness of our anti-drug policies. Now enough of the lesson, I'm going to turn in for the night."

"Me too. *Hasta mañana*," Masure replied.

He watched Evans leave the bar then took a good look at the golden mask beside the table before retiring. It dawned on him that the Inca were chewing coca leaves long before the Spanish Conquistadors had invaded the land.

Chapter 14

The Caribbean coast of Colombia stretches northeast from Panama on the Gulf of Darien to Venezuela at the Peninsula of Guajira, a distance of approximately twelve hundred miles of ragged bays dappled with quaint little fishing villages and cities reminiscent of the Spanish Main. Pirates preyed on unwary yachtsmen. Smugglers bootlegged undaunted by the laws of the land. Every night boat loads of duty free electronic goods, cigarettes, and precursor chemicals made the run from Panama to the interior. Tons of marijuana and cocaine made the return trip northward by sea, air, and land to the soft borders of Mexico, the United States, and Canada. Smuggling was a way of life, as deeply ingrained in the culture as the Spanish Language. Two cities guarded the Colombian coast with inadequate coastal patrols; Barranquilla, home port to the Ballesteros's ships, the *Don Blás* and the *Don Blasón*, and Cartagena, playground of the rich and famous.

Cartagena de Indias was once the homeport of the Spanish Navy in the Western Hemisphere. Lieutenant Duran savored the seventeenth century walls and Iberian style houses that lined the narrow winding streets originally designed to repel pirates. He slowly strolled through old town, carefully watching for a tail. Between Master Chief Masure and Maria Christina he was suspicious of anyone headed in his direction. Masure saw a trafficker behind every bush and Maria Christina was worried that her father would find out about their relationship before she had the chance to talk to him.

Duran had rented a cheap hotel room in old town but it had gone unused most of the time. He spent his nights in Maria Christina's penthouse and his days, when not with Maria, exploring the haunts of pirates and buccaneers. He picked up his pace when he reached *Avenida Santander*, the main road that paralleled the sea and jogged down the beach to *Boca Grande* where the rich and famous lived. At a small cabana on the beach he stopped and ordered a soft drink. From his seat he could see Maria's penthouse on the twelfth floor. It was on the beachside of the building with a million-dollar view of the pounding Caribbean surf. The signal was not flying so he watched the breakers and sipped his drink, mentally planning his training schedule for the *Bloque de Busqueda*.

His mission was to teach the BBs to scale the side of an underway ship at night with live ammunition in their weapons. The SEALs called it shipboarding. The Colombians called it anti-piracy tactics. Duran mused over pistol and rifle range exercises that would support his ultimate objective and then mentally visualized dry-run assaults on mock targets and moored ships. But he couldn't see the BB's boarding an underway ship at night. It was just beyond their capability.

Training them to play professional baseball would be easier and less expensive, he thought.

Jack looked up at the penthouse just as Maria came out onto the balcony. She looked down at the beach without seeing him and tied her beach towel to the rail to dry. It was their signal that it was okay to come up. Jack gulped down the rest of his soda and jogged across the busy avenue with the heat of youth in his loins. The more Maria learned about sex the more voracious and insatiable she became. He felt a shudder of desire as he entered the lobby of her building. No woman had ever affected him like Maria Christina and he intended to marry her no matter what the consequences.

Acting like a local returning from the beach, he crossed the main lobby and took the stairs to the second floor. When no one was looking he slipped into the service elevator at the end of the hallway and punched the number for the fourteenth floor. When the door closed he stared at his reflection in the stainless steel surface. He didn't like the image that greeted him. He was tired of clandestine rendezvous with the woman he loved. Waiting for the slow moving elevator to reach the top of the building, he anguished over his situation.

This is no way to begin a lasting relationship, he said to himself. *I would kill any man who courted my daughter like this. Damn! Why doesn't she just invite me to her house and get it over with. Perhaps,* he thought, *she's afraid her old man will spurn me because I'm not Colombian. But hell, if an American is not good enough for her, who is?*

Jack was pondering the prospects of marrying into a rich aristocratic Colombian family when the door opened. He checked the hallway to make sure no one was watching and slipped up the stairs. A blast of wind hit him in the face as he walked out on the roof of the fourteen-story building. A warm wind was blowing briskly off the sea. In the distance he saw a large cruise ship ablaze with lights. It was the Caribbean Queen with a load of U.S. tourists anxious to visit the next port of call up the coast in Venezuela.

Jack quickly glanced around the rooftop to be sure he was alone and made his way to the edge of the building above Maria's balcony. He took a light rope out of his daypack, looped it over a heavy pipe protruding from the roof, and let both ends dangle down to Maria's balcony. Holding both bites of rope tightly together, he tested the pipe as he had done on a half dozen occasions. Satisfied, he sat down on the edge of the building and eased himself over the side, carefully grasping both bites of the rope together to lower himself hand over hand. With the rope only looped around the pipe, once on the balcony he could pull on one side and retrieve it. He was halfway down to Maria's balcony when a *sicario,* nicknamed the

Punisher, ran from his hiding place at the back of the building. Straight razor in hand, he went directly to the rope and cut through it in a single stroke. With a smile on his face he watched it sizzle over the side of the building, pulled by the weight of a man he was paid to kill. The Punisher crossed himself and ran away with the fear of God in his heart.

Maria screamed as Jack caught himself on the railing of her balcony. With his body dangling precariously over the side of the building, he held on with iron claws forged by fear. The adrenaline coursing through his veins gave him super human strength. In one fluid motion he pulled himself up and over the railing and collapsed on the deck. With eyes enlarged by fright he gasped for breath.

"*Damn that was close!*"

"*Jack! Carido! What happened? What happened?*" she cried, startled by the closeness of death.   "I don't know. The rope just gave way," he gasped. He breathed out with a gush of relief. "Whew. We've got to stop meeting like this."

When he regained his composure he kissed her lightly on the lips and struggled to his feet. With Maria fawning all over him like a mother over a hurt child, he peered over the balcony.

"Jeez, it's a long way down."

A section of rope was draped over the railing, dangling down the side of the building. He pulled on it until he came to the end. What he saw caused a lump in his throat.

"*Maria! It's cut!*" he blurted, holding it up to the light coming from apartment. "A clean cut." The clean cut of a sharp knife was obvious even to Maria who was still a bundle of jagged nerves.

"Jack. Who would?" she stopped in mid sentence.

"Let's get the hell out of here. I'm not sticking around to find out."

"Okay. I'll send Enrique for something to eat so we can take the stairs."

Maria went into the hallway and rattled off orders in rapid-fire Spanish. When the guard cleared the hallway, they sneaked down the stairs to the lobby and ran across Avenida Santander to the boardwalk. With Jack nervously watching behind them, they half-walked, half-ran down the beach toward old town. A couple of miles down the boardwalk Jack hailed a cab.

"*Crespo. Pronto!*" he ordered, as they climbed inside. The cabby sped off toward the airport driving with abandon.

"Jack, there's something I have to tell you," Maria whispered, as the cab sped down Avenida Santander.

"What, Baby?"

"My family is, well, you know, my family is very wealthy."

"Yes," he replied, just as the cab screeched to a stop at an intersection. He anxiously checked the corner and relaxed when the driver pulled away in a hurry. "Rich or poor, I don't care," he said sincerely, holding her face in his hands. "I love you, Maria. As long as you are with me, I am okay with what the future brings."

He kissed her lightly on the lips while watching out the back window with one eye. She squeezed him tightly and returned the kiss with frantic passion as if it was their last kiss. When the embrace ended she tried to tell him about her father's cartel. She knew her father's business had a shady side. So did her mother but it wasn't something discussed around the family dinner table. To survive, most Medellin businessmen had to play the game.

"Jack, my father has a lot of business interests," she whispered. "Cattle, coffee, flowers, real estate. Some of the men who work for him are very dangerous people. It is possible that they traffic in illegal goods."

"What are you trying to tell me, Maria?"

"There are men who work for my father, that," she stammered, "that would harm you if they knew about us."

"Traffic in what kinds of illegal goods, Maria?" he asked.

"All kinds of things. Everyone in Medellin does it. No one really takes the government seriously, Jack. They think the *Bogotañeos* have exploited the *paisas.* They believe they have to fight oppression by smuggling goods in from Panama. Jack, you have to understand. They have been doing it for hundreds of years. *Se es la vida.* Many, many people illegally import radios, TVs, stolen cars, and liquor. It is a way of life. Drugs have been found on my father's ships," she said abruptly.

She was trying to tell him about the Ballesteros Combine but she couldn't. Combine was the Medellin word for cartel. It was a word meant for the biggest and most powerful enterprises. Her father was simply the chairman of the board and if he made bad decisions, he would be removed, perhaps with a knife or a gun. *Acero o plomo* -- Steel or lead, in South America meant to kill with a knife or a bullet.

"Drugs?" Duran asked, with eyes wide open.

"Jack, it is very difficult for my father to keep his workers from using his ships and airplanes for drug smuggling. He has asked your government for help in stopping criminals from using his businesses, but the people of Medellin are not so sympathetic with such ideas. Many businessmen believe they have a right to sell whatever they want to sell. Your country is the champion of the free market. They believe it is hypocritical for the United States to put restrictions on products that your people want to buy."

"Maria, drugs kill people. They aren't products like coffee or flowers," Duran argued.

"They don't see it that way, Jack. They think the U.S. has grown rich at the expense of Colombia. My involvement with you will be seen as a threat. The *Bloque* are their enemies, Jack, because they try to stop what they believe is free commerce. And since you train them you are the enemy too. They will kill you if they find out about us."

She didn't want to lie to him but she couldn't tell him her father, like many businessmen in Medellin, was a narcotics trafficker.

"And I am a gringo. Right?"

"Well. Yes. Americans are seen as hypocrites who have raped all of South America of its riches. If these men find out about you they will kill you, *mi amor*."

"*Will Maria?* Someone just tried to kill me. You saw the rope. It was cut. *Clean!*"

"Oh Jack. I'm so afraid. I'm so afraid for you. Maybe it was someone who works for my father."

"Then we have to tell your father," Duran asserted.

"*No!*"

"If we are going to have any kind of life together it has to include our parents, yours and mine. We have to talk to them."

"No, Jack. I can't. Not now," she cried.

"Why?"

"I just can't take you to Medellin and say, *Popi*, this is Jack and we are going to get married. I just can't right now. I have to prepare him."

"Why?"

"Because he wouldn't understand, Jack. Oh, honey, I love you so much if anything ever happened to you I could never forgive myself. Let's run away. Let's go to Miami or New York and get married. I have money. Let's don't tell anyone," she pleaded, kissing his face. "We don't need anyone's approval."

Maria's heart fluttered as she thought of *Gato's* cold warning and his all-knowing eyes. She wanted to tell Jack everything but she was ashamed of the family business, ashamed of the part her father kept secret from her and her mother. She wanted to tell him her father made several million dollars every day selling cocaine to willing buyers in the United States, but she couldn't. She was going to tell him, but not in the backseat of a taxi speeding toward the airport. She knew he wouldn't understand. Like her father, he wouldn't understand the world in which she lived.

"I can't just run off, Maria. I am in the U.S. Military, assigned to train a Colombian unit. I can't just run away. My government would find me and put me in jail."

Duran stared into her eyes trying to read between the lines. He couldn't. Love blinds. He stroked her cheek and kissed her softly in a tender moment. When the kiss ended he said, "It doesn't matter. Nothing matters as long as I am with you. Nothing matters as long as you love me. Let's make a plan, a long-term plan. Next week I'll begin the second phase of my mission. When it's over, I'll be going back to Virginia. Come with me. I'll get out of the Navy when my obligation is up and we can start a new life."

"Oh, Jack. I love you so much, I would go anywhere with you," she said, holding him tightly. "If anything happened to you I would die too."

"Nothing is going to happen to me Maria. I'm bullet-proof," he smiled with bravado, not really feeling the confidence his handsome square-jawed face showed to her.

Jack suspected that the Ballesteros's great wealth came from something more than cattle and coffee. He had seen it in Maria's eyes. There was a guilty look in her eye when she deceived him, a glint of shame when she deflected drug smuggling from her father onto his employees. She couldn't walk him through the front door and introduce him to her family because he was the enemy. Jack Duran knew he was a good catch for any woman. He was handsome, educated, well off, and an officer in the United States Navy. Most South American women would have been proud to show him off to their families, rich or poor. He decided to snoop around the Ballesteros holdings in Barranquilla and Cartagena.

Jack paid the taxi driver at the airport and waited until he pulled away before hailing another cab.

"*Plaza de la Independencia, por favor. Con prisa.*"

"*Sí, señor. Por supuesto*," replied the cabby with a grin. Driving *con prisa*, with haste, was the national sport of Colombia.

Once back on the narrow winding streets of old town Jack felt more at ease. He paid the cab driver and led Maria on a meandering tour of the back streets. A block short of his hotel he pulled her into a dark recess in the alleyway between two buildings and watched the street for a few minutes to ensure no one had followed them.

"Maria, I love you. I want you to know that no matter what happens, I will always love you," he whispered.

"Oh, Jack. I love you too, more than life itself, *mi amor*," she replied, pulling him close.

In the dark of the alleyway she kissed him with fiery passion. For several minutes they embraced like young lovers with no tomorrow. When Jack was sure no one had followed them, he led her to his hotel room. With renewed commitment and the hunger of young desire they lay in each other's arms all night making love in fits of wild passion.

Chapter 15

Masure took a plug of tobacco out of his shirt pocket. "Chew?" he asked.

Evans declined with a frown. Masure shrugged and bit off a piece. He tucked it in his cheek like the old Indian he had done with his coca leave in front of the hotel. Evans eyed him with disgust.

"Hell, they'll just think I'm chewing coca, Boss," he grinned. "Between the *maté*, the tobacco, and this horse-piss they call beer, I'll whip the shit out of this headache."

"Or kill yourself. Nicotine is an alkaloid like cocaine, you know. Both are psychoactive plant extracts," he explained.

"Psycho-what?" Masure blurted, playing dumb.

"Psychoactive. In scientific terms, a substance which fucks with your brain chemicals," Evans growled in a testy mood.

"I am so glad you explained it in terms I can relate to."

Evans had a headache too and it made him grumpy. So Masure left him alone with his thoughts as they nursed a couple of beers. He listened to the guitar player and scoped out the women in Sinchi's. They had both slept late then taken a light meal in the hotel before hitting the streets of La Paz. Evans had led him on a circuitous route about the city as he check dead drops and talked to friends. At the end of a long day of hiking up and down the cobbled streets they ended up back at the Sopocachi, both with agonizing headaches from the altitude. After a power nap they rendezvoused at the bar to wait for their dates.

Masure caught Evans's eye and turned to see two women across the smoky room. They had Hispanic features, long Indian-black hair, full lips, and olive skin. When Evans stood up, Masure followed suit.

"Rita," Evans said, while waving at her.

When the older of the two women spotted the commander, her face brightened like a schoolgirl. She was thirty-ish and pretty. Slim and healthy, by dress and manner she looked like she belonged to the University faculty. When she reached the table Evans extended his hand. She grasped it and pulled him close. With a warm embrace she kissed him on both cheeks and then lightly on the lips. Then she verbally berated him.

"Derek Evans, I got so excited when I found out you were coming to La Paz I almost forgot I'm still angry with you," she said, with mock temper.

"*Por que, mi amor*," Evans feigned.

"You promised me dinner before you left La Paz," she pouted. "And you didn't call me to tell me you were leaving."

"Ummmm. Rita, my most profound apologies. *Se me ovido.* I was babysitting a group of eggheads," Evans pleaded in self-defense, "and I just ran out of time."

"The next time I see Carol, I'm going to tell her you think she's an egghead."

Evans eyes locked onto Contreras like radar. He wanted to ask her if she had seen Carol lately. But he resisted the temptation.

"Rita. I am sorry. I was just doing my job."

"You were too busy lusting after Carol to remember your promise to me," she sassed, with a little Spanish schoolgirl pout.

Evans ignored the comment. "Pat," he said, deflecting the verbal assault, "it is my pleasure to introduce you to Rita Contreras, Professor of Botany at the University of San Andres."

After a warm handshake, Rita introduced her best friend, Sonia Diaz who took the seat adjacent to Masure.

Through greetings and polite talk Masure learned that Professor Contreras had been part of several large expeditions sent into the *Chaparé* region to study plants for Syntec Pharmaceuticals. From the tone of the conversation he could tell that Rita had a thing for Evans and he suspected she had brought along her colleague to clear the decks when the time was right.

After a decent interval of polite conversation Evans carefully steered the conversation to the issues of Cocaine Inc. by explaining Masure's shock at drinking *maté* for the first time and seeing the old Indian with his cud. Contreras picked up on the topic without reservation. She understood the coca culture from an academic point of view and enjoyed the banter of conversation that went with explaining it to the uninitiated. Masure was her fifth SOC Inc. pupil.

"*Señor Masure*, you have to understand the Andean culture," she explained. "Almost every Indian in the Andes chews about an ounce of coca a day. It's an integral part of the lives of the Quechua and the Aymara."

"Are they the descendants of the Incas?" Masure asked.

"Yes. They have worked the mines since the days of the conquistadors. Mining in Bolivia is a horrible life. Some Indians farm potatoes and maize, and scratch out a living herding sheep and llamas on the Altiplano, but when famine strikes or the mines slow down they stream into La Paz and other cities looking for work. There they are easy prey for *traficantes*. In desperation many go down to the jungles to raise coca."

"For chewers or for traffickers?" Masure asked.

"For their children," Evans interjected forcefully. "For survival."

Contreras smiled. "Chewing coca is called *acullicu* and it is a very powerful cultural symbol viewed more or less as an adult social skill in much the same way you North Americans consider drinking alcohol or smoking cigarettes."

Contreras had a professorial manner of speaking. She locked her eyes onto Evans with passion. As she lectured Masure she undressed the Commander with her gaze.

"In rural areas of the Andes virtually every worker carries a small pouch call a *k'intus* in which they keep their coca leaves. Without social stigma they chew a few leaves after every meal. In the mines they pause for coca breaks just as you do for cigarette breaks."

"What does it taste like," Masure asked, being polite. He didn't really want to know.

"It tastes like spinach," interjected Sonia Diaz, Contreras's companion. "I'll get you some if you like."

She had been carefully watching Masure since her arrival, inching her way closer as the evening progressed.

"*No!* No thanks," Masure replied, shaking his head.

He had spit out his plug of tobacco when he saw that the women were headed his way. Suddenly he was fearfully there was a large chunk of tobacco stuck between his front teeth. With each beer, Sonia Diaz was looking better, despite the gap between her front teeth. Masure's philosophy toward women was simple. Any port in a storm and Sonia Diaz was the closest port. He was warming up to her until she asked if he knew Fred Swan. He smiled politely, wondering if Fred had broken ground in the Sopocachi. He had.

"It's not the taste that drives the chewers. It's the mild narcotic effect somewhat like nicotine. They believe it gives them strength and that it wards off the cold and the effects of high altitude," Contreras continued.

"It does," Sonia insisted.

"They masticate the leaves into a wad, almost ritualistically, and hold it in their cheek, like tobacco chewers," Contreras explained looking straight at Masure.

Damn, there must be something stuck between my teeth, he thought. He took a big swallow of beer and surreptitiously swished it between his front teeth hoping to remove the offender.

"When the cud is just the right consistency, they add a little vegetable ash, graystone or crushed sea shell to release the alkaloids which are absorbed into the bloodstream through the mucous membranes of the mouth."

Masure grimaced and frowned.

"Stick, the dose of narcotic from *acullicu* is minuscule," Evans added. "The difference between chewing leaves and snorting cocaine is like the difference between sipping apple cider and guzzling down a water glass of one hundred proof rum."

"Why do they call you Stick, *Señor Masure?*" Sonia asked.

Evans smiled. "Oh, ah, no real reason," Masure quickly replied.

Contreras looked from Masure to Evans before continuing her lecture. "Like caffeine, nicotine, and opium, *Señor Stick,* cocaine is an alkaloid. It is a psychoactive compound produced by the plant to protect itself from animals and insects. Most cocaine comes from one of two varieties; erythroxylon coca and erythroxylon novogranatense coca."

"Professor, you've lost me," Masure frowned.

"Me too," Evans smiled.

"Both varieties grow on the eastern slopes of the Andes," Contreras explained. "Our Bolivian plant has glossy, greenish brown leaves, somewhat elliptical in shape. That is the species in your *maté.* The Indians believe it is the best chewing coca."

"The best plants come from an area just north of La Paz called the Yungas," Sonia Diaz interjected. "It's beautiful there."

"That's where the world's legal crop of coca is produced," Evans added.

"The Indians claim that Yungas leaves are sweeter and tenderer. If you want, I can get you some tonight," Diaz volunteered.

"No. Well, maybe just a little bit so I can taste it."

He could tell she was driving a wedge down the center of the table. The reason was obvious every time Contreras looked at Evans. He kept asking himself if Sonia was territory Popeye had traveled. He didn't want to walk in Popeye's moccasins even if she was the only port in the storm.

"Some of the Yungas crop goes to the chewers of the Andes and some is exported to the United States to the Stephan Chemical Company of Maywood, New Jersey. They extract the cocaine and distribute it as a pharmaceutical," Contreras lectured.

"Stick? Do you know what happens to the leafy residue that's left over?" Evans asked.

"Nope. Haven't got a clue," Masure said, feeling like he was under attack from two professors of dope-ology.

"They send it to Atlanta, Georgia where it's used in Coca Cola's secret recipe, *Formula Seven-X.*"

"*Ah!*" Masure exclaimed, enlightened by the revelation. "Coca Cola will never taste the same again."

They all laughed at his facial expression.

"Most of the Yungas crop though," Contreras continued, "is bought by traffickers. The poor Indians are left with the dregs, the Peruvian plant. It also grows in Bolivia and Colombia. It has smooth pale green leaves that are oval in shape. The Indians don't like the flavor but that's about all they can afford."

"Will there be a taste test after this lecture?" Masure asked with warm smile.

"Life is a big test, *Señor Stick*. It pays to know one's environment," Contreras countered, with a stern expression like she was speaking to a sassy student.

"I agree. What I don't understand is why the government doesn't just destroy the coca crops and be done with the problem?" Masure commented.

"First," Evans said, holding up one finger, "It's a legal part of their culture and has been so for thousands of years. Second," he said as another finger appeared, "coca bushes are a part of the natural ecosystem. You'd have to destroy the entire highland rain forest to kill them all, maybe even the Amazon. Third," he said, shaking three fingers, "the coca crop is the only thing between many of the Indians and starvation. The traffickers have turned the crap into a damn cash crop."

"Gosh. I'm sorry I asked, grumpy," Masure complained.

"In order to combat something that's bad for the U.S. we don't have the right to stomp on an entire culture. Just for a minute, imagine that you are a dirt-poor Indian living in abject poverty. But there is a crop you can plant that yields four or five harvests a year. Your ancestors have been growing it for a thousand years and it flourishes in acidic rain-washed soils that wither all your other crops. And like tea leaves, all you have to do is send your kids out to pluck off a few leaves four or five times a year and put them in a sack. You don't even have to take it to market. Someone will come to your little hooch in the jungle and pick it up, and give you money to buy food and clothes. Imagine that. Imagine you're that impoverished, illiterate, superstitious Indian out on the steps of this hotel. There is no stigma against chewing coca and there is no stigma against growing it. There never has been. And you don't care who buys your leaves. All you care about is eating, surviving. Killing the likes of Pablo Escobar won't stop this freight train either. You see, demand drives Cocaine Inc."

Rita Contreras's eyes were alight. She liked and respected Evans, even if he was a macho sexist male chauvinist *puerco*. He understood the magnitude of the problem. That was much more than most gringos she knew.

"I understand," Masure said.

"No you don't," Evans snapped. "Not yet. Not till you've fallen in a coca pit filled with a mash of fetid leaves. Not till you've seen the eyes of a starving kid who depends on the narcos for survival."

For several seconds everyone was silent as Masure looked from person to person. Rita changed the conversation.

"So, Derek, am I the reason for this visit or are you on some great new adventure?" she asked.

"Rita, a trip to Bolivia wouldn't be complete without seeing you," Evans deflected. "How could I ever explain the culture of coca without you?"

"Did Popeye and Pegleg grasp the problem?" Contreras asked.

Masure's eyes lit up as he thought of Ray Keith arguing his case for killing all dopers. He chuckled out loud at the thought. Contreras cut him a glance knowing what was on his mind. Ray Keith would never be convinced that the answer to America's dope problem couldn't be found in the barrel of a gun.

"Well, not exactly. You did manage to move Keith's position just slightly to the left of Attila the Hun," he replied, with a sly smile.

Masure's suspicion that Contreras had given the lecture to every member of SOC Inc. was confirmed.

A desultory conversation ensued for half an hour ranging from Incas to Arabs. After the women had absorbed a few strong drinks Evans began to maneuver the conversation. As deftly as he had brought up the subject of Cocaine Inc. he carefully steered the discourse toward the *Chaparé* and Syntec Pharmaceuticals. Eventually he asked the question that was burning in his mind.

"Rita, have you seen any of the scientist from Syntec lately?" His eyes focused on her pupils like a laser.

She sucked air across her teeth. "They are not due for several months," she answered, like a politician not wanting to be caught in a barefaced lie.

Her eyes blinked and her pupils constricted slightly as she look to her right and instantly back to Evans's unblinking gaze. Contreras was uncomfortable and it was obvious she didn't like deceiving the Commander. He instantly knew a proper interrogation would require deep and gentle probing.

She's being evasive, thought Evans. *She doesn't want to lie to me. That means, Carol is in Bolivia. The question is where? I'll have Decker keep tabs on Rita while I beat the bushes in the Chaparé. Maybe if I can get her alone, she'll talk to me.*

Evans dropped the subject.

It was Sonia Diaz who finally broke up the evening after several more drinks. She insisted that she had a big day ahead and needed to go home. Acting the gentleman, Masure offered to walk her home. At Sonia's door he made polite conversation for a few minutes, and when he sensed that she didn't intend to invite him inside, he eased up on the charm just in case she was Popeye's Bolivian squeeze. He offered to call her when he returned to La Paz and high tailed it back to the hotel.

The night was clear and the moon was hovering over the eternal snows of Illimani as he hurried along the cobbled streets. The entire canyon, up to where it met the Altiplano, was ablaze with streetlights. And above, there were brilliant stars that sparkled in the clear mountain air. When he got back to the hotel the old

Indian was asleep near the steps, stretched out on a piece of cardboard and covered with a woolen blanket. Masure shivered. The conditions in which the old man lived would have killed most men his age.

Evans and Contreras were not in Sinchi's so he had another beer and listened to the guitarist for a few minutes before going to bed. At one in the morning he was awakened by the sound of a rhythmic thumping on his bedroom wall. Then he heard the soft sound of Rita Contreras cooing in pleasure. He pulled the pillow tightly over his head and went back to sleep. Evans was taking the art of interrogation to new depths.

Chapter 16

In Colombia, paid gunmen are called *sicarios*. They take their nickname from fantasy figures like the Terminator, Rambo, Dirty Harry, and the Punisher. Most are young men in their late teens and early twenties with no saleable skills other than killing. They live on the edge in a brutal world of violence where life expectancy is low. *Sicarios* charge as little as fifty-dollars to kill a man and their services are always in high demand. Unscrupulous businessmen use them to kill off competition. Jilted lovers use them to eliminate rivals. Politicians use them to assassinate opponents. Even honest cattle ranchers recruit them to combat guerrillas and to evict squatters. The best paying employers by far are drug traffickers.

There was no moon and few stars out as Risitos set pickets of *sicarios* around the airstrip. The Punisher took station near Ramón Savajé's Mercedes and played with his MAC-10 like a kid with a new Christmas toy. He was just one of fifty gun hands hired to protect the Savajé's shipment but he thought of himself as a rising star within the organization. He was an accomplished killer who specialized in shooting from the back of a moving motorcycle but he wasn't above using a straight razor to cut a rope and let a man fall to his death.

Risitos assumed his position at the van parked at the end of the runway and smoked a cigarette laced with cocaine. He waited until the exact second before giving the signal to illuminate the airfield. On cue, *sicarios* stationed around the field shined their flashlights south, creating a lighted runway for fifteen seconds. They repeated the signal at two minutes intervals. When they heard the plane's engines, they left the lights on until the aircraft touched down.

The twin-engine turbo prop hurled down the makeshift airfield and taxied back to the headlights of the waiting van as fast as the pilot could press the airplane. Time was his enemy. The anxious pilot was in a hurry to get back in the air. He had filed a flight plan that over flew the *finca*, so he was on course, and in the mountains of Colombia it is impossible to track an aircraft one hundred percent of the time. What worried him was time. If he stayed on the ground too long he would fall behind schedule and draw attention to his aircraft.

As soon as the engines stopped a group of *sicarios*, armed to the teeth, drove out in a small truck and began topping off the fuel tank. Others walked security beats around the airstrip and up and down the dirt road leading up to the *finca*. Risitos stood in the dark watching several men hurriedly load the aircraft. To ensure no one had pinched off a kilo or two during truck transit from the *llanos*, he had personally counted the bricks of cocaine as they were packed into the specially constructed barrels. When the barrels were loaded in the plane he signaled Ramón with his flashlight.

From the back of the big Mercedes Ramón coordinated the final arrangements to the deal. He always waited until the last minute to tell the pilots where to drop the load as well as the recovery crews where to pick up the merchandise. Several of his shipments had been busted at destination in the U.S. and he was suspicious of everyone except his brothers, *Lucho* and *Risitos*. Because of the busts, the Savajés had turned to the Mexican trampoline for deliveries to the United States. They bought *pasta basica* from Peruvians and Bolivians, processed it into cocaine hydrochloride in the jungles of the Colombian Amazon, and sold the finished product to Mexican Mafiosos.

The Mexicans had extensive knowledge of the soft border between Mexico and the United States. The backcountry bordering Texas, New Mexico, Arizona, and California was violated nightly by hundreds of illegal aliens seeking opportunity in *el Norte*. Drug traffickers simply broke their shipments down to individual loads and paid, or coerced, poor farmers into taking the biggest chance of their lives, carrying finished cocaine across the border into the United States. Sometimes they bribed U.S. Border Patrol agents and smuggled huge quantities into the U.S. in one shipment. But mostly they used what the Mexicans called *mulos,* mules to pack the product across the border. Ramón Savajé didn't know how the Russians operated but he knew enough to know they were running things in Eastern Europe and Asia. To service that supply chain he dropped most of his product at sea to waiting fishing trawlers. Russian thugs did the rest.

Ramón took a die out of his pocket and threw it in the floorboard of the car. It landed on the number five. He removed six folded squares of paper from his shirt pocket and selected the one with the number five on it. He rolled down the window and yelled, "Fabio."

Racy salsa music attracted the Punisher's attention when Ramón rolled down the window of the air-conditioned car so he was ready for action to serve the master.

"Sí, Señor Savajé," he said, rushing over to the car door.

"Take this to Risitos," he ordered. "*Immediatamente*."

Something in Ramón Savajé's eyes frightened the Punisher, something sinister, evil. His instincts told him to deliver the message and keep on running but there was no place to go. The Savajés could find him anywhere in Colombia. Besides he had killed several men for them so he considered himself to be one of the boys. He controlled his emotions.

"*Sí, Señor*," he answered.

133

As he jogged into the darkness Ramón dialed a number in the Medellin exchange.

"Hola."

"Lucho?"

"Sí, Ramón."

"Numero cinco,"

"Sí, Ramón. Numero cinco," repeated the voice on the other end of the line.

The Savajé brothers immediately terminated the connection. Number five was one of six preplanned locations along the coast of the Yucatan peninsula that they had coordinated with their Mexican associates. The slip of paper contained the precise GPS coordinates Ramón wanted the pilots to drop the cargo before landing to refuel in Cozumel for the last leg of their journey to the United States. When the plane landed the aircraft would be empty of cocaine. It would pick up passengers and a load of cash.

The water off the Yucatan coast was shallow and the barrels containing the cocaine were outfitted with a pinger system that allowed divers to easily locate and retrieve the merchandize. Ramón had chosen the drop zone at random by rolling a six-sided die. Once selected, he had called Lucho who passed the coordinates to the Mexicans by secure fax. The same modus operandi worked with Russian trawlers only the pilots dropped floating barrels for the fishermen to retrieve.

When the aircraft took off Risitos joined Ramón and together they watched their merchandize disappear into the night sky. The plane was only twenty minutes behind schedule.

"Esta bueno, mi hermano," Ramón mumbled.

Using his flashlight as a signaling device, Risitos dismissed most of his *sicarios.* He snorted two lines of cocaine with his brother before turning on the Punisher like a trained pit bull. Fabio Ruiz was standing under a small tree dreaming of the day when he could afford to do cocaine like his rich employer when Risitos called him over like a dog.

"Fabio!" he snapped at the young killer.

"Sí, Risitos," the Punisher answered with an air of importance.

In Medellin the slang for murder is called *scoring a goal*. Fabio Ruiz had killed twelve men in his young life and he wasn't afraid of anyone except drug lords. He feared them because they had the power to order a hit on anybody and the means to execute it anywhere in the world. He knew the Savajés had a long reach because he had done two contract killings for them in Miami, Florida.

"Get your ass over here! Ramón wants to talk to you," Risitos yelled from the front of the car.

"Sí, Risitos," the young man replied.

The Savajé brothers were standing in front of the Mercedes when Fabio walked up like a cocky little Banta rooster confident in its virility. He was expecting a new, more important assignment from his infamous narcoterrorist bosses.

"Don Savajé," he said, very respectfully with a mock salute. He strutted with a little juke like a cock trying to impress his hens.

Ramón leaned back against the hood of the car, his brain sizzling with cocaine, and studied Fabio's face, which was illuminated by the headlamps.

"Fabio, it has come to my attention that you work for the Ballesteros," he growled, like a mafia don.

Fabio's knees nearly buckled and he lost his breath. His dreams of cocaine by the pound, money, and beautiful women evaporated like mist in a hot summer sun. Before he could mouth a protest three *sicarios* stuck the barrels of their MAC-10s in his ribs and disarmed him.

"*No, Señor Savajé!*" he sniveled. "*No, Señor!* I never work for the foucking Ballesteros." He protested, with more bravado than he felt. "The Ballesteros are foucking *putas!* I only work for you, *Señor*," fear oozing from every pore.

The gunmen searched his person for weapons, removed a straight razor, and handed it to Risitos.   "He's clean, Risitos," one of the thugs said.

"*Bueno.*"

"But *Señor Savajé*,"

The *sicarios* behind Fabio Ruiz kicked him in the back of the legs and his knees buckled. He forced him to the ground with a hand on each shoulder. On his bended knees, eyes wide with fear, Fabio began pleading for his life like a man praying at an altar.

"But *Señor Don Savajé*, what have I done to displease you, *Señor*?" he pleaded.

He held his hand together like a priest and with the headlights of the car blinding him, he begged.

"Please, *Señor*. I have done nothing wrong. I have done nothing."

"Tie him to the tree," Risitos ordered.

The Punisher begged for explanation as his *sicario* associates lashed him to the tree trunk. They trussed him up with his hands behind his back and tied him so tightly it cut off circulation. As the Punisher peered into the darkness trying to figure out what he could have done to anger such a powerful man, Ramón answered his query.

"It has come to my attention the Ballesteros paid you to kill a man in Cartagena," Ramón said, out of the darkness. "A Yankee."

The lights of the car silhouetted Ramón's short stocky little body. To the Punisher Ramón was the reincarnation of Lucifer himself. He had seen the results of those who had crossed him and he was sweating fear. Risitos had cut out a man's tongue and thrown it in the yard of the local DEA for his children to find. Ramón was infamous for his ruthlessness. He had killed a man with a heated spike that he slowly pounded into the man's skull until it destroyed his brain. What was worse, he had murdered the man with his family listening to the torture on a cell phone. Ruiz's blood ran cold with sheer terror

"*Señor Don Savajé*," the boy cried. "It is true that I took a small contract to keel soam fouckem Yankee who is fouching the Ballesteros girl, but it wasn't from the fouckem Ballesteros. It was from one of her fouckem lover boys," Fabio explained.

"*No!* It was from that *jefe de putas, Gato Gaviria!*" Risitos snapped, projecting saliva on the boy's face.

"But *Señor Savajé*, I did not know, *Señor*. I only take the money to keel de fouckin' Yankee. I hate fouckem Yankees. You know that, *Señor*. I scored two goals for you in Miami. I didn't know the fouckem contract came from that *puta*, Gaviria," the youth begged.

"You disappoint me, Fabio. You must think I am stupid," Ramón said calmly. "First you lie to me. You know the rule. If you work for me, you don't work for anyone else. I pay you well, Fabio. You say you work only for me. Then you tell me you take a contract to keel a Yankee who is foucking *Maria Christina Ballesteros!*" he yelled. "And you expect me to believe you did not know the money came from *Gato la puta*. First, you say to me you only work for me. Then, you tell me you take a contract to keel soam fouckem Yankee. And for who? *For the fouckem Ballesteros girl!* What am I to believe Fabio? Huh? What am I to believe? I am disappointed in you. If you work for the Ballesteros to keel for the girl, maybe you work for them to spy on me? Maybe you are working for them now?"

"*No, Señor. No Señor*," Ruiz protested, trembling with fear. "On my mother's soul, I never work for the fouckem Ballesteros."

Risitos backhanded the youth, nearly knocking him unconscious.

"*Ramón is speaking. Do not interrupt*," he yelled, spitting saliva on Fabio's face.

"Maybe you have told them information about my shipments. Maybe you are the reason I have to use the foucking Mexican trampoline."

"*No, Señor Don Savajé. No Señor*. I never told nobody about your business and I will never take a contract without your permission, *Señor*," the Punisher begged.

"Ahhh, of that I am certain Fabio. Of that I am absolutely certain. Risitos," Ramón snapped. "Make an example of this fouckem idiot."

"*Por supuesto, hermano. Con mucho gusto.*"

Fabio began begging but he didn't have time to finish his plea. Like a cat, Risitos sprang to action. He planted his right knee into the youth's groin and stuck both of his thumbs in the boy's eyes. There was nothing the youth could do but scream as Risitos gouged them out in a brutal act of savagery. He let the boy scream for two minutes before he cut off his penis with a straight razor. I was the very razor the Punisher had used to kill four men and attempt to kill Jack Duran. Then, he forced the appendage down the boy's throat with the barrel of a pistol. Tied to the tree the Punisher died a thousand deaths. The faces of his victims didn't flash before his useless eyes. As he gurgled, choking on his own penis, all he could see was his mother's face begging God to have mercy on his condemned soul.

* * *

Roth's Tactical Analysis Team intercepted Ramón Savajé's cell phone and plotted its general location. The young officer seated at the bank of high-tech electronic equipment had no idea a major cocaine transaction was going down nor could he have envisaged the horror that was taking place. He simply recorded the conversation, picked up his telephone, and dialed a number in the Bogotá exchange. A smoky deep male voice answered the phone.

"*Digame*."

"The Savajés are up to something," the TAT duty officer reported. "Ramón just called the Medellin exchange and passed some sort of code to Lucho. All he said was '*number five,*' then hung up. A few minutes later Lucho sent a secure fax to Cozumel, Mexico."

"Doesn't mean anything to me," Roth replied.

"We tracked a turbo prop into the area where the call originated. Lost it behind the mountains. When it re-appeared it was about fifteen minutes behind the projected track. I'll send the coordinates, flight plan, and the tail number to SOUTHCOM."

"Good," Roth praised.

"I think the DEA should check this one out at destination," the duty officer suggested.

"Agreed. Alert them and keep me informed," Roth ordered.

"Yes, sir."

"Out here."

Roth hung up and immediately called Alysin Harris in Washington, D.C. to report the information. For the next three hours Harris worked the whole system to determine if there were any Russian trawlers near the aircraft's flight plan or transiting the Panama Canal. She wasn't really interested in the payment so much as the delivery of something more deadly to the Colombians.

There is no unified worldwide criminal conspiracy, nor is there a single unified international crime fighting effort with a James Bond ready to take on powerful shadowy underworld figures. Efforts to stop national and international crime are fragmented and as piecemeal as the acronyms that litter the morning newspaper, CIA, FBI, DEA, BATF, Customs, I&N, Interpol, MI6, ad nauseam. Trust is on the side of the law enforcement so information is sometimes shared. Fortunately, trust is the biggest obstacle to a transnational criminal front. In a deal between two mafia organizations everyone is armed to the teeth and expecting to be cheated or killed. Violence is the norm. Trust the exception.

The rebirth of the profit motive in the former Soviet Union and Eastern Europe, combined with weak governments in Asia, Africa, and South America create fertile ground for criminal enterprises. While on the one hand, extensive international travel and soft international borders produce unparalleled prosperity, as goods seek new markets and people sale their labor to the highest bidder, the combined effect creates enormous opportunities for criminal endeavors. Moreover, the development of the computer and communications technologies, electronic funds transfer and the worldwide connectivity of financial institutions, allow huge sums of money move in an instant. A billion dollars can evaporate in the time it takes a few electrons to circle the globe. Secure fax and cellular telephones make it all but impossible to trace criminal deals and money transfers. Sophisticated financiers with fancy degrees and homes in Paris and Luxembourg launder millions of dollars in seconds with impunity.

Ramón Savajé was two steps behind the technology curve. Unlike *Gato* Gaviria who purchased his electronic gizmos in Europe, he bought his eavesdropping devices from the Bogotá Spy Shop, every one of which had been provided to the shop by Tom Roth. One of his cover occupations was a salesman of advanced electronics. The Savajés could not have imagined the extent to which electronic eyes and ears were violating them, nor could they comprehend the electronic spies that patrolled the sky above. Before the turbo prop cleared Colombian airspace, a C-130 Hercules reconnaissance plane based out of the Panama Canal Zone converged on a parallel course across the Caribbean. Flying at thirty thousand feet, the Hercules was too high above the small plane for the pilots to see or hear. They proceeded on course toward Cozumel unaware they were being filmed from above. The crewmen in the Hercules could even see through the clouds with electronic equipment so powerful it turned night to day.

* * *

Two hundred miles south of Cozumel, the *Flash* was cruising on station waiting for action when the radio operator at Southern Command called, "Viper, Viper, this is Baseplate, Baseplate, over."

"Baseplate, this if Viper, roger over," Lieutenant Alex Gomez reported.

"Viper, come to course three-one-five, speed eight-zero knots."

"Roger, Baseplate. I copy, course three hundred and fifteen degrees, speed eighty knots," Gomez repeated.

"Roger Viper. Baseplate, out."

The *Flash* rose up out of the sea and cruised on her hydrofoils for two hours as the trafficker and the spy plane closed her course. Forty miles south east of Cozumel the dope runners opened the side door of the turbo prop and pushed out the barrels they had loaded at the finca.

"Baseplate, this is, Eagle Six-One. Tail Two-three just splashed cargo."

The radioman in the spy plane passed the exact time and coordinates of the drop to headquarters.

"Roger, Eagle Six-One. Maintain surveillance of Tail two-three. Break. Viper, Viper, this is Baseplate, Baseplate, over."

"Baseplate, this is Viper, roger over," Gomez answered.

The operations coordinator at Southern Command ordered Gomez to investigate the drop site.

The skipper of the *Flash* was Lieutenant Alex Gomez, a Cuban-American by heritage and a combat veteran of El Salvador and of several other low intensity conflicts. His years of experience serving with the SEALs had given him the instincts of a warrior and the skepticism of a scientist. He cruised at eighty knots until he was ten miles from his target. There he waited for the pick up boats to show. Two hours after taking station he spotted four cigarette boats cruising at high speed headed southeast out of Cozumel. They navigated directly to the drop zone and stopped dead in the water.

God, this is too easy, he thought. "I wish Boomer was here," he said out loud. "He'd love this op."

Gomez and Boomer Savarese had served together for years and he missed the burly warrior like a brother lost at sea. For several minutes he watched his scope and from time to time his mind wondered while he waited for the dope runners to retrieve the cargo from the shallow water.

I wonder where Boomer is? he mused.

When the traffickers were clustered, Gomez eased the *Flash* closer, cruising in a stealth mode until he could see men in his night scope. The magnification was so good he could see them hanging over the side struggling with the barrels in the rolling sea. They couldn't get the barrels aboard the sleek cigarette boats so they were opening them up alongside busily shuffling packages from barrels to boats. Gomez knew what he was watching in his night-eye. He waited until they were almost finished before calling SOUTHCOM.

"Baseplate, this if Viper, over."

"This is Baseplate, roger over."

"The customer has retrieved the merchandize. It appears to be a substantial quantity of illegal drugs. They are breaking the shipment up into four fast movers. Interrogative as to time on target of the Coast Guard, over?"

"Viper, Sea Stallion will be on station in four hours, over."

"Roger, Baseplate. Be advised, in two hours the cargo will be scattered all over the Yucatan Peninsula. I'll need to detain the boats if you expect the shipment to be here when the cavalry arrives, over."

"Roger, Viper, wait, out."

For several minutes the radio was silent while the duty officers at Southern Command sought a decision as to what to do.

"Viper, this is Baseplate, over. PER GRA on weapons live. Fire only to incapacitate. Maintain station until the Coast Guard arrives. How copy, over?" asked the operator at Southern Command. He had just granted Gomez permission to engage the boats.

"Good copy, Baseplate. Viper out."

Gomez grinned and looked at his coxswain. "All ahead one-third."

"All ahead one-third, aye," responded the coxswain.

He eased forward on the throttles and the sleek stealth boat rose up out of the water like a big cat charging a herd of wildebeest.

"Shooter, as we pass by place a few rounds in the engine compartment of each boat. Do not fire to destroy."

"Roger, L.T." said the big black man seated behind the console. "Easier said than done."

The *Flash* closed the distance at thirty knots and blew by the four fiberglass boats like an ill wind. The targeting computer controlling the minigun slew the weapon from boat to boat blasting each with a two second burst that sent hundreds of 7.62 projectiles careening through their plastic hulls. Two boats exploded in giant fireballs as tracer rounds ripped through fuel cells, igniting a volatile mixture of air and gasoline. The other two boats went dead in the water, shredded like cheese. Gomez brought the *Flash* about and stood off three hundred yards. Using his P.A. system he hailed the remaining craft.

"Do not attempt to resist. Do not attempt to throw your cargo overboard. If you do, you will be destroyed. You may assist any survivors in the water."

Gomez maintained station until the Coast Guard was a few miles from the scene of the incident. Before they were close enough to clearly identify his craft he turned the *Flash* about and sped off into the darkness at sixty knots.

Chapter 17

Ten minutes after the plane lifted off from La Paz it passed alongside Mount Illimani and broke over the crest of the Cordillera Occidental. A few minutes later it began its descent into Cochabamba. In the distance Masure caught sight of the tropical highlands and the jungled lowlands below the mountains. A lush living carpet of green stretched from the foothills to the horizon as far as the eye could see. Before them stretched the Amazon and thousands of square miles of jungle, an area nearly the size of the continental United States.

"So that's where they mine white gold." Masure said, amazed by the scale of the Bolivian jungle.

"A lot of it," Evans replied. "For hundreds of years, perhaps for millennia, the Indians have cultivated it for *acullicu*. It didn't take a great feat of genius to turn it into a cash crop."

Evans took a sip of his coffee just as the plane took a nasty bounce. He balanced it deftly in his right hand and waited for the plane to settle down before taking another sip. Masure smiled sheepishly as Evans yawned from lack of sleep.

"Bolivia," Evans continued, "is the poorest country in South America so it was relatively easy for drug traffickers to establish coca as a cash crop."

Evans used the term *Cocaine Inc.* to collectively describe the big trafficking enterprises. The shadowy underworld of drug cartels mostly operated as rivals as compared to an organized corporation. He accepted that. Their collective effect was what he called, "Cocaine Ink and Heroin Incorporated."

"The ghetto at the opposite end of the pipeline is rooted in poverty, ignorance, and desperation. Even if it were possible to kill all the coca bushes in the Andes, Cocaine Inc. would just set up business in some other poor country, maybe in South East Asia or Africa. It won't stop here because it doesn't start here."

"I don't understand."

"Demand. Users. As long as there is a demand there will always be some poor son-of-a-bitch willing to take a chance at big money, no matter what the punishment is for trafficking," Evans said, with a yawn.

Masure studied the terrain that lay below the aircraft. It was fertile rolling farmland covered in crops. In the distance below the plateau the jungle stretched to the horizon. After a few minutes of reflective silence he commented. "Sonia Diaz told me the Indians believe coca stimulates their sexual prowess."

"Oh, yeah? Did she offer you a chew and a roll in the hay like she did

Popeye?" Evans asked with a sly smile.

"I never kiss and tell, Boss. You know that," Masure grinned. "I get more pussy that way. But I'll tell you this. I was in bed early enough to hear your interrogation of Professor Contreras."

"Interrogation?"

"Yeah. You were probing her all night long for details."

"We were discussing the cultural aspects of cocaine," Evans said, referring to their conversation about the terrain.

Masure dodge his diversion. "Not much of a discussion if you asked me," he continued goading Evans. "Sounded like torture with a friendly weapon."

"I didn't ask you for comment," Evans snarled.

Masure ignored him. "All I heard was the bed thumping on the wall and the Professor murmuring something, or was it moaning something? Oh yeah. Something like, *Ohhhh! Derek, it feels so gooooood!*"

"You, Knucklehead. We're not talking about my love life," Evans cautioned, with a smile.

"Oh? So that's what you were up to? In Sinchi's you asked her about Syntec Pharmaceuticals. I caught that little jab and faint. You're looking for someone down here and you think she can help you find him. That's why you set up that little get together at Sinchi's. And when direct questioning failed, you tried a little friendly persuasion of the intimate kind. You dirty old dawg."

Evans gave Masure a hard look.

"Assumption is the motherhood of,"

"Oh, I'm right on," Masure insisted, cutting him off. "I know how you operate, Commander."

"Bolivians would no sooner accept a prohibition on coca than Americans would stomach a ban on coffee," Evans said, ignoring Masure's attempts to uncover SOC Inc.'s mission. He took a sip of his brew and yawned.

"Okay. So you don't trust me," Masure said with a shrug. "I can't help you guys if I don't know what you're up to."

"I don't need any help," Evans growled, with a mean expression. "You're the one who asked for a PM." He continued his lecture with piercing eyes. "They chew huge wads of the crap to stifle hunger,"

Masure cut him off again. "It helps them overcome the drudgery of heavy work," he said, finishing Evans's sentence. "And supposedly," he grinned, "it stimulates their sexual prowess." He smiled deviously. "Does it work?"

"How the hell should I know, Buckaroo!" Evans chuckled.

"Boss, I got the picture. Believe me."

"It's a woman, by the way," Evans confessed.

"What?"

"We're looking for a woman, a colleague of Rita's. And mine," he said as an after thought.

"Why?"

Evans shook his head in disbelief and exhaled with a gush of displeasure. "Need to know, partner. Need to know. You get paid to train BB's. I get paid to do what I do and right now that's to find this woman." Evans handed Masure a picture of Carolina Galán.

"*Wow!* Some looker. You balling her too?" Masure asked, studying the photo.

"I wish," Evans grinned. "She's one of those genius types that dreams in chemical formulas. I doubt she has a passing thought about men."

"Don't bet on it," Masure cautioned. "They all fantasize about men like us. Old, young, rich, or poor, they all get the urge."

"I'm mighty happy to be included as one of the desirables. I presume we're getting into your area of expertise, huh?" Evans asked facetiously.

"Yeap," Masure smiled. "You think she's down there? In that jungle?" he asked, looking out the window.

"Yeap. Or I wouldn't be here putting up with your shit."

"Is she involved with illegal drugs?" Masure asked.

"A large portion of the coca harvest is processed into cocaine and smuggled into the U.S." Evans continued, ignoring Masure's insistent rummaging into his affairs.

"I got it. I got it," Masure cut. "Take a little kerosene and water, pour it over dried leaves, stomp the shit out of it, and when it turns nasty, pour in a little sulfuric acid. Wala. *Pasta basica de cocaina.*"

Evans looked at Masure and shook his head.

"Naval Intelligence. Professor Contreras. You, and about a dozen other experts," Masure volunteered.

"Alright, Buck-O. You can catch the next flight back to Bogotá. You've earned your associate's degree in dope-ology."

"I want a master's degree, Boss. I haven't seen the enemy yet."

"And you won't," Evans snapped, "unless you go to a drug rehabilitation center."

"I haven't seen a snot-sucking drunk Injun dancing in a *pozo* pit. I haven't seen a *cocalero* family on the verge of starvation. I haven't seen the LBG's in action. I haven't seen *Screaming Eagle* or *Hawkeye* or *Bortac* or the *Bolivian Queen* or a bunch of other bullshit I picked up on in a bar full of drunken hotshots hell bent for leather."

LBG was an acronym the DEA called the Leopards. It stood for Little Brown

Guys. Screaming Eagle was a system of electronic listening posts used to identify and intercept suspect aircraft ferrying narcotics. The outposts were manned by U.S. Air Force personnel and scattered about on mountaintops all along the Andean chain. The Bolivian Queen was one of several mobile floating bases used to control hundreds of small craft that plied the huge rivers of the Amazon Basin. Interdicting narcotics shipments, precursor chemicals and other contraband was a difficult if not impossible job in the Amazon. From intelligence apparatus to border patrol personnel, Uncle Sam had thrown the spectrum of modern tactics at the Andes. To accommodate the engine of war the coca crop was simply expanded.

"You are just full of bombshells this morning, partner. Is your testosterone out of control?"

"Yeap," Masure grinned. He stretched in his seat and yawned. "The guy in the room next to mine was pole vaulting all night. I couldn't sleep a wink for all the moaning and groaning."

Evans chuckled. "Then you best choke your chicken, partner, cause it's the only safe sex where we are going."

"Don't you know?" Masure agreed with big yawn.

After a thirty-minute flight the plane bounced to a landing at Jorge Wilstermann Airport in Cochabamba. They quickly navigated the terminal and caught a cab to the bus station where they caught the first bus headed into the interior. The seven-hour bus ride from Cochabamba to Sinajota was a utter test of endurance, like riding a bone-jarring buckboard down a rocky trail. The half-paved, half-dirt road was so full of potholes the old Mercedes bus had to crawl down the steep grade at a snail's pace, bumping and grinding all the way. On each side of the road enormous naked mountains towered into the sky disappearing into billowy white clouds blowing off the Amazon. It was the end of the dry season and the rains were coming early. From time to time, when the bus rounded a curve, Masure caught sight of the *Chaparé*, the mysterious, primitive jungle of Bolivia. It looked like an endless emerald green carpet of life laid out below an aquamarine sky.

About a half-hour from Sinajota the bus stopped at a checkpoint at the edge of the forest. Bedraggled children rushed out from everywhere trying to make a quick sale. They scurried about the legs of unkempt Leopards like cockroaches when a light is turned on. The kids were pushing everything from fried fish to fried bananas while the Leopards pushed the margins of corruption.

The anti-drug police of Bolivia were notoriously corrupt and abusive. Their livelihood depended upon taking bribes and thievery to supplement their meager pay. They mounted the bus like lazy thugs. If they found money, they kept it. If they found dope, they kept it. If they saw something they wanted, they took it. Eyeing Evans with suspicion they avoid both American's and their baggage. One particularly ugly officer, who was missing his front teeth, glared at them for several minutes wondering if he could shake them down for a few bucks on the pretense of finding something wrong with their passports. Evans's look dissuaded him. He had shaken down enough strangers to know who to pick on and who to avoid. He walked back to his shack leaving his men to carry out the necessary plunder.

Evans bought a bunch of bananas and a dozen Mandarin oranges from a couple of the young merchants. The purchase incited others to mob the bus trying to make a sale until an ill tempered corporal smacked one of the boys with a backhand. He snarled viciously at the youngsters and they retreated like whipped dogs.

During the inspection three young troops took an interest in a pretty young Indian girl. They took extra time searching her bags, all the while demanding to know where she had hidden the dope. They frisked her body, paying special attention to her breasts and crotch. She stood passively without emotion, letting them violate her privates without protest, knowing that to do otherwise would invite arrest and rape. Interrupting the molestation, Evans offered the soldiers and the woman some of his fruit. His size and strength intimidated the LBGs and his menacing glare shamed them. Like a good Catholic, one young soldier crossed himself and moved on to the next passenger.

A half-hour down the road from the first checkpoint, the bus screeched to a stop at Sinajota, a shabby little town fifteen minutes drive from the DEA base at *Chimoré* where Evans had spent six months teaching small unit tactics. It was just after dusk when they climbed down from the bus. Bowler-hatted Indian women were still packing away their street side stalls of counterfeit Nike tennis shoes and Levi blue jeans. Sinajota was a sprawling corrugated tin-roofed town midway along the Cochabamba-Santa Cruz highway. It was strategically located on the edge of the jungle and it was the last stop for provisions before leaving civilization. Not much happened during the day. It was a vampire kind of town that came to life with the darkness when *la pichicata* ruled. Once called Little Chicago because of the shootouts that regularly took place on its unpaved streets, it had seen the heyday of the coca trade and had been passed by for towns deeper in the interior.

Evans noticed that the big time traffickers who sported gold chains and pearl-handled .45s were gone. But not the hot Latin salsa music that blared from the seedy little bars and billiard halls that lined the streets. Salsa beckoned the rowdy to play. A cacophony of sounds blended with passing trucks and motorcycles headed for Santa Cruz and points east, or Cochabamba and points west; anywhere but Sinajota. The money that had once flowed freely in the red clay streets had dried to a trickle. Desperate young men, who by day slept in rabbit hutch like compartments scattered throughout the town, were congregating in the bars to drink and hope for a deal with *la pichicata*, the merchandise.

Evans collected his bag and motioned for Masure to follow him down the street. He walked to the far end of town where the shacks merged with the jungle before taking a side street toward a huge barn that sat at the end of a wide dusty red clay road. It was bustling with activity like a tobacco barn in Kentucky.

"*Venta de Coca*, partner. That is the center of commerce for this shitty little town," he said, shaking his finger at the coca market.

Dozens of campesinos were trading *pichicata* like candy. Merchants were arguing over price like tobacco farmers in North Carolina or wheat farmers in Nebraska. Laborers toiled with large nylon sacks of dried coca leaves, grabbing them with hooks like bales of hay. Children jumped and played on the bags of leaves amid the drone of voices trying to make deals. A pungent spinach-like odor assaulted them, reminding Masure that he was starving.

Evans motioned him over to a small open-air bar that catered to the laborers of the coca market. He spat out a string of Spanish at the bartender and watched carefully as the man dipped into boiling pots for potatoes and corn on the cob. Satisfied with the hygiene, Evans took a seat and motioned for Masure to sit opposite him. In moments a waiter appeared with an assortment of hot foods and two cold bottles of Peceña beer.

"Don't drink the water, man," Masure commented, in his best Mexican accent.

The heat of the tropics was oppressive. Sweat was tricking down his forehead and it was after sundown. He wiped his face and then the top of his beer bottle before taking a big pull on the cold beer.

"You see those sacks over there?" Evans asked, pointing at the coca market.

"How could I miss 'em?"

A young campesino, naked from the waist up, hooked a bulging bag and heaved it onto a scale for weighing.

"They call it *la carga.* Each one is approximately a hundred pounds of dried leaves. Let's listen and see what that one goes for."

Evans strained to hear the blur of Spanish as the merchant and farmer argued over price.

"I think it went for about eighty bucks," Evans said, when the deal was struck. "Price is down from the last time I was here. The supply must have increased."

"So the law of supply and demand is busy at work here in the jungle, huh?" Masure asked.

"You bet. Supply is up. Price is down. Farmer goes hungry. That simple. The whole damn area is considerably depressed from the last time I was here," Evans said, looking around the town. "During its heyday Sinajota was rolling in money. Gun toting cowboys used to have gunfights in those bars over there," he said, pointing across the dusty street.

He took a bite of his corn on the cob and washed it down with a big gulp of beer. Then he bit off a big chunk of boiled potato to sample the texture and washed it down with another swallow of beer. Breaking off a piece of bread, he dipped it into the piping hot *sopa de papa lisa*, a hearty beef and potato soup relished by the Indians of the Altiplano, and slurped it up like a native. Masure copied his every move.

"How does it convert?" Masure asked, wiping his chin.

"What?"

"I mean the coca leaves. How much cocaine would that eighty dollar bag make?"

"Roughly. A hundred pounds of leaves stomped down with about three gallons of kerosene, four pounds of lime and a pint of sulfuric acid would yield about one pound of paste. Paste is about 40 percent pure cocaine, so, that bag would make a little less than half a kilo of finished product."

"*Jesus!* A kilo that costs forty grand on the streets of L.A. starts out here as less than three eighty dollar bags of leave?" Masure exclaimed incredulously. "There must be ten million dollars worth of cocaine in that barn."

"A lot more than that. And there are hundreds of coca markets just like that one scattered throughout the Andes. The price of *la carga* fluctuates wildly depending on supply and demand. I've seen it go as low as ten bucks a bag and for as much as a grand."

"*Holy shit!* That must wreak havoc on the people."

"You bet it does. Bolivia is a cripplingly poor country with only its coca crop between subsistence and starvation. The government has agreed to fight cocaine trafficking, but people have to eat. The truth is, they depend on the coca crop. Corruption is inevitably built into the system. Combine that with an inflation rate of a gazillion percent, a corrupt police force, and narcos that will kill a man for talking too loudly, and you begin to understand the hopelessness of the common man."

"Wow. The poor bastards are abused by everybody," Masure commented.

"No, not all the time. The traffickers are usually generous, as long as they get their way. Brutal, but generous with their money. They build schools, and bridges, and all sorts of things to win the hearts and minds of the people. They throw huge parties with bands and booze, and while the Leopards rape and pillage, they donate to the widows and the poor."

"What the hell are we doing down here, Boss?" Masure asked, referring to U.S. policy. He shook his head.

Evans decided to throw him a curve ball.

"We're going bar hopping, man. My favorite place is the *Lucero*. It has swinging bat-wing doors like an Old Western saloon and psychedelic pictures on the wall."

"Sounds like my kind of place. Any pussy?"

"Forget it, dude. Is that all you got on your mind?"

"It's not my fault. You see, there was the couple in the room next to mine and,"

"Would you cut the crap? We're going to the *Lucero* to meet an old friend and then we're going out on an op."

"Oh no! No. I need some sleep, man. I can't go out on an op. Besides, I never go into the jungle unarmed," Masure protested.

"You can sleep tomorrow on the bus, on the way back to Cochabamba."

"Oh no. No. No. No. Not the ride from hell again?"

"It's either that or a slow boat down the *Rio Mamoré* slapping mosquitoes and pium flies. Five days of boredom."

Masure scowled and resigned himself to a long night.

"Finish your beer," Evans ordered. "It's time to go bar hopping."

Chapter 18

The old man was bent over talking to his favorite coca bush when she walked up behind him. All his special plants had names and he cared for each of them the way he did his five grandchildren and his daughter-in-law. They were his means of survival in his old age, the coca bushes, the children, and Dr. Galán.

"Rodrigo?" Carol Galán said respectfully.

"*Sí Dueña*," he answered, trying to stand up straight like a gentleman in the presence of a great lady.

To Rodrigo, Dr. Carolina Quintero Galán was a goddess, like Viracocha, the bearded white Inca god who could fly like a bird. At sixty-five he was bent and gnarled like an old tree, far beyond his time. Hard of hearing, he squinted to read her lips from underneath the wide-brimmed straw hat that protected him from the scorching tropical sun.

"I'll be going down to the river now," she said. "I won't be back until tomorrow afternoon."

"I will go with you, *Señorita*," Rodrigo volunteered.

The trip down through the jungle to a navigable section of river was several hours walk and he feared for her safety. Packing in supplies was no chore for a great lady, a famous doctor. He knew she had important work to do inside her little bottles. Rodrigo understood. He was a shaman and he knew her magic was powerful.

"*No, viejo.* I can manage by myself this time."

"*Sí, Dueña.* But you must be careful of the snakes," he warned. "*Y los zepes,*" he continued, referring to the Indians who packed coca leaves about the forest.

Rodrigo blessed Carolina Galán. She had brought him many riches and had cured him of the sickness that had robbed him of his strength. Every morning he blessed the day he met her. As was the custom of Bolivian Indians of the Altiplano, to please Ekeko, the dwarf god of abundance, he had carved a miniature Dr. Galán complete with a miniature laboratory. There were tiny bottles and little scientific instruments to exact detail the way she had set up her makeshift lab. To please the earth goddess and encourage her to send good luck, he had buried a dried llama fetus under the corner of the house he had built for her.

"*Por supuesto, viejo.* I will be careful," Galán replied, with a brilliant white smile that warmed his heart.

"*Y los banditos,*" he continued his warning.

"*Sí, Rodrigo,* I will be careful," she muttered, patting the pistol strapped to her right leg.

He watched with fatherly worry as she walked back toward his wooden-planked, stilt house. He was worried because his son had been killed by Leopards, or bandits, or by greedy *cocaleros,* while on such a trip through the jungle. Miguel had gone to Sinajota carrying a hundred-pound bag of coca leaves, the family's only source of income for the best part of the growing season, and he had never returned. The merchants of Sinajota two hundred miles south paid eighty dollars for a hundred pounds of coca leaves and that was enough to feed the family for almost a year. *La carga* had been their only source of salt, and sugar, and maize, and life. Without *La Dueña* they would have starved the year of Miguel's disappearance.

Rodrigo and his son had come down from the Altiplano when the strikes had hit the mines. They had worked as stompers in the *pozo* pits of others to get enough money to buy coca seedlings to start their own farm. Together, they had fought snakes and jaguars, and other desperate *cocaleros* to build up a small plot of land near Sinajota. Then the Leopards attacked in their spotted uniforms. At first they just wanted a small share of the harvest. Then more and more, until they drove them from their land. They stole their coca, their cooking pots, their clothes, and their food. So Rodrigo had moved his family deeper into the jungle, deeper than *la zona roja,* the red zone, far beyond the claws of the corrupt Leopards, deep into the *Chaparé* until he could see the vast savannah of the *Beni* below his mountain and on a clear day the Amazon beyond. There, he started again with a fist full of seedlings and a pocket full of hope. When his wife Rosa died, a part of him died too. Then his son disappeared. But there was Juanita and the children to care for, so he had to labor on. Rosa was buried under his favorite coca bush and he talked to her everyday.

In the years since Dr. Galán had come into his life, he had improved their one room plank house to several rooms and had expanded his coca crop to more than five times its original size. He had even planted beans, corn, and other vegetables. Four men worked for him full time now, thanks to her generosity. They were retched souls, a mirror image of himself when he had climbed down from the Altiplano hungry and desperate for work. There was no electricity on the farm, or running water, or an indoor toilet, but that didn't matter to Rodrigo. There was food to fill their bellies, and wonders beyond his dreams; screens on the windows to keep out insects. His grandchildren were learning to read the tracks in books, tracks he could not understand. He looked up with pride at the cluster of thatched-roof houses perched high up on stilts, reflecting on the change in his life. He had had one built for her. It was set back from the others and hidden so she could have privacy to perform her magic in her laboratory. He wouldn't allow the children to visit her house, even though it was only a hundred meters from the coca fields. It was a place of magic, a place where she conjured up medicines that could rid people of the demons that possessed their bodies.

"I am sorry you did not see this, Rosa," he mumbled to his dead wife. "You would be proud to live in such a house. "And, Miguel, my son. I know you died at the hands of your killers keeping our secret."

He thanked God in the Catholic way and then he thanked Viracocha in the ways of his Inca ancestors.

The children and the chickens were pecking about beneath the house, playing in the scorched red clay of the *Chaparé*. It was the end of the dry season and the land was parched by the equatorial sun. The plain board structures he called home were built high up on stilts to keep away snakes and other jungle animals that came in the night. Rodrigo watched with pride as Carol Galán hugged each of his grandchildren and told them which tracks to read in the books she had given them. Miguelito, the oldest, helped her with her backpack and tagged along with her through the pale green carpet of coca leaves leading down to the edge of the clearing. Then, he watched with a gnawing apprehension as she disappeared down the jungle trail alone.

The jungle is no place for a lady, he thought. *What if La Dueña doesn't return? The children are too young to help in the coca fields and I am too old.*

He eyed his workers with suspicion. They were an ignorant lot, not to be trusted without Miguel around to keep them in line.

Maybe La Dueña will teach me to shoot the gun before she leaves.

He hitched up his grubby black pants and retied the twine that secured the cloth about his waist. He paused just long enough to stuff a handful of fresh coca leaves in his mouth before continuing his labor of love.

"*Mil gracias*, Rosa," he said, thanking the plant for the leaves.

La Dueña has changed, he thought, squatting down to tend the Rosa plant.

"Rosa," he said, speaking to the plant. "She is more relaxed, more *simpatico* than her other visits. Maybe she will stay this time. But there is fear in her heart. I can see it. Rosa, why is she so afraid of strangers?" he asked his dead wife. "Why does she have her supplies delivered to a secret place and not to her house?"

* * *

Carol Galán confidently hiked down the jungle trail, secure in her ability to handle anything in her path. She felt the Colt .45 strapped to her right leg and mentally rehearsed the lesson Derek Evans had given her at least thirty times. It was a skill she had insisted on learning against his chauvinist judgment. It had taken her more than a year to master the simple technique and she was proud of it.

Grip, smack, click, squeeze to a surprise break, she said to herself. The words comforted her. Deep down inside she was afraid of the jungle.

Evans's words returned to her like a broken record. *An empty weapon is like a car without gas. I repeat, an empty weapon is like a car without gas. It's just a worthless chunk of metal. Always, I repeat, always, keep your weapon in condition one. Never point your weapon at anything you are not willing to destroy. Remember. All weapons are always loaded. I repeat! Treat all weapons as if they are loaded and you will never make a mistake. Grip it like this.*

Grip, her hand went to the pistol. Smack. She could feel her right hand smack into her left as her two arms formed a triangle like the turret of a tank. It was the perfect shooting stance. Then her right thumb clicked down the safety in one smooth motion. Click. She could almost feel his strong arms and hands shape her body into a perfect shooting platform. She could almost hear his voice, smell the scent of his body. For a moment she wondered if her difficulty in learning how to use the pistol was a subconscious excuse to feel his arms around her.

Keep your finger off the trigger until you are ready to fire! Front sight focus! Front sight focus! Now, squeeze to a surprise break. His words echoed in her mind.

She could feel her finger slide into the trigger housing and gently squeezed until the weapon discharged in a moment of complete surprise. She could do it all now in less than a heartbeat and hit a ten-inch target at fifteen yards.

Grip. Smack. Click. Squeeezzze to a surprise break. Evans would be surprised, she thought, *the arrogant chauvinist jerk!*

Popeye's words echoed in her mind. *Yeah though I walk through the valley of the shadow of death, I will fear no evil, for thou art with me, my fully-load, hair-triggered Colt .45.*

Evans would be surprised to see me now. He thinks I'm such a klutz.

An image of Rita Contreras leaving Evans's room at the Sopocachi Hotel invaded her mind and she momentarily boiled with anger.

"I don't understand this primitive emotion," she said out loud. "He just chose Rita instead of me. It's that simple. A man will lay next to any woman who offers herself to him. It's in their genes."

Carol hiked down the trail for several hours without a break, carefully scanning the areas below like Popeye had taught her. At noon she took a break and ate the corn cakes Juanita had packed for her lunch and washed them down with purified water. She carefully re-stowed her gear and continued her journey without really seeing the jungle that teemed with life all around her. She was focused on the most dangerous animal in the jungle. Man. Avoiding men.

Another hour down the trail she spotted several Indians carrying heavy bundles of coca leaves. She took to the bushes until they disappeared in the forest below. The navigable sections of the rivers and streams that drained into the *Rio Chaparé* were used to transport coca leaves out of the jungle and goods into the region. Like her, the men were headed for a navigable section of water but for the opposite reason. She was going to a cache site she had worked out for receiving provisions and equipment from Rita Contreras. The Indians were delivering someone's coca crop to market.

At two in the afternoon she reached the first section of navigable water on a small river that fed *Rio Chaparé*. Ultimately, all the streams and rivers of the region flowed into the Amazon and on then on to the Atlantic Ocean three thousand miles to the east.

She took off her hat and backpack and climbed down a steep narrow path adjacent to a thundering waterfall that prevented boats from traveling any further up stream. At the base of the falls she checked her cache site to see if her supplies had been delivered. It was empty, so she climbed back up to her LUP to wait. LUP was a SEAL term she had learned from Popeye. It stood for Lay Up Point, a secluded location to hold up and watch the surroundings. Exhausted from the climb, and depressed by her circumstances, she sat down in her hide-site to wait for the shipment she desperately needed to complete her analysis of the substance.

Life is so unfair, she thought, trying to keep the images of the terror she had seen in her lab from surfacing. *So unfair.*

Only dugout canoes, *peke-pekes,* could make it so far into the highland rain forest. She had selected her LUP so she could see the jungle and the stream below the falls. She took out her binoculars and searched the river, listening for the puttering sound of a long-shafted engine. It was the end of the dry season and she could see a squall in the distance moving in from over the Amazon.

It could rain tonight. That would please Rodrigo. His crops need water. But it doesn't please me. After the rain, the mosquitoes feed. God, I hate mosquitoes!

Biting bugs were inescapable, especially the tiny whining pium flies which had an uncanny knack for finding holes in her mosquito net. They left small itchy blood blisters wherever they bit. She hated mosquitoes so much so she had shipped in yards of nylon screen for Rodrigo.

Carol strung up her jungle hammock in a secluded area, taking care with the mosquito net and the poncho that covered it. Then she sat down to wait for the *peke-peke*. She continued searching the stream below the falls for signs of movement in the far distance where it bent into the undergrowth. The sky, and the jungle, and the sound of the water going over the falls were beautiful but she couldn't see the beauty of nature. She couldn't see it for the clouds in her mind, the fear, the knowledge, the loss of her employees and her life as she had known it.

"I can't focus," she murmured to herself. "Why can't I think clearly?"

She watched a bee service a flower but she couldn't see the beauty in it. Compelled to know she retrieved a leather pouch from her backpack and removed the small Ziploc bag containing her remaining quantity of C_{31}.

"No," she muttered. *I promised myself I wouldn't do it again. And I'm not going to do it.*

She put the baggy back in the leather pouch but she didn't put the pouch in the backpack. Instead she placed it on her lap subconsciously knowing what she was going to eventually do. She didn't have to. She needed to. She wanted to know the secrets of nature.

I'll cease this superficial analysis and look deeper at nature without moralizing or dragging myself into farfetched similes or similitudes. I will comprehend the fundamental reality of wild nature without the use of a neuro-stimulant.

The bee caught her eye again. It emerged from the flower covered with golden pollen.

Ahhh, yes. The universal acceptance of opportunity. But what is it? It's not just opportunity. It's not just survival of the fittest. Or is it? Darwin was so shallow. A chauvinist. A product of his inflexible time.

Carol pondered and fidgeted for half an hour, twice pulling the plastic bag from the leather pouch. Each time she did, she reminded herself she had promised not to touch it again.

If I am walking through the jungle and someone calls out my name, hey you, Carolina Galán. You there! I won't turn around. No, I won't turn around. I'll just keep walking. If I hear someone curse me or threaten me, or moralize about some aspect of my life, I won't turn around. I won't even look back for a second. But if someone says, hey you there, Carolina Galán. Do you want to know? Do you want to know the secrets of the universe, the meaning of life? Then, I would turn around. Yes. I would turn around because I want to know.

She removed the plastic bag from its leather pouch and gazed at the lustrous crystalline substance inside. It was just a whitish gray lump of carbon, hydrogen, nitrogen and oxygen, with an atom of magnesium imbedded. And it was magic.

"C-twenty-one, H-twenty-three, NO-three, MG-one" she said out loud, reciting the chemical formula. "Not so very different from heroin or cocaine in substance, but so very different in effect. Heroin and cocaine are evil. But you bring peace and focus to human thought, and beauty, and knowledge, and wonder," she said out loud, talking to the substance in the bag.

She removed the small lump of matter and held it in one cupped hand, rotating it slowly with her fingers as if playing with a worry stone. The sweat in her palms of her hands was enough to activate the narcotic effect. The substance flowed into her body by osmosis. She understood the process, and so not to receive a high dose, she quickly placed the substance back in its protective package. Little by little focus came to her thoughts. With gentleness the dead calm of the jungle stirred slightly and burst into life caused by the wings of a butterfly floating by. She saw a breeze, she had not felt before. It was an imperceptible signal from some great jungle spirit that enjoyed playing with her thoughts. It came to her as if six great veils slowly lifted from her eyes allowing her to see more clearly.

The first veil revealed sound. From the cacophony of the jungle came the sounds of the underworld, a new sound like tuning radio frequencies to a single channel. She focused. From the roar of noise a strange little rasping sound detached itself, a scraping, a picking, a rustling in the leaf litter beneath her. But before she could discover the source an explosion of sound descend from the trees above as hundreds of parakeets winged in for a landing, squawking and chirping in the glory of life. The explosion of noise startled her but curiosity compelled her to seek out the source of the scratching. It beckoned her like her search for the secrets of the universe. Systematically, she searched the forest floor until she detected the source of the distraction. It was a beetle sorting the leaf litter for food. All around the Lilliputian hunter she saw the offerings from the canopy above. The rot and crumble of the trees were hiding places and food for a vast array of life forms she had not seen. So near, yet so far, she began to recite their names out loud.

"Slime molds, ponerine ants, scolytid beetles, bark lice, basidiomycete fungi, earwigs, embiopteran web spinners, zorapterans, entomobryomorph springtails, japygid diplurans, schizomid arachnids, pseudoscorpions."

Life she had not seen was all around her. The next phenomenon to come into focus was color, unreal color, living pigment which seemed to appeal to more than one sense, and which satisfied like a cool drink of water on a hot summer's day. A big bird flew overhead with steady wing beats tuned to the jungle below. It caught her attention. The instant it came into focus it flashed out brilliant turquoise, living turquoise in motion. She heard the sound of turquoise in her mind. It landed in the tallest tree and called to its mate in a voice she understood. She saw the sound. Then the jungle began to vibrate green, deep living green, every color of green her mind could fathom, shades of living green bursting with life, chlorophyll-green flowing through millions of living veins.

And then fragrance. The veil of fragrance was lifted, fragrance so delicious it was orgasmic. She drank in the fragrance of a million flowers bursting in living color. Then taste. She could taste the fruits on the trees from the fragrance they emitted to attract animals. She touched a flower blooming next to her. It was just a small singular flower unremarkable to a passerby. She felt it for the first time and she saw the veins in its leaves and the texture in its pedals. And then the great finale of the pyrotechnic display of life came into focus. Sound had smell, and smell had feel, and feel had color, and color had taste, and taste had sound. And knowing.

"Seeing, smelling, feeling, tasting, hearing..., knowing," she murmured. "Knowing!" *How is it we are here? How is it that life is here? All the world surrounds me and I'm trapped inside my head. But I think I understand. We, Homo sapiens, are going to keep growing and evolving, yes, evolving if we don't destroy ourselves with our technology or our tremendous biological potential. It's an inexorable fact of life. All creatures evolve. What is to become of us?*

She recalled her journey through the rain forest, the sights, the sounds, and the smells. Looking at the beetle with new eyes she picked up a hand full of soil and felt is for the first time. Its raw existence came into being. She saw the colors and the textures and the balance of life.

"Self replication is the cornerstone of any definition of life," she said out loud. "Birds do it. Bees do it. Fungi do it. No matter how simple the organism, it must do it. But I haven't done it. Why?"

Self-replication is the principle and DNA is the key molecule to life on this planet, she thought. *It defines almost every living thing that we know. The biological world is now the realm of chemistry. My world. But what is the true nature of that world? What is life? What are we? Are we simply the descendants of a self-perpetuating molecule that has taken on bizarre forms, that double helixical structure of self-replicating nucleic acid we call DNA, the selfish gene. It's all around me. It is the jungle. We are a tiny part of that selfish substance, the part that has reached self-awareness.*

The concept struck her like a beam of light.

"Sentience is the perfection of nature. We are the living brain of nature. Nature seeing nature through itself. But what am I but a sac of organic molecules suspended in a bag of salty water. How is it that I know? Has it always been? Matter, energy, and intelligence in universal balance? It's not E equals MC squared, but I over E equals MC squared. Intelligence as a function of matter and energy that is in constant balance in a never-ending universe. Why is it we are here? Because the function has always been so. We are a part of the biomass, the sentient part. All things DNA are programmed to self-replicate. Birds do it. Bees do it. Humans do it. Humans love to mate. They mate all the time, by night and by day, through all phases of the female's reproductive cycle. Humans throughout the world will mate with any other human if given half a chance. The barrier between races and cultures melt away when it comes to sex. Why? Biological power. They don't mate to have offspring, at least not consciously. So why?"

Love comes in at the eyes, wrote Yates, *and is ejaculated as seminal fluid,* wrote *Galán,* she thought. She chuckled at the brilliance of the thought as she imagined half the genes necessary to produce a human being wriggling down a living tunnel the length of a man's penis.

"It's programmed into us by DNA. Self-replication is the most constructive," and then the thought struck her like a bolt of lightning, *and the most destructive force in the living world. The drive to procreate transcends all. It controls us as it controls other species. We just won't admit it. We want to believe in free will. As a species if we don't learn to control it, it will destroy us. Maybe even the planet. Your thoughts are rambling, Carol. Get a gripe.*

She looked at the forest around her. And then she asked herself, "What drives you, Carolina Quintero Galán?"

Derek Evans's handsome face flashed into her mind. Rugged, sincere, confident, manly. She felt a stir in her body, a longing she didn't fully comprehend but she realized it was the selfish gene exerting itself.

"Yes. The essence of manly. Hardheaded, self-assured, confident and willing to mate with any female who gets near his penile projection. He can't help it. He's not capable of understanding the drives wired into his reticular complex. But it's not a matter of understanding, is it? It's a drive beyond understanding, a drive so deeply imbedded in the reticular complex no one really understands it," she babbled to herself. "Males of all species are programmed to mate with as many females as possible. Man is no different. Man just suppresses the desire. Females on the other hand are programmed to be selective, to choose a mate whose genes have the best chance for survival."

A new emotion overwhelmed her and it wasn't the magnificent perfection of the jungle. It was a raw human emotion. Fear.

"Self awareness brings with it the baggage of human emotions. Like and dislike, love and hate, joy and sadness, loneliness and despair. I understand. My anger is related to the drive to self-replicate. Locked deep within me is the drive to self-replicate, a drive I have suppressed for my career."

Then she thought, *My fantasies about Derek Evans are just subconscious bubbles boiling to the surface and my anger with Rita is simply resentment, or envy. Something inside, something ineffable attracted me to the man. Only God knows why. He's such an ass. Jeez, that's a strange thought, Carol. God. A strange concept.*

The sound of a *peke-peke* aroused her attention. She heard it in the distance straining against the current and it caused a flood of emotions. Fear seized control. Overwhelming fear. Her hands began to tremble and her breath came in small shallow puffs.

"Fear is a human emotion to be controlled. No fear is. What am I saying? All living things feel fear. Fear is the essence of survival. Those we call courageous, like Commander stuck-on-himself, know-it-all Derek Evans just know how to smother that fear with calming thoughts."

She took a deep breath and drank in the fragrance of the jungle and the fear subsided. A calm came over her body and her stomach stopped churning. She picked up her binoculars and gazed out over the gorge. The chemical fire in her brain was waning but it was not gone. At the sight of the *peke-peke* a new reality set in. They were coming. They were coming for her.

The image of her chemistry lab tucked away in a nondescript building north of San Diego invaded her mind. Her research assistants were busy mixing liquids in a beaker when the door flew open. Her body began to tremble and her stomach began to churn as the horror returned in color and sound. Spectrographs, recording every flicker and flare, seized her attention, but she could not control the fear. It invaded again and it overwhelmed her emotions. And then Laura began screaming. It was inside her head. She knew it. But she couldn't stop it. She heard it as if it was happening in real time. She saw it in her mind's eye as if it were real.

Through a small window in a heavy metal door she saw the man with the horribly disfigured face. He was looking at her. His lips were missing. His mouth was foaming. The gruesome image of Risitos Savajé's face flooded her brain. Then, out of breath and foaming at the mouth, he stood at her car door aiming a big black pistol at her. The movie inside her mind replayed with blood and horror in fast forward, over and over. It frightened her to the depths of her soul. Then the killer fired the pistol point blank at Laura Shula. Only it wasn't Laura Shula. Carol felt saliva on her face. For a second she was Laura Shula, in the last seconds of her life.

Like an animal in flight for its life, she ran. She ran into the darkest recesses of the jungle. From bush to bush, tree-to-tree, she scurried for her life until, exhausted, she bounced chest first off the trunk of a tree and fell on her back. And still the men kept beating and tearing at the lab. Panting for breath, laying on the ground with slime molds, ponerine ants, and scolytid beetles, she struggled to control her emotions, to focus her mind on a small patch of blue sky peeking through the leaf canopy.

"Fear is a human emotion to be controlled," she recited, like a mantra. "Fear is the essence of survival," she repeated out loud in a quivering voice. "Those we call courageous know how to smother fear. I can do it too."

She took a deep breath and focused her eyes on an orchid growing in the branch of the huge tree. She drank in its fragrance and the fear subsided as quickly as it had seized control. A calm came over her entire body and her stomach stopped churning.

Carol got up off the ground and walked back to her LUP with the inner calm of a priest. She coolly picked up her binoculars and without fear studied the gorge below the falls. Green and yellow macaws swooped low over the thickly jungled banks, fleeing from the approaching aliens. A blue kingfisher made an arrowy descent right in front of the *peke-peke* and emerged with a small fish grasped crosswise in its beak. Like a dart, it too headed for the safety of the jungle. Egrets flew from the trees in terror, alarmed by the sight of the men. But Dr. Carol Galán wasn't afraid anymore. She was in control.

I will never touch that stuff again, she swore to herself with conviction. *Never.*

The intensity of the puttering increased until the *Resbaloso* ran the dugout aground near the base of the falls. It was the place they had agreed upon so long ago. As they had done on several occasions, *Viscoso* held the boat while *Resbaloso* carried the bundles into the foliage and hid them in the cache site she had chosen. He looked for a message from her but found none.

She watched from seclusion as they shoved off and headed down river twice as fast as they had come up. When they were out of sight she climbed down the cliff and made her way to the cache site. She opened the bundles like a child on Christmas morning, and rejoiced at the sight of a new portable spectrometer. Finally she had the tool she needed to solve the mystery, the shape of the C_{31} molecule.

Taking the supplies and equipment back to her lab would take several trips even with Miguelito's help, so she moved the bundles to a new location deeper in the jungle and took only the spectrometer with her. It was too important to leave behind. She climbed back up to her LUP before reading Rita's letter. When she did, fear seized control of her entire body again. Uncontrollable fear. Her heart pounded and her temples throbbed. She stared at the words not believing the ink on the paper.

Carol, Derek Evans is back in Bolivia, Rita wrote. *I saw him at Sinchi's last night. I believe he is looking for you. He didn't say so directly but I could tell by his questions that he is looking for you. But don't worry. I didn't tell him anything. Carol, perhaps you should contact him. He's a good man and I know he'll help you. Think about it, won't you? He'll be at the Backthorne's by the time you read this letter.*

Why is he here? Why is everyone after me! Everyone! Why? Why? she thought.

She knew the reason. The realization kept visiting her like a phantom. She had caused it all. It was the Internet, or the telephone, or one of her lectures. Narcotic traffickers had been monitoring her every move. They wanted the formula, or to kill her to keep the formula secret.

They think I know how to make it. Oh, Jesus, are they wrong!

Chapter 19

Evans led Masure back to the main part of town and down the street to a noisy open-air dance hall called the Morning Star, *El Lucero*. Inside he selected a table and ordered a couple of beers. Everyone eyed them suspiciously but the music played on. Four men standing at the bar took special interest in them.

"See those guys over there?" Evans asked, pointing at the bar. The men appeared to be annoyed by the gesture. One snarled his lip and said something to others.

"Yeah."

"DEA. I can spot 'em in the dark. They're stationed at *Chimoré*, a big Leopard base about fifteen minutes from here. And those over there, they're small time dealers in illegal goods. Kerosene, sulfuric acid, even toilet paper is controlled down here. They make a living supplying sheet plastic, chemicals, food, you name it, to the past labs scattered throughout the *Chaparé*. The agents keep some of them on the payroll for Intel. And those over there, the ones with the messed up feet," he said, pointing to a group of young men dressed in dirty jeans and tee shirts. They were barefoot. "They're stompers. The chemicals ulcerate their feet. I've seen infections so bad the only cure was amputation."

"Damn. That's brutal. Hell of a way to make a living."

They chatted for a while over a din of salsa music. The locals were blowing off a little steam and a number of them were tanked up. A young mestizo dressed in jeans and an oversized tee shirt with a Miami Vice logo staggered into their table and fell on the filthy floor at Masure's feet. Spilled beer ran off the table onto his head. Masure helped him up but for some reason the youth took offense and decided to fight. Evans intervened by grabbing the young man's arm and waist. He spun him about-face and with a simple wristlock forced him to sit down at their table. With steady pressure Evans held him in an iron grip. When the man calmed down, Evans yelled at the bartender in Spanish.

"Barkeep. Two more beers and a drink for my friend here."

The drunk said something unintelligible and Evans cranked down harder on his wrist. The boy winced in pain and Evans eased up on the pressure.

"Make it two drinks for my brave little friend here," he hollered in Spanish. "And one for the house," he continued, slapping the youth on the shoulder with his free hand.

Evans took the youth to his feet with the wristlock and ushered him toward the stinking filthy bathroom that consisted of wooden trough nailed to the wall.

The DEA agents at the bar watched the exchange with amusement. They kept eyeing the SEALs suspiciously. Finally, when Evans returned to the table one of them sauntered over as if he was a hired gun in the Old West. He was a hawkish American of Latino descent and he spoke English with a thick Mexican accent common to the borderlands of Texas.

"What you doin' down here, *gringos*?" he demanded, with a level gaze on Evans.

"None of your fuckin' business, *gringo!*" Masure bristled, taking offense to the tone of the man's voice. The agent kept his eyes on Evans and ignored Masure, which angered the Master Chief even more.

"Vacation," Evans replied.

"Now that you know why we are here, fuck off," Masure added, ready of fight.

"I'm not buyin' the bullshit," the agent replied, looking at Evans

"No one is asking you to buy anything, asshole," Masure growled.

"This is no garden spot for gringo tourists, man."

"Listen, pal, we go where we want to go. We do want we want to do, and we don't take orders from a chicken-chokin' DEA scumbag," Masure snarled.

"Tough guy, huh? Military?" the agent asked, still looking at Evans.

"Tough enough to whip your ass, poncho and the fuck-heads with you." Masure stood up ready for action.

"You want something, *amigo*?" Evans asked in a calm polite tone.

"No, Commander. Your reputation precedes you. Just checkin' you out," the agent said.

He watched Evans's eyes for response to ensure he had the right man.

"Major Miamani wants to meet you at the Sinajota Hotel at twenty-one hundred. The last time he was in here a drunk Injun shot him in the chest. He's got a lot of enemies around here, you know."

Evans eyed the young agent and nodded. "Thanks."

"Sure thing, Commander. And thanks for the beer." He eyed Masure squarely. "You two enjoy your vacation, *gringo*."

He grinned at Masure then headed back to the bar.

Just before nine Evans and Masure left the bar and walked to the best hotel in town. The lobby smelled of cheap perfume and beer. They registered for two rooms, and were about to put away their bags, when an old pickup truck screeched to a halt in front of the hotel. It was headed in the wrong direction on the wrong side of the street. A short Bolivian dressed in a spotted camouflage uniform beamed a smile at Evans from the driver's seat. He had a typical Bolivian face, mostly Indian with a hint of Spanish. He jumped out of the truck and rushed inside to greet the Commander with a bear hug.

Slapping Evans on the back like a long lost brother, he asked, "Ebans, you mean-ass son-of'n-beech. What brings you to Little Chicago, *hermano*?" he beamed.

"Vacation, Jamie."

"Don't sheet me, Ebans, you son-of'n-beech. Only a crazy man comes to Sinajota for vacation." He laughed.

"I came to see you, you ugly little greaser," Evans said. He punched Miamani in the arm.

"For this I am thankful, *mi amigo.*" Miamani looked at Masure and then back at Evans. "I got your message, *hermano*, and I have an easy op set up, like old times, huh. Your friend will see the other side life. Let's go bust some dopers and then drink soam beer."

"I heard you got shot in the *Lucero*, Jamie," Evans said, still eyeing Miamani. Evans pushed him away for a better look. "You look pretty good for a marked man."

"I always looks good, Ebans. You know dat!"

Miamani quickly unbuttoned his shirt and pulled it open so Evans could see his bullet wounds. He pointed to them with pride. Six round scars were scattered about his chest and stomach along with a number of zippers where surgeons had opened him up.

"The dirty bastards tried to kill me three times since you left, Ebans. But I fix 'em. *Los bastardos!* They who do dis, now fed the piranhas in *la Rio Mamoré*," he grinned. "You know the deal. Fouch heem what tries to keel me!"

"Jamie, I'll send you some lightweight body armor. Wear it. Okay?"

"Choor, *amigo*, choor. I wear it." Miamani beamed a proud smile.

With the truck still running in the street, Evans ushered Miamani to a bench in the hotel lobby and showed him a picture of Carolina Galán.

"Jamie. Do you remember this woman? She came through here with me a couple of years ago."

"*Sí. Es una Señorita Professora, no?* The one who is de friend of *Professora Contreras*. You take them to stay at the Aussie's, no?"

"*Sí.* Jamie. I need to find her." Evans locked his eyes on Miamani and watched his pupils. "I'll pay for any information that helps me find her."

"Ebans," said Miamani, shaking his head with a sad face. He studied Carol Galán's picture for a few seconds. "Then you do not know, *amigo.* There are many people looking for dis woman." He handed Evans the picture. "The narcos have a big reward for her, dead or alive. The DEA are looking for her. There is even a picture of her in the Special Forces hooch at *Chimoré*. What has this *chica* done to deserve such a fate, Ebans?" Miamani asked.

"Nothing, Jamie. Nothing. She was trying to do something good for the junkies of the world and it backfired in her face."

"Oh. I know this problem, Ebans. Damn, but do I know this problem. Because I will not take de corruption it is backfired in my face, no?" Miamani looked Evans squarely in the eyes. "I cannot help you, *mi amigo*. I know nothing of dis woman."

"You have heard nothing from the DEA, the SF, or your informants?"

"If she is in the *Chaparé*, Ebans, she is deep beyond *la zona roja*. She is not in the southern *Chaparé*."

Miamani studied Evans face for a moment. He had an extensive network of informants throughout the region which was the reason Evans had sought him out.

"There is just one bit of intel I have that may be of interest to you." He pulled Evans closer. "I have a *zepe*-informer who lives in the northern area, near to the Aussie's ranch. He told me that some of the cocaleros up near the *Beni* have screens on their windows. That is very unusual for the *Chaparé*, no?"

"Sí, *mi amigo*. Most unusual," Evans said, deep in thought. He remembered how much Galán hated mosquitoes. "Do you know the area, Jamie?"

"No. But you do. It is the same area where you took *las professoras*. The area beyond *zona roja*."

Evans was deep in thought when Miamani asked, "Good intel, no? What is your plan?"

"I'm going to stay with the Aussie and search the northern *Chaparé*."

"Ahhh. So you already know this information?"

"No, Jamie. I'm just walking old trails, hopin' to find her before the bad guys do," Evans replied, with a worried expression.

"Is the Aussie coming here to get you?" Miamani asked.

"No. But he knows I'm coming. I have a couple of men staying with him searching the area south of his ranch."

The Aussie was a Bolivian citizen of Australian descent. He was a gnomish little man with beady eyes and a heart of gold, and he owned a ranch the size of Rhode Island right on the edge of the highland rain forest. Evans had used his ranch as base camp for his Syntec Pharmaceutical expeditions in the northern *Chaparé*.

"How are you going to get to the Didgeridoo, Ebans?" Miamani asked, referring to the Blackthorne ranch.

"I'll rent an air taxi in Cochabamba."

"You can fly from Sinajota, now you know. I have a friend who will take you to see that worthless keeper of cows. Tomorrow if you want. But tonight is

164

cobertura, mi amigo, and we have dopers to bust."

Cobertura was local slang used to identify the days when policemen were paid to allow the traffickers to conduct business without interference. Jamie Miamani was one of the few Leopards in Bolivia that wasn't on the take. For his incorruptibility he was a marked man. Marked for another bullet when the Americans lost interest in him. Marked to be passed over for promotion. Marked to be watched carefully when important deals were going down. Marked for death when the time came to pay him back for not playing the game like a good Bolivian citizen.

Miamani cut loose a string of Spanish directed at the hotel proprietor that made Masure's ears sizzle.

"*Si algo falta te voy a cortar los cojones!*" he ordered, pointing at the SEALs' baggage. It amounted to, *if anything is missing when I come back I'll cut off your balls.*

Evans, Masure, and Miamani piled into the front seat of the pickup truck and roared out of town in a cloud of dust. Two Toyota pickups followed them with more than a dozen troops. They had no idea where they were going, which was Miamani's secret to success. A few miles outside of town the incorruptible little Leopard pulled off the main road onto a smaller dirt track that led into the jungle. He bounced along for half an hour with his headlights on, winding down a jungled gorge that would soon be impassible during the rainy season. The last part of his journey he drove the dangerous track without headlights, slowly creeping along in the dark. There was a full moon but from time to time clouds covered the land, threatening rain.

Jamie stopped at a plank shack. A kerosene lantern was on the porch. His soldiers tumbled out without a word, M-16s at the ready and took up positions all around the area. They fanned out in a circular perimeter. Miamani hastily retrieved three M-16s from behind his truck seat and handed one to Evans and one to Masure, along with a couple of extra magazines of ammunition.

He motioned with a wave of his arm and in silence he tracked off into the jungle with Evans, Masure, and ten men in tow. A few meters down the trail an old Indian stepped out of the bushes and stood directly in his path. In the moonlight he looked like a scarecrow dressed in rags. Evans brought his rifle to the ready but checked his fire when he saw the man was there to meet the Major.

With the old man as scout, they tracked deeper into the jungle. Several miles from the trucks the old man stopped at a footbridge, a small tree dropped over a deep gorge carved out by a fast running stream. Paste labs need lots of water and when Evans saw the old man stop and point across the footbridge he knew they were close. In the poor light penetrating the single canopy jungle, Jamie led the way across the footbridge without the procedures Evans had taught him for crossing danger areas. He paralleled the stream for a couple of hundred meters until the ground leveled out. He slowed up the pace and crept through the jungle like a cat. Masure heard music and he tugged at Evans's arm.

"You hear that?" he whispered.

"Yeah. Rock concert for the monkeys," Evans whispered.

"No. Rolling Stones," Masure corrected, misunderstanding Evans's comment.

As they crept closer to the lab Evans chuckled. Mick Jagger was singing *I can't get no, satisfaction* to the accompaniment of jungle frogs and crickets.

They silently crept through the jungle until they could see two young men with their trousers rolled up above their knees stomping around in a shallow pit dug in the ground. It was just a hole in the dirt lined with plastic sheeting but it was the key to making coca paste. As Mick Jagger crooned away at *Jumping Jack Flash*, they danced in a lethal tea-colored brew of leaves, water, and kerosene. When the song ended one of the boys stopped dancing and said something to an old campesino that was stirring a thick liquid in a half-barrel with a large wooden paddle. The old man stopped what he was doing and handed the dancer a cigarette. It was stuffed with tobacco and coca paste, a concoction known as *bazuko* in South America. Knee-deep in kerosene, the boy lit the cigarette and inhaled deeply. After several puffs, he shared it with his partner. Together they finished the weed and gulped down a couple of mugs of *chicha* beer provided by the old woman that fed the camp. When the break was over the youths started the tape player and jumped back in the *pozo* pit. As they danced in the fetid mush the soldiers closed the cordon around the coca lab.

At the far end of the camp there was a smaller pit surrounded by several blue plastic barrels and several large tubs. Evans pointed at the smaller pit and whispered.

"See the small pit?"

"Yeah," Masure whispered.

"That's *agua rica*, rich water. It's caustic as hell. When the shit hits the fan stay away from there."

"Got it."

"And stay away from the flammables. If there's any shooting something might go off low order. One of those big containers is full of sulfuric acid. The others are probably kerosene."

The Leopards slowly closed in on the camp searching for the lookout as they crept through the jungle. Luck was on their side. The observation post was back at the footbridge and the picket was just a boy, age twelve. He had abandoned his post to get something to eat and was seated on a stump beside the old lady.

When Jamie was satisfied his men were in place, he fired one shot in the air and yelled. "*Manos arriba!*"

The two drunken youths jumped out of the paste pit like frightened jackrabbits and bolted for the jungle. The first one to make it to the bushes ran face first into a rifle butt. The force of the blow knocked him to the ground. He rolled around in the dirt, half-conscious, moaning in pain. The second dancer threw up his hands and began begging for his life. "Don't kill me! Please, don't kill me!"

The soldiers dragged them back to camp like a pair of scruffy dogs.

"Leopards, please don't kill us!" the old man begged. "Please don't kill us. We are just poor campesinos trying to make an honest living."

"Making coca paste is against the law, *viejo*," Miamani replied. "That's not honest. You know that."

"But we have to eat," the old woman cried. "Please, don't take us to prison. We have done nothing wrong."

The soldiers cuffed the prisoners with plastic Zip ties and sat them on the stream bank. The old woman kept wailing at the soldiers to let her go until one of them smacked her in the back of the head. She stopped for a few seconds then started crying and begging again.

Using machetes the soldiers hacked down the camp and threw everything that was flammable into one of the paste pits. They dumped kerosene and acid in the pits and set the mess ablaze. As the fire roared the spunky little Bolivian major conducted a field interrogation.

"What is your name?" he demanded of one of the youths.

"His name is Juan," the old man said.

"*Liar!* His name is Alvaro," Miamani yelled, shaking his finger in the old man's face. "His name is Luis. The boy's name is Paco. And her name is Melida Garzon. Carlos, I let you go last time and here you are again," he said to the old man in an exasperated tone.

Carlos Garzon was a professional cook. A man paid to make *pasta basica* -- coca paste.

"But we have to eat," the old woman cried. "We have children to feed."

"*Quien es el patron?*" Miamani demanded, seeking the name of the owner of the coca leaves and the supplies. He wanted the man who financed the operation.

"We cannot tell you that *leader of the Leopards*. If we do, we will be killed," one of the youths cried. His eyes were blurry and red with the fire of *bazuko* and his words were slurred by intoxication.

"Then whisper it in my ear boy or you go to jail this time."

"The jungle has ears, Leopard. Before my feet heal, I would be dead in your prison."

"If I let you go will you tell me?" Miamani asked.

"If I tell you, Leopard, I would not get past the check point at Villa Tunari before one of your men killed me."

"Then you go to jail, boy," Miamani snapped.

"Better to go to jail and live, then tell on the *patron* and die. Besides, *leader of the Leopards*, in jail you have to feed us."

"Let's go," Miamani ordered.

When the boys stood up Masure got a good look at their feet. They were cracked and raw. Sores the size of quarters were oozing fluid and blood.

Chapter 20

Shortly after the twin engine turbo-prop crossed into Bolivian air space the terrain changed abruptly from the dense tropical jungles of Rondonia to the enormous African-like savannah of the *Beni*. Gaviria sipped his rum and Coke and studied the terrain. He was a cattleman at heart and he loved staying at the Bolivian ranch. There were more than a hundred thousand head of mestizo cattle on the spread and five hundred square miles of range. Horses and cattle and open spaces appealed to him. He puffed on his cigar and looked down at the wide Mamoré River floating by sixteen thousand feet below. He thought of the rubber barons who had once ruled the land. They had barged their product down river to Manaos in Brazil until synthetic rubber and competition from Southeast Asia destroyed the market. Now cattle ruled the land, cattle and cocaine.

We're going to be dinosaurs like the rubber barons, he thought, *if Ramón gets the formula. The Savajés will market it like candy until it is widely known on the streets.*

Cut by huge meandering rivers thickly cropped with jungled banks, the *Beni* was a lonely land of extremes. During the dry season, from June to December, the land baked in an equatorial oven. Temperatures soared above one hundred degrees and the relentless sun scorched the savannah bone dry, cracking the thin topsoil and bleaching the grass to a tawny lion brown. During the wet season from December to June, torrential downpours ran off the hard packed clay soil like water off asphalt. Two thirds of the province became inundated and the rest turned to a sea of mud. There were no paved roads in the *Beni*. Only dirt tracks deeply rutted by lumbering trucks that mired up in the sticky red clay. During the rainy season the only way to get product to market was by airplane.

The turbo-prop banked to the left to avoid a billowing column of smoke rising from the savannah. Ranchers were firing the pastureland. Three hundred miles to the south Gaviria spotted the Ballesteros ranch up near the base of the highland rain forest. He couldn't make out any details but he could see the base of the mountains. The ranch was located on high ground, the best in the province. For a moment he questioned his decision to personally pursue Dr. Galán in Bolivia. He had plenty of men to chase down leads. La Paz was just one of several unresolved matters. He knew Carol Galán could be anywhere. It was his love of the ranch as much as his instinct to follow Derek Evans that compelled him to fly to Bolivian.

Why Bolivia? he thought. *Why would she come down here of all places?*

The phone records he had purchased from Gilberto Mesa in Miami listed the calls Galán had made from her home and office in the months prior to her disappearance. Several were to the University of San Andres in La Paz. Other intelligence, provided by his own spies in Washington, D.C. indicated that the FBI and the DEA believed that she had left the United States. The DEA had contracted several private organizations to look for her in Europe, Africa, and South America, and to Gaviria's surprise, SOC Inc. had not been one of the companies on the list. He assumed that Evans was feeding information to his country. The men in Evans's company had actively recruited several people in the Ballesteros organization, none of who knew about the organization's secret business. But it was only a matter of time until they succeeded. SOC Inc. had not cultivated the right intelligence sources yet and therefore had not outlived its usefulness to Gaviria.

The greedy bastard, he thought, as an image of Gilberto Mesa crossed his mind. *All the money in the world won't do him any good if he's rotting in a stinking Yankee prison.*

Gato balled up his fist in anger as he thought of his meeting with the Cali cartel's spymaster. Mesa worked primarily for Cali combines but it was well known that his services were available to anyone with enough cash to pay for them. He owned the Miami Spy Shop and in the world of electronic espionage he was the best in the business. Mesa was the mastermind behind the intelligence system that had penetrated the highest levels of the Colombian government. He had even succeeded in bugging the U.S. Justice Department, the FBI, and the DEA. *Gato* often collaborated with him, comparing intelligence on mutually beneficial subjects. It was a shaky alliance that existed for situations of mutual interest.

Gato had been angry enough to kill Mesa when he left Miami. The man had personally insulted him, made him wait, refused to cooperate, and even threatened to exposure the Ballesteros business as a front for drug trafficking. Moreover, he had demanded a huge sum of money for the information he had acquired on Dr. Galán, most of which Gaviria already possessed. Mesa had actually accused *Gato* of botching the hit on Dr. Galán's lab in San Diego even though he knew it was the Savajés who had hit the lab. Seething with anger Gaviria calmly met Mesa's demands and left the restaurant. But before he departed Miami he issued a contract to a group of Cubans with close connections to the CIA to expose Mesa's electronic espionage business. He paid them twice what he had paid Mesa for the information on Galán. It wasn't the money. It was the principle.

Fire and water. Water and fire, he thought, as he looked out over the smoking savannah. Grass fires were burning all over the province, set by ranchers to clear away the scorched brown grass of the dry season before the rains came. Smoke billowed into the sky so high the pilot had to divert the aircraft several times to keep the runway at Trinidad in sight.

Soon the rains will come, he thought. *We have to move more than ten thousand slabs of beef and sixty tons of coca paste before this land turns to mud and water, or we'll have product stuck on the ranch for six months. And I have to find the woman,* he mused, *before the gringos do, or the Savajés, or some other cartel.*

Gaviria's thoughts turned to business.

If we are the only ones who possess the formula we can manufacture the drug at sea aboard the Don Blás and the Don Blasón and sell it along with cocaine through our existing distribution system. What was it Don Ballesteros said? 'Product diversification.' It's simple if we have a monopoly. Professor Contreras is the key. That's why Evans in Bolivia. He's on to something. I'll have the Cataños snatch her and bring her to the ranch. The Doctor can make her talk, he thought, remembering the Panamanian Doctor he kept on retainer. *A little sodium penathol and then she can entertain the boys before the piranhas.*

Carlos's voice carried up to *Gato's* seat at the front of the aircraft and it made him think of Ramón Savajé.

Sooner or later I'll have to deal with that crazy little bastard, he thought. *It's time to eliminate the Savajés. The hell with Don Ballesteros. Lately he's been neglecting business. If he wants to be a figurehead, so be it. He knows Ramón is dealing with the Russians. If that crazy bastard gets his hands on a nuke we lose. I have to take care of the Savajés soon. Then, I'll ask Don Ballesteros to politely be president and leave the business to me.*

At his direction Carlos had planted listening devices all over the Savajés's houses and vehicles. Consequently, Gaviria was usually two steps ahead of Ramón. The hit on Carol Galán's lab had come as a surprise and only two days ahead of his own plans to abduct her.

I doubt Ramón knows I have him bugged. He's not technically adept. He'd rather rely on brutality and terror to get his way.

Gaviria decided to redouble his efforts to keep track of the Savajés. Then he thought about the submarines.

If Ramón finds out about the subs he'll expose us to the Yankees. Damn Don Ballesteros's eyes! If anyone discovers them they lead directly to the corporation. They are attributable pieces of North Korea junk and they break the first rule of covert operations, non-attributability.

Gaviria was still musing over business when the plane touched down. The airport at Trinidad was little more than a depot for the transshipment of beef. His aircraft hurled down the runway to a crude refrigerated warehouse. Near the building the pilot revved up his engines and reversed the props to stop the plane's forward momentum. The propellers stirred up a red cloud of dust that swirled up around the aircraft. Men standing by with an air-conditioned car shielded their eyes from the blast, and as soon as the aircraft stopped rolling, two boys rushed to the door to lower the steps so that Gaviria could dismount with comfort.

Stevedores were running back and forth carrying slabs of beef from the warehouse to an awaiting cargo plane. The hundred-degree heat melted the thin layer of frost on the beef so their cotton shirts were drenched in blood and sweat. It was a gruesome sight made worse by flies. One of the welcome party, the senior manager of the facility, asked Gaviria if he wanted to inspect the warehouse. *Gato* shook his head and with a foul expression on his face declined the invitation to inspect the nasty meat locker. Without a word he walked directly to the awaiting Mercedes and climbed inside.

"Welcome back to Trinidad, *Señor Gaviria*," the chauffeur said. "*El Centro?*" he asked pleasantly.

"*El Ganadero!*" Gaviria ordered, ignoring the friendly greeting.

Ganadero was the Spanish word for rancher, and apart from cocaine, ranching was the biggest business in the *Beni*.

Located on mainstreet, the Ganadero, which American agents called the hotel Gonorrhea, was also the temporary headquarters of the U.S. Drug Enforcement Agency in northern Bolivia. Gun-toting Americans rented two entire floors and lived in air-conditioned comfort when not raiding the surrounding countryside for *zepes and lavaperros*. They bought information like the ranchers bought antibiotics for their cattle. But the legs of their old huey helicopters, stationed at the Trinidad airport, were far too short to cover the entire *Beni*. What they caught were the little guys who struggled to make a meager living cooking up coca paste or transporting raw materials for the coca labs. The big traffickers simply set up businesses just beyond the range of the helos and fed the DEA a steady diet of zepes to keep them occupied.

The major *traficantes* owned huge *fincas*, like the Ballesteros spread, that were untouchable, both beyond the range of the helos and beyond the clout of the U.S. Government to acquire permission to conduct raids.

* * *

Trinidad is a classic Spanish colonial town set in the heart of South America. It is constructed around a large tree lined plaza dominated by a cavernous Catholic cathedral. The two enormous white towers buttressing the religious relic reflected a pink salmon glow down mainstreet to Ray Keith's observation point. Across the main street, the fiery red sunset of the dry season, enhanced by the smoke of the burning savannah, painted the Ganadero with a rosy blush of crimson and vermillion.

Ray Keith sat on the boardwalk with his one good leg dangling down to the street and his artificial leg lying beside him on the wooden planks. In Trinidad, the buildings and sidewalks are set above street level so the roadbeds can serve as channels for run off during torrential downpours. With exception of the cathedral and the Ganadero, most of the buildings around him were single story with high ceilings and slow moving overhead fans. Their red tile roofs jutted out over the sidewalks, providing protection from both sun and rain.

There were few cars on the streets and those that were honked incessantly. Gaviria's car stood out from the beat up trucks and mopeds smoking up and down the boulevard. Engine noise combined with radios playing deafening Brazilian sambas filled the air. From time to time the music was interrupted by personal messages for remote ranchers.

This message is for the Galendez ranch. Paco, the barge is on its way with twenty head of zebu. It should arrive late tomorrow afternoon.

There are few telephones in the *Beni* and the radio station helped remote ranchers communicate. Short wave radios were the norm but only affordable by the big ranchers.

* * *

The sun was setting in a fiery red ball when *Gato* Gaviria's car rolled up to the front steps of the *Ganadero*. Representing the Ballesteros Coffee and Cattle Consortium, he commanded the best room in town and treatment like royalty. Ray Keith appeared not to notice the arrival across the street. He spat out a big gob of tobacco juice that landed with a plop on the brick pavers below. The juicy bomb barely missed the ant he was shooting at.

"Damn," he cursed. "Missed again."

The brown stain joined fifty other splotches the ant had to navigate to reach its objective, a smashed banana Keith had planted in the gutter as bait. He wiped a string of saliva out of his blond-red beard and rubbed the nasty on his dirty threadbare jeans. Years of tobacco use had permanently stained his scraggly sallow beard. Maniacally, he bobbed his head and juked his body to the samba beat of the salsa music blaring from the nearby bar as he nonchalantly watched the big Mercedes pull away from the hotel. On the side of his artificial leg he surreptitiously jotted down the time of Gaviria's arrival at the hotel. With mission complete he leaned back on a large flowerpot to rest his back, dreaming of a cold beer and the little Indian whore he had met just after arriving in the provincial capital of thirty five thousand people.

* * *

The staff of the Ganadero welcomed Gaviria like royalty and showed him directly to his suite. As he passed the second floor of the hotel, he noted the dozing Leopards guarding the iron gates that sealed off the floor from the other hotel guest. It amused him.

Americans. So naive, he thought. *If I wanted to kill you bastardos, I would raise this entire fuckin' hotel while you sleep with your Bolivian whores.*

On the third floor landing he stopped, leaned his hand against the door jam and checked the bottom of his expensive Italian shoes. He snarled at the bellboy as if looking for a piece of gum sticking to the sole of his shoe. There was nothing there. It was only a ruse to cover the movement of his hand. The boy didn't notice the small square piece of tape Gaviria left behind on the door facing. It was a signal for his paid DEA agent to make personal contact. Money talks. Big money shouts.

* * *

Ray Keith had worked for Derek Evans for two years, mostly in a surveillance role, and he had raised the simple assignment to a fine art. Using his disability as a disguise, he could blend into the street scene like a discarded scrap of soiled paper. Keith had lost his leg while on active duty with the SEALs at a time when he was near the pinnacle of his profession. Just before his accident Senior Chief Ray Keith had placed first in the most prestigious pistol contest in the world. He celebrated his achievement by popping off a few caps in the desert near the SEAL Camp at Niland, California and was minding his own business riding his Harley down the back roads of the Imperial Valley when a drunken migrant broadsided him in the dark. The accident ended his career and cost him a leg. The Navy cared for his injuries, fitted him with an artificial leg, and medically discharged him to fate. For a SEAL used to a life of guns, parachutes, and adventure, Ray Keith's discharge was tantamount to a death sentence. When Evans found him, he was soaked in booze and sorrow, and wasting away in a twenty-one foot Air Stream trailer parked near the Salton Sea.

Keith wiped the sweat off his brow, and in keeping with his cantankerous nature, which compelled him to complain about everything, cursed the heat, Bolivia, the ants, and the samba music. In his concentration to bomb the ant and note down the arrival of *Gato* Gaviria, he completely missed the approach of the two men sneaking up behind him. He was cursing the moped drivers buzzing up and down the street when a booming voice assaulted him with a verbal insult.

"Damn, if that ain't the sorriest sight I've ever seen in my life," Boomer Savarese exclaimed. Arms akimbo, he shook his head in disgust when Keith glanced up like a dimwit, grimaced, and pretended to ignore the abuse.

"You think it's a hippie, a doper, or a crazy?" Fred Swan asked with a scowl. He took a pinch of snuff from a round tin he carried in his back pocket and tucked it behind his lower lip.

"Judging by the stench, I'd say it's a broke dick alkie down and out on his luck. But I wouldn't rule out a crazy. Think we should buy him a beer?" Savarese asked.

"I reckon so," Swan replied, scowling at Keith. "He looks like a gringo. Vaguely familiar."

"More like a scorched lizard that's been squashed by a tandem truck," Savarese groused.

"Wasn't it a drunk Mexican, what done the damage?" Swan asked, not expecting an answer.

"I'm packin', I'm packin' *goddamnit!*" Keith growled, referring to the 1911 Colt .45 concealed in his artificial leg. "I don't won't to hear no more about drunk beaners," he snarled with a wild-eyed look.

"Kinda testy, don't you think?" Savarese asked.

"Yeap. Looks like trouble to me," Swan added.

"Are you two yokos through with your compliments on my disguise?" Keith sassed.

"Disguise?" Savarese quipped. "Is that what you call that filthy get-up?"

"You damn straight I do. And it works like a charm, too. A rich feller came by here a couple of hours ago and gave me a whole fist full of money. Look," Keith said, holding up his panhandling cup. "I see it," Savarese chided, looking at the huge wad of Bolivian bills. "I'd say you've got about four dollars U.S. in that cup, Pegleg."

"Maybe less," said Swan. "And with inflation by this time tomorrow it won't be worth two bits."

Inflation was running at more than a thousand percent. The money in Keith's panhandling cup was depreciating by the second.

"Quick! Help me up, damnit. Let's go spend it a'for it's worthless like this whole damn country," Keith exclaimed, staring at the wad of worthless Bolivian money.

"Help yourself up, asshole," Swan snapped. "You got one good leg."

"I got two good legs and the little one's seeing lots a action," Keith smiled, grabbing his crotch.

He showed them his best wild-eyed look, like a crazy Charlie Manson with a long blond ponytail, and spat a gob of tobacco at an ant down in the street.

"*Got that sucker!*" he cried with glee.

"Little one? Your short leg? Boomer, remind me to bring Pegleg a microscope so he can find his dick."

"I was gonna buy you a beer, Popeye, but now I'm gonna spend all my money on my little Injun gal."

"Where did you find her, *La Peña Grande*?" Swan asked, referring to the seediest cathouse in Trinidad.

"Yeah. So what?" Keith growled, as he strapped on his artificial leg.

"If she took up with the likes of you, she sure as hell has to be one desperate little bitch," Swan chuckled. He wiped a tear off his cheek. "You'd better save that money for her."

"Some people are more deserving of my company than others," Keith argued.

Fred Swan had lost an eye while serving with the SEALs during *Desert Stroll*. He covered the injury well with a glass eye but it still teared uncontrollably. He was a handsome man, well proportioned and muscular like an Olympic athlete. Unlike Keith, who wore a long shaggy reddish-blond beard and a ponytail, Fred Swan was clean-cut and clean-shaven. He had a boyish Brian Pitt look about him that attracted women like a magnet. He watched Keith finish strapping on his leg and reached down and pulled him to his feet like a football player helping a teammate up off the turf.

"I'll buy the beer," Savarese said, staring at the facade of the *Hoya Negra*, the Black Hole, a dank little joint set directly across the street from the Ganadero.

Afro-Caribbean music vibrated from the seedy little bar. The samba beat set Keith to gyrating on the boardwalk. Savarese shook his head in disgust then sauntered off through a maze of street side stalls selling everything from papaws to pineapples. Keith shrugged his shoulders and raised his eyebrows. Swan smiled.

"Let's go a'fore he changes his mind. I'm parched," Keith exclaimed.

"After you," Swan said.

He spit out a stream of tobacco juice at one of Keith's ants before following him down the boardwalk toward the bar.

Chapter 21

Ronald Savarese was a big man. As hard as a rock, he was six foot two and two hundred and twenty-five pounds of solid muscle. He had a Sean Connery type face, brutally handsome with keenly intelligent eyes. His physical presences proclaimed he was not the kind of man to lock horns with for any reason. He sported a wide handlebar mustache and a long black ponytail streaked with a hint of gray. Years of operating with the SEALs had earned him a deserved reputation as a brawler and a badger capable of tearing men apart when angered. He had the look of a heavyweight boxer, the eye of a hawk, and the wit of comedian. People naturally stepped out of his way and for good reason.

He worked his way into the dark, smelly little bar, and took a seat where he could see the Ganadero Hotel across the street. With a gnarly expression on his face he ordered up three beers and pointed at three young women who smiled lasciviously. Before Keith could pull up a chair he had picked out the prettiest girl for himself and she was seated on his lap, cleaning the top of his beer bottle with a napkin. He took one look at her voluptuous breasts, barely concealed under a thin summer dress, and put on a grin that stretched from ear to ear.

"*Would you look at the torpedoes on this little bitch, Popeye?*" Savarese grinned, mesmerized by the lovely brown bosoms bulging out the skimpy cotton dress.

"You like?" she asked, with a luscious smile.

"Oh, I like," Savarese grinned, surprised the girl spoke English. "I like a lot," he exclaimed, flipping out a five-dollar bill. "Let's have a little peek," he suggested.

The girl snatched up the fiver in a flash and stuck it up underneath her panties before anyone could see. Then, with both hands, she pulled down the top of her dress exposing the most perfect pair of breasts Savarese had seen in weeks. Her long Indian black hair flowed down over them in a cascade, partially covering one breast. In the dim light she radiated a youthful beauty Savarese couldn't resist. She had small dark nipples that caused his eyes to grow in size and his mouth to fall open in awe. She was no more than twenty years old, and like many of the desperate females in Bolivia, she did whatever it took to survive. Recognizing Savarese as a high rolling America customer, she was out to please.

"*Look at these jugs, man!* Aren't these the most beautiful tits you've ever seen?" he asked, parting her hair for a better look.

Swan smiled and nodded his head in agreement.

Keith snarled and said, "I've seen better humps on a camel."

"I'm in love," Savarese exclaimed, licking his lips. "*I'm in love*."

"That's what you said last time we came to town, and the time before that, and the time before that," Swan groused. He took a big pull on his beer and shook his head. Then, out of the corner of his eye he spotted several of the Ballesteros bodyguards crossing the street. "Hey. Looky what we got here," he said, nodding toward the street.

"Bad company," Keith sizzled, eyeing the men.

Savarese was too busy appraising the young girl's assets to pay any attention to the street scene outside the bar. Three of the men split off and entered the Black Hole. Carlos Cataño spotted Swan and grabbed his brothers by the arm then waved warily at the trio.

Approaching the table he asked, "Hey, *gringo*. What de fouch you doing in Bolivia, meng?"

Savarese, who had never worked with the Cataños, stared at them with a cautious eye. Keith, who had maintained a low profile in Medellin, Colombia, spat a gob of tobacco juice on the floor.

The Colombians were short and pale faced for South Americans, and they dressed narco-style with Guayabera shirts and expensive Italian shoes. They all sported gold chains and expensive watches as status symbols.

"Carlos, Juan, Pablo," Swan said, gesturing with his hand, "this is Boomer, and Pegleg, *mis compadres*. Gentlemen," he said in a formal voice to Keith and Savarese, I present *Señor Araña, Señor Coyote, y Señor Alacrán*."

The Colombians grinned, pleased by the introduction. They enjoyed their sinister reputations. Savarese sneered at them and immediately turned his attention back to the young lady seated on his lap. She was attending to his every need, hoping for a big payday. Keith shook hands with them and went back to his beer.

"*Putas!*" Pablo yelled at the girls at the bar. "*How's 'bout soam fuckeem service! Now!*"

He was a surly individual who was always spoiling for trouble. He pointed at three girls and beckoned them over like dogs.

Keith studied the men from behind his bottle of beer. Carlos was sinewy and hawk-nosed and the large *nevus flammeus* on one side of his face looked like a smashed insect. The poor light in the bar accentuated his craggy, pockmarked face like craters on the moon. Juan was mangy looking like a cur dog, and like his handle indicated, nervous and fidgety. He kept looking from side to side and behind, as if someone was out to back-shoot him. Pablo was greasy and needed a shave. He was just plain ugly mean. When three bargirls reluctantly walked over to the table, Carlos ordered a round of beers and took a seat at the table without an invitation.

"So, meng, what's you fuckeem gringos doin' in this fuckeem shithole, meng?" he pressed, in his thick Colombian accent.

"Looking for women, *Señor Araña*," Swan grinned, eyeing the young lady on his lap.

His companion was frumpish and squat bodied, and she was missing one of her front teeth.

"Fouch you, meng," Juan laughed, slapping the table. "That little *verraca* you're pokin' in Medellin looks a lot better than that bitch, meng. Really, what chew guys doin' down here, meng? You lookin' for dee woman, no?" he suggested, with a knowing eye.

Carlos shook his head at Juan with a menacing expression. Swan understood the insinuation and ignored the question. But Savarese didn't. He didn't like men who bullied women and the Colombians were yanking the bargirls around.

"None of your goddamned business, *hombre*," Savarese bristled like a junkyard dog.

"I don't tink I like dis one, Popeye," Carlos said, shaking his finger in Savarese's direction. "Does this one work for sock ink too?" he asked, intending to use his influence to get Savarese fired.

Swan nodded yes. "So *amigo*, how's target practice, eh?" Swan asked, trying to defuse the engagement.

Try as he might, Swan had been unable to improve the Colombian's shooting technique. They were strictly spray and pray shooters who possessed an unlimited budget for ammunition.

"This is how I target practice, meng," Pablo replied, like a coiled rattler ready to strike.

He held out a beautiful, hand-tooled six-inch switchblade. He pushed the button and a razor sharp shaft of steel flashed into place like magic. Showing a rack of ragged gray teeth in need of a good dentist, he smiled proudly. Pablo Cataño thought the instructors from SOC Inc. were overpaid *gringos* who were out of their element and it showed on his face.

"That's a beaut, *Señor Alacrán*," Swan praised. "A real beaut."

"Pablo has keeled many meng with that knife, *hombre*," Juan volunteered, glaring at Savarese. "That's why we call him de scorpion."

Pablo's wavy black hair was slicked back with a thick coat of brilliantine and it reflected the gloomy light of the bare light bulb above the table. He grinned at Savarese menacingly. Savarese locked eyes with him.

"Go tell someone who gives a fuck," he bellowed, over the sound of the racy salsa music.

Pablo's eyes narrowed as he focused on Savarese like a fighting cock with erect spurs. They stared at each other like two alpha wolves bristling to fight. Swan got their attention.

"By the way, Carlos, what are you guys doing down here?" Swan demanded. "Are you looking for that doctor woman too?" he asked, grinning at him with a knowing eye. "Big reward, huh?"

The three Colombians glanced back and forth at each other and eyed Swan suspiciously for a few seconds. They figured the SEALs were out for the reward on Dr. Galán. The word was out all over South America.

"*No amigos.* We are not looking for anyone. *Señor Don Gaviria* is inspecting de ranch and we go where he goes," Carlos lied.

"I thought your job was to watch Maria Christina?" Swan asked.

"Sometimes *sí*, sometimes *no*. We do what *Señor Gaviria* tells us to do," Carlos explained. "Now he says we inspect the ranch. So, we inspect the ranch."

"The ranch is here in the *Beni*?" Swan asked, trying to control the conversation.

"*Sí.*"

"How big is it, man?" he pressed.

Swan and Decker, the man Evans had stationed in La Paz, had soaked up a lot of suds with Carlos and Juan, and he knew how to handle them. Pablo was another matter. He was always like a hooded cobra. But Swan had never seen him strike. Just talk. SOC Inc. had provided specialized training on a regular basis for more than two years and he understood their bravado.

"As big as a fuckeem country, meng," Carlos exclaimed. "More than a hundred thousand cows."

"*Jesus Christ!*" Keith growled. "That's a lot of hamburger, dude."

"You should not say such a thing, meng," Juan cautioned. "It is not good to use the Lord's name in vain." He crossed himself like a priest.

Keith shrugged his shoulders. 'It's not nice to kill people either, meng," he said in a mocking voice. He chuckled at the paradox and took a sip of his beer.

For an hour they traded beers and stories, with Pablo and Savarese eyeing one another like fighting cocks circling for battle. Swan kept pumping the Colombians for information and Carlos kept pumping the SEALs. After several beers Carlos again asked Swan if they were after the reward on Dr. Galán. Swan continued to play dumb, but by mannerisms told Carlos that they were in Bolivia for the reward money. But no matter how hard he tried to steer the conversation, it always devolved to bragging and brutality. Colombian bodyguards lived a violent life and they enjoyed the machismo that accompanied their stories of violence. Every war story Pablo told, Juan reinforced with blood and gore. After the fifth round the

Colombians were slurring their words and abusing their female companions, a faux pas Savarese dislike to no end. To Savarese women were a treasure to be loved and cared for. His problem was that he loved them all.

"How many meng you keel, esse?" Pablo asked, slurring his words at Savarese. His chin lifted up like a bullfighter.

Boomer ignored him and whispered in his love interest's ear. She giggled and hugged him, an act that angered the inebriated Colombian because he thought Savarese was making fun of him.

"What did he say?" he yelled at the girl in blistering Colombian Spanish, shaking his finger in anger. "What did that shit-eater say about me?"

The girl shrank deeper into Savarese's huge embrace.

"Put that finger away asshole or I'll break it off and feed it to you," Savarese growled calmly.

"What did you say to her, meng?" he demanded in a drunken fury.

Savarese ignored him.

"I'm talking to you, meng. I've keeled twenty-seven fuckeem peoples, meng," Pablo threatened.

Savarese continued to ignore the henchman, which increased his anger.

"*Es verdad, hombres,*" Juan cautioned. "He keeled deem with de knife, meng."

"You ever see de life of a peoples leave, meng?" Pablo asked in a deadly serious growl.

Savarese continued to ignore him. Enraged, Pablo's eyes bugged out and his face contorted. He hated *gringos* and he had taken an instant dislike to Savarese. He slammed a knotted fist down of the table and stared at Savarese with quivering lips.

"At the time of death, meng, *el tiempo exactamente!* The eye change, meng. You ever see this, *gringo?*" Pablo taunted, staring at Savarese with red eyes.

His knife appeared and he toyed with it, glaring at Savarese. But Savarese just ignored him. He gently kissed the girl on her neck and whispered in her ear. She looked at Pablo and giggled. The insult was more than the Colombian could stand. His lips began to twitch above his ragged teeth.

"I'm talking to you, *comemierda!*" he yelled, slamming his fist down again.

Everyone heard the click as the switchblade locked into place. The flash of steel gleamed in the dim light of the dingy bar. With a mad smile, he slowly toyed with the knife, pointing it at Savarese like a scorpion's stinger.

Boomer smiled. "You know this sound, meng?" he said, mocking the Colombian's accent.

The click of a safety on a 1911 Colt .45 sounded beneath the table. Pablo's eyes widened and he swallowed hard. The metallic click reverberated inside his head.

Slowly Savarese extended his arm until the barrel of the pistol was visible. Then, another click sounded underneath the table as Keith thumbed the safety off his pistol. He smiled manically and spit a stream of tobacco juice on Pablo's knife hand.

"Rule number one, you campesino fuck," Savarese growled like a junkyard dog. "*Never bring a knife to a gunfight!*"

The Colombian sat frozen like a statue. Doubt crossed his face.

"*Comprendes?*" Savarese asked.

Ignoring the knife in Pablo's hand, he jammed the barrel of his pistol into the Colombian's ribs and slowly slid it down his ribcage to leg. Pablo flinched, as the cold steel nudged up against his testicles.

"Go ahead, meng. Cut me," Savarese dared.

With the pistol aimed at Pablo's manhood, Savarese turned his head like a bullfighter ignoring an angry bull. He gently kissed the girl on her neck. When he turned back to face the Colombian, he mocked him.

"Go ahead, *meng*. Cut me." He turned and looked at Juan. "Have you ever seen the eye of a *peoples* with his dick blown off, *meng?*"

Pablo grinned. "Okay, meng, Okay. Okay," he said, with his fake smile. He raised his eyebrows, dropped the knife, and raised both his hands in the air.

"*Okay, my ass!*" Savarese growled.

In a lightning move, the big SEAL lifted the pistol from Pablo's crotch to his chin. With all the power in his body, he struck the Colombian under his jawbone with the top part of the pistol, lifting him completely out of his chair. Pablo sprawled out on the filthy floor knocked cold by the force of the blow.

"*You two!*" he yelled at Carlos and Juan. "Get that asshole out of my sight," he ordered, "or I will shoot his dick off."

Without argument Carlos and Juan dragged their brother outside and disappeared up the street.

"Boomer, that was a bad move, man," Swan said, shaking his head. "A real bad move. We gotta get out of town, now. Drink up, we're going back to the ranch."

"Tomorrow. I have some unfinished business with my little friend here."

The girl was still in shock from the turn of events.

"*No!*" Swan snapped.

During their military careers, Savarese had always out ranked Swan. But Swan had tenure with SOC Inc. and Savarese read his eyes loud and clear.

"Roger, little buddy. I roger that. Ambush, huh? You think the three *amigos* will sic *la policia* on us?"

"That is the least they will do, dude. Backing him down was enough. *Sicarios* understand that kind of shit. But not knocking his ass out in front of a bunch of whores. He'll be looking for blood when he wakes up," Swan answered.

"Why hell, I should have killed him," Savarese replied.

"Let's mosey over to the Cafe *Beni*," Keith suggested. "It's a DEA hangout. No one will bother us there. On the way I'll ask Mr. Tineo to radio the ranch for a plane."

"Good idea," a Swan greed. "But I suppose you'll want us to buy dinner?" Swan asked.

"Yeap," Keith grinned. "A big juicy steak."

"I'm sick of steak. That's all we been eatin' out on the Didgerido," Savarese complained, referring to the Aussie's ranch.

"Boomer, you're startin' to sound like Pegleg. No one in his right mind complains about eatin' steak, man," Swan said.

"*I ain't eatin' steak!*" Keith blurted. "I been eatin' beans and tortillas. Why do you guys always get the cush jobs?"

"Cush jobs, my ass. You've been eatin' beans and tortillas and a little Indian princess while we been gettin' saddle sore, asshole," Savarese snarled, jealous of Keith's city assignment.

"Let's go," Swan ordered. "You two can finish this argument somewhere else."

Swan and Keith guzzled down the last of their beers while Savarese said good-bye to his lovely. Before leaving the Black Hole Savarese gave his new friend a twenty-dollar bill, big bucks for a little peek.

They cautiously left the bar like a platoon of SEALs on patrol and walked down mainstreet. The Cafe *Beni*, a saloon off the central plaza, was the rancher's in-town watering hole. It was located near the Cattlemen's Association and on the way Keith ducked into the office to relay a shortwave message to the Aussie requesting a lift.

Chapter 22

There were horses tied to a hitching post outside the Cafe *Beni* and old jeeps parked here and there. The Seals entered in separately with Keith Ray acting as rear security. Inside, the air was smoky despite the fifteen-foot high ceiling and the long bladed fan that slowly cut through the haze. Ranchers in Texas-style boots crowded around a dozen tables, swapping lies and making deals. The trio took a table near the window where they could watch the street.

Several DEA agents were eating at a nearby table and one of them recognized Savarese. He gave the burly SEAL a knowing nod and continued to eat his meal without verbal contact. After the men ordered steak and beer from a hawk-nosed waiter, Savarese got up to use the bathroom. The agent followed inconspicuously. Boomer was standing at the trough urinating when the DEA man walked up and stood beside him. Savarese let loose of his penis, wiped his hand on his shirt and held it out. The agent stared at his paw and shook his head.

"Aguillar," Savares said, in his best fake Mexican accent, "it's just a little piss, man. Not aids."

The frowned.

"What the hell are you doing down here, Boomer?" he asked.

"Well I ain't choking my chicken, Jose," Savarese answered noncommittally.

"That I can believe," Aguillar replied.

He was a borderlands Texan serving a tour in the *Beni*. Aguillar had met Savarese while working out of Brownsville, Texas, when Savarese was serving with a special action unit stationed out of the Panama Canal Zone. They had collaborated on an operation and afterwards gone out drinking and womanizing.

"So how's business, *Señor Aguillar*?" Savarese asked, shaking his penis with great vigor.

There was something about Aguillar Savarese didn't like but he was a fellow warrior fighting in a just cause so he tolerated him. Savarese didn't particularly like any of the other services from the Army to the FBI. The DEA ranked low in his book, just above the BATF.

Aguillar looked over his shoulder before answering. "This is a hot area, Boomer. Real hot. Almost all the cocaine that leaves Bolivia passes through this province."

"I didn't know that, dipstick," Savarese mouthed-off, derisively.

"Screw you, Boomer."

"Not a chance." Savarese grinned, then his face turned serious. "How are they

184

movin' the product, Jose? Goat, llama, boat?"

"Why are you asking me, hotshot? I thought you had the answers," the agent sassed.

"I don't have all the answers, buddy. But I got a solution." He patted the pistol concealed beneath his shirt, then formed his hand into the shape of a pistol and sighted down his finger at the agent's face.

Aguillar looked at him and raised one eyebrow. "How about all of the above. There are hundreds of airstrips scattered all over the province, scores of rivers and thousands of boats. The police and the military look the other way to put it charitably."

"Why don't you shoot some of the bastards?" Savarese suggested, as he looked the agent in the eye without blinking. "It messes up their game plan, you know."

The agent misread the expression. He wanted to know if Savarese was part of the covert action unit working the Andean chain. He misread Savarese's look to mean he was active in the cause.

"That's your job, Boomer," Aguillar said. "I'm strictly into intel, man." He glanced over his shoulder again. "You guys have sure put the fear of God in the pilots who fly the Andean route."

Savarese studied the man's face but made no comment. The boat unit he had served with out of the Canal Zone was known for its lethality. A similar air unit was working the Andes. Hundreds of aircraft had simply disappeared into the jungle, forcing the traffickers to use other means of transport to move their product north. The agent wrongly assumed Savarese was a part of the covert mission.

"What is your mission, Jose?" Savarese asked, turning deadly serious.

"I'm just an ear and an eye. I watch the bankers and businessmen flying in and out of Trinidad. They are not all into buying cattle, buddy. Some come up here with suitcases stuffed full of pesos to exchange for coca dollars. They can buy greenbacks for ten percent less here then in La Paz. This province is bursting at the seams with greenbacks."

"Is the cattle business purely decoration?" Savarese asked.

"For the most part. There are a few legit ranches. But for every one on the square there are twenty that provide cover for dopers."

"How 'bout the Aussie? He legit?" Savarese asked.

"I think so."

"And the Ballesteros?"

"Clean, as far as I can tell."

"Are we slowing down the traffic, Jose?"

"Hell, yeah," the agent replied. "These people don't give a shit about the law, man. All they understand is brute force. Keep knocking them down."

"How about you? Making any progress?"

"All I do is process info and pass it to you guys." Aguillar tossed his head back in a manner that annoyed Savarese. "You'd be surprised at the people who talk to me in private; women who are pissed off at their dope-dealing boyfriends, dealers who squeal on their rivals, all kinds of shitheads. The word on the street, man, is that you guys are putting the fear of God in the pilots. They can't get anyone to fly the birds."

Savarese had him hooked and he knew it. He pressed for more information.

"Is your unit making any arrests?" he asked.

"No. We don't do that kind of shit anymore, man. Too dangerous. Can't get clearance. Always some excuse. You know the deal. I make myself available to anybody who wants to talk and I've got a big budget for bullshit. I'm strictly mining for information that's not available to SIGINT or COMINT."

SIGINT and COMINT were short-talk for signal and communications intelligence information gathered by electronic means.

"You bring in some fast boats?" Aguillar asked, pumping Savarese for information.

There was a special unit working the Andes that coordinated radar, satellite, and other means of tracking aircraft, and there was a covert action unit shooting first and asking questions later. But it was Peruvian. So many of the trafficker's planes had been shot down that they had taken to the hundreds of rivers that drained the Andes. The boat the agent had seen off Brownsville, Texas was a state of the art stealth craft and he wrongly assumed Savarese was in South America as part of a covert action unit sent to address the changing tide in narcotics trafficking. Savarese knew he was leading the agent on and he wasn't about to give away his game face.

"Hey, Jose. I retired, man," he said in a joking manner.

"I ain't buying that shit, man." He looked at Savarese not believing him. He studied the Seal's face for clues. "What are you doing in this shithole?"

"Looking for a woman, dude."

Aguillar recalled the reward for Dr. Galán. "The scientist?" he asked.

"Why not? Pay's good. Heard anything?" Savarese probed.

"Only that she got a big price on her head."

"How about lead, Jose?" Savarese pressed. "I need the money to pay my alimony. The eagle doesn't shit enough for me, man."

"Me either. Are you really a goddamned bounty hunter or is that just another bullshit cover story?" Aguillar asked.

"I'll can't tell you or I'd have to kill you, man." Savarese grinned.

"So what is the latest scoop on the doc?" asked Savarese.

"Like I told you, man. I haven't heard shit, not so much as a whisper that the bitch is even in Bolivia. All I know is, she's got a big price on her head, dead or alive, depending on who's paying the bill."

"I only accept shekels from my uncle, *brother,*" Savarese volunteered.

"Me too," mumbled the agent.

"I'm strictly a salary stiff but if I could pick up a little coin on the side, I'd give up my day job."

"I'll tell you what I'll do. If I hear anything I'll pass it along, fifty-fifty if you get her off my tip."

"Fair enough," Savarese agreed.

"Where can I find you, man?" Aguillar asked.

"Through the Aussie.

Aguillar chucked. "I knew it. You got any stealth planes out there? Any of those odd looking boats you had up around Brownsville?"

"How do you think I got down here, shit for brains?" Savarese gestured with his palms, leading the agent on. "Gotta go, *amigo,*" he said, turning to leave. He sauntered out of the latrine and back to his table.

"What'd you do in there," Keith asked. "Fall in the crapper? You guys have to skedaddle, man. The plane is gonna be here any minute."

"He's soaked us for a beer and a steak, and now he wants to make it with his little Injun whore while we cool our heels in the middle of the jungle," Swan chided.

Keith grinned. "I'll bet I'm gettin' more and better'n you."

"Ahhhh," Savarese growled like an angry dog. "I ain't taking that bet cause I ain't getting' any, thanks to your Colombian friends."

"I know you Boomer Savarese. You'd better stay away from Guillermo's daughter," Swan warned. "Tangling with that *hombre* would be like wrestling a forty-foot anaconda."

Swan got up and threw some bills on the table. As they headed out the door Keith spotted the local police and eased back into the restaurant out of sight. Smelling trouble, he moseyed up to the bar and ordered a beer while watching the exchange through the window. The fat *alcalde,* dressed in a dirty khaki uniform, approached Savarese and began questioning him politely. He wore his hat too far back on his head. Above his belt, his swollen belly was showing through his shirt like a huge ball of protruding blubber. Keith couldn't make out the conversation but by the look on Savarese's face the situation was not good. When they headed for the police station, he followed at a cautious distance.

Keith hobbled down the street, around the block, and worked his way near an open window in the ram shacked police station. From his concealment, he saw the

Colombians across the street chatting. They were grinning. Pablo said something to his brothers and they all headed down the street toward the Ganadero.

Inside, Keith saw Swan and Savarese sitting quietly on a bench being interrogated by the *alcalde*. At first, Savarese pretended to speak poor Spanish. His sudden lack of understanding of the language angered the fat policeman. Then, Swan offered the customary bribe. The man was deathly afraid of the Colombians and he had already taken a bribe from them to rough up Savarese. But upon seeing the size of the Americans, he had changed his mind. They looked like more trouble than the bribe was worth. Under guard by two men with rifles, he had a third man search them. Straight away the trooper discovered the Seal's pistols which set off alarm bells. When Swan produced a valid permit, he refused to accept it, smelling a large bribe. Then, he made a huge mistake. He pointed one of the pistols at Savarese and accused him of being a trafficker. He was just about ready to suggest the terms of a settlement when Savarese attacked.

"*You fucking swine!*" he cut loose in perfect Spanish. "*If you point that gun at me again, I'll stick it up your fat ass!*"

The brazenness of the verbal assault surprised the corrupt sheriff, but he pressed his advantage.

"*Señor Traficante*, I am placing you under arrest for narcotics possession," he said, gesturing at a plastic baggy of marijuana one of his troopers produced from behind Savarese.

"So that's your game, *hombre*. A frame. That's the best you can do?"

Savarese walked closer to the short fat man. When the pistol was two feet from his face, he glanced back over his shoulder at Swan, taking measure of the four men standing around them. In a blur he parried the pistol and twisted it out of the *alcalde's* hand. Like cat in motion, he stepped back and planted a horse kick into the chest of one of the guards. The force of the kick lifted the small Bolivian two feet in the air and sent him crashing against the wall. Using the impact of the kick as counter force, he spun around and smashed another guard in the face with a right back fist. Both were rendered unconscious in two heartbeats. As Savarese jammed the pistol in the fat cop's face, Fred Swan took the other guard out with one quick right cross to the chin.

"Alright, *amigo*. How much do you want?" Savarese snarled like a madman.

"*Nada! Señor. Nada!*" the surprised policeman croaked.

Savarese holstered his pistol under his shirt and dug into his jean pocket. He pulled out a wad of bills and peeled off two U.S. fifties buried inside.

"How's this?" he asked.

Without protest the *alcalde* took the money and stuck it in his pocket.

"Have your teeth fixed, *amigo*," Savarese suggested, as he gave him another two bills.

He turned to Swan. "Let's go, Popeye. Poncho, here has made a small fortune tonight."

"Right behind you, partner," Swan said, as he grabbed for his pistol.

At the door Savarese stopped and turned to face the corrupt policeman.

"Don't ever fuck with me again, *hombre*. His face contorted and his cheeks quivered in an animal act, as his focused on the man like lasers. "I'll kill your wife. I'll kill your kids," he growled like a junkyard dog. "I'll kill your whole damn family while you watch. I'll even kill your fuckin' dog. Then I'll kill you. *Comprendes*?"

Sí, Señor Savaresi!" the cop gushed. "*Entendido perfecto!*"

He was happy with the deal. Two hundred U.S. dollars was more than he made three months.

Chapter 23

The Casa transport banked sharply and swooped down for a landing on John Blackthorn's two hundred thousand-acre spread. Evans scanned the tawny lion-brown expanse of grassland five hundred feet below. Ostrich like birds, called ebuses, scurried into the undergrowth alongside a small river flowing down from the emerald green highlands of the *Chaparé*. Masure awoke from his nap and yawned as they flew low over cattle pens, silos, and hangars, and by the mud-brick houses of ranch hands. A small cluster of cattle grazing peaceably near the dirt airstrip stampeded helter-skelter as they skimmed close to the ground to check the condition of the runway. At the end of the field gray-feathered rheas strutted nervously in large flocks as aircraft powered up and circled back.

The pilot set the plane down gently on the bumpy dirt strip and in a swirl of dust taxied up to a large hangar containing several small aircraft and four ancient cargo planes. Wrecked DC-6s, cannibalized for parts, littered the area around the hangar.

Most of the large ranchers in the *Beni* left their holdings in the hands of managers and maintained households in La Paz, Surce, or Santa Cruz. But not the Aussie. He lived and worked his land with a passion. John Blackthorne was a Bolivian born citizen but his roots were on the other side of the world. In the 1930's, his father had moved to South America to get away from the long arm of Australian law. He chose the *Beni* because of its remoteness and purchased a huge track of land that lay up next to the rain forest. Fearing extradition he spent the rest of his years living on his ill-gotten property. His bones were buried on a hill overlooking the enormous ranch he had named the Didgeridoo after an aboriginal musical instrument. The inscription on his tombstone read, *"Here rests John Alvin Clarke, a bold and adventuresome rogue, who saw a chance and took it."*

Old man Clarke, alias John Blackthorne, had bought the land for pennies on the acre. In his day the land was considered useless because it was so isolated there was no way to get product to market. Cut off by highland jungle to the south, the Andes to the East, and the Amazon to the north and west, there was no way to get beef to market. To make ends meet, he had butchered his cattle for their hides and let the meat rot in the fields. Over the years he had improved the ranch and the breed of cattle that fed there. But during his lifetime the ranch had not paid a return on his investment. That was left to his son, John Junior.

Educated in Sidney as a veterinarian, John Junior was Bolivian by birth and Australian by nature and mannerism. He was a short, squat, gnomish little man with beady eyes and a cockney pointed noise. He spoke English with an Aussie accent and Spanish like his Bolivian mother. In constant motion his nervous energy had turned the Didgeridoo into one of the finest and most profitable ranches in all of South America. And he had done it honestly without coca dollars. The keys to his success were surplus WW II aircraft he used as cargo planes to fly his beef to market. Without pressured cabins they wheezed their way through high-mountain passes to reach tin miners in the Andes and the markets of La Paz, Potosi, and Surce. Blackthorne even fed the gold miners of Brazil, flying his meat to market over vast tracks of impenetrable jungle.

Evans dismounted the plane just as John Blackthorne barreled up in a cloud of red dust. He jammed on the brakes of a salvaged WW II jeep and screeched to a halt ten feet from the fuselage of the Casa. Beaming a smile he tipped back his Indiana-Jones hat and gave Evans a backhanded saluted like an Aussie soldier. He bounded out of the jeep like a young man and rushed over to Evans as if greeting a long lost son.

"*Hey, mate!*" he yelled, shaking Evans's hand enthusiastically. Then he hugged him and slapped him on the back. "Just in time for dinner." He looked at Masure and asked, "Who's the new bloke? Another one of your merry men?"

"Just a stray dog I picked up in Bogotá," Evans replied.

Blackthorne grabbed Masure's hand and squeezed it like a vice. For an old guy he had the grip of a prizefighter.

"Any bloke that's a friend of the Commander's is a friend of mine," he said to Masure. "Welcome to the Didgeridoo." Then he turned back to Evans and said, "Let's get on up to the shack. Maria's got some sort of lizard cookin' on the barbie. When she heard you were in bound she nearly had a hissy fit."

Masure's eyes sharpened at the word lizard.

With Blackthorne at the wheel, they rumbled off with the old jeep smoking and coughing in protest. Over the sound of the groaning engine, Blackthorne told Evans about the altercation in Trinidad. "I had to send a plane for Boomer and Popeye last night," he said

"Oh?" Evans frowned. "Why?"

"It seems there was a bit of a little fracas in town. Boomer whipped up on some Colombian in the Black Hole and *la policia* got involved."

"Colombians? In Trinidad?" Evans grunted, displeased by the news.

His thoughts immediately focused on *Gato* Gaviria's men. He knew they would be hot on his trail. But he was surprised that they were already in Bolivia.

"Swan said it was one of the blokes he's been training up in Colombia. Boomer whacked this dingo in the Black Hole, and later, whipped up on the police. Do you remember that fat policeman I introduced you to a couple of years ago outside the

Ganadero? The one I told you makes his living shaking down strangers?"

"Savarese roughed up that butter ball?" Evans asked, incredulously.

"No. But he beat up some of his boys and paid a healthy stipend for the pleasure. I'll patch up things with the *alcalde*, but it'd be a good idea if he stayed out of Trinidad for a while."

"John, I appreciate your help, and I'll pay for the extra fuel," Evans said, referring to the cost of flying an airplane to and from Trinidad.

"You most certainly will not," Blackthorne scolded. "You're damn welcome, Derek Evans, and it's me who should be thanking you," Blackthorne argued, insulted by the offer.

Blackthorne wheeled the jeep through a gate that fenced in the runway and gunned the engine. It backfired several times. Bucking like a bronco, it lurched up a dirt road that led toward a red tiled mansion set high on a knoll. After he had run through the gears and the vehicle was back up to speed, he focused his beady little eyes on Evans.

"It's me who owes you, Commander. You should see Maria's face when she opens up your care packages. That's thanks enough for me. She treasures the magazines you send her and she worships the videos, especially them damned musicals." He frowned and shook his head with a guilty look on his face. "She gets so desperate for company out here."

Maria Blackthorne couldn't have children of her own so she collected orphans from all over Bolivia. The Blackthorne ranch was actually full of children of all ages and lots of ranch hands, but there was no town life, no TV, no church and the nearest neighbors were almost a hundred miles away.

"Yeap. I can't tell you how much we enjoy your company," Blackthorne continued. "Always excitement when the SEALs come to the Didgeridoo."

A flock of rheas ran from the fence line, frightened by the noise of the engine backfiring as Blackthorne downshifted to take on a steep hill. Evans hung on to his seat as the jeep bounced over a nasty bump at thirty miles per hour and went airborne for a few seconds. He looked back to see if Masure was still on board. With wide-eyes Masure glared at him and shook his head, showing his dislike for the mad hatter's ride.

"Have you seen Professor Contreras lately?" Evans yelled, over the sound of the straining engine.

"She was down to visit Maria about three weeks ago, just before Swan and Savarese arrived. She comes to visit quite regular. Two or three times a year. She's been like one of the family since you brought her down here."

Evans mind was working overtime.

"Any sign of Dr. Galán?" Evans pressed, hoping for good news.

192

"None. And I offered a handsome reward for information that might help you." Blackthorne glanced over at Evans with his beady little eyes. "I hate to tell you this, son, but I don't think she's down here. If she was, it's likely I'd know by now."

"If you don't mind, John, I'll stay on a few weeks and search for her myself. I want to visit the places I took her during the plant gathering expeditions."

"Hell, I don't mind if you stay on permanently. You know that. Stay as long as you want. Your mates too. They have been busy *hombres* when not molesting the police in Trinidad," he chuckled. "That Swan is one smart rascal. He's covered the area like a blanket for the last two weeks. And Boomer, the man missed his calling. He should have been a comedian. He keeps us in stitches around the supper table."

Since his assignment in Bolivia, Evans had maintained contact with the Blackthorns. He periodically sent magazines, books, and movies to Maria and tools to John. He even sent the old man special weapons and ammunition. Evans had met them at the Sopocachi Hotel in La Paz during his six-month tour of duty at *Chimoré*. Depressed from teaching tactics to corrupt UMOPAR soldiers, he had gone to La Paz to recharge his batteries. At breakfast one morning he had met the Blackthorns and they had invited him to their ranch. With nothing better to do he took them up on the offer and made lifelong friends during the visit.

Blackthorne stepped on the brakes and stopped the jeep with a screech in front of a huge two-story mansion that looked like a plantation manner from the Old South. It was framed like a picture by a deep green jungle rising up into the mountains to the south. To the north it overlooked the vast savannah grassland of the *Beni*.

Blackthorne led them through the house. Airy in construction, to take advantage of the long hours of sun during the dry season, the house had high ceiling fans, hanging down from huge wooden beams. The floors were laid in the finest Brazilian tile and the furniture was heavy and rustic like the pioneer days of the Old West. Huge luxurious tropical plants decorated the open spaces, reaching up for the light beaming in from skylights fifty feet above. He led them to the back courtyard constructed around a crystal clear swimming pool.

"Maria," he yelled, from the far end of the pool. "Look what the dingos drug in."

A plump, overweight woman in her mid sixties smiled broadly when she saw Evans and rushed over to kiss him like a long lost son. Like her husband, she was not an attractive person to look at, but the warmth of her smile and twinkle in her eye told Masure she was good people. She was squat-bodied and high cheek-boned like the Indians of the region but she had a hint of Spaniard in her eye, a gift from a long dead conquistador. Before introductions were through Masure had a cold beer in one hand and fist full of jerky in the other. She coddled over Evans for ten minutes while offering him everything from a beer to watermelon.

"Fred and Ron are out exploring the jungle, but they'll be back for dinner. We're having *surubi*," she said, eyeing Evans like a mother.

Surubi was a local catfish known for its delicate white meat. Evans loved the flavor and she knew it.

"Maria, you sure know how to make a man feel welcome," Evans complimented.

"Boomer is sick of steak, so Juanita is preparing some of her specialties. We're having barbecued rhea tomorrow," she continued.

"As long as it's not capybara, I'll eat it," Evans grinned, referring to the largest rodent in South America.

Capybara meat was known for its foul taste.

Evans reached into the bottom of his bag and pulled out a stack of magazines that weren't available in South America. Her eyes opened wide in awe and she hugged him like a mother receiving a present from a prodigal son. It was obvious she was delighted to have guests and Masure soon relaxed in a lounge chair, feeling at home in a castle in the middle of nowhere, unsure if it was lizard jerky or beef he was chewing on.

The Blackthorns were cut off from the world. That was the way of the *Beni*. The distance between ranches was so great social life was non-existent. Without roads or TV, their primary source of news was the shortwave radio, BBC's Spanish language broadcasts, and newspapers flown in from La Paz. Both John and Maria were starved for company and the conversation around the pool jumped from politics to movies to social problems with as much direction as a Mexican jumping bean. The old couple asked endless questions about the world outside Bolivia. Just before dinner, Swan and Savarese joined them, saddle sore from an excursion into the *Chaparé*.

"Hi, Boss," Swan reported, as he walked up with a swagger.

"How's your hammer hanging, Commander?" Savarese asked, shaking Evans's hand vigorously. He raised his eyebrows and hung his head down when he saw that Maria was present. He took one long look at Masure and glanced back at Evans. "I see you're collecting white trash again." Savarese looked at Masure and raised one eyebrow in a curious expression. "What are you doing down here, Stick? The Navy finally see the light and kick your sorry butt out?" he asked, extending his hand. While shaking Masure's hand he turned to Maria Blackthorne. "Maria, with this guy around, we'll have to put an armed guard on every eligible female for a hundred miles."

She eyed Savarese with a grin and looked at Masure. "I can see why, too," she
194

smiled.

"I volunteer for the security detail," Savarese continued.

She eyed Masure with a motherly expression and turned on Savarese.

"Boomer, you don't fool me one bit. You're the anaconda in my chicken coop," she said, shaking her finger at him. "But you don't have to worry about me and John. We're enlightened. It's Guillermo you'd better be careful of," she warned. "You go fooling around with one of his daughters and you'll be married or he'll have a machete after you."

Guillermo was Blackthorn's foreman and he had several daughters who had been making eyes at both Swan and Savarese.

Savarese gulped hard. "No ma'am. I don't have any ambitions of that nature," he exclaimed. "I'd rather fight that fat *alcalde* in Trinidad, and all his men at the same time, than tangle with Guillermo and his machete."

Evans chuckled and winked at Savarese. "She's got your number big guy. You best keep a low profile, here and in town."

"But Boss, you can't be good, if you're not bad once in a while," Savarese objected.

He rolled his tongue around inside his jaw salaciously on the side Maria couldn't see.

Over dinner the men learned the history of the Didgeridoo and the business of cattle ranching in the *Beni*. Blackthorne had crossed the humpbacked zebu with the local criollo cattle to produce a mestizo that was more productive. The criollo had good flavor but it took five years to fatten for slaughter and produced less meat than the zebu. The crossbreeding resulted in a hardy strain that was bigger and ready for market within three years. Blackthorn's problem was in getting the product to market.

Later, over coffee and cognac in the living room, they talked of piranhas, revolutions, and ranching.

"It's the cost of fuel that cuts into my profits, Derek," Blackthorne said. "Someday a highway will be built to La Paz, and maybe a paved road to Santa Cruz, and on to Argentina and Brazil. Then the *Beni* will be another Texas. I could double, triple, even quadruple the size of my herd if I could only get the meat to market by road all year round. That day has to come, boys. But until it does, I have my old World War Two cargo planes to depend on."

"Why can't you just truck your cattle to market over the dirt roads, Mr. Blackthorne?" Masure asked.

"Stick, in a few weeks when the rains come, half the *Beni* will be underwater for months. You might have noticed that all the roads leading out of Trinidad are built up on dikes. If the town wasn't surrounded by levies the whole place would be underwater for three months of the year."

"Masure hasn't been to Trinidad, John," Evans explained. "And after the trouble we've had in town I don't think any of us should go there for a while." He looked at Masure and back at Blackthorne. "John, Masure needs to get on back to Colombia soon. You think he could catch a hop to La Paz on one of your meat runs?"

"You bet. If he can stand the smell of aged beef," Blackthorne said, puffing on his cigar. "I got a run going out in the morning."

"Stick, you best be movin' on," Evans said.

"Yes, sir," he agreed.

"You'll be riding with the best beef in all of South America, son. Free ranged cattle on prime land," Blackthorne bragged proudly. He swirled his cognac and took a sip.

"One thing is for certain. Those hamburger factories will never eat all the grass in this country," Savarese commented.

"There's plenty of fodder to feed 'em, boys" Blackthorne agreed. "Plenty."

"This land doesn't need much investment, does it?" Swan asked. "I mean, a network of paved roads would open this country up like a ripe melon."

"That's right and now is the time to invest if you're of the mind, Fred. You can buy prime land for next to nothing," Blackthorne advised. "You know what they say over on the Brazilian coast, don't you?

"No."

"Go west, young man. Go west."

Swan shook his head no. "It's the stability of the government that bothers me, sir. Seems like a mighty risky investment."

"Yeah," Masure added, "not to mention the dopers."

"And don't forget the outlaws. A fellah could get gut-stuck just lookin' at a pair of jugs," Savarese interjected.

"Paved roads would drive the cocaine traffickers off, boys, and bring in more investment," Blackthorne argued. "The sad truth is without roads there is no stimulus for a rancher to improve the quality of his meat. A filet mignon from a tender calf sells for the same price as a tough steak from a ten-year old steer. The tin miners don't much care as long as they eat."

"This is the most productive land I have seen in this country," Swan said. "You'd think the government would be quick to develop the area. In comparison, the Altiplano is a cold windswept desert."

"The damn government has done absolutely nothing for this province," Blackthorne complained vehemently. "And the reason is plain and simple. Corruption. They wouldn't give an honest rancher one peso toward the purchase of an airplane to deliver his product. For more than ten years they have promised us a paved highway to La Paz. You know where that project is today? It's gathering dust in some government filing cabinet. There is not one kilometer of asphalt road in the whole of the *Beni*. If we had to depend on the damned Bolivian government this province would look exactly like it did two hundred years ago when we threw the Jesuits out. Now the cocaine business, that's another story, boys. It competes with ranching up here and it gets lots of government help."

"How's that, Mr. Blackthorne?" Swan asked. "It's hard to believe the Bolivian government would knowingly help narcotics traffickers."

"Why?" Blackthorne said, emphatically. "They know who the big traffickers are. They turn a blind eye for a piece of the action. Money, boys, money. That's what talks in Bolivian politics. They don't want this land to be developed. You take Suarez for example. Old Nicolas created something to be proud of. He controlled the rubber business until the Brits stole some of his trees and set up plantations in Ceylon and Malaysia. Then, your scientists figured out how to make synthetic rubber and that put the natural rubber farmers slam-damn out of business. But even after the rubber market collapsed the Suarez name was a name to be respected in these parts. They had huge ranches that operated at a profit. Then his grandson, Roberto, that handsome high rolling bastard got control. He sported about with the likes of Frank Sinatra and the high rollers of Bolivian politics, and destroyed his family's name. He pretended to be a cattle rancher, but his real business was narcotics. He made so much money he was about to buy the presidency when some of your boys exposed him. He'd bought off nearly every official in the Bolivian government by the time he was arrested. It was only pressure, the threat cutting off U.S. aid that finally brought him to justice."

"The lure of easy money is hard to resist, even for a family like the Suarez's," Evans interjected. He took a swig of his cognac and tried to explain the situation in historical terms. "In the nineteen eighties, when cocaine prices boomed in the U.S., ranchers of this region came under tremendous pressure. Some had their ranches taken over at gunpoint. Others, willingly started trafficking for the huge profits that could be made overnight. Most just tried to survive. John here, would have none of it. He fought off the traffickers and the government, and he won."

"I came by this land by ill-gotten money, rest my father's soul," Blackthorne confessed. "The least I can do is to give a little back to society. For as long as I live the Didgeridoo will turn a legal profit and provide people with a decent product at a fair price."

"What happened to Suarez?" Swan asked, inquisitively.

"He's in jail in La Paz, if you can call living in a penthouse with his family jail. The last time I saw him he flew on to my ranch unannounced, grabbed a truck from the hangar, and drove up to my front door with two German-speaking bodyguards. I hardly recognized him he was so emaciated from drugs. He said he felt bad that he owed me money and he opened up a large suitcase filled with American greenbacks. I said, 'Roberto, this is some kind of mistake. You don't owe me any money. I never lent you any money.' Then, he told me it would be a good idea if I accepted the money and kept my mouth shut when some of his airplanes set down on my property about fifty miles to east of here. I told him I'd keep my mouth shut and that I'd shut his permanently if he didn't get the hell off my land and stay off. Facing the barrel of Guillermo's rifle from the second floor he thought better of the situation and left with his dirty money. And that was that. The next thing I heard he was arrested by Bolivian police down on one of his ranches north of Trinidad."

"Speaking of ranches, Mr. Blackthorne, do you know what they call a cow that doesn't have any legs?" Savarese asked.

"No, Boomer," Blackthorne said, humoring him.

"Ground beef. Get it?" he chuckled

The SEALs shook their heads in disgust but Blackthorne thought it was funny.

"Seriously gents, from a Bolivian point of view the war on drugs is a joke," Blackthorne said. "It's some sort of choreographed funny-show designed to impress U.S. politicians and the news media. The object of the game is simple; keep U.S. aid money flowing while taking bribes from the drug barons."

"To my understanding," Masure said, "the Colombians get the lion's share of the profits."

"That's true, Stick," Evans said. "But Bolivian drug dealers still make several billion dollars a year from the coca crop and that's more than the entire value of the country's legal exports. That kind of money corrupts all but a handful of people, and you gentlemen, are drinkin' with one of the few incorruptible men in this whole damned country."

"Then let's have a little toast," Swan suggested. He held up his glass and said, "John Alvin Clarke, a bold and adventuresome rogue, who saw a chance and took it."

"Here here!" replied the gallery.

Savarese took a gulp and said, "To men of honor, women with gorgeous tits, and understanding fathers."

"I'll drink to that, Boomer" Blackthorne chuckled. "But I wouldn't get your hopes up that Guillermo is one of those understanding fathers."

Savarese gulped. There was no way to keep a secret on an isolated ranch in the *Beni.*

"Boss, how's about I mosey on up to Colombia with Masure?" Savarese asked sheepishly.

Evans smiled. "Nope. We're going horseback riding in the jungle, partner. First thing in the morning."

Chapter 24

Gato Gaviria showered and shaved before meeting several officials of the provincial capital of Trinidad. After greasing a few palms and extending Don Ballesteros's best regards, he returned to the Ganadero Hotel and gravitated to the roof top terrace for a beer. With drink in hand he strolled around the rooftop pool and gazed out over the city. Unspoiled by department stores or high rises, there were no tall building to spoil the view. At the edge of town the lights ended abruptly in a huge black empty expanse of savannah and jungle. Trinidad was an isolated city and the Ganadero was the only classy nightspot for hundreds of miles.

Gaviria eyed several lovely young girls dressed in skin-tight mini-skirts. Only the cream of Bolivia's females frequented the Ganadero. He watched with amusement as the most beautiful women in the province hustled DEA agents of every age, size, and ethnicity, some so unattractive as to be down right ugly. An American, handsome or homely, was a ticket out of poverty. He made eye contact with a beautiful woman no more than twenty years old. She glanced at her American boyfriend who was swilling down a beer, then surreptitiously signaled Gaviria in that seductive Latin way women speak with their eyes. He would receive a visit when she was through pleasing the American agent.

Gaviria bought several drinks for a young woman, who aggressively sought his attention, then excused himself to use the restroom. Using the absence, he entered the *whiskeria* and ordered two more drinks. Standing at the bar, one of the Americans took a special interest in him. The DEA agents job was to make contacts, recruit people, and buy information. He spoke in Spanish with a borderlands Texas accent.

"You remember that secret unit I told you about, the one that operates those special boats out of Panama?" the agent asked, barely moving his lips as he spoke.

"Yes," Gaviria whispered, as he looked down at the bar.

"I saw one of the boat drivers in the Cafe *Beni*. His name is Ronald Savarese. Nickname Boomer. He said he was retired but I don't believe him. Wherever this guy goes, Mr. Gaviria, he fills up body bags."

"What is he doing in Trinidad?" Gaviria asked, without looking at the agent.

"He's probably with that covert action unit that I told you about at our last meeting, the one that's been shooting down airplanes all along the Andean route. Any bird that deviates from flight plan is challenged and if the pilot doesn't comply immediately, bang, he's blasted out of the sky. This guy is one bad dude, Mr. Gaviria."

"You said he drives boats. Now you are telling me he flies airplanes too?" Gaviria asked, suspicious of the information.

"The unit he is in has special boats and airplanes," the agent explained.

Gato immediately thought of the *Flash* and her sister boats. "Does the U.S. Government have special boats in the Amazon?" he asked.

"Perhaps but not like the one he skippered out of Panama. Those vessels operate in international waters. He's probably working as an advance or with their secret air unit, maybe coordinating the deployment of special boats. Covert action units like his don't play by any rules. If they get on to you, you're dead. They'll shoot down your plane, scuttle your boat, blow up your house, kill your wife, your kids, that's the way they operate, *amigo*."

"Don't ever call me *amigo*, Aguillar," Gaviria looked the agent in the eyes for the first time.

"Sure thing, Mr. Gaviria. What ever you say. No problem."

"What about the ranch?" Gaviria whispered, his lips barely moving.

"Still the same. Johnson can't get permission to raid any of the big movers and shakers in the province. All the busts are within easy range of the hueys. He thinks there's shit going down on all the big *fincas*, except for Blackthorn's. By the way, that's where this guy Savarese is staying."

The Ballesteros ranch was beyond the range of the DEA's helicopters.

"*Claro*. And the system? What have you learned about the new system?"

"It's top secret. He keeps it locked up in his room and won't let anyone near it. It's called the *Command and Management System*. It's just a computer that uses special software called Hawkeye. We use digital cameras to take pictures of planes, boats, people, anything of interest. Johnson uses Hawkeye to send the data for analysis, I think to La Paz, and perhaps to Washington. They evaluate the information and sic the dogs on anyone they think is packin' dope, nasty dogs of war like Savarese."

"And the woman?" Gaviria asked.

"Every agent in South America has her picture on his wall. The Company dudes have worked over the border guards and customs. Nothing. Not a squeak. Even this character Savarese asked me for information about her. I doubt the bitch is in South America."

"*Claro*. I will be very, very generous if you help me find her first."

Jose Aguilar's eyes grew in size. He was a GS-11 and government pay was poor even with the special pays and per diem of an overseas assignment. He had grown up in borderlands poverty and had gotten his government job because he was bilingual. His morals and lack of education were not critical factors for employment with the DEA. Taking kickbacks was commonplace in the Latino cultures of South and Central America where most of Aguillar's relatives still lived. Gaviria was already paying him twice what Uncle Sam paid him on the condition that none of the money showed up in his personal lifestyle. Aguillar was careful to cover his extra paycheck. If not, the Cataño brothers would have bleed him dry long ago out behind the Black Hole.

"You got it, Mr. Gaviria. If the bitch is in Bolivia, I'll find out."

Gaviria left his DEA informant at the bar and with two drinks in hand walked back to the rooftop terrace to his lady friend. Carlos was running his mouth as usual and Juan was busy molesting a young girl that looked about fifteen years of age. Pablo was missing. *Gato* didn't know it but Pablo was in his room with a painful jaw and a headache.

They are stupid men, he thought. *Only Carlos shows promise*.

The Cataños had no idea *Gato* had several DEA agents on the payroll, as well as the hotel management, and half of the officials in Trinidad.

Juan is stupid and Pablo is a sexually pervert. All they care about is drinking and bragging. They have no vision. If they weren't kin I would kill them, he thought.

He finished his drink and tried to get Carlos's attention. But he was too engrossed with his lady friend. Finally, he sent the waiter over to his table. Gaviria motion for him to follow, slipped his companion the equivalent of a twenty-dollar bill, and went to his room. A few minutes later Carlos knocked lightly on the door and waited for *Gato* to invite him in.

"Enter," Gaviria ordered, hand on his pistol.

Carlos opened the door, and like the chairman of the board, *Gato* beckoned him over to his desk.

"I want this woman, Carlos," he said, handing the gunman an envelope. "No fuck ups. Understand?" he continued, shaking his finger. "Grab her off the street and take her to the safe house in Cochabamba. Don't let that perverted brother of yours touch her," he threatened, "or I will skin him alive. He can have her when I am finished with her. *Comprendes?*"

"*Sí, Gato. Claro.*"

"Take her directly to the house out behind the hangar and don't let anyone see her. Get word to me by of the cargo flights and I'll send a special plane for you."

Carlos nodded and opened the envelope. He took out several pictures of Rita Contreras. Her address, phone number, and habits were listed neatly on a note card.

"Carlos."

"*Sí, Gato?*"

"Keep this in the family. Use Juan and Pablo but no one else. I'll see to the pilot. After you snatch the woman I want you to go back to Medellin," he said, eyeing his cousin. "I want you to personally keep tabs on the Savajés."

"I'll have to give Risitos something," Carlos said, referring to information.

He knew by the look in Gaviria's eyes that war was close.

"Tell him I'm making a deal with the Russians for a nuclear weapon."

The color drained out of Carlos's face. Gaviria saw the fear in his eyes.

"Ramón will go fouckem crazy, man," Carlos exclaimed. "He thinks Russia is his turf."

"I know that. I want him to go mad with rage."

"But *Gato*."

"Carlos," Gaviria interrupted, "grab Contreras and take her to the ranch. Then I will tell you exactly what I want to do. *Comprendes?*"

"*Sí.*"

"*No te preocupes*. I'll have a hundred *sicarios* backing you up," Gaviria added.

"I am not afraid of Skelator, *Gato*," Carlos bristled, with more bravado than he felt. He lifted his chin defiantly. "But it would be wise to have a few extra men. Risitos is using too much coca. He is paranoid. He gouged out the Punisher's eyes?"

"Oh!"

"*Sí*. Then he cut off his dick and shoved it down his throat."

"Why? Why would he do such a thing?" Gaviria asked, knowing the answer.

"They say he took a contract from another cartel and Ramón wanted to make an example."

Gaviria gestured with an upturned palm.

"You see what I mean, Carlos. Such brutality is very bad for business, *primo*. Very bad. We must eliminate the Savajés before they bring us down."

Carlos smiled. "You want Ramón to go crazy so he will make a mistake? No?"

"*Sí*, Carlos. *Exactamente*. When he rants and raves, we listen, no?"

Carlos smiled remembering the bugs he had planted all over the Savajés holdings.

Gaviria knew his cousin was afraid of the Savajés. He had good reason. He was feeding the Savajés information on order. He was a double agent. Gaviria knew Ramón was planning something big and it included exposing the Ballesteros Cattle and Coffee Consortium. War was imminent.

After Carlos left his room *Gato* began worrying about the submarines. They were the weak link in his transportation system because of their connection to the ships. Airplanes could be ditched, boats could be sunk, dirty cargo could be blamed on bad employees, but specially designed submarines pointed the finger directly at the Consortium.

I've got to sink those damn things before they take us down, he thought.

At two o'clock in the morning there was a faint knock on Gaviria's door. Pistol in hand, he opened it just wide enough to see the girl's lovely face. She scanned the hallway in both directions. When she faced him he pulled her inside and locked the door.

"What have you learned, Marta?" he asked in a whisper.

He stood so close to her she could feel the heat from his breath.

"They have a new thing in Mr. Johnson's rooms. No one is allowed in there," she whispered.

Johnson was the head DEA agent in the *Beni*. Gaviria pulled her closer.

"You have to do better than that, Marta," he mumbled, almost incomprehensible. "Remember, your brother's health."

In the dim light of the room he watched fear cross her face. She toyed with her hair like a little child, then reached out and touched his cheek sweetly. Slowly she stroked his face and put her hand behind his neck. She pulled him closer and kissed his cheek and ear in faint passion, working him like an American DEA agent. To arouse him she pushed her pubis against his leg and with a little tease of her hips humped him. In disgust, Gaviria pushed her back. Again, fear crossed her face. She knew what he was capable of doing but she didn't have any useful information to report.

"He tells me they are having a big problem, *Señor Gaviria*. They have so much information they cannot, how do you say, put it all together. So they give *Señor* Johnson a *computadora* to help him. That's all I know, *Señor*," she pleaded.

"What kind of computer?"

"I don't know, *Señor Gaviria*. I know nothing of such things. He says, Johnson talks to men in La Paz, military men at the American Embassy with it."

Gaviria had been able to listen in on Johnson's conversations outside Trinidad until the wily agent installed a new system that scrambled the information. His best electronics experts hadn't been able to break the code.

"What do they call it?" he asked, already knowing the answer to the question.

"They call it CMS. They make photographs and send them to La Paz."

Gaviria understood immediately. In the parlance of the spy, he was cross-referencing the intelligence. She was describing the digitized system of information transfer Aguillar had told him about. Johnson was feeding key information to the U.S. intelligence system and the military experts in La Paz were processing it. Gaviria imagined a large room at the American Embassy in La Paz filled with intelligence specialists, electronic equipment, and charts of South America. In a flash, he understood why he had been so successful. He shipped beef and coca paste in the same aircraft on routine flight plans. In route, the coca paste was tossed out of the aircraft near processing labs in the Colombian Amazon and the meat was delivered on schedule. Random inspections of his aircraft only turned up slabs of beef. The scent of the meat masked any lingering odor of coca paste from the drug dogs.

It is time to move the processing labs to sea, he thought. *We can process the coca paste into cocaine on board the Don Blás and the Don Blasón.*

In Gaviria's mind the trick to Cocaine Inc. was to stay one step ahead of the Yankees. And intelligence was the key. He felt the girl's closeness and the warmth of her young body. Then, he felt his loins stir.

"His tour is almost over, *Señor Gaviria.*"

"So."

"He's wants to marry me and take me with him," she said, in a soft sultry voice.

"Then marry him. Go where he goes. You will be useful to me as long as he works for the DEA."

"*Sí, Señor Gaviria.* Thank you for your blessings," she murmured quietly.

In the dim light Gaviria stared at her beautiful face. Young and full of life's force, she was almost angelic in appearance. He felt a deep longing in his loins and it was too late to choose a whore. But *Gato* Gaviria would never knowingly have intercourse with a woman who slept with a Yankee DEA agent. He grasped her hands and slowly slid them down his chest to his groin. He put one of her baby soft hands on his hardness and she understood immediately what he wanted. With deftness born of practice she kissed him on his neck and nibbled on his ears. She slowly unzipped his expensive trousers and carefully removed his throbbing organ. Softly stroking him, she kissed his neck and ear, while breathing and moaning in fake passion. She worked him to ecstasy, dropped to her knees, and with tongue and lips, drove him to orgasm.

Chapter 25

In physique and personality *Benianos* are very different from the natives of the Andean highlands. The Indians of La Paz are squat-bodied, with deep brown, almost purple complexions and unsmiling gazes that signals their aloofness from the wealthy, powerful, light-skinned minority descendants of the Spanish. In contrast, *Benianos* are lithe and bronze, garrulous by nature, and prone to easy laughter. They like to dance and sing, especially to the sound of trumpets playing slightly off key. Most are simple people who live a day-to-day existence, hand to mouth.

For many, the DEA agents that worked the area were a source of income and with luck, a U.S. passport out of the country. In terms of income the agents were rich men. Local women, especially those with a pretty face, made a few extra dollars giving Spanish lessons and providing special services, which explained the reason why many of the babies in Trinidad had very light-skinned complexions. During their off hours the agents often visited the Hoya Negra, the brothel across the street from the Ganadero, and when they did the girls went wild with excitement hoping for a big payday. La Hoya Negra was Spanish for Black Hole, a local euphemism for vagina.

Ray Keith, with his hobbling gate, disheveled appearance and earthy manner, made friends easily in Trinidad. He took up residence in the poorest section of town and frequented the local bars and eateries. Like hens in a chicken coop the prostitutes of Trinidad chattered and squabbled, and those that worked the high-class establishments like the Ganadero knew those that hustled the working class brothels like the Black Hole.

Ray Keith's favorite bar was *La Peña Grande - the Big Rock*. He was seated at the best table in the establishment when he spotted his two *peke-peke* friends coming through the door.

"*Hola! Viscoso! Resbaloso! Qué pasá,*" he shouted across the room.

They looked as if they had just returned from a long run into the jungle. Their nicknames were Slimy and Slippery because they always managed to avoid arrest while delivering illegal supplies to the paste labs scattered about the province. Paste cooks were always in need of sheet plastic, barrels, toilet paper, and the other essentials of camp life, many of which were controlled by the government. Both men grinned when they spotted Keith in the dim light of the bar and they made a beeline to his table. They loved the attention he gave them and he was always good for a couple of beers when he had the money.

"Hola, *Señor* Keith. How is Chiara?" limy asked.

Chiara was Keith's woman.

"She's over there," Keith said, pointing at the bar.

"*Chiara!*" he yelled, over the sound of racy salsa music.

He waved at her, held up two fingers, and pointed to Slimy and Slippery. She nodded yes and ordered two more beers.

Keith was at home in the tumbledown shack in the unlit outskirts of town. The people accepted him because of his relationship with the Indian girl and his missing leg.

"What have you two chicken-chokers been up to, Slimy?" he asked, of the skinnier of the two men. "I haven't seen ya in days."

The youth was little more than skin and bones. He beamed a smile and answered.

"Same old thing, *Señor Pirata*. Five days on the river, five pesos."

They had nicknamed Keith, the pirate, because of his pegleg.

"Why don't you do something else for a living?" Keith asked, just as Chiara walked up with a tray full of beers. She served them then nestled in beside Keith without a word.

"What's to do, *Señor Pirata*?" Slippery asked. "In the *Beni* there is only cows and coca, and we don't like cow-sheet, meng." Both men laughed.

"Don't get caught, *amigos*. I don't have enough money to bribe that fat assed cop to get you out of jail."

"Don't worry. We don't get caught," Slippery replied.

Keith winched. "I'm not worried. That'd be stretchin' it a bit too far, seeing as how it's not my ass on the line. I'd just hate to see you two yard birds rotting in that fat cop's jail."

"Don't worry, *Señor Pirata*. We are slippery and slimy," they grinned.

They high-fived each other like two teenagers in a B-grade movie.

"Hey, who's paying you two *hombres* to take all that weird shit into the jungle?" he asked, with a serious expression. "I need some work, man."

"*En boca cerada no entran moscas,*" Slippery chuckled, repeating an old Spanish proverb: *In a closed mouth, flies can't get in.* He took a big swig of his beer and puckered up his lips.

"You boys are up to somethin' that's gonna get you in deep shit. I'd better go along with you next time to keep you out of trouble," he suggested.

"No. No, *Señor Pirata*. This is our secret. Besides, your pegleg might poke a hole in our boat," Slimy argued.

Keith dropped the subject. He bought them several more drinks and chatted with them for half an hour. Several times he tried to trick them in to talking about their client, but they didn't fall for his tricks. Recently, they had been wearing better cloths and eating well so he knew they were up to something profitable.

When he had gathered all the information he could without compromising his intentions, he yawned and said, "I'm hungry, Chiara *mía*. Let's go downtown and buy some barbecued monkey-meat before I spend all my money on these two *coyote-ugly chicken-chokers*."

They smiled at the compliment not realizing chicken-choker was Keith's term for masturbators.

"We'll see you boys later," he said standing up to leave.

"*Hasta luego, Señor Pirata*," they chimed. "*Gracias por las cervezas.*"

"*De nada.*" Keith hobbled outside into the unlit street with Chiara Norte following like a trained puppy dog. She took his hand and they walked toward *El Centro* on a stroll that took them by the gossipers of town.

In Trinidad it was the custom of the people to lean out of their ground floor windows and chat with passersby. With Chiara Norte by his side Ray Keith was accepted as a *Beniano*; poor, gregarious, and fun loving. They stopped a half a dozen times to gab with people about everything from the weather to the price of rice and beans. It wasn't long until he had learned who was sleeping with whom, both agents and traffickers. Discretely, through Chiara Norte, he bought drinks and food for those that liked to gossip. Not much. Not too little. Just enough to make friends and feed hungry bellies without drawing attention to himself. Explaining that he lived on a pension as a result of his missing leg, he would spend his last dollar to buy a destitute whore a bite to eat. Then, pretending to be broke when his pension money ran out, he would panhandle for a few bolivianos down on mainstreet. During his down times, the whores would return the favor and buy him food and drink. Keith chose the seedy side of town because it was fun and it fit his personality. With Chiara Norte as cover, he infiltrated the underworld of Trinidad, the world of *zepes and lavaperros*. He knew *Viscoso* and *Resbaloso* were delivering unusual supplies to the *Chaparé* and he suspected it was Carol Galán. It was just a matter of time until he discovered where they were going on their forays into the jungle.

On the way to the Black Hole for his evening drink, they stopped at the cattlemen's association for his pension money. With Chiara seated comfortable on the boardwalk outside, Keith entered the office and greeted a short gentleman about sixty years of age. The old geezer looked up from his desk and smiled. He was reading a two-day old La Paz newspaper and nursing a cup of coffee when Keith hobbled through the door. His craggy face, partially blocked by spectacles, brightened at the sight of the gnarly American. He sat back in his chair and patted his ample round belly that jutted out over his soiled khaki pants.

"*Señor* Keith, *mi amigo.* How are you today? Would you like a cup of coffee?" John Blackthorn's best friend asked.

"I'm just great, *Señor Tineo.* And no thanks on the coffee. I'm headed for the Black Hole for a cold one. Want to come along? I'll buy, assuming you have my pension money."

"*Nooo! Señor* Keith. If my wife heard I paid a visit to *La Hoya Negra* she would be mean to me for a month."

"Now Mr. Tineo, surely she trusts you not to hanky-panky at the Black Hole?" Keith asked with a grin.

"She is a very wise old woman, *Señor* Keith," Tineo grinned. "She knows that all men like to hanky-panky. But alas, the hanky is not worth the panky at my age."

Keith chuckled. "I've got Chiara Norte with me. She's the only hanky-panky I can get in this whole damn town. All the women of accommodating morals talk too each other," he complained.

"Ah huh. I know what you mean. Chiara will cut off your *cajones* if you go foolin' about with another fallen dove. You know *Señor* Keith, a man could do a lot worse than that little heifer. She's just a little country girl from Riberalta looking for something more out of life then a few chickens scratching in the yard and a drunken husband to beat her on Saturday nights. I've been checking her out for you. She's a good girl and she's taken quite a fancy to you."

"Yeap. But I'm twice her age."

"Count you blessings, *Señor.*"

"That presents a passel of problems down the road, Mr. Tineo."

"Worry about what happens when you get down the road, *hombre.* Here," he said, handing Keith an envelope. "I got some money for you, but it's worth a whole lot less today than it was yesterday. Inflation is running at about ten thousand percent," he grumbled.

"Hell, Mr. Tineo. Let's go spend it a'for it's worthless."

"Buy that little ole' gal a new dress and something good to eat."

"Now wait a minute, Mr. Tineo. I don't want to spoil her. Besides, I like that skimpy little dress she's wearin'. It tickles my imagination," Keith beamed.

Tobacco was stuck between his front teeth.

The old man looked out over his spectacles with a frown causing Keith to raise one eyebrow. "Well, come to mention it, I was thinkin' of buying her a motorbike so she could visit her family once in a while, and maybe a little house down near Riberalta, *before I leave town, mind you!*"

"That's how we *Benianos* beat inflation, you know. We buy stuff and stick it under the bed. You'd be surprised how many Hondas there are stored underneath people's beds," Tineo said. He liked Keith. Everyone liked Keith. He was just an infectious sort of fellow.

"Not to change the subject Mr. Tineo, but do you have any news from the ranch?" Keith asked, while he was counting his money.

"Yeah. They want you to make contact with an agent named, Jose Aguillar. He frequents *La Hoya Negra*. Chiara will know which one he is. He's an old drinking buddy of your compadre, Savarese."

"Anything else?"

"No. That's the only message," the old man said.

"Well, I can do better'n that. I got a line on some *peke-peke* fellers who have been making long runs up into the *Chaparé*. I've been buyin' 'em beans and beer, so you can tell Commander Evans he owes me a bundle of money for all the booze I been feeding these yard birds," Keith complained. "But any who, they been taking some mighty strange stuff up into the jungle, stuff like scientific things, and winder-screening, and crap like that. A'fore too long, I'll find what they're up to and where they're going. I don't want to push 'em just yet. Tell the Cap'n to send me some money so I can get 'em good and drunk."

"Anything else?"

"Nope. That ought to do it."

"I'll be going out to the Didgeridoo tomorrow. I tell him," the old man said.

"Oh, one more thing, Mr. Tineo. About a month ago a woman packing a Mexican passport showed up at the Riberalta Motel. She stayed in the area a few days then left on a bus. As far as I can determine she didn't come here. And get this. She fits the description of Doc to a tee."

"Commander Evans will be glad to hear that," Tineo said, with a surprised expression. "That'll be the first good news he's had since he got here."

Keith turned and hobbled toward the door. "Sure you don't want to come along, Mr. Tineo?" he asked, stopping in the doorway. "Beer's on me."

"No, no. Not me," the old man replied. "I might find myself in the back room. Some of those fallen doves are mighty pretty."

"I see you know what goes on in those back rooms," Keith grinned.

"In my younger days, *Señor* Keith," the old man chuckled. "In my younger days. Believe me, I've plucked the tail feathers off of a few fast Fannies."

Keith chuckled. "I don't doubt that, Mr. Tineo. I'll see you later," he said, ambling out the door.

"*Hasta luego, mi amigo*," the old man replied.

Keith and Chiara strolled on down the street stopping to chat with several locals along the way. As they neared *El Centro,* the center of town, Keith asked Norte if she knew the DEA agent Evans wanted him to contact.

"Chiara, do you know a *gringo* named, Jose Aguillar. He's Mexi-Merican. Lives in the Ganadero."

"I don't know heem. But he's a bad man," she warned, in her cute little voice.

"If you don't know him, how do you know he's a bad man?" Keith asked, hobbling along beside her.

"I know," Chiara insisted. "He's a butterfly."

A butterfly was a man who flew from woman to woman, using each woman for sexual favors.

"That's not something I can hold against a man," Keith argued.

"This one is a bad man. They say he takes money," Chiara continued.

"From who?"

"From the big narcos. From the Colombians."

"He's an American agent for Christ sake," Keith gasped.

"*Señor* Ray, he used to have a girlfriend from Riberalta. My friend. She says he talks in his sleep. He has nightmares about the Yankees and the Colombians keeling heem. She says he takes money from the Colombians."

"I'm supposed to talk with him. Make friends with him," Keith said, watching her facial features.

"*No, Señor Ray! No! Do not do it!*" she begged. "He is not like you. He is a bad man. He beats hees woman and he takes money from the narcos. I can find out anything he can find out, *Señor* Ray. You don't need heem. Just ask me. I will find out for you," she pleaded. She squeezed his hand. "Don't talk to heem, *Señor* Ray," she said, alarmed by the thought of Keith dealing with Aguillar.

"Let's have a drink and talk about it," he suggested.

"No, *Señor* Ray. I' not going der. I don't want anything bad for to happen to you. Don't talk to heem. You promise me. You will stay away from heem," she pleaded, stopping on the boardwalk. She looked at him and refused to go any farther until he agreed.

"Okay, Chiara. Okay. But if he comes in the Black Hole tonight, point him out," he said, staring across the street at the Hotel Ganadero. "I want to know which one he is."

Keith and Chiara had visited the Black Hole on numerous occasions and he knew most of the agents by sight if not by name.

"You know which one he is. He is de one who wears the pointy boots and de mean sunglasses."

"Ah, I know the one."

He took her hand and walked down the street to the Black Hole. They entered the bar to the cheers of the whores who greeted them warmly. Chiara Norte was one of the working girls of Trinidad and Ray Keith was viewed as her prince in shining armor, even if he looked like a fleabag. Chiara was no longer doing tricks with drunken farm hands to get enough to eat, thanks to Ray Keith.

The Black Hole was a nasty little bar with tiny rooms in the back. It smelled of damp sheets and stale beer and it vibrated to the music of the tropics. They took up a table in the corner with several whores and Keith proceeded to teach them a dice game he had promised. A half-hour later several agents entered the bar and were greeted to howls and hoots. Chiara pointed out Aguillar among the men. From the look on her face Ray could tell she was sincere in her loathing for the man. He was tall, made taller by high-heeled pointed Texas boots. His angular face and high cheekbones gave him a sinister appearance. Keith watched him for half an hour without making eye contact. Like the other agents, he was loud and boisterous, and he spent his money freely, but the women avoided him. The girls who worked the bar knew men and it was their job to keep them entertained by dancing to racy salsa music, teasing and flirting with them. But they avoid Aguillar. Several of the agents went into the back rooms with their little friends and returned with happy faces. But not Aguillar. He just drank and taunted the girls who ignored him.

"Chiara, do you really think that man is bad?" he whispered in Norte's ear.

"*Sí, Señor Ray! Sí! Mira!* It is in hees face, like *los bastardos* from La Paz. He beats my friend," she said, with a cold loathing in her voice. "Hees a very bad man."

Keith was drawn to honest everyday people and he was particularly fond of Chiara Norte. She had taken good care of him, washing his clothes, combing his hair, cleaning his beard, and she didn't seem to care that he only had one leg. Her honesty and openness appealed to him. In the weeks he had been sleeping with her he had come to trust her judgment and to value her opinions, so he decided not to make contact with Jose Aguillar contrary to Evans's orders. There was something in Aguillar's face, something in his eyes and mannerisms that bothered him. He knew Evans had access to the top DEA dog in the *Beni,* Johnson himself. Aguillar was a paid low life, like himself, and Evans didn't need him.

"Why screw with a snake if you don't have to," he mumbled to himself.

He decided to drop a dime on Jose Aquillar. He finished his beer, grabbed up his little Indian girl, and hobbled outside. Halfway down the street she commandeered a ride on the back of an ox cart that took them to the small room they shared in a seedy hotel near *La Peña Grande.* It was the kind of place that *peke-peke* men and ranch hands stayed when visiting Trinidad for a night on the town. Chiara took off his boot, washed his body with a face cloth, and made love to him until he was convinced she was the best woman he had ever met in his entire life.

Chapter 26

Classic third world tropics, Carol Galán thought. *The rains come in torrents, the showers in trickles. Oh what I wouldn't give for a hot shower, a decent meal, and an intellectual argument with a handsome man.*

Cooped up in her board house, she had worked non-stop for weeks to discover the mysteries of C_{31}. In a test tube the substance commandeered cocaine molecules like a vacuum cleaner on high, binding with them and rendering them impotent. She believed that a slight change in the molecular structure would render it non-psychoactive and yet still have the binding properties she desired. But first, she had to reproduce it.

It had been raining off and on all day and the coming of the rainy season added to the melancholy and fear she felt inside. Frustrated, she flicked a mosquito off her arm and abandoned her makeshift lab table. Collapsing in a bamboo chair she rested her head in hands overwhelmed by the weight of emotional despair.

"Right now science is as remote a concept as room service," she said out loud.

Carol had been talking to herself for weeks. She spoke fluent Spanish, but she thought in English and she was hungry to speak with someone on an intellectual level. She needed the stimulation that came from discussing difficult problems with other scientists. And she missed the banter of argument with colleagues in chats on the Internet.

"What am I doing wrong?" she asked, looking at the lustrous gray lump of matter inside the plastic bag. Only a bean-sized quantity of the substance remained.

"I've duplicated all the initial conditions recorded in the lab notes. Why can't I reproduce it? Why won't the magnesium atom bind?" she cried in frustration.

Dr. Galán was an expert in reproducing chemical compounds. She was part of a new science of discovery, a revolution in chemistry. Her contributions to the field were significant, particularly in developing methods of determining the precise molecular structure of useful compounds. She was an expert in ascertaining the shape of molecules, and shape was the determinant in whether or not a substance had medicinal value.

All the big pharmaceutical companies were interested in exotic medicinal plants and the most logical place to begin a search was with the shamans of the world. Men like Rodrigo, whose knowledge of traditional medicines of the Inca culture, knew which plants were useful and which were not. Their magic potions had been discovered by trial and error in countless human experiments that extended over eons. Shamans like Rodrigo were a short cut in the development of useful drugs.

Free Enterprise

The battle against microbes is as old as humanity itself and for most of man's history the microbes have won. Many of the bacterial infections we consider commonplace were once routine causes of death. It is only since the advent of mass-produced antibiotics, starting with penicillin during World War II, that humanity bested the microbe. But microbes mutate very quickly and after fifty years of antibiotics, they developed resistant strains to the standard arsenal of drugs. The renew interest by the big drug companies in the shaman's plants was fueled by a turning tide in the battle between man and microbe, and in part, by advances in laboratory technology that allowed scientists to work at the molecular level.

Conventionally, interesting plant extracts derived from native fauna were administered to sick animals and scientists waited and watched to see what happened, if anything. If the result was positive they analyzed the extract to determine what compounds were in the plant. But as they learned more about the disease process, about viral and bacterial replication, and how these processes could be blocked at the molecular level, new techniques developed, techniques Carol Galán had pioneered. She quickly moved beyond the standard bioassay shotgun technique of administering plant extract to a living organism, to breaking down the shaman's plants into its basic compounds. With her computer she could compare the compounds to thousands of bioactive substances and select those compounds with promise from the hundreds the plant produced. Once discovered, she could decipher the compounds precise molecular structure and synthesize it in a test tube. And unlike natural models, which are fixed by nature, she could modify a synthetic drug to increase its effect or reduce its toxicity by manipulating its precise molecular shape to better fit receptor sites within the body.

Then, she got side tracked into a government program. Coca is the only naturally occurring local anesthetic known to mankind and it has many useful properties. The coca leaves she was working on in her makeshift lab had more than five hundred different chemical compounds in them and each had to be isolated and identified, and then, there was the problem of discovering the synergistic effect of combinations of compounds.

The elements in heroin, cocaine, nicotine, and caffeine are essentially the same. Carbon, hydrogen, nitrogen, and oxygen. C_{31} was similar with exception of an atom of magnesium. In the presence of cocaine it combined with the narcotic, producing a molecule too big for the brain's receptor sites. C_{31} was designed to rid the body of $C_{21}H_{21}NO_4$. Instead, in the absence of cocaine, it activated brain functions like no other drug.

"Something is missing," she muttered to herself. "Something my instruments are not picking up. Perhaps there is some inter-structural ionic effect."

She thought she understood the molecular structure of C_{31}, but she couldn't reproduce it in her lab. Frustrated for the hundredth time, she collapsed head in hands. In despair she sobbed for a few minutes. Then the rain stopped. She needed to get away from the lab to think clearly. Like an exhausted student she gathered up her kit and slipped silently outside. She wanted to be alone so she quietly slipped into the jungle at the back of her hut and made her way around the coca fields to the trail that led down to the river.

Several miles from Rodrigo's farm there was a bluff that overlooked the savannahs of the *Beni*. It was her favorite thinking place. She made her way there and gazed out over the expanse. A thousand feet below stretched a wet emerald carpet of life that blended into the lion brown grasslands of the savannah. Off in the distance, the *Rio Mamoré* snaked away toward the horizon.

Soon the savannah will turn green, she thought, *drenched by the seasonal rains of winter.*

Though cooler in the rain forest, the humidity was high and she was sweating profusely, so she took off her poncho and spread it out on her favorite moss covered outcrop. The sun was low in the sky and it was backlighting the clouds, painting them with brilliant colors. As she sat her backpack on the ground and shifted her 1911 Colt pistol to a more comfortable position, she was conscious that she had brought the substance with her. She hadn't touched it for weeks, keeping a promise she had made to herself. In the iron will of her conscious mind she had brought it along to look at, to study, to ponder what she was doing wrong in the lab. But in the recesses of her unconscious mind, just below the level of her thoughts, she knew why she had taken it along. She wanted to know. As the sky turned from pink to a shade of vermillion, the light playing on a brush of clouds seized her attention. But she couldn't see the beauty of life anymore. She couldn't focus her mind enough to smell the flowers.

I want to know. I want to see clearly what I cannot see without it. I want to see sound, and taste sight, and smell touch. I want to know, her unconscious mind was crying.

She pulled out the small leather pouch and removed the plastic bag containing the magic lump of carbon, hydrogen, nitrogen, oxygen and magnesium that was forged into some strange unfathomable shape. And without self-argument, she removed it from the plastic bag and held it in the palm of her hand. Like a worry stone, she rotated it for half a minute before returning it to its container. The narcotic passed through her skin and flowed through her body. Like tiny missiles the molecules went directly to her synaptic junctions. Sound became light and light become taste and her senses merged into one. She drank in the beauty of the environment like a thirsty woman in a parched desert. For her the world vibrated anew. And then, her mind began to wonder, and no matter how hard she tried to focus on her work, she couldn't do it.

"An entity in time. I'm just an entity in time. I control nothing," she murmured.

My senses are enclosed in a framework of categories, categories of predetermined thought. My mind is enclosed in a field of time. C-thirty-one breaks down those precast concrete walls, made smaller and more confining by my life's experiences. Without it I'm in a mental straightjacket inside my head. That's why I keep doing it even though I promise myself that I won't touch it. It allows me to transcend normal thought patterns. But how? I can almost see it fit into a lock in the synaptic junctions of my brain. It must cause the release of neurotransmitters. Perhaps all of them simultaneously. I can actually taste the wetness of the clouds and hear the life of the jungle.

For a few seconds she observed the beauty of nature all around her.

"So what is consciousness? What is it?" she said out loud.

In the Cartesian mode, I think, therefore I am. Am I some little woman inside my head with a feeble little flashlight that directs the firing of neuronal nets? Is that little woman with the flashlight a single neuron? Is she me? My ego? Is she a single neuron or a net of neurons? It can't be just stimulus and response. I'm not just stimulus and response. I'm not just cause and effect. Am I? I am. I think, therefore, I am. Consciousness is not like a central processing unit in a computer directing the flow of electrical activity. The brain is hopelessly interconnected, cross-wired for information processing and information storage. I am ten-thousand neurons firing semi synchronously. Yes. The little woman inside my head, the one people call Carol Galán, is a hundred-thousand, a million neurons, hopelessly cross-wired to chaos, all firing semi synchronously. Maybe ten million or a billion. It's this synchronized activity that releases brain chemicals. Some exist long enough to synthesize a memory trace, a little chemical pearl of knowledge. That's short-term memory. If the pearl hardens, if it's important to existence, it is placed in long-term memory and becomes part of me, part of the information available to the millions of firing neurons that I call me. Ancient man must have felt the same things, passed through the same stages; childhood, sexual maturity, failure of the body, and the fear of death. I think, therefore I am. Born from a warm sac of H-two-oh, a warm protected watery world, and evicted for cause.

Galán fell on her back, imagining the rhythmic convulsions of her mother's uterus pushing her out toward the light.

When she finally regained control, she thought, *the terror of existence is birth and death. First, there is a difficult trip into the world down a living tunnel toward the light. That first experience is sheer terror, pressing terror. The reality of the self is that it said, I am. And after it said I am, it was afraid, alone. What am I thinking? Carol. Look at the beauty of the sunset and don't be afraid. You are not alone.*

Fear coursed through her body so she sat up and pondered the beauty of the world. For a few moment she saw it anew. Below her a small eagle took wing and she reveled in the beauty of its flight. She could feel herself flying over the jungle like the bird. Then, the predator plunged into the canopy. To her horror, when it re-appeared it had a small monkey in its talons, squirming and struggling for life in the iron grip of its executioner.

"The brutal precondition of all life is death. Life lives by killing and eating life. It's the yin and the yang of existence, the darkness and light, the male and female, the right and wrong. Life and death," she mumbled. "Precast concrete walls."

Then her mind jumped track like a scratched CD.

"I am missing an ion. That's what I need to create the molecular structure. There are two atoms of magnesium. One inside the lattice I cannot see," she said out loud.

But why do I want to reproduce it, Carol? To help mankind see better? To help addicts ride themselves of the craving for cocaine? It's not cocaine that drives the need to escape reality. It's the desire to know more than the self. Do I want to synthesize this substance to help mankind see better? Nature took care of that. Do I want to make it for myself? Oh God no! No! I'm not addicted to anything. I won't ever touch it again. I mustn't.

Carol stared at the grayish lump of matter and fear consumed her. For solace she felt the pistol strapped to her leg but it provided no comfort. She had promised herself the same thing ten times and each time she had broken the promise.

"What was it Rodrigo said? 'The narcos have a narco god, *Dueña*. It protects them.'"

I am so close to figuring it out, she thought. *But do I really want to know? The narcos do. They want to exploit mankind and they have a narco god that protects them. What a terrible thought! But are they so bad? They are just selling something people want to buy, a trip beyond personal reality. My thoughts are rambling. I'm hiding in a jungle in the middle of South America and I am alone, and afraid. I don't know the true meaning of life. I don't know what I'm doing here. I don't know who killed Byron and Laura. I don't know who's after me --- the government, the traffickers, Evans.*

Carol Galán began to cry. She couldn't stop herself. She didn't know why. She wasn't crying for the baby monkey being torn asunder by the eagle's beak. She wasn't crying for her dead colleagues. She was just crying, looking out over the emerald green expanse of rain forest, watching the light of day wan to darkness.

"Consciousness and energy are one and the same. The Hindus have it right. There are three things in the universe; matter, energy, and intelligence stuff, all blended in magnificent harmony. Joseph Campbell had it right too. Religion is just the software man uses to see meaning in life, to see the intelligence stuff beyond matter and energy. Drugs are a kind of hardware."

But software and hardware aren't the answers. They are means unto an end. One has to go beyond the precast concrete walls of the mind. Ever since man dreamed his first dream he has tried to enter the dream world, chemically. And it leads nowhere. Or does it?

"Drugs aren't the way to transcend the duality of life," Carol Galán cried. "They only destroy the vision."

She looked out over the darkening jungle.

Okay then, Carol Galán. Throw it away, said a tiny little voice inside her head.

Energized by the thought she picked up the plastic bag and held it out over the cliff face as if compelled by some higher order function of her foggy brain.

"All you have to do is let go, Carol, and it's gone forever. Without a sample, you'll never be able to reproduce it and neither will anyone else. Let it go. Let it go," she mumbled.

But she couldn't let go. And there was a reason. An unconscious reason. A powerful, consuming reason. She was addicted to the substance. She put it back in her backpack and gathered up her gear without thinking. She was afraid to let herself think the unthinkable. *I am addicted to a thing of my own creation,* was the thought she was suppressing.

The sun was below the Andes and darkness was fast approaching when she came down enough to head back home. She quickly put on her backpack and hurried up the trail toward her lab. As she neared Rodrigo's old homestead she heard a horse snort and hooves trample the wet ground. Startled by the sound she ducked into the foliage like a frightened antelope. Eyes wide with fear, she quietly crept through the undergrowth to the edge of the clearing, weapon in hand the way Evans had taught her.

On the other side of the abandoned coca field twenty yards in front of her, three men were leading their horses by the reigns, walking around in the open. At last light she strained her eyes to see their faces.

"*DEA*," she thought.

One man walked to the location of the old house and examined what was left of the structure. Then he led his horse into the clearing where the coca had been cultivated. The jungle had quickly reclaimed the exhausted ground. There was something familiar in the way he moved as he waded effortlessly through the low grasses and small plants that had colonized the field.

If they spotted this clearing from the air, they'll soon find Rodrigo's new home and his other fields.

Rodrigo's new house was only a half-mile away, next to the largest of his cocoa fields. The man studied the ground before mounting his horse. The other men followed his lead and climbed up on their steeds. They eased their horses up close together and one of the men spoke.

"It's too late to make it back down that goat trail."

The leader didn't answer. He kept studying the jungle surrounding the clearing, staring directly at Carol Galán. Her heart skipped a beat and her temples began to pound when she realized that he was looking directly at her. She strained to see his face. At last light the man was only a shadow, a green-black form mounted on a horse.

Why is he looking at me? she thought.

She knew there was no way the man could see her in the undergrowth.

Why is he staring at me?

She held her breath for fear he could hear her breathing.

"Hey, Boss."

"Yeah, Boomer."

The sound of Derek Evans's voice hit Carol Galán like a sledgehammer. Her knees buckled and the air gushed out of her lungs. One of the horses sensed her presence and complained with a snort and a stagger. Evans continued to stare in her direction, seeing only a green-black wall of foliage against the darkling sky. But his senses told him something else.

"It's too slippery to make it back down the canyon in the dark. We need to make camp up here, tonight."

"I agree," Swan said.

"Yeah," Evans agreed. "Let's make camp in the clearing near the edge of the cliff. The breeze off the savannah will keep the mosquitoes down."

"Roger, that. I hate mosquitoes," Savarese grumbled in a hushed tone.

Evans eased his horse off. He passed twenty feet from Galán hide-site and headed down the trail she had come up. When they were out of earshot she ran across the clearing and back to her lab. For hours she paced the floor wanting to make contact with Evans. She couldn't sleep and she couldn't eat, knowing he was so close. He had sensed her presence and she had felt his thoughts. They weren't bad thoughts. Then paranoia and fear consumed her, the down side of C_{31}. She had to duplicate the substance before anyone found her. She had to find another place to hide. Then, she thought of betrayal.

Maybe Rita told him where to find me. Oh my God! What if she told him where I am? Maybe he's just looking for me in all the places he took me during the expeditions. He took me to Rodrigo's house, the old house. But why does he want to find me? He's not a bad man. Tomorrow. I'll talk to him tomorrow. No. I can't. But I have to. He'll find me anyway.

Galán's thoughts rambled for hours. Finally, she took a hand full of sedatives and gulped them down. She vacillated from making contact to fleeing into the jungle until the drug took effect. She awoke the next morning to the sound of a rooster crowing. She had a terrible hangover and the jitters like a junky. When she finally got up the courage to walk down to the cliff, Evans was gone.

Chapter 27

It was early evening when Sonia Diaz sat down on a park bench across from the University of San Andres to wait for Rita. They had made plans to have drinks at Shinchi's. While she waited for Rita to finish teaching her evening class, she warily watched a gang of hoodlums idling away their time cat-calling the college girls that ambled up and down the sidewalk. Suddenly, the gang tensed as they spotted a middle-aged man dressed in a business suit walking slowly toward them. Like coiled snakes ready to strike, they eyed the man with disdain. They weren't afraid of Bolivian police. At the slightest hint of danger they would scatter into the dark narrow alleyways of La Paz like cockroaches when a kitchen light is turned on.

As the businessman walked by the thugs, he winked at one of the boys and continued up the street to the corner near where Sonia was seated. He stopped by the lamppost and looked back in the direction of the ruffians. Glancing around nervously he took a few crumpled bills out of his pocket and let the boys see the money. One of the gang jumped up and walked brazenly up to the man, unafraid of the consequences. Life in a Bolivian prison was pure hell but the risk of getting caught was low and not enough to outweigh the profits of free enterprise. Taking a tiny white packet out of his jacket pocket, the boy simultaneously grabbed the dirty money and pressed the drugs into the man's hand. Darting up a winding alley, he was long gone before the man in the suit could hail a cab.

Sonia was so intrigued by the street scene that she lost awareness of her surroundings. She watched the cab speed away up the avenue with the well-dressed drug user inside and when she glanced back across the street she saw Rita approaching the intersection. As Contreras neared the crosswalk, Sonia had a strange feeling even before she saw a man with a purple birthmark on his face walk up behind Rita. Something in the way he moved told her he was no mere pedestrian.

"*Sonia,*" Contreras shouted cheerfully, from the other side of the narrow street.

Sonia returned the wave, eyes fixed on the man at Rita's back. He was a skinny, pock-face man with an alien look about him like that of a Colombian. Unlike the dark skinned Bolivians of the capital, he was pale-faced and dressed like a narco. He held one hand up over his head and signaled someone in a car up the street.

The driver gunned the engine and the sedan lurched forward, tires squealing.

The noise caught Rita's attention and she stepped back up on the curb bumping into the pock-faced man. Before she could say, *"excuse me,"* he wrapped both arms around her and lifted her off the ground. A second later, the vehicle screeched to a stop directly in front of them and a passenger jumped out. With Rita kicking and screaming the two men forced her into the backseat, and in a cloud of smoke and noise, sped away.

Sonia couldn't believe her eyes. It had all happened so quickly that she didn't have time to scream. One second Rita was smiling and waving and the next she was gone. Stunned, Sonia began to scream at the top of her lungs.

The street hooligans were gone when the police arrived and so was Sam Decker. He had recognized Carlos Cataño when he had walked up behind Rita but there was nothing he could do to prevent the kidnapping. It happened too quickly for him to intervene. None of the college students on the street could remember the make of the car. Even Sonia's report was scant on details and of little use to the police.

Barranquilla is Colombia's second largest seaport, set ten miles inland up the Magdalena River. Infrequently visited by tourists, it is a city of more than a million inhabitants engaged in the nation's commerce. The streets bustle with the choke and smoke of industry. Pollution fills the air and hawkers noisy the streets trying to make deals. And like the Big Muddy serving New Orleans, the Magdalena River meanders down from the interior of the country carrying the fruits of the land. Unfortunately, in Colombia, those fruits include marijuana, cocaine, and heroin.

Barranquilla was the home to the Ballesteros Shipping Company and their two ships, the *Don Blás* and the *Don Blasón*. In their holds they carried the finest coffee in the world. Under their keels, they hauled another stimulant, one capable of shattering lives and corroding the fabric of societies.

Outside Barranquilla, the *Bloque de Busqueda* slowly crept through thick foliage until they were twenty yards from an isolated warehouse. Surrounded by jungle, the building was poorly lit and secluded from view of the rutted road that served the river valley. It was a perfect location for private enterprise of a shady nature. Near the entrance the soldiers spotted two dark clad figures in civilian clothes standing near the entrance. They were smoking Cuban cigars and chatting quietly, taking in the evening air. From time to time their voices carried into the jungle.

The two men couldn't see the commandos in the bushes but they could feel them. They didn't smell the BB's and they didn't hear them but they knew they were there. Years of experience had given them a sixth sense like jungle animals. They were enjoying the night air and their expensive cigars when the feeling came upon the older of the two, a gut feeling that told him the quiet of evening was about to be shattered by the sound of gunfire. Masure nodded at Duran and cut his eyes toward the bushes. Duran returned the signal, and as he put out his cigar, he scanned the edge of the clearing surrounding the warehouse.

"Let's go inside," he ordered quietly.

As soon as the door closed behind them they sprang into action, taking up defensive positions on opposite sides of the building. Out of habit they checked their sidearms. Masure whistled quietly with air across his lips and pointed to his eye with his finger. He put on clear Oakley sunglasses and moved behind a stack of pallets. Duran put on his protective glasses and stood in the open waiting for the commandos to storm through the door.

Outside, like a pride of lions on the hunt, the commandos inched their way toward the building in two squads, trapping their prey in a deadly kill zone designed to prevent anyone from escaping the building, while minimizing the chances of fratricide. From north and east, the two squads quietly closed the remaining twenty yards to the warehouse. They stacked at opposite corners of the building like two bristling organisms tensed for battle. One squad took up perimeter security down two sides of the building and covered the road leading into the compound. The other squad stacked on the entrance, leaving two men to cover the other two sides of the rectangular building.

Lieutenant Rodriguez evaluated the disposition of his troops and nodded to his point man to check the door. The wily Colombian soldier silently acknowledged the order and reached out carefully for the doorknob. He rotated it slowly to see if it was locked then signaled the lieutenant when he was satisfied that it was not. Rodriguez took a deep breath and exhaled slowly. He checked his weapons, then gave the order to enter the building. It only took a slight movement of his hand to set in motion one of the most dangerous operations conducted by the Colombian military.

The point man burst through the door and immediately peeled left down the west wall just far enough for those behind him to enter. The man on his back peeled right and covered down the south wall, rifle at shoulder ready. The next man covered west and north toward the center of the building. The next button-hooked to covered east and north toward center, but checked the door by slamming into it with his back, a move intended to pen any potential adversary between door and wall. Rodriguez stormed down the fatal funnel. With weapons at shoulder ready they began yelling at the opposition force.

"*Al suelo! Al suelo! Al suelo! On the floor!*"

With lightning speed, Masure drew his pistol, ducked for cover behind the stack of pallets and began firing at the commandos. Red splotches began to appear on the soldiers' body armor. Before any of them could react the first four men through the door had been shot several times. A split second later the commandos opened up, returning fire in a barrage of noise and smoke. Rodriguez threw a flash crash in Masure's direction. The Master Chief used the explosion as cover to escape. He ran from obstacle to obstacle through a hail of bullets, shooting on the move. When a second grenade exploded, he jumped to his feet and threw himself out an open window. In one fluid motion he rolled to his feet to face two Colombian riflemen from the second squad.

"*Mis manos arriba, amigos!*" he smiled, reaching for the stars.

Inside the building, the commandos yelled out crucial information.

"*Clear right!*" one yelled.

"*Clear left!*" shouted another.

"*All clear!*"

"*All clear!*"

"*Five men coming out!*" Rodriguez bellowed.

The commandos stormed out of the building the same way they had entered, weapons at the ready.

"*Last man out!*" he rear security man shouted.

"Okay. Okay. Okay. Back inside. Gather up," Jack Duran ordered, wiping his cheek where he had caught a splotch of paint from one of the simulated rounds. The flesh wound burned and he was bleeding where some of the plastic had imbedded in his skin.

Master Chief Masure climbed back through the window and joined his boss. He re-lit his cigar and waited for the men to gather up around him. When all the BB's had mustered by counting off in sequence, he began a step-by-step critique of their actions at the objective. Five minutes later he concluded with a lecture, pointing out the red splotches of paint he had placed over the hearts of the first four commandos in the assault-train. He could have shot Lieutenant Rodriguez too. He had spared him the embarrassment of being killed by an enlisted man in front of his own troops.

"I could've shot all of you in the head, but," he yelled, pointing to the nasty mark on Lieutenant Duran's cheek, "I conformed to the rules of engagement and didn't shoot above the torso. Men, this is a thinking man's game. You have maybe a second, maybe a second and a half at best, to put it all together. Some things have to be automatic, like muzzle control, target discrimination, front site focus. *But there's one thing that cannot be automatic!*" he yelled.

In a flash of movement he drew his weapon and took aim at a building stanchion. His finger was clearly visible to his students and it was not on the trigger.

"The one thing that cannot be automatic is pulling the trigger," he said, sighting down the weapon. "Pulling your trigger has to be a conscious decisions."

Masure fired his weapon and a simulated round painted the center of the stanchion. He faced the men with a stern expression, clicked his weapon to safety and reholstered his pistol.

"If you involuntarily pull your trigger every time you go through the door, sooner or later you'll shoot a good guy, maybe even one of your own. Lieutenant Duran had his hands in the air. He gave up. I didn't. He never touched his weapon. I did. You shot the shit out of him and missed me. See," he said, holding his arms out so they could all see he didn't have any red splotches of paint on his body.

"Let's see Lieutenant," he said, turning to Duran.

He pointed out five paint rounds on Duran's chest and the one on his cheek that had drawn blood. The rounds were designed to leave a blood-red splotch of paint on uniforms and facemasks without doing damage, but on bare skin they hurt. The rules of engagement for the exercise had clearly specified no shooting above the chest.

"In most cases, C.Q.B. is conducted in a confined space," Masure continued. "When you're in a ten foot square room with four other guys, you are only one slip away from disaster. One slip. This is a thinking man's game, gents. *Muzzle control!* Never, ever, sweep your teammates with a loaded weapon. *Target discrimination!* Always identify friend from foe before you pull the trigger. *Front site focus!* Control your weapon. Know where your round is going before you *squeeezzze* your trigger."

Masure paused and studied the faces of his students. He liked them. He had put them through the most dynamic training they had ever experienced in their military careers and he had personally coached each man to improve his individual warrior skills.

"Okay. Tomorrow we'll do a little target discrimination exercise on the range that I guarantee will pump up your adrenaline and make you think under pressure," he said, with a deadly serious expression. He puffed on his cigar and blew out a smoke ring. "We are startin' to put things together now, gents; boats, helicopters, fastroping, diving. The next thing we are going to do is put it all together in a static operation. By that I mean a ship that's pier side. Then, we're going to do it underway in the daytime. And then at night," he said, making a face. "Men, night underway shipboarding is the most dangerous and difficult operation you'll ever conduct. One slip and you've blown it. Let's start thinking before we pull the trigger. Okay? That's all I have lieutenant," he said, turning over the floor to Lieutenant Duran.

"Don't worry too much about the placement of your rounds, gents," Duran said. "We'll improve that on the range. As the Master Chief just said, watch your trigger control. Your entry technique was excellent and overall your performance was outstanding. Good job Lieutenant Rodriguez. You guys are catching on fast," Duran complimented, not really believing his words. He didn't believe they would ever be proficient enough to take down an underway ship at night. "Would you please dismiss your men and then let's talk about the next phase of training."

"*Por supuesto, Señor Duran,*" Rodriguez replied, like the *Bogotañeo* gentleman he was.

The soldiers gathered in one corner of the warehouse with Duran's men and began discussing tactics. When they were alone Duran pressed Rodriguez.

"Juan, do you remember the difference between static and dynamic shipboarding?" Duran asked.

"*Sí, Jack.*"

"When we were training in Panama with scuba we did some short night swims in the bay. Then, in the pool we learned to derig underwater. In the next stage of training we'll conduct an underwater swim in full gear and derig under a ship before boarding and seizing the vessel."

"*Comprendo, Jack.* It is in our schedule, no?" Rodriguez said, confused by the direction of the conversation. "My men are ready. They are very excited to conduct such a mission."

"Well, I have a big problem, Roberto," Duran said.

"*Que?*" Rodriguez asked, with an expression of concern.

"I requested a target ship from the Ministry of Defense six months ago and none has been assigned," Duran explained.

Rodriguez smiled broadly. "*Ahhh! No es un gran problema, Jack.* In Barranquilla the sheeps come and the sheeps go. The Ministry cannot say which sheep can be de target. When you want one, you say which one you want and it is yours. *No problema.*"

"But you don't understand, Roberto. We must coordinate the operation carefully. We have to think *safety*. We have to go aboard the ship and make sure it doesn't get underway and kill you and your men while you're underwater. For safety, we need to shut down ship's work and stop the sea suctions, and stuff like that."

"The admiral say, when you want a sheep, you say which one, and I am to send men to make the captain stop what he is doing until we are finished. Sheeps come. Sheeps go. We only use it for a little while," Rodriguez said, with raised

226

eyebrows.

"Okay," Duran chuckled, surprised by the ease of coordination.

U.S. Military operations took weeks, sometimes months, to clear.

"I'll choose a ship and send some of my men with yours to ensure safety. Thanks Roberto. I'll see you back at base, Okay."

"*Hasta luego, mis amigos*," Rodriguez smiled.

He walked off toward the soldiers gathered near the entrance. As he neared, his men snapped to attention.

When he was out of earshot Duran shook his head and said, "Do you believe this shit?"

"What's the prob, L.T. Sheeps come. Sheeps go," Masure mocked.

"Give me a break," Duran grumbled. "This is serious business. Get Spear and the rest of the land graders over here. I want to hear what happened during the infiltration phase."

"You want to know what went wrong, L.T.? I'll tell you. Everything. Remember Masure's Law?"

"You mean Murphy's Law," Duran argued.

"No, I mean Masure's Law. Murphy was a goddamned optimist. It goes something like this. *Shit happens! Count on it. Something will always go wrong and it will go wrong at the worst possible time. So be prepared.* A good unit deals with the problems, sir. A good unit overcomes the inevitable obstacles of a mission. These little rascals aren't so bad. In fact, they're pretty damn good. The only thing holding them back is leadership and he's doin' better every day."

"I don't think they'll ever be ready for night underway shipboarding," Duran argued. "They're scared of the water at night. Loaded down with gear, they'll be petrified. Anyone that falls in the drink is dead."

"That's what we're down here to teach 'em L.T. And we're gonna do it."

"Without killing someone I hope," Duran cut.

"You might have noticed Lieutenant, that no one in Bogotá is particularly concerned about the use of body bags," Masure counseled.

Duran acknowledge agreement with a grimace. "We'll I am," he said.

"Me too. I like these little rascals. They're spunky. I'm not going to let any of 'em drown on my watch."

The death of the soldiers in the ambush had had a profoundly affected Duran. Colonel Tulley and his counterpart had quickly papered over the tragedy as if nothing had happened. That too had stuck in Duran's craw.

"You don't understand, Stick. We're running out of time. We have to press on and they're not quite ready for shipboarding."

"I understand L.T. You're under pressure from Tulley. You're going to make him a star with the general and that's going to get him promoted to general when he leaves Colombia. I've been doing this shit for a long time and I know how it works. And, I know how far we can press these guys. I'll have someone there to catch 'em if they fall."

"Roger, Master Chief. Thanks. You know I have confidence in you. It's just that this business is so damn unforgiving. One little mistake and someone is going to die."

"Not on my watch," Masure growled. "And you can take that to the bank."

"Round up the crew. I want to hear what happened during the infiltration phase of the op, then we'll grab a cold beer on the way back to base."

"I got a better idea. Let's round 'em up, go down to the Green Door, and really hear what happened out there," Masure with a grin suggested.

"Alright. On the way we'll check out the port district for possible target *sheeps*," Duran mocked.

"Now you're talkin' Lieutenant."

* * *

Alpha Platoon and several of their Colombian counterparts piled into a six-by-six canvas covered army truck and rumbled down the potholed road to the seedy nightspot favored by the *Bloque*. It sold Colombia's best rum, *Ron Viejo de Caldas*, for five dollars a bottle, and women for ten dollars a night. Jack Duran, Chuck Spear, and Stick Masure followed the commandos in an open jeep. When they reached the Green Door the truck stopped and the commandos piled out. Masure waved at them as he drove by and continued down the road for half a mile. He turned right into the port district and maneuvered the jeep around several heavy trucks laden with cargo containers waiting to enter the gate. Seeing their uniforms the gate guard instantly waved them through. Masure doubled back parallel to the wharf that ran alongside the river and drove for half a mile before stopping the jeep for a good look at the ships that lined the river. Huge cranes were loading and off-loading cargo containers from a dozen ships tied up along the quay.

"What do you think of that one?" Duran asked, pointing to a typical freighter.

"Sheeps come and sheeps go," Masure said, mocking Rodriguez. "You can have any one you say."

Duran frowned. "Get serious. What do you think?"

"It's okay, L.T. but there's too much going down around here. We'd play hell trying to maintain control with all this shit going on." Stevedores were busy with heavy equipment all over the area. "We'd be better off with one of the ships at the end of the wharf."

"I agree," Spear agreed. "We need a ship on one end or the other or sure as hell

228

we'll get someone chewed up in a screw."

Tugs and small boats were coming and going up and down the river. Spear's concern was valid and Duran knew it. Right away he had seen that his biggest problem would be stopping business long enough to conduct a simulated mission.

"Let's have a look at the far end of the port district," Duran suggested. "Maybe it's not so busy up there."

Masure gunned the engine and drove for more than a mile up river. The last berth was perfect for a military exercise. It was poorly lit, relatively secure, and easy to approach from up river where boat traffic was light and further out toward the middle of the channel. Masure drove around the staging apron and stopped the jeep facing the ship. She was a typical freighter with a clear foredeck for cargo containers and an aft superstructure that rose up several decks to a pilothouse. A brow hung down her starboard side to the wharf. Stevedores were walking up and down the gangway busy with ship's work.

"This one is perfect, L.T." Masure said.

"I agree," Spear said. "The only thing that worries me is the current. With an outgoing tide it can get up to eight knots."

"We'll just have to restrict the time of the mission to slack tide," Duran said. "To keep Colonel Tulley happy and off our backs all we gotta do is one underwater infil."

"Yeah. And we'll have to restrict the approach to down river to prevent problems with the other ships," Spear added. "But it's workable."

"Looks good to me, too. But to play it safe I'll get in the water and check it out first. Now, let's go get a beer and some grab ass," Masure suggested, eager to join the men at the Green Door.

"Roger that," Spear concurred.

"Drive by the stern so I can read the name of the ship," Duran ordered.

"Roger," Masure replied, shifting the jeep in gear.

He drove up near the stern of the vessel so Duran could see the name emblazoned on the hull.

"Got it," Duran said, before Masure stopped the jeep. "The *Don Blás*."

"Stand by for boarding, *mis amigos*. *Los BB's* are coming aboard," Masure sang out jovially. Then he stepped down hard on the brakes.

"What's wrong?" Duran asked.

"Boss, I don't think we should dive 'em here. Look at the water. It's worse than the damn Potomac. We'd better plan on a surface infil."

"Colonel Tulley will raise holy hell if we don't do at least one underwater approach," Duran argued, thinking out loud. "That's our forte, you know."

"I agree with the Master Chief," Spear said. "We might as well paint their facemasks black. Three feet below the surface there won't be any light at all."

"These guys are pretty good but they're not that good," Masure said, as he stared at the swirling river.

"Just a second ago I was the one worried about getting someone killed. Remember?" Duran quarreled.

"I remember, sir. But look at that shit. It looks like creamed coffee."

"Let's find out for ourselves what the conditions are," Duran said. "The turbidity changes from day to day with the rains."

"Roger. But fair warning. We may have to do this op during daylight hours," Masure argued.

"Whatever, Master. Tomorrow at slack tide, you and I will get in the water and check it out. If we can't see anything, I'll order a surface infil. If Tulley raises hell, well, that's tough shit."

One of the missions Duran was supposed to conduct was an underwater assault, using scuba to infiltrate a stationary target. It was one of the primary reasons the SEALs were training the BB's and not the Special Forces. Colonel Tulley had been closely following every operation they had accomplished since the ambush in the jungle and he had been a hard man to please. Any deviation or delay in schedule brought on a rash of verbal abuse. Duran endured the ill treatment and found solace in Maria Christina's arms. He just tuned the colonel out and carried on with teaching the Colombians as best he could.

"Good decision," Masure said. "Now for a little beer and a little grab ass?"

"No. We've got to dive tomorrow," Duran warned seriously. "No booze."

"*Ahhh, Boss, come on!*" Masure snarled. "I need a little action or I won't be worth shit tomorrow."

"Who says you're worth a shit anyway, Master Chief," Duran kidded, making light of Masure's mood.

Masure gave him a hard look, mean eyes, no smile.

"Well, since you're so sensitive, I suppose we should check behind the green door to see what the troops are up to, but just for a little while. Besides, I still want to know what went down during the infil," Duran said.

The lieutenant was breaking the rules: No alcohol within twenty-four hours of a diving operation.

"Now you're talking, sir. Nothing like a little truth serum to loosen up the tongue," Masure grinned. He shifted the jeep into gear and popped the clutch.

"Roger the adjective, *little*," Duran emphasized.

Masure knew it was against naval regulations to consume alcohol before a diving operation. He wasn't really interested in the booze. It was the women he wanted to see. He gunned the engine and barreled off alongside the wharf.

"You know, if Maria Christina finds out you paid a visit to the Green Door she'll cut off your *cajones*," Masure shouted, over the sound of the engine.

"One beer and it's back to the base for me."

"C'mon L.T. Lighten up. I was just kidding. I didn't mean to spook you. She'll never find out you were in the sleaziest bar in Barranquilla."

"Oh yes, she will. That girl's got eyes in the back of her head," Duran said, cutting his eyes over his shoulder.

Duran hadn't seen the beat up Ford that had followed them from the warehouse district. But he felt a presence, as if someone was watching him. The close call he had had climbing down to Maria's penthouse had put the fear of caution in him. As Masure exited the port district gate and headed up the road, the Ford fell in behind them, and followed them to the Green Door. The two *sicarios* trailing Duran waited until the SEALs enter the bar then followed at a cautious distance. It was the biggest contract Gaviria had ever given them. They were so busy trying to engineer trouble that they failed to notice the two motorcycles that had followed them to the bar. The two young men parked the bikes down the road and followed the *sicarios* through the green door. They were Jack Duran's private unsolicited bodyguards. Maria Christina Ballesteros had something better than eyes in the back of her head. She had money to burn.

Chapter 28

By the time Decker's report and the day old newspaper reached the Blackthorne ranch in the *Beni*, Rita Contreras was already in Cochabamba. As Blackthorne translated the Spanish newspaper, Evans read Decker's letter to himself. Two bits of information stood out from the newspaper article. *The abductor was a pock-faced man with a purple birthmark on his cheek.*

"The Cataño brothers, Boss," Swan said.

"Yeah," Evans agreed. "Decker saw it go down," he said, as he handed the letter to Fred Swan. "The question is, where did they take her?"

"Carlos said they were down here to inspect the Ballesteros ranch. Maybe they took her there."

"Let's go have a look," Savarese suggested.

"The Ballesteros *finca* is adjacent to mine, over to the west of here about a hundred and fifty miles," Blackthorne added. "It's a lot like my ranch, with an airfield and a number of buildings set back on the high ground near the jungle."

"How big?" Swan asked.

"About five hundred square miles," Blackthorne replied.

"Wow. And she could be anywhere on that ranch."

"Why would Gaviria want that woman?" Savarese asked. "It doesn't make sense to me," he said, with a puzzled expression.

"Carol and Rita are friends," Evans explained. "She often called Rita. Gaviria probably bought Carol's phone records, correlated the numbers and tracked Rita down. He wants to have a private chat with her to see if she knows where Carol is hiding."

"They'll make her talk, Boss," Swan warned.

"Yeah," Savarese grunted. "When the three banditos get tired of pokin' her they'll feed her to the piranhas."

"I know. I know," Evans growled, frustrated by the situation. "And then they find Carol." Indecision crossed Evans's face. "Rita knows where she is, John. I could tell she was hiding something from me. That's why I had Decker shadowing her." Evans exhaled heavily. He wasn't used to failure and he was worried.

"I'll do anything I can to help you, son," Blackthorne said.

"She's on the ranch. Will you fly us over there?" Evans asked.

"Damned straight. I'll put you down on top of their hacienda if you want," Blackthorne blurted excitedly. "I'll even help you shoot the narco bastards."

"No, no, John," Evans cautioned, shaking his head. "I got a better idea that won't attract so much attention. My agency contact promised me full support. Let's see if he'll come through."

"Boss, those jerk-offs never live up to their word," Swan cautioned. "We can't count on them. Besides, they don't know shit anyway."

"Yeah they do, Fred. They've got very big eyes and huge ears and that's what we need right now. If we can locate her, we can save her," Evans said. His mind was racing, wondering if there were voice recordings of an air to ground conversations. "Fred," he snapped.

"Yes, sir."

"Set up a SATCOM radio. I have a frequency and a codeword that is supposed to get me access. There's a Screaming Eagle Unit working this AO. If they'll grant us access, they can tell us what flights have come and gone from the Ballesteros ranch in the last few days. They'll even have recordings of the radio conversations between aircraft and the ranch."

"You got it, Boss. It'll take me a while to set up the antennae and figure out the availability of birds," Swan replied, referring to the satellites passing overhead.

"Set up the secure fax, too."

"Roger."

Evans looked at Savarese. "Ron. I want you to fly up to La Paz and pick up Decker. You guys fly down to Cochabamba. There's a sports parachutes club near the airport. Buy, rent, borrow, steal; do whatever it takes to pick up a couple of squares."

Savarese grinned. "I know what you're thinking," he exclaimed, with gleaming eyes. "We gonna drop in and kick some ass," he said, giving Swan a high five.

"Yeah. Before you go, check out the equipment Fred brought down. There should be some NVGs, a thermal imager, and a shotgun microphone system. We have to know exactly where she is before we hit 'em."

"What about weapons?" Savarese asked.

Blackthorne looked at Boomer and smiled proudly. "I'm what you might call a gun aficionado, mate. They are my dope and the Commander here is my source."

"But we need some special shit, Mr. Blackthorne. AR-15s with night scopes, cans, down-loaded rounds, that kind of stuff."

"I got it. Your choice! 7.62, 5.56, nine-mill, and just about anything else from a buffalo rifle to a 50 cal." He looked at Evans and chuckled. "The best thing you ever sent me Commander, was that laser illuminator and the night scope. Hell, I can hit a jaguar at a hundred meters and choose the eye I want to stick it in."

For Christmas one year, Evans had sent Blackthorne an AR-15 with a Trijicon scope. The old man wasn't joking. He could light up a cat at a hundred meters and place a laser dot exactly where he wanted the bullet to hit the animal, and the cat would never know he was illuminated. The lum was infrared.

"You wouldn't happen to have a couple of cans and some down-loaded rounds, would you?" Savarese asked, referring to silencers and bullets with light-loads of powder that propelled their projectiles at sub-sonic speeds.

"Yeap. Mind you it's not my gear. It's stuff the Commander left behind on one of his secret missions," Blackthorne revealed.

"What the hell were you doing down here with stalker-shit, Boss?" Savarese asked, surprised by the revelation.

"Ask me no questions and I'll tell you no lies." Evans leveled his gaze on Savarese. "Check out the gear, Boomer. The ammo is old, so pop off a few rounds from each batch, and check the accuracy of the scopes while you're at it."

"I gotcha covered. I just wish I had a little bomb-bomb to go with the bang-bang." He smiled salaciously and projected his jaw out with his tongue.

"At first light I'll fly up to La Paz and get your other mate. With a little luck I'll have 'em in Cochabamba by noon and back here before four," Blackthorne said.

"Excellent. Then we'll drop in at last light tomorrow night and set up an O.P."

"Boss, why just two parachutes?" Swan asked. "What about Savarese and Decker?"

Evans looked at Fred, directly into his one good eye. "We need a way out, Fred, and you know the country better than Boomer. I want you to take a string of horses and meet us in the jungle up behind the Ballesteros ranch. We'll pick out a couple of rendezvous points and coordinate link-up by radio. If we can get her out quietly, we'll ease out the back door and meet you in the jungle. If we have to go hot, well you know the deal."

Savarese cut him off. "We'll kill every narco son of a bitch in sight and beat feet with one of their airplane."

"Not exactly, Boomer. Fred?"

"Yes, sir."

"You're the cavalry," Evans said. "You'll have to make the decision to save our ass if shit hits the fan."

Evans could see Swan was disappointed. He wanted to jump into the Ballesteros ranch for front line action. But teamwork requires all kinds of players. In military operations the ground crew is just as important as the flight crew. Swan understood. Teamwork was in his blood. He gave Evans a mock salute and resigned himself to a long horseback ride through the jungle.

"What about Sam?" Swan asked, referring to Decker.

Evans had stationed Decker in La Paz as liaison with the embassy and to keep an eye on Rita Contreras. Decker had a pacemaker in his heart and was in no condition to infiltrate by parachute or horse.

"I want him here Fred, to man a base station. We'll need a fixed point for HF comm. He'll provide the link between me and you and if we get in trouble Mr. Blackthorne can drop us supplies, maybe even pick us up if we can find a suitable landing zone."

"Hell, I'll bomb the bastards. I'll hang an AR-15 out the window and shoot the shit out of 'em," Blackthorne offered.

Evans smiled and ignored the old man's bravado.

"And Keith?" Swan asked.

"He's got his finger on the pulse of Trinidad. We don't need him for this op," Evans reasoned.

"They'll know it's us, Boss," Swan said. "Sure as shit."

"May be. We can't beat these guys by playing by the rules. They have enough money and contacts to buy a small country. If we can't do this thing in the squelch mode we'll have to go bloody and leave no one alive. I don't want to bring anything down on the Blackthorns."

"Let's take this one step at a time Commander," Blackthorne interrupted. "If Rita is on that ranch you get her out and I'll come and get you out. If I have to I'll set down on their runway and we'll shoot our way out and worry about the consequences later."

Evans nodded with a troubled expression on his face. John Blackthorne was a champion and he understood the dimensions of the problem. He was just too hardheaded for his own good.

"Thanks, John. Say, when you fly up to La Paz can you drop Fred off with some horses so he can get a head start?"

"You bet. There's a dirt strip out on the western corner of my property. It's high and it's dry. But it's about sixty miles from the Ballesteros spread as the buzzard flies. That's a far piece to ride."

"I'll do it," Swan said.

"Guillermo can fly you and the horses out this afternoon. That'll give you a head start."

"Great," Swan said.

"On your way to La Paz, can you fly close enough to the Ballesteros ranch for Boomer to get a look?" Evans asked.

"Yeah, as long as the clouds cooperate. The rains have already started. In a week or so it'll be raining cats and dogs non-stop for months."

"Good enough. Boomer, pick out a D.Z. within walking distance."

"Roger, Boss," Savarese acknowledged.

"Now for the hardest part, gents," Evans said. They all looked at him perplexed. "Trying to get good intel out of a bunch of tight-assed spooks," he explained with a grimace.

* * *

Rita Contreras rolled her head back and forth on the filthy cot, slipping in and out of consciousness.

"Please. Please," she moaned, pulling on the straps that restrained her arms and legs. She twisted to one side, as the man sitting on the edge of the bed fondled her breasts. "Stop. Stop," she pleaded.

Fleeting images fogged her mind. Images of terror. Images of bad breath and bodies pressing against her, holding her down in the backseat of a car. Then blackness as someone placed a rag over her face, smothering her with the smell of ether. Her head ached and her chest was congested. She gasped for breath and moaned a deep guttural sound like an injured animal. Drooling out the side of her mouth she opened her dilated eyes to a world that seemed to waver and drift in and out of focus. A man with ragged gray teeth leered down at her, hands all over her breasts.

"*Por favor, por favor*," she moaned, drifting in and out of awareness.

The sound of voices echoed inside her mind like men speaking from far away through a long pipe. She tried to make out what they were saying but the words wouldn't fit together.

"Nice tits," Pablo exclaimed. "I think I'll have some of this bitch right now," he said, opening up her blouse for a better look.

Carlos and Juan stood over the bed staring down at Contreras. Her eyes were wide open, not really comprehending her situation, still glazed by anesthesia and fear.

"*No, Pablo! No!*" Carlos ordered. "The airplane will be here in a few minutes."

Carlos had done everything he could to keep Pablo away from Contreras. His perverted brother was growing impatient by the minute. He looked up and sneered.

"I want some of this fouckeem bitch, meng. *Now!*" he yelled, pulling down her brazier.

Rita's full round breasts gleamed under the light of a bare light bulb hanging in the center of the filthy little room. Both Carlos and Juan felt a stir in their loins as they eyed her exposed flesh. Then Carlos remembered Gaviria's warning.

"Pablo, *Gato* said he would kill you if you hurt her," he said.

"Fouck heem. I'm not gonna hurt the bitch, meng. She's gonna like it," Pablo argued.

He bent over and sucked on one of Rita's exposed nipples.

"*Please! Stop*," she begged, slurring her words like a drunk.

She squirmed on the cot trying to get away.

Pablo sat up on the side of the bed and laughed. "See, meng. I told you. She likes it. See. She likes it, meng."

"Pablo, when *Gato* is through with her he said you could have her," Carlos argued. "Leave her alone!"

"Yeah, meng. We can smoke soam weed and take turns," Juan suggested.

"Alright. But me first," Pablo snarled, with a glare.

"I don't want the bitch," Carlos said. "You two can have her. She's nothing but trouble."

He wet a face cloth with a little ether and placed it over Rita's mouth and nose. She struggled for a few seconds, then went limp.

"You're gonna kill the bitch with that shit, meng," Pablo yelled. "Then I'll never get to fuck her." He snatched the cloth out of his brother's his hand. "I don't fuck dead bitches, meng," he growled.

"Why?" Juan goaded. "You'll do anything else from a goat to an old woman." He laughed by himself, as Pablo glowered.

"The plane will be at the airport soon. Let's go," Carlos ordered, untying one of the wrist restraints.

Pablo flipped out his switchblade and cut her loose with three easy slices. He wrapped her in the bed sheet and pitched her over his shoulder like a sack of beans.

"Just remember, *mis hermanos*, me first," he snarled.

"Who cares, Pablo," Juan grumbled. "The juicier the better, meng."

"I care. Maybe you bastards have some kind of venereal disease or something."

"Fouck you," Juan snapped. He opened the door so Pablo could carry her outside. "You're the pervert."

After snatching Rita off the streets of La Paz, the Cataño brothers had driven non-stop to a safehouse outside Cochabamba. From there they sent a message to Gaviria by one of the freight planes ferrying beef to the city. The last leg of her journey was a one way trip from Jorge Wilstermann Airport in Cochabamba to the Ballesteros Ranch in the *Beni*. She had a date with a Panamanian doctor who was infamous in the underworld for making people talk one way or another.

* * *

Sam Decker did a final check of the operational gear while Evans and Savarese put on their parachutes. When he was finished he looked up toward the nose of the airplane and gave John Blackthorne a thumbs-up. The old man waved at him and ducked into the cockpit. A few minutes later one of the engines on the old DC-6 sputtered to life and coughed. Smoke billowing back behind the prop, momentarily covering the fuselage in a cloud of noxious fumes. Savarese made a sour face at Evans and held his breath. Then, the other engine grumbled to life and another cloud of blue smoke streaked by them.

"*Let's go do it!*" Evans yelled, over the sound of thundering engines.

Savarese snapped to attention and gave Evans a backhanded salute. "*After you, sir,*" he yelled, in his best fake Aussie accent.

Evans climbed on board the ancient airplane wearing a sleek high performance parachute that didn't look large enough to contain two canopies. A main and a reserve were crowded into a little package the size of a pillow. Savarese followed him through the hatch wearing his chute with the leg straps undone. He turned around in the door and helped Decker load their operational gear.

Savarese had bought two Cruise Lights from the parachute club in Cochabamba and all the other equipment they needed to conduct a freefall parachute infiltration. The small, compact bundles on their backs contained square canopies capable of making seventeen knots of forward speed in full flight. The parachutes were constructed with toggles that connected to the canopy. The toggles allowed the user to distort the shape of the wing and steer the chute as easily as driving a car. In the hands of experts like Evans and Savarese, they were infiltration vehicles capable of secretly delivering men and equipment to a drop zone the size of a tennis court. When SEALs talk about move, shoot, and communicate, a parachute is one of the vehicles included in the verb *move*. Both men had made thousands of parachute jumps in their careers beginning in the days when the military only possessed round parachutes. The squares made the job infinitely easier by comparison.

Decker passed up their operational gear, neatly packed in two kit bags that were rigged to hang from their parachute harnesses. Then he handed Savarese two weapon bags. With the engines thundering he did a final equipment check before giving Evans a thumbsup. Evans checked his watch and nodded back to Decker that it was time to launch the mission.

Decker half saluted and walked forward through the cargo bay of the airplane. It was old and patched together by field expedient measure. Years of hauling slabs of beef had given it character. When he reached the cockpit he tapped Blackthorne on the shoulder and leaned on the back of the pilot's seat. The old man looked up at him and smiled, ready for war. His adrenaline was pumping at a high rate and he was ready for action with two AR-15s and a pile of magazines at his side. The weapons were not necessary but the SEALs weren't about to let the wind out of the old guy's sails. He was enjoying his part in the adventure too much to spoil his mood.

"*Ready?*" he bellowed at Decker.

"*Yes, sir,*" Decker hollered, nodding his head in the affirmative. Decker leaned over and spoke directly into Blackthorn's ear. "Mr. Blackthorne, I'll be back up once we're airborne to give you course corrections."

"*Roger that, mate. I'll have you off the ground in five minutes.*"

Blackthorne taxied to the end of the runway, turned about and immediately opened up the throttles. He roared down the runway and lifted off in a thunder toward to the west. The sun was low and about to set behind the Andes. Darkness was fast approaching. Behind him, angry clouds were building up over the Amazon, threatening rain. When he reached two thousand feet he looked back at his ranch. The fires he had built around his dirt airstrip flickered against the darkening savannah creating a lighted runway to welcome him home.

I hope it doesn't rain, he thought. *If it does, we're in big trouble.*

He didn't like using vehicle headlights to mark his runway. Vehicles were obstacles to run into on a nasty night. When he reached altitude at fourteen thousand feet above ground level, it was near last light and the Didgeridoo was too far away to make out detail. Only his makeshift runway was visible, flicking in the distance.

Decker rigger-checked the parachutes and helped rig the equipment bags and weapons to the men's parachute harnesses before returning to the cockpit. When they were near the Ballesteros ranch, Savarese leaned out the open hatch for a better look. A blast of wind hit him in the face like a hurricane. He ducked back inside and pointed at a cluster of buildings off at an angle to their course. Evans nodded acknowledgment and studied the layout of the ranch through the open hatch. At fourteen thousand feet the houses of the ranch hands were Lilliputian in size. Two buildings stood out from the rest on the darkening savannah; the aircraft hangar and the main house. Savarese pointed to a small clearing in the jungle about five miles behind the ranch. With a nod Evans approved of his choice of drop zones.

Savarese stuck his head outside the fuselage again and looked down at the ground. For a couple of minutes he studied the movement of the airplane over the ground in relation to his drop zone. Then he waved at Decker up in the cockpit. He held up his hand with all his fingers spread wide, until Decker rogered for the signal. Then he pointed to the right side of the aircraft with his thumb.

"*Come right, five degrees, Mr. Blackthorne,*" Decker yelled.

"*Right five degrees, aye,*" Blackthorne repeated excitedly.

He eased the plane over five degrees and steadied on the new heading.

Savarese adjusted the course two more times as they approached the drop zone. When the plane was nearly over the D.Z. he backed out of the aircraft, holding on to the sides of the hatch with both hands so he could look down between his legs at the ground. Standing inside the cargo bay, Evans held on to his shoulder straps with both hands.

"*Ready!*" Savarese hollered.

"*Ready!*" Evans yelled.

"*One! Two! Three! Go!*" Savarese bellowed.

He kicked his legs out and grabbed Evans's shoulder straps as he fell out of the aircraft. Evans pushed and hurled himself out of the airplane, holding on to Boomer with both hands. In free fall, facing each other they balanced their attitude with their legs, using their feet like rudders on an airplane.

It takes a few seconds to reach terminal velocity at about one hundred and twenty miles per hour so they covered the first thousand feet in ten seconds, the second thousand in five. Both men studied the drop zone below and decided that it wasn't necessary to track to reach it. Tracking allows a man in free fall to glide across the sky about one foot horizontally for every foot of fall. Savarese had maneuvered the aircraft to an ideal location in relation to the wind. For about forty seconds they fell toward the surface of the planet holding on to one another. For most of the time they seemed to hover like birds soaring in the darkly sky, buoyed up on a bubble of air. When objects on the ground began to quickly increase in size they cut away from each other and tracked off for a few seconds to increase the distance between them.

At about twenty-five hundred feet above the jungle Evans reached back on his right side, while simultaneously balancing himself on his left hand to keep himself horizontal to the ground, and pulled a small pilot chute out of its sock. He tossed it out and back to his right with a flick of his wrist. At a hundred and twenty miles per hour the small parachute caught the air and shot up above him like a bullet pulling the pins that secured the main parachute in its container. It continued to string out the main canopy in a line above him, then pulled off a long nylon sock that sheathed the main. As the force of the wind caught the bottom of the chute, it blossomed like a flower opening up to give life.

With a jerk, Evans was yanked to a feet down position. He quickly looked up to check his canopy to ensure he hadn't blown out a panel during the opening shock, then glanced around the gray sky for Savarese. The wily Master Chief had waited longer to toss out his drag chute. He was a full five hundred feet below Evans in free flight headed away from the D.Z. when Evans spotted him against the dark jungle. He watched as Boomer pulled down hard on his right toggle. The nimble little parachute responded immediately swinging him out in a large arc like a carnival ride. Evans followed suit, turning back to face the fast approaching drop zone. He eased off his toggles to see which way the parachute would turn. If left alone a high performance canopy will run with the wind.

Even at night an experienced parachutist can determined the direction of the wind over the ground. It was at his back. With wind direction established, his thoughts turned to speed over the ground. He looked at the drop zone and then below him, sighting a large tree over his toe. It stuck up higher than the others. Using it as a gage, he estimated his speed over the ground. The parachute was designed to fly at about seventeen knots in no wind. By the motion below him he estimated his speed at about twenty-five knots and thus the wind speed over the ground at eight knots, no problem for an easy stand up landing.

At five hundred feet he lowered his kit bag down below him on a tether line so it would hit the ground first. Then he deftly maneuvered the parachute over the clearing and turned about to face the wind. Just after his equipment bag touched the ground he flared the chute by pulling down hard on both toggles. He landed on his feet as easily as stepping off a curb. As soon as his feet were on the ground, he let up on one tog and pulled down hard on the other, driving the canopy into the ground. Immediately, he began pulling in the parachute by daisy-chaining the shroud lines. He folded the canopy into a small package and slung it over his shoulder along with his equipment bag. Just as he finished Savarese walked up behind him. Around them the jungle was alive with the noise of insects and animals.

"What took you so long," Savarese whispered.

"I'm not as fat as you," Evans sassed.

Savarese ignored the cut. "God, I love this shit," he whispered. "Let's get another jump in before we kill these bastards," he joked.

Evans ignored the bravado and walked into the edge of the jungle. He unpacked his AR-15 first and carefully checked the Trijicon scope before taking out his operational equipment and packing the parachute away in the same kit bag. Using an infrared flashlight manufactured in Russia, he illuminated the tree line all around the small drop zone and checked the AO with a set of ANPVS night vision goggles. The infrared flashlight invisibly lit up the whole area like a searchlight. The high-tech goggles turned night to day.

While Evans was checking out the infrared spectrum, Savarese scanned the clearing with a thermal imager. It detected heat. He saw monkeys and birds in the trees and numerous rodents scurrying about the exhausted field but no evidence of humans. They were alone.

"Clear," he whispered.

"Let's conduct a weapons check before we move out," Evans ordered.

"Roger, sir. Stand by for one round."

Savarese sighted in on a tree trunk across the clearing and placed the internal laser dot of his scope on a knot. He gently squeezed the trigger and the weapon fired in a moment of surprise. The only sound was a thud as the projectile hammered into the hard wood on the other side of the clearing.

"Right on, Boss. I'm good to go," he whispered.

"Stand by," Evans said. Evans squeezed off a round and it smacked into the tree trunk. "Me too," he said.

Evans checked his pistol before putting on his backpack. He took one quick check of his compass and pointed. "That way," as he trekked off toward the Ballesteros ranch.

Chapter 29

In the American psyche the word *intelligence* is inextricably linked to the word *spy.* It conjures up images of James Bond, danger, romance and intrigue in far away places where spies meet in seedy little restaurants to exchange secrets that change world events. Nothing could be farther from the truth. Contrary to the sexy British image, the intelligence business is tedious, boring and dull.

In the wake of the Cold War governments changed the nature of intelligence operations. They re-focused their efforts on international criminal organizations and on legitimate business interests, especially the ones on the cutting edge of technology. In virtually all of the world's finest intelligence services, the heavy action shifted from the operational side to the analytical side of the house. Satellites silently listened and watched from outer space, peering down at selected areas analyzing crop size, the amount of timber taken, the actions of fishing fleets, as well as the disposition of military forces. Desk bound analysts sifted and sorted the imagery along with newspapers, magazines, trade journals, communiqués, and thousands of other open source materials. It was a boring occupation.

Tom Roth's assignment was a little more exciting. He had an overseas posting. As a case officer he was responsible for a number of informants and for coordinating the information gained from communications intercepts in South America. Posing as a businessman specializing in advanced electronics, he supplied the Bogotá Spy Shop, a front company with special cameras and assorted spy gadgetry. The bugging devices were all strategically tuned to reception equipment located at the CIA Tactical Analysis Team headquarters within the embassy. The Bogotá Spy Shop's biggest customers were the drug barons. Unbeknownst to them, Roth was selling them the very bugs he used to spy on them.

Roth entered TAT headquarters in the embassy compound, drew a cup of coffee, and marched straight to his deck to a huge stack of communications intercepts. The hardest part of his job was sorting through the glut of information. Most of the intercepts were of no value. Some were of drug barons talking to their wives or lovers, a maid calling home from her narco-boss's house, or an innocuous conversation in the backseat of a car. Others were cryptic and veiled. Of the thousands of conversations only a few had intelligence value. He picked up a stack marked "Savajés" and thumbed the pile. It was more than four inches thick.

For an hour he poured over the reports trying to discern the deceptive and vulgar language of the dope dealers. Eventually a pattern emerged. Then one of Lucho's conversations made him sit up bolt straight at his desk. The crook was negotiating the purchase of a large fishing boat docked at Buenaventura on the west cost of Colombia. That, in and of itself, didn't mean much. But together with the other information he had gleaned turned the glut of information into intelligence. The Savajés were putting together a huge shipment of cocaine and heroin and they were marshalling it on the West Coast in Cali territory. He pick up his secure phone and called Dr. Alysin Harris at Langley, Virginia.

"Harris," answered a sexy sultry voice.

"Roth here. The Savajés are putting together the largest shipment I've ever seen," he reported. "Last week Ramón brokered a gathering outside Medellin. He made deals with more than a dozen small players. And this week Lucho is buying a fishing boat."

"Let me guess," Harris replied. "On the West Coast?"

"Yes."

"That doesn't surprise me," she said. "We're tracking a fleet of Russian trawlers based out of Vladivostok. The weapon is probably aboard one of them. Get me the specifications on the fishing boat, right away," she ordered.

"Sure thing. You think they would risk a transfer on the high seas?" Roth asked.

"Yes, of course. The Russians are not going to do a deal in a Colombian port."

"What's the plan?" Roth asked.

Harris took a deep breath and exhaled heavily into the receiver. "T.B.D." she replied, with an annoyed tone. T.B.D was short talk for To Be Determined. "Let's hope for a severe storm that sinks them all the bottom of the Pacific Ocean," she said, with a note of sarcasm. "What's the latest on Dr. Galán?" she asked, changing the subject abruptly. Her tone was demanding and abrasive as if ordering around a weak subordinate.

"Nothing new. As far as I know Evans is still poking around Bolivia. He used the codeword. I gave him access to local intel yesterday. Gaviria's down there too."

"What?"

"Yeah. He took a company plane to Bolivia a few day after Evans left for La Paz."

"Hum."

"I think he's dirty," Roth said, referring to Gaviria.

"That doesn't mean the entire organization is dirty," Harris argued.

"No. But it means we've hung Evans out to dry."

"He can take care of himself," Harris said.

"It's not him I'm worried about. It's me. I told you what he said. He doesn't seem like the kind of guy who makes idle threats. Perhaps I should give him a heads up?"

"Don't. The treat was only a bluff. Besides, if his gets Galán, he make a bundle," Harris said. "That'll keep him happy."

"I don't like it."

"You don't have to like it, Roth," Harris, said raising her voice. "And it would help a great deal if you could penetrate Gaviria's inner circle."

"He buys all his bugs outside Colombia, and you know I can't recruit a source inside the family. They are family," Roth said, raising his voice. "Blood kin. That's the rule." Roth paused before asking the question that was burning inside his head. "Has Evans?"

"He's a contract employee, Roth," she said, cutting him off. "Get me some pics of that fishing boat. Send them by secure fax, right away," she ordered. "Harris out."

Evasive. Disingenuous, he thought. Then Evans's words came back to him. *It's not an advance, Roth. I don't work for free anymore. And as for the Ballesteros combine, you tell Harris the information I've been providing just dried up.*

* * *

Master Chief Masure was on the shooting range when Lieutenant Jack Duran drove up in a military pickup, followed closely by another truck loaded with diving gear. Masure saw them but waited until the shooting stopped before signaling a stand down.

After the assault on the warehouse and a long night drinking at the Green Door, the Colombian soldiers were suffering from a lack of sleep. It was a condition that permitted Masure to gauge their performance under pressure. So he had started the day with gut wrenching calisthenics in full gear. Afterwards, he drilled them on a range where his men controlled pop up targets with long nylon lines. Most of the targets were bad guys but occasionally, at the most inopportune time, the poster of a woman with a baby or a businessman with a briefcase would appear to see if the soldiers would shoot automatically. After the pop up range he had put them through quick reaction drills in an area littered with urban debris such as old cars, stacks of pallets, and industrial barrels. In full gear, one by one, he had them run a hundred meters and then do twenty-five push-ups before patrolling down a trail that twisted through a debris field. Out of breath from physical exertion, the drill tested each soldier's individual response under stress. Halfway through the course, he had each student simulate a jammed weapon, forcing the man to drop his rifle and use his pistol. As the soldier drew his sidearm Masure would pull up a poster of a businessman or an innocent women. Those that shot without thinking were given additional training to improve their discrimination skills. Over and over, for hours he drilled them, until they were exhausted.

After lunch he ran them through the Close Quarters Battle course, again controlling pop up targets of innocent people and armed thugs. The CQB house was just a huge pile of used tires stacked into the shape of a multi-roomed building without a roof. Sheets of plywood served as barriers and doors. Working as squads he walked them through entry situations, gradually building up their speed to real time. Masure was about to knock off for the day when the Lieutenant drove up, followed by Spear, Simons, Carroll and Peters in the second vehicle. Masure walked over to where the vehicles were parked.

"Master," Duran said, "I just received a call from Colonel Tulley. Lieutenant Rodriguez and I have to go to Cartagena to give a briefing at naval headquarters. You decide on the shipboarding op and give me a call."

Masure yawned and rubbed his forehead. "You think that fat tanker is capable of grasping the fundamentals of shipboarding?"

Duran ignored the derisive comment about a superior officer. No one respected Colonel Tulley, not even his Colombian counterpart.

"We still haven't resolved the visibility issue, Master Chief," Duran pressed. He was all business and Masure sensed his mood. "You and Lieutenant Spear check out the river and get word to me soonest."

"Roger that, sir. I understand the pressure you're under. If we can dive the river safely I'll let you know."

"I'm not sure where we'll be staying," Duran cautioned. "As soon as I know I'll base ops and leave a message for you."

"When are you coming back, sir?" Masure asked.

"Sunday morning."

"Roger. Watch your ass. There are a lot of banditos on the road," Masure warned.

"How did Lieutenant Rodriguez do today?" Duran asked, looking around for his counterpart.

"Damned good. He's down at the staging barracks whipped like little puppy."

"Our briefing is scheduled for tomorrow morning so we've got to get a move on."

"Aye-aye, sir. See you in a couple of days," Masure replied.

As Duran drove off, he started issuing orders to Alpha Platoon. "Ryeback," he said, turning to address the platoon's leading petty officer, a large lanky man who acted as foreman. "Police up the range and see that they clean their weapons thoroughly." He looked around at the men and grinned. "After chow gather up all the troops, and I mean all of the troops, and meet us at the Green Door. No excuses. We need to do some serious team building with our counterparts and now it is time to soar with the eagles and hoot with the owls."

"You bet, Master Chief," said the lanky petty officer with a broad smile. He was looking forward to seeing two naked dancing girls shake it to hot salsa music.

"We'll check out the river and meet you guys in a few hours. And Ryeback?"

"Yes, Master."

"Don't let anyone cop out. I want a full muster when I get there."

"Got you covered, Master Chief," Ryeback replied with enthusiasm. "While the officers are away the men are going to play," he whispered under his breath to the nearest petty officer.

The muscular young SEAL winked at him and pointed at Lieutenant junior grade Spear.

"Don't worry about that one. He likes to play," Ryeback said, making a circular motion with his hand to gather up the troops for a briefing.

Masure over heard the comment. "Ryeback, there is more to team building than just movin' and shootin'. Warriors have been bonding around a campfire and a little grog since the beginning of time. Get with the program. Coppice?"

"You bet, Master Chief," Ryeback replied.

"Well then get your ass in gear," Masure growled, as he climbed into the expanded cab of the pickup.

"Let's go Simons," he ordered. Simons barreled off toward Barranquilla like a crazy Colombian hopped up on rum.

The road was choked with Friday evening traffic. It took them nearly an hour to cover the thirty miles from their secret training base to the port district on the Magdalena River. It was getting late when they drove up to the gate. The soldier spotted their uniforms and immediately raised the barrier for them to enter. Lazy guards rarely hassled military personnel, Colombian or American. They drove through the wharf area and beyond the busy loading docks to an isolated spot a hundred yards up current from the *Don Blás*. Simons parked the truck in a clump of trees and while the men unloaded and checked the gear, Masure studied the river.

"It doesn't look so bad today L.T.," Masure commented, as he looked down at the water.

The bank was muddy and jungled on the edge, but the water was relatively clear for a South American river.

"Turbidity is a function of how much it rains in the mountains," Spear said.

He was a graduate of Notre Dame and he had an insatiable interest in science.

Spear was an excellent young officer who had earned respect among the men of Alpha Platoon by performing well under pressure. Masure trusted his knowledge and his skills as a SEAL operator.

"Turbi-whatever the hell you say, sir. I figure we'll be able to see about two feet if we're lucky. And underneath that ship, we'll have to feel our way," he continued with a grim expression. He was tired from standing all day on the range.

"That's enough for a daylight mission, Master," Simons said.

"But not enough for a night op," Spear countered.

"Let's go see before it gets dark," Masure said, as he turned for his gear. "Simons," he growled.

"Yes, Master Chief."

"I'm not getting under that son of a bitch. We'll get in the water here and let the current carry us along the outside of ship. Pick us up in the open berth just to this side of the second ship."

"Roger, Master Chief. I'll be there," Simons said.

In the last berth the *Don Blás* was tied up parallel to the river at the end of the wharf. The *Don Blasón* was moored behind her with one empty berth beyond them.

"What if one of them gets underway?" Simons asked, concerned for their safety.

"I'm not going to be in the water long enough for them to haul in their mooring lines, dick breath. We're going to streak by that sucker with the current and beat feet for the Green Door."

"Do you want me to go aboard and stop ship's work?"

"Hell no. You couldn't do it if you tried. Just check the river for boat traffic before we dive. If I hear anything we'll hug the bottom until it passes."

Simons and Peters helped Spear and Masure put on their scuba bottles, and then prepared the safety equipment for Petty Officer Carroll. Carroll was acting as the safety diver, complete with all equipment, but he wouldn't enter the water unless there was an emergency. As Diving Supervisor Simons was in charge of the operation and although the lieutenant was the senior man and technically responsible, the real control of the mission rested in the hands of Master Chief Masure. Simons checked the lifejackets, knives, and regulators before giving the divers permission to dive.

"Good to go, Lieutenant," he said, finishing his inspection.

Spear and Masure eased off the muddy bank and into the warm water of *Rio Magdalena*. The sun was still above the horizon but the light was waning fast. They put on their swim fins, spit in their facemasks to prevent fogging, and when they were ready to descend, Masure looked back at Simons. The agile young Petty

Officer was standing on top of the truck checking the river for boat traffic.
"It's all clear, Master," he said. "If a ship or boat comes too close I will toss an M-80 in the water."
M-80 was the military designation for a large cherry bomb type firecracker the SEALs used for recall. The sound of the explosion carried through the water signaling divers to surface for instruction from their diving supervisor.
Regulator in mouth, Masure and Spear gave Simons a thumbs-up.
"Commence dive," Simons said loudly.
Simons logged the time and watched their bubbles on the surface of the river until they began to move quickly down current. Then, he and the other men drove to the bow of the *Don Blás* and watched the bubbles pass by. From the disturbance on the surface of the water he knew exactly when the divers were alongside the ship even though he couldn't see them under the murky water. Stevedores on the wharf and crewmen on the deck of the ship stared at the SEALs curiously, wondering why military men were in the port district. Simons slowly drove by the *Don Blás* and assumed his watch in the open berth behind the ship.
Visibility in the water was less than three feet so Masure and Spear floated along with the current just below the surface. Spear held on to Masure's web belt while the Master Chief navigated with a compass and a depth gage. By sound and by the shadow cast by the ship and the wharf, Masure knew when they were near the vessel. Sound carries better underwater than it does in the air and from experience he could almost navigate by the noise emitted from the ships' generators.
He surfaced for a peek just as they came down on the bow and ducked back underwater like a frog slipping up on an insect. Only his facemask broke the surface and it was visible for just an instant. Masure let the current carry them into the side of the ships, and using a gloved hand, fended them both off as it carried them down stream at half a knot. Amidships he swam down to check the visibility under the curve of the ship and ran into something unusual for a freighter. At ten feet he felt a rectangular surface that seemed to be an artificial projection of the ship's hull. Instead of a curved surface that descended to the keel he encountered a seam.
Masure was miffed. He couldn't see what he was dealing with so he let the current carry them to the back of the projection. Swimming against the current he navigated along the edge toward the keel of the ship. When his hand bumped into a small screw, much too small to belong to the *Don Blás*, he grabbed Spear's arm and grunted loudly so the officer could hear. Working his way across the vessel he ran into another screw. The water was so murky he had trouble visualizing what they had discovered but he had a gut feeling it was some kind of submarine

attached to the bottom of the ship. He felt upward to the hull of the *Don Blás* and discovered the mating seam between the ship's hull and the submarine.

"*Sub*," he grunted.

Even underwater divers can talk to one another. Spear understood him even though Masure's voice was distorted and the noise of the ship above them was loud.

"*Let's go*," Spear grunted.

He put his fist in front of Masure's facemask and signaled him it was time to leave with haste. Masure let go of the sub's screw and let the current carry them down river. When the light intensity increased he knew he was in the open area between the ships so he let the current carry them along the wharf a distance of twenty yards, far enough down river to avoid the ship. Simons was waiting on a large camel used to fend ships away from the wharf when Masure surfaced three feet away. He noticed the wild-eyed look in Master Chief's eyes, logged the time the dive ended, and helped the divers out of the water.

"Let's get the fuck out of here," Masure whispered.

"Simons, quick," Spear said, "Pass the gear up to Carroll. We gotta beat feet."

They passed the scuba bottles up to Carrol who was standing on the pier and threw their fins and facemasks up on the wharf.

"What wrong, Master?" Simons asked.

"I'll tell you later," Masure replied, as he scrambled up onto the wharf.

"Let's move it, Simons," Spear ordered.

"I movin' as fast as I can, sir," Simons complained.

Masure glanced back at ships along the wharf. Men on the deck of the *Don Blás* and the *Don Blasón* were staring down at them in disbelief as if they had never seen divers in the water before.

As soon as the gear was loaded the SEALs piled in the truck.

"*C'mon Simons, goddamnit*," Masure yelled, as he slammed the door. "Let's make like a hockey player and get the puck out of here."

Simons popped the clutch and when the truck was up to speed asked the most obvious question, "What the hell is wrong with you two? Piranhas nibble at your dick?"

"You're not going to believe what was on the bottom of that ship," Spear said.

"Try me, sir," he said, dodging a forklift loaded with pallets.

He glanced in his mirror to see if any gear spilled out of the truck.

"A sub," Masure said.

"What! You guys have got nitrogen narcosis," he said.

Simons glanced at them for explanation. They were still wearing their swimming trunks and their hair was dripping water.

"It's wide and flat like a Mark-Nine boat, and it's huge," Masure explained.

The Mark Nine was a flat shaped wet submersible the SEALs used to deliver mines and torpedoes.

"That doesn't make a damn bit of sense," Simons said, as he glanced over at the young officer. "A wet submersible? Here? That's ridiculous. I've got to take you two guys to a recompression chamber. Fast!" he said, perplexed by their strange behavior.

"No. It's a dry sub of some type," Masure insisted, "and it's hooked to the bottom of that cargo ship."

"Why the fuck would a submarine be attached to the bottom of a ship?" Simons bellowed. He dodged a big truck loaded with containers. For a second he thought about the possibilities and then it hit him. "Belay my last. Dope smugglers. Right?"

"That'd be my guess. Now get us to the Green Door, pronto. We got to get the guys and get our asses back to the base. At least fifty people saw us make that dive," Masure said with a worried expression.

"So what?" Simons asked.

"So these guys don't fool around, Simons. They'll kill us in a heartbeat to keep that boat a secret."

"Oh," gulped the young petty officer. He pressed down harder on the accelerator.

Simons drove through the port district as fast as he could and screeched up to the main gate. Two police vans were waiting at the exit. Before he could back the truck up armed policemen surrounded them. They ordered the SEALs out at gunpoint and frisked them. There was nothing the men could do but comply. Before they had a chance to protest they were handcuffed and loaded in the back of a van.

For half an hour they road through the streets of Barranquilla, twisting and turning until it was well after dark. When the van finally stopped and the door opened Masure realized how much trouble they were in. They were back at the gangway of the *Don Blás*. At gunpoint three thugs ordered them out of the van. It was completely dark outside and the lights on the ship and the wharf had been turned off. Several more men sporting MAC 10's appeared and roughly shoved them up the ship's gangway one at a time. Without a chance of escape the *sicarios* herded them into the superstructure of the ship and locked them inside a steel compartment without any portholes.

Chapter 30

The sound of the door opening startled Rita Contreras to consciousness. Her head ached and her mouth was parched. Throughout the day she had heard men talking outside and airplanes landing and departing but no one had entered her room.

"Water," she moaned. "Water."

She was tied spread eagle to a cot like a prisoner on a rack and the bare mattress beneath her was wet with her sweat.

"Please give me water," she begged.

There was a pitcher of water on a small table nearby but she couldn't reach it. She had sweltered all day in one hundred-degree heat with water only inches away, life giving water she was unable to drink. She was near death from heat exhaustion when the door opened.

The light came on and in a daze she stared up at the naked light bulb in the center of the room. Like her life force it varied in intensity as the ranch's generator fluctuated in power. She vaguely recognized the man standing in the doorway as one of her tormentors. He was an ugly Colombian with a purple birthmark on his face. He stared down at her with hawk like eyes and held the door open for an older man who wore his hair back tango-dancer style in a tight ponytail. An old man, small in stature and meticulous in dress, followed him into the room. Her heart skipped a beat when she saw the black bag in the doctor's hand.

"Professor Contreras, I am pleased that you accepted my invitation to visit the ranch," Gaviria said pleasantly. His voice was so soft-spoken Rita didn't understand his words. She stared up with glassy eyes and begged in a dry rasping voice.

"Water, please. May I have some water?"

"Of course, Professor. Carlos," Gaviria ordered.

Carlos poured a glass of water from the pitcher next to the bed and held her head up so she could drink. She gulped down the warm liquid like a person dying of thirst in the desert. Choking and coughing, she drank a second glass before she came to her senses. Then she looked up at Gaviria and asked, "Who are you? What do you want?"

"Professor Contreras, I have a few questions for you, that you must answer," Gaviria said with piercing eyes. "First, I want to know where Dr. Galán is hiding?" he asked matter of factly.

"I don't know what you're talking about. I don't know any Dr. Galán,"

Contreras replied.

"Ah but you do, *Señorita*. You are her friend," Gaviria scolded, shaking his finger at her as if she were a naughty child. "She spoke with you on the telephone many times from her lab in San Diego. You see Professor, I have her phone records," he warned.

"I don't know where she is?" Contreras whimpered.

"I think you do. That's why you're here."

"She called me and told me she was coming to La Paz. But I haven't seen her," she lied.

Carol had described in detail what had happened in her laboratory in San Diego. Rita assumed that the same thugs had kidnapped her. There was a hollow in the pit of her stomach.

"Let me go. I don't know where she is. I, I don't know anything."

Gaviria looked down at Rita in mock pity. Her hair was all a mess and her clothes were soiled and soaked with sweat.

"Doctor," he said, stepping aside.

The little man sat down on the edge of the bed and opened his bag. Rifling its contents, he took out a syringe and a vial of clear liquid. He held it upside down toward the light and drew out a measured dose.

"*Señorita*, you will tell me everything you know about Doctor Galán," he said in a thick Panamanian accent. "But I must warn you. This is a very dangerous drug. It could kill you. It would be better for you to tell the man what he wants to know," he said gently.

"But I don't know anything. I don't know where she is. Please. Please don't hurt me," Rita pleaded, wriggling in her restraints.

"Very well," the Panamanian said.

He intended to give her the drug anyway. People under its influence didn't lie as well. The Doctor was simply trying to establish a base line. He checked the syringe again and squirted a little of its contents in the air. Then, he injected the drug into Rita's forearm. A cold sensation moved up her triceps and into her shoulder. Then, it hit her brain like a sledge hammer. She wanted to cry and she wanted to laugh at the same time. But she couldn't. Then she wanted to die. She could hear the questions, over and over, as if she was in a labyrinth and the voices were coming from every direction. Then, she heard a familiar voice answering the questions and she wanted to die because it was her voice and she couldn't make it stop.

After thirty minutes of interrogation Gaviria was satisfied that Rita didn't know where Carol Galán was hiding. But she had told him crucial information, the names of the men she had hired to take supplies into the rain forest.

"Juan. Pablo," he snapped.

"*Sí, Gato,*" the henchmen answered in unison.

"I want those two men," he demanded, referring to the *peke-peke* drivers. In the morning you two go to Trinidad and get them. Quietly. *Comprendes?*"

"*Sí, Gato. Claro,*" the brothers answered.

They knew by the tone in Gaviria's voice that this was a top priority mission.

"Doctor, I'll have a plane take you home in the morning. Pablo can make the Bolivian pigs talk," Gaviria said, referring the *Viscoso* and *Resbaloso*. Pablo grinned with pride. "Let's have a brandy before retiring?" Gaviria continued.

"*Mil gracias, Señor Gaviria. Mil gracias,*" the old man replied with a soft smile.

Such work didn't bother him. Gaviria paid him more for one job than he could make in three months in Panama. As they filed out of the room Pablo asked the question that had been burning in his perverted mind.

"Gato, what about de woman?"

Gaviria glanced at Contreras lying on the filthy cot and then back at Pablo.

"Do with her as you please, Pablo, but make sure no one finds the body," he ordered, shaking his finger.

His stone cold killer eyes seemed to pierce Pablo Cataño's soul. With delight the thug flipped out his switch blade, felt the edge, and flashed his ragged gray teeth in a maniacal grin. Still partially under the influence of the drug Rita heard her fate and began to sob like a child. There was nothing she could do but cry and pray for a quick death.

Carlos glared at his sick younger brother. When he looked at Gaviria he saw loathing in his eyes. *Gato's* cheek twitched and his lips quivered in disgust. "Carlos," he said thoughtfully.

"*Sí, Gato.*"

"Come up to the house. I have something I want to discuss with you privately."

The mark on Carlos Cataño's face turned a darker shade of purple.

"*Sí, Gato. Por supuesto.*"

Carlos was worried about Pablo. *Gato* didn't like him and Pablo was too dumb to know it. He was also worried about his own life. His dealings with Risitos had put him on the edge. When Gaviria had ordered him to leak information to the Savajés about drug shipments, he had almost quit the family and moved to Venezuela. Only Don Ballesteros himself had been able to persuade him that the family sanctioned the mission.

Carlos, Pablo, and Juan had gone to school with Ramón, Lucho, and Risitos. They had played on the same soccer teams and had dated some of the same girls during high school. At one time they had been best of friends. Then business got in the way. The Savajés turned ruthless and became heavy users of cocaine. Then Risitos had been badly mauled by a bomb that had so disfigured his face that it caused people to stare at him like a freak.

Carlos had carried out his orders. Over drinks and old times he bragged about his job and the Ballesteros business. At first he just let little bits of information slip out, then more and more. Finally Risitos made him an offer of money and he accepted. Don Ballesteros had let him keep the money, which was little consolation for the risk he was taking. When the Savajés found out that they were being misled and that he had planted bugs all over their property they would put a contract on his head.

Through Carlos, *Gato* fed the Savajés information and eavesdropped on them for information he leaked to the DEA. He passed the intelligence to Tom Roth. Whenever he moved a big shipment, he always gave the Yankees something to chase. If he didn't have information about one of the other cartels, he sent out small decoy shipments that he blame on low level employees. While the Yankees chased the lure, Gaviria infiltrated tons of cocaine into the United States.

Snatching a couple of dirt poor Bolivians from Trinidad was an easy job for Juan and Pablo but it was a mission that he would have normally given to the three of them. The fact alone told Carlos that *Gato* had something else on his mind. The Savajés. Carlos was gambling with his life that Ramón, Lucho, and Risitos would die a violent death before they found out he was double-dealing them. War was close. That he could feel. What he didn't know was that *Gato's* invitation had just saved his despicable life.

Gato cut Pablo an evil glare and left the room. The Doctor and Carlos followed like aides on a general's staff.

Evans watched as Gaviria's vehicle departed the hangar and meandered back up the road to the main house a mile up the hill. Then he listened to Juan and Pablo arguing about methods of disposing of the body.

He shook his head and mumbled out loud. "Not that body, assholes."

"Boss?" Savarese whispered, baffled by the statement.

Unlike Evans, who was wearing earphones, he couldn't hear what was going on inside the building. They had carefully searched almost every building on the ranch with electronic eavesdropping equipment before locating Rita Contreras, mainly by observing the Cataños.

"They're arguing about how to dispose of the body," Evans explained. "What time is it?"

Savarese removed the tape covering the dial on his Rolex watch and read off the time. "It's twenty-two thirty."

"At best we got eight hours. Let's work our way along the fence line and up the back side of the hangar."

"It's clear. Nothing but livestock," Savarese whispered, as he scanned the terrain with a thermal imager.

"There's no reason for guards out here in the middle of no where. I think the best approach is to just walk up to the house like a couple of ranch hands."

Savarese put down the imager and picked up a set of night vision glasses.

"I gotcha," he concurred, studying the lay of the land with the NVGs. "If anyone spots us sneakin' around they'll get suspicious. But if we just mosey along naturally, they'll think we're *caballeros*."

Evans put the headset back on, aimed the microphone, and listened for a few minutes.

"What are they doing?" Savarese asked.

"Arguing over who gets to jump her bones first," Evans replied.

"I know who'll win the argument. *El Alacrán*, the skuzzy little pervert."

Evans ignored him.

"Hey," Savarese challenged. "I'll bet you a thousand bucks that I know who gets it next."

"It won't be one of those sorry bastards," Evans growled, as he gathered up his gear.

"Oh…, I'm bettin' on you, *mi Capitán*."

"Aaah," Evans growled. "Let's go kill 'em before they rape her."

All Evans could see of Savarese's face was his gleaming white teeth.

"You need to camouflage your teeth before you go on another op with me, partner, or stop grinning like a possum eatin' shit," Evans said.

"Man, I like this job! Let's get some."

Evans shook his head and strolled off toward the hangar.

The fog in Rita's brain was clearing when Pablo entered the room. He leered down at her and smiled broadly showing his gray jagged teeth. A strange looking cigarette hung from his lips. Rita could read his eyes. In terror she began pulling at her restraints. Tied to the four corners of the bed, she was in no position to do anything but scream.

"Please. Let me go. I have some money in La Paz," she begged. Her eyes were wild with fear. "I have five thousand U.S. dollars. It's hidden in my apartment. I'll show you where it is if you let me go."

"Ha, ha, ha," Pablo laughed. "I don't want choor money, bitch. I want soam of your pretty ass."

"*No! Please! Please! No! Let me go!*" she pleaded.

Pablo reached down and ripped open her blouse. Then he pulled out his knife and held it in view. Rita's heart skipped a beat when the blade clicked in place.

She almost fainted with fright. Pablo sat down on the edge of the bed and slowly ran the tip of the knife up and down her breastbone. He took a deep drag and blew the smoke in Rita's face. The faintly sweet pungent odor of marijuana choked her. He took another deep drag and slowly exhaled the smoke into her face forcing her to inhale the narcotic. After several breaths she felt a gentle rush of warmth overwhelm her body. Then he teased her with the edge of the blade. He ran it down to her brazier, slipped it under the strap, and cut it in two. With eyes wild with fear she begged and prayed to God for mercy.

Staring at her exposed breasts he sneered, "You might as well enjoy it, pretty lady. It's going to happen."

Using his free hand he fondled one breast and kissed the other with his stubbly mouth. Rita began to scream as loud as she could.

"*Pablo! Shut that bitch up, meng,*" Juan yelled, from outside the room, "*or I'll come in there and put a dick in her mouth!*"

With an angry expression Pablo placed his hand over Rita's mouth and smothered her scream.

"*Fouck you, Juan!*" he yelled at the closed door.

Lashing back with the only weapon at her disposal, Rita bit his hand viciously. Wincing in pain the Colombian dropped his knife and slapped her with his open palm so hard she nearly lost consciousness. He ripped off her blouse and using the sleeves gagged her tightly. Then he slowly cut off all her clothing, taunting her with the tip of the blade as he defiled her privates. He ran the knife down her chest and up and down her thighs pausing at her clitoris, teasing her with the backside of the blade. Rita closed her eyes and prayed to God for a quick and painless death. But Pablo couldn't hear her prayers. And he couldn't hear the thudding noise in the outer room. He was breathing too hard. His eyes focused on Rita's open vagina. He visualized her making love to him and liking it. He saw her licking his body with her tongue, his anus, his scrotum, his nipples, his belly, his penis, until the sensation was so exquisite it seemed real. Then he looked down at his phallus, short, stubby, and hard.

"You want soam of this, bitch. You gonna like it."

* * *

Jack Duran and Roberto Rodriguez traveled along the rutted back roads of the Magdalena River valley headed for a junction with the Trans-Caribbean highway, which connects Santa Marta in the east with Cartagena in the west. Jack had driven the road many times but he deferred the driving to Roberto. As a native he understood the subtle rules of the road and careening around slow moving farm equipment and horse carts like a racecar driver was fun to him. To Jack it was nerve racking. Roberto pressed the government pickup truck hard and soon had Jack wearing white knuckles. In the excitement of the wild ride neither man noticed the Ford sedan that was following them, or the motorcycle that was behind the car.

"Jack, I'm hungry. Let's get something to eat before we get to the highway."

"What ever you say, Roberto. Just slow down a little bit, okay?"

"Choor, *amigo*, choor," Rodriguez grinned.

He stepped on the accelerator and barreled around a slow moving mini bus filled with passengers only to face an overloaded produce truck. Jack's heart skipped a beat as Roberto whipped in front of the bus just in time to avoid a head on collision.

"Damn, that was close. After we eat, I'm driving," Duran insisted.

"If you insist. But the way you drive Jack, it will take us two days to get to Cartagena," Rodriguez replied.

"At least we'll get there alive," Duran murmured.

Rodriguez was exaggerating. The trip from their secret base to naval headquarters was only four or five hours drive, depending on traffic.

A few miles down the road Rodriguez stopped at a restaurant. It was little more than a shack located at a crossroads but it served good local food. When off duty the BB's frequented the place. Rodriguez parked the truck outside in a location where they could watch it from inside the restaurant, and being comfortable with the local people he left his overnight bag in the back of the pickup. Jack followed his lead but maneuvered himself so he could see the truck from his seat in the restaurant.

Rodriguez ordered enough food for five men and ate like a racehorse. They chatted in Spanish and English about training issues all through dinner, finally deciding on the best way to brief their superiors. Neither of them saw the young *sicario*, called the Fixer, approach the back of the pickup truck. He had been waiting for weeks for just such an opportunity. He timed his approach by running along side a mini bus pulling into the parking lot. He jumped in the bed of the truck like a grasshopper and lay on his back. Hidden from view he rifled through both bags not sure which one belonged to Jack Duran. With his mission complete he waited for just the right moment to leap out and returned to his partner. When he reached the car he giggled like a teenager.

"That'll fuck 'em good, man," he grinned.

His partner pressed on the gas and eased away from the busy intersection. Once out of sight he drove as fast as he could to the next checkpoint along the highway.

The men on the motorcycle didn't know what the Fixer was up to but it seemed harmless. They watching him jump in the back of the truck, and though his actions appeared strange, they didn't appear life threatening, so they continued their protective vigil. They were discussing what they should do about the incident when Rodriguez and Duran walked out of the restaurant, got in the truck, and sped off down the rutted road. They followed as ordered.

It was dark when Duran drove into a small town mid way between Barranquilla and Cartagena near the Trans-Caribbean Highway. He pulled up to a checkpoint that filtered traffic coming out of the central part of the valley and waited for the guard to wave them through. Internal security personnel, responsible for checking vehicular, traffic never stopped military personnel in uniform. When the guard asked Rodriguez where they were going, both men were surprised. Rodriguez answered in the arrogant *Bogotañeo* manner that he used to intimidate lowly enlisted soldiers. But the soldier wasn't intimidated. Duran didn't have a clue that his life was about to change.

"Would you please pull over," he said.

He gestured to an apron beside the road where customs officers searched vehicles for contraband. Jack complied and several fat policemen shuffled over to the truck. They searched the cab, the engine compartment, and tapped all over the vehicle looking for hidden compartments. Discovered nothing, they courteously requested permission to search their persons and their baggage. That's when the nightmare began for Jack Duran. In each bag they pulled out a half-kilo of snow-white cocaine hydrochloride. Rodriguez protested but his verbal abuse made matters worse. Jack just stared at the dope wondering how it had gotten into his bag.

A half-hour after the nightmare began, Jack Duran found himself in a Colombian jail. It was nasty and wet, and it smelled of urine and vomit. By midnight the cells around him were full of drunks, moaning and babbling, crying and vomiting. Insects crawled up and down the dirty walls and all over the filthy mattress lying in the corner of his cell. His latrine was a feces crusted bucket. Jack wasn't allowed a phone call and he didn't know where Lieutenant Rodriguez had been taken. But he knew from stories about Colombia that the worst was yet to come.

* * *

Savarese turned the knob and pushed the door open. Evans stepped into the room, eyes scanning like radar, his rifle aimed at Juan Cataño's head. The Colombian was bent over peeking through the keyhole to the bedroom. He was smoking a joint and playing with himself. Savarese slipped through the door right behind Evans, rifle at shoulder ready. Juan turned around expecting to see Carlos, and before the realization occurred to him that the men standing inside the doorway were hostile, it was too late. Evans squeezed the trigger and the weapon discharged with a puff of smoke. The projectile struck the Colombian in the center of the forehead and spit in to four pieces. It sounded like a baseball bat striking a slab of beef as the bullet hammered through the bone and turned his brains to mush. Death was instantaneous. The force of the blow slammed *El Coyote* back into the door with a thud. But the sound didn't bother Pablo. He was breathing too hard. As Evans pushed the corpse aside with his boot, the body quivered in spasms on the dirt floor like a chicken with a severed head.

"*Wait your turn, Juan!*" Pablo bellowed, from inside the tiny bedroom. "*Stop watching me, meng!*" he yelled.

Evans quietly slid back his receiver and manually chambered another round. Down-loaded ammunition doesn't have enough back pressure to cycle an AR-15.

In a low crouch at the side of the door, Evans turned the knob and shoved it open so Savarese could enter, rifle at shoulder ready. He instantly followed him through the door peeling to the right. Pablo was naked, kneeling between Rita's legs preparing to penetrate when Savarese rushed into the room. At first he thought it was Juan. Then he saw Savarese, his face blackened by charcoal, eyes piercing like a predator after blood. Pablo's heart stopped for a few beats and his mouth fell open in disbelief. Savarese grinned as he watched Pablo's stubby little penis deflate. With the barrel of his rifle he motioned for the Colombian to get off the bed. Pablo slowly backed off, hands in the air, and began grinning like a madman. While Savarese dealt with the Colombian,

Standing naked against the wall he taunted Savarese. "Hey, meng. What the fuck you doing here, meng? Is this choor woman?"

"No. I'm just want to see what a campesino-fuck looks like without a dick, *meng*," Savarese replied, mocking the Colombian's bad diction.

He slowly lowered his rifle and placed the little red dot on Pablo's chest. The Colombian's eyes widened in horror and his mouth fell open as he watched the red dot descend toward his crotch. Out of instinct he dropped both hands to cover his privates. They reached home just as Savarese squeezed the trigger. The projectile hit the back of Pablo's hands shattering the bones before ripping into his scrotum.

"Uuugghhhh!" Pablo groaned, as the bullet tore into the base of his penis knocking the breath out of his lungs and staggering him to the wall.

His eyes bugged out and he dropped to his knees groaning in agony. Savarese stepped forward and planted a front thrusting kick in his face to stifle a scream of pain. The force of the blow bounced the Colombian off the wall and he fell face forward on the dirt floor, still clutching his privates with his shattered hands. In a half-conscious state he groaned on the floor, blood oozed from his mouth and nose.

Evans used Cataño's knife to cut Rita free.

"Oh, Derek. I thought I, I thought," she gasped when he removed the gag.

He pulled her naked body up off the filthy cot like a rag doll and asked gently, "Can you walk?"

"Yes," she mumbled still in shock. She took one step and collapsed.

Evans grabbed her by the arm and waist and ushered her out of the room leaving Pablo Cataño's fate in the big Seal's hands.

Ronald Savarese loved women and he hated men who brutalized them. He stared down at Pablo, cleared his throat and spit on him.

"Hey, meng. Wake up, meng," he said, shaking the Colombian with his boot.

Pablo squirmed on the filthy dirt floor clutching his mangled manhood. As he regained consciousness he stared up at the huge American through glazed glassy eyes.

"We can do this the easy way or the hard way," Savarese said, putting his boot on Pablo's neck. "How many people have you keeled, meng?" he asked, in a mocking Colombian accent.

In distress, Pablo stared up at him like a wounded animal begging for mercy with its eyes. None of his act fazed Savarese.

"Ahhh! Cat got you tongue, *Señor Alacrán*? Too bad," he said with mock pity.

Savarese jacked another round into his chamber, aimed the rifle, and fired point blank. The projectile ripped into Pablo's leg like a jagged knife severing the artery at mid thigh. Blood began pumping out all over the floor. Pablo tried to scream but Savarese pushed down on his throat until he gurgled in near death. He eased up the pressure.

"How many people have you killed, meng?" he asked again.

"*Veinte-siete, maricon*," Pablo gargled in agony.

"How many women have you raped?"

"*No lo se*," Pablo moaned. "*No lo se, comemierda!*"

Comemierda was the worst slang word in his vocabulary. It meant shit-eater.

"So many you can't remember, you campesino-fuck?"

"*Fouck you, gringo*," Pablo groaned, gasping for breath.

Savarese jacked another round into the chamber and aimed the weapon at Pablo's crotch.

"Lessen number two, asshole. Never get caught with you pants down, *you campesino-fuck*."

He squeezed gently on the trigger and the weapon discharged. The bullet smashed into Pablo's pelvis sending a shower of bone fragments ripping through his scrotum and rectum. With the Colombian squirming in agony underneath his boot, he stepped down on his throat and crushed his larynx.

"Die slowly, *comemierda*," he growled.

When Savarese slipped out of the room, Evans was helping Rita Contreras put on Juan Cataño's cloths while simultaneously watching the open door. Savarese walked across the room and slipped quietly outside. Starlight illuminated the empty airfield and the cluster of buildings around the hangar. He scanned the area for signs of activity, then reported back to Evans.

"All clear, Boss" he whispered.

As soon as Rita was dressed they tracked off into the darkness working their way around a cluster of houses that were the homes of ranch hands. Taking turns, half-carrying Contreras, they returned to the D.Z. where they had landed. Evans laid Contreras down on his kit bag and helped her drink from his canteen.

"Boomer, string an antenna and call Decker. Set up a rendezvous with Swan at checkpoint alpha."

Checkpoint alpha was one of the locations he had coordinated with Fred Swan for link up.

"Tell 'em we'll be there before daybreak."

"Roger."

"And tell Decker to get word to Keith to get those *peke-peke* drivers out of town fast."

"*Peke-peke* drivers?" Savarese asked, confused by the order. "What the hell is a *peke-peke* driver?"

Evans ignored him and continued to aid Contrares. Savarese didn't have a clue what Evans was talking about. He hadn't heard the interrogation, as Evans had through the eavesdropping equipment. Evans wanted to beat Gaviria to the deliverymen and radio waves were faster than horses. "Just relay the message, Boomer. Keith will understand."

"Sure thing. Whatever you say, Boss." He rifled through his kit bag pulling out radio equipment and mumbling under his breath. "*Peke-peke* driver? What the hell is a *peke-peke* driver?"

Chapter 31

Gaviria, the Panamanian doctor, and Carlos Cataño were having brandy and cigars when a servant knocked lightly on the study door and entered the room.

"*Señor Gaviria* this came with the evening mail from Colombia," he said, handing *Gato* several envelopes. "One of them is marked urgent."

"*Gracias,*" Gaviria replied.

He acknowledged the clerk's diligence like a proper Colombian gentleman then dismissed him. The Ballesteros spread ran two flights a day from the ranch and three in and out of Trinidad. The return trips from Colombia often brought in the mail and supplies that weren't readily available in Bolivia.

Gaviria sipped his brandy and took a puff on his cigar before opening Don Ballesteros's urgent message. When he read the words informing him of the security breech on the ships, he exploded with anger. He balled up his fist and pounded the arm of his chair. Carlos and the Panamanian doctor were taken aback by his sudden change in mood.

"*I told him this was going to happen! Those goddamned boats!*" he roared.

"What happened, *Gato*?" Carlos asked, miffed by his deranged behavior.

"Doctor, would you please excuse us?" Gaviria demanded, his eyes burning with angst.

"But of course, *Señor Gaviria*," the old man said, eager to leave the room.

He took his cigar and his drink and shuffled out of the study.

Gaviria got up and paced the floor like a cheetah in a cage. When the heavy wooden door closed behind the doctor, he unloaded on Carlos. He needed someone to talk to and Carlos was the bait for his trap.

"The Yankees have discovered the submarines. We must move fast to protect the business."

"But if they already know about them, what can we do?" Carlos asked.

"*Sink them, Araña! Sink them to the bottom of the fucking ocean!*" he roared.

"The ship captains can do that, *Gato*," Carlos argued, with a puzzled expression. "They don't need us to do that, and besides, we haven't found the woman yet."

"The woman can wait. We are going to solve three problems at once," Gaviria growled, exercised by the thoughts he was entertaining.

"What three problems?"

"The boats, the gringos, and the Savajés."

"I don't understand," Carlos exclaimed. "What do the boats have to do with the

Savajés?"

"We are going to send the submarines to the bottom of the sea with the Yankees and the fucking Savajés inside. No boats, no gringos, no Savajés, no problems. And we blame the Savajés for the missing Yankees," he snarled.

Carlos crossed himself as he thought of a watery grave at the bottom of the Caribbean. The thought occurred to him that he was going to be the bait that lured the Savajés to their graves. He took a gulp of his brandy.

"What's wrong, *Araña*? Losing your nerve?"

"No, *Gato*. If my head is going to be in the hangman's noose, I want to know what's going down, *primo*," Carlos answered, with more bravado than he felt.

"The Savajés are idiots. They bring the Yankees to our doorstep. They are coca addicts that delight in killing those they dislike. I have tried to reason with them and they have insulted us. *I want them dead, Carlos!*" he yelled. "*Dead!*"

"The Savajés have more than a hundred *sicarios, Gato*. It will not be easy to kill them," Carlos warned.

Gaviria ignored Cataño's warning and continued pacing the floor.

"You are wrong, *mi primo*. It will be easy. Very easy. Because they are greedy *bastardos*. When the trout is the hungriest, that is the time he should be the most wary of a fat insect landing on the water." Gaviria sneered.

"I am the fat insect, no?" Carlos asked.

"No, Carlos. You are the fisherman. The Savajés will be wary, but they will not be able to resist the insect. It is their nature. Greed. And that is what will kill them.""

Carlos stared at him seeking explanation.

"I want them to feel the sub sinking deeper and deeper. I want them to know they are going to die," he growled in a mad rage. "Do you understand?"

Carlos's mind was racing but he managed a knowing grin. With the Savajés dead he would be out of the vice the family had put him in.

"*Comprendo,*" he replied.

Gaviria stopped pacing the floor long enough to look his cousin in the eyes.

"I want them to hear the metal creaking and groaning before the water rushes in and crushes their miserable fucking bodies," he growled, with glowing eyes. "I am going to give each of them a *key* of cocaine so they can fully experience the exact moment of death."

Carlos was speechless. He didn't know what to say but he was interested in seeing the Savajés dead. The veins in Gaviria's neck were bulging and his eyes were distant and vacant as he visualized his plan in detail.

"*Gato*, I'll find the woman," Carlos suggested, hoping Gaviria would leave him in Bolivia until the war was over. His birthmark had turned a darker shade of purple because he knew what Gaviria was going to say.

"No, Carlos. You are the fisherman who will cast the insect on the water," he grinned manically.

Gaviria had been planning to do away with the Savajés even before he received Don Ballesteros's urgent message. He was waiting for Ramón to make the exchange with the Russians. He had planned to hit them just after Ramón took possession of the nuclear weapons that he was attempting to purchase.

Carlos gulped down another swallow of brandy.

"The woman?" he asked.

"*Si, mi primo.*"

"But we don't have the woman, *Gato,*" he said, puffing on his cigar.

"The Savajés don't know that, Carlos."

Carlos beamed. "An imitation fat insect."

"*Exactamente.*"

"I never liked the bastards *Gato,* even when we were kids. *I will help you keel dem,*" he said with conviction.

"Carlos, you surprise me," Gaviria smiled. "I think it is time for you to move up in the organization."

He was thinking that it was time for Don Ballesteros to run for president and that it was time for him to take over the business.

"I'll go help Juan and Pablo dispose of the professor," Carlos suggested.

"*No!*" Gaviria snapped. "Let them have their perverted fun. Beside, I want them to get the boatmen from Trinidad before Evans smokes them out. Go upstairs and wake the pilots. We leave immediately for Medellin."

"But *Gato,* the pilots will not fly at night."

"Oh, yes they will, *mi primo,*" he said, checking his pistol. "*Yes they will.*"

* * *

When Evans returned to the Blackthorne ranch two days later he was greeted by bad news.

"Boss, Keith can't find those *peke-peke* drivers."

Wearily, Evans flopped down in a chair and eyed Decker.

"I got more bad news. Yesterday, this came in," he continued, handing the Commander an urgent message.

Evans scanned the secure fax and slumped deeper into the chair, mentally and physically exhausted. For a long time he was silent.

"What is it?" Savarese demanded.

Both Swan and Blackthorne were riveted on Decker.

"The Ballesteros girl called the office in San Diego. She told Al Kovack that

Lieutenant Duran was arrested."

"What for?" Swan asked.

"Cocaine possession."

"Not good," Swan croaked. "Not good at all."

"And now for the really bad news. Master Chief Masure and four of his men are missing," he continued. "She thinks they were kidnapped."

"Couldn't be Gaviria. He hasn't had time to set it up," Swan said.

"Don't bet on it, little buddy," Savarese disagreed. "Not long after we hit the Cataño brothers, his plane lifted off from the runway."

"Boss, after I received the fax, I called Kovack on a secure line. He said the girl sounded frantic. She desperately wants to talk to you," Decker continued.

"Sounds like a shit-heap to me," Savarese exclaimed. "What next?"

They all looked at Evans. "John, will you fly us to Colombia?" Evans asked.

"You betcha, mate."

"Cap'n, we're getting close to Doctor Galán," Swan said. "I can feel it. Gaviria's probably got the *peke-peke* men and that means he's two steps ahead of us."

Swan was wrong. The boatmen were off on a long trip into the *Chaparé* delivering supplies to a coca lab.

"The bastards will get her if we leave," Savarese said.

"Maybe. Maybe not," Evans mumbled.

"They'll get her, if they have to kill every man, woman, and child in Trinidad," the big man argued.

Evans thought for a second. "Teams and shit, man," he said, indicating his priority was with helping find the missing SEALs.

But his thoughts were very different. He knew he was throwing away his best chance at the million-dollar reward. He was exhausted and torn between former teammates and Carol Galán. "Gather up your gear," he ordered, forcing himself up out of the chair. "We'll leave as soon as Mr. Blackthorne is ready."

"Thirty minutes, mates," Blackthorne said.

As Evans packed his operational gear for the long flight to Colombia, he thought about the circumstances that embroiled him.

Gaviria is behind this. He knows we're the ones who hit the ranch. He set this up so I would call off the search for Carol. He's dictating the rules of the game. But what is the game? Tennis? Marco Polo? Chess? Yeah. Chess. That's his kind of game. Carefully crafted moves to manipulate me. Reminds me of Harris. He wants me out of the picture. Okay then. I'll hang it up for a while. So what's his next move? He'll make it look like small time thugs nabbed the SEALs. They'll ask for a ransom and after an indecent interval some mysterious benefactor will pay the money. He doesn't want American blood on Colombian soil. They don't want that kind of heat. He'll snatch the peke-peke men if he hasn't already and he'll torture them until they tell him where she staying. Then he'll grab her. But he won't kill her, not until he has what he wants. So I'm gambling he won't find her so easily and that if he does she won't cave in right away. So what have I got? Three or four days, a week a best to get up there and back? I hope the Ballesteros girl has some solid information.

Evans felt a hollow in the pit of his stomach as thoughts ran through his mind at high speed. His logic was excellent, but fundamentally wrong. Gaviria had no idea he and Savarese had killed his two cousins. He had departed the ranch before the bodies had been discovered. Finding Dr. Galán would have to wait until after the war between the cartels.

I'll wake up Rita and lay it on the table. Maybe she'll tell me where Carol is hiding, he thought.

On the long trip back to the Blackthorne ranch he had spoken with her on several occasions about Carol but each time she had insisted that she didn't know where she was hiding. Evans shouldered his gear and walked down the hall to her room. He knocked lightly and waited for a response. But there was none. He knocked harder and waited. Finally he opened the door and entered. Rita was sound asleep, dead to the world. He shook her several times before she awoke.

"Oh, Derek," she moaned. "I was dreaming."

"Rita. I am sorry to bother you. I have to leave soon and there is something I need to ask you. I know how you feel about keeping promises but if you know where Carol is you have to tell me. Her life is in danger from the same men who kidnapped you."

"Derek, I don't know where she is." She looked at his sincere eyes. "All I know is that *Viscoso* and *Resbaloso* pick up supplies at my mother's house and take them into the jungle. They drop them off at a waterfall. That's all I know, *querido*."

Evans kissed her lightly on the cheek. "Get some rest," he said gently.

"Be carefully, *querido*."

"I will," he promised as he left the room.

Before leaving for Colombia he sent an urgent message to Keith to make all efforts to find the *peke-peke* men in Trinidad and Riberalta.

* * *

Jack Duran sat in his filthy jail cell listening to the den of noise created by the other prisoners. He couldn't sleep and he couldn't eat. The privy bucket in the corner of his cell made him sick to this stomach. Every time he looked at it, it made him think of Colonel Tulley. His mind kept replaying the events of the last three days over and over like a broken record. The first to visit him had been Maria Christina. She brought witnesses to swear that the drugs had been planted on the two officers. Then came Colonel Tulley.

Guilt or innocence is not the question here, Lieutenant Duran. This is a dicey political problem. Look at it this way. You are down here to train men to fight in the war on drugs and you get caught red-handed with half a kilo of cocaine in your possession. How do you think that appears to the Colombian Government or the U.S. Ambassador?

But Maria has witnesses who will swear they saw someone plant the drugs in our baggage, Jack had argued.

Your rich girlfriend has tried to bribe every government official between here and Bogotá. I hardly think she's an impartial player, Lieutenant.

His fat face had contorted and his eyes had hardened.

Think of it from the U.S. Government's perspective. It doesn't really matter if you're guilty or innocent. This incident stains us all. Remember the old saying Lieutenant, perception is reality.

Duran had snapped. *Then reality be damned, sir!*

As you were, Lieutenant. I'm not the problem here and it's not my butt that's in a crack. I'm just the bearer of the bad news, son. The Colombian Government is insisting on seeing this case to trial.

What about Lieutenant Rodriguez?

That's a short story, Lieutenant. Your counterpart is in Bogotá with a stable of fancy lawyers. His family is well connected and I suspect the charges will be dropped soon. The policemen who discovered the drugs are now saying they found it all in your bag.

Duran had stared at Tulley lost for words.

That's bullshit, Colonel!

Listen, Lieutenant. I think we can get you out of this jail cell if you plead guilty and request a U.S. Military courts martial.

What? But I haven't done anything. I'm not going to plead guilty to this shit!

I'll remind you, Lieutenant, you were caught red-handed with a kilo of cocaine in your vehicle.

Duran had shaken his head in utter disbelief. *So the whole damn thing is going to be pinned on me?*

I'm afraid so. And either way you slice it, your career is over, boy. The Navy will be forced to see this case to courts martial. But I wouldn't worry too much, with a good lawyer, you'll probably beat the charges.

The words kept echoing in Jack Duran's mind, over and over, like a broken record. *Your career is over. Perception is reality. You were caught red-handed with a kilo of cocaine in your possession.*

Then Tulley had told him about Masure and his missing men. Jack had argued for ten minutes trying to get the colonel to send the police to check out the port district and the ship. But Tulley had refused.

We've got enough problems without stirring up anymore more shit with the Colombians. They'll turn up with hangovers after a weekend binge. And you can tell that sorry excuse for an E9 not to do anything stupid, like trying to break you out of this jail. I know how you people think. You'll get out in due time. But we're going to do this by the numbers. Do you understand me, Lieutenant?

Something's happened to them! Duran had insisted.

But Tulley had refused to listen.

When Maria Christina returned with news of her latest efforts to free him, he asked her to contact Commander Evans's office in San Diego. Duran had been surprised to learn she knew the commander personally. At first he couldn't believe Evans owned the company that was training the bodyguards he had been fooling for so many months.

Duran was feeling sorry for himself and pondering over his problems when Evans entered the cellblock. He recognized the Commander's voice speaking Spanish to a guard at the end of the hall. He jumped up to peer between the bars just as Evans walked down the corridor to his cell door.

"Duran," he said, when he was adjacent to the cell. Evans looked tired and worn out.

"Here, sir. Thanks for coming."

Evans squinted to see Duran's face behind the bars. The cell and the corridor were dank, and it took a few seconds for his eyes to adjust.

"Are you alone?"

"Yes, sir."

"I can't stay but a minute. I just wanted to let you know you'll be out of here by tomorrow morning. But we're going to have to stretch the truth just a little bit."

"I don't follow you, sir," Duran replied, in a defeated voice.

"Your leading petty officer, Ryeback, is holding two little *sicario* assholes, one that goes by the handle of the Fixer and they are singing like songbirds. As I understand it from Lieutenant Rodriguez, the two of you arrested the Fixer and his partner at a restaurant on your way to Cartagena and called Ryeback to pick them up. Rodriguez says you two were maintaining the chain of custody of the evidence when you were stopped at the checkpoint. Does that about sum it up?"

"If that's the way you say it happened, sir, that's how it happened. And Commander, thanks," Duran said, breathing a sigh of relief.

"Don't thank me. Thank your girlfriend and a whole lot of her money. I just persuaded the little assholes it was in their best interest to tell the truth. Now for the big problem; your missing men. Maria thinks they are being held on one of her father's ships."

"They were supposed to check out the diving conditions around the *Don Blás*. It's the last ship along the wharf."

"Maybe they saw something they shouldn't have seen," Evans thought out loud.

"What are you going to do, sir?" Duran asked.

"Board her and take a look for myself of course," Evans replied through a yawn. "I have to go now, Lieutenant. Hang tight."

"Thanks, Commander."

"Luego," Evans said, as he turned to leave.

Chapter 32

The black Mercedes motored through the slums of Envigado and down the hill toward Medellin. Several motorbikes led the way, darting in and out of the side streets like army ants on patrol. As they traveled along the Savajés picked up more men who joined the convoy in front and in back of the car. Carlos Cataño's demand for six million dollars for Dr. Galán had come as a complete surprise. The car twisted and turned through the streets of Medellin gathering up a small army of thugs.

"I don't like it Risitos. This is too easy," Ramón said, over a din of raunchy salsa music.

"The Cataños want out, Ramón. The Ballesteros and the Gavirias keep all the money and pay them chump change to take the risks. Besides, you know *Araña*. We've kicked his shitty little ass since he was three years old. He doesn't have the *cajones* to double cross us."

"I'm not worried about the three idiots, Skeletor. It's *Gato* Gaviria I'm worried about," Ramón lamented.

"That *jefe de putas* is still in Bolivia."

"How do you know that? And why is he still in Bolivia if the woman is here in Colombia? If they found the bitch, why is he still there?" Ramón worried.

"I don't know, Ramón. Carlos said he is coming back tomorrow."

"Why? I don't like it. I'm calling Lucho for more men," Ramón grumbled.

"*Chuleta, Ramón!* We have fifty men," Risitos exclaimed, projecting saliva on his brother's face.

Ramón snarled and wiped off his cheek. "I smell a trap," he insisted.

"Okay, *hermano*, okay. You stay at the restaurant. I'll pick up Carlos and go get the woman by myself. *Since you are so afraid of the Cataño brothers!*"

"Fouck you, Risitos. It's not the Cataños I'm worried about. They are too stupid to plan a trap."

"I know that. Look Ramón. I know this place. It is near the Jose Cordoba airport. I'll have twenty men surround the fouckem place before we make the deal, bro. *He knows that!*"

"The woman will not be there, *estupido*. Carlos is not that fouckeem stupid."

"He doesn't know we are going to keel dem, Ramón, and take the woman. He will expect the money as usual," Risitos argued.

"He can't be so fouckem dumb to believe we are going to part with six million fouckem dollars like *putas!*"

"Ramón, you stay at the restaurant. I'll get the woman," Risitos snarled.

"*No!* I want to see Carlos's face before I decide. If he is lying, I'll know it. If he so much as farts, I'll blow his fouckem brains out," Ramón growled.

"That's okay with me, Ramón. Just don't get any of shit on me," Risitos said, gesturing with his hand.

The Mercedes meandered through the streets and pulled into the alley behind the Las Margaritas, a busy restaurant owned by a well-known trafficker named Fabio Ochoa. Motorbikes sped up and down the narrow alleyway and around the block ahead of the car looking for anything out of the ordinary. One of the bikes screeched to a stop behind the restaurant and the kid on the back motioned to someone standing in the shadows with the barrel of an Uzi.

Carlos Cataño stepped out into the beam of the headlights. He shielded his eyes with his hand and waited for the motorcycle to rattle off up the alley. The car idled up to where he was standing and the bulletproof glass on the rear passenger door rolled down.

"*Hola, Araña. Como estas?*" Risitos asked, over the sound of racy salsa music.

"Where's the money?" Carlos mumbled, nervously as he scanned the alley in both directions.

"It's in the fouckem trunk, bro," Risitos blurted, through his exposed teeth. "Where do you think it is?"

"I want to see it," Carlos demanded nervously.

"Here? In the fouckem alley? Are you fouckem crazy, Carlos?" Risitos snapped.

"No money. No woman," Carlos growled defiantly.

"You don't trust me, *amigo*? After all the years we've been friends, you don't trust me?" Risitos asked, with mock insult.

"Risitos, I don't trust anyone, anymore. I just want out and money is the only way," Carlos, argued with as much bravado as he could muster. His face was tired, exhausted, worn thin.

Ramón glared at him from behind Risitos and whispered, "I'm beginning to believe this fuck, Risitos. Look at his face, meng." Without taking his eyes off Carlos he snapped at the guard in the front seat. "*Mogrey!*"

"*Sí, Señor Savajé.*"

The gunman jumped out of the car and opened the trunk so Carlos could peek inside. He opened up two of four large suitcases packed full of used greenbacks. Carlos nodded and walked back to Risitos's window. He bent over so they could hear him over the sound of the music.

"Here's the deal, *amigos*. Pablo and Juan are watching the woman. They are waiting for my signal to take her to the airport."

"What? The airport? You want do a deal at the fouckem airport, bro?" Risitos asked incredulously. "*You crazy, meng?*"

"No. Not crazy. Careful. I told you the airport. Here's the deal, man. You drive to the departure ramp and drop the money off at the curb."

"No way, bro. No fouckeem way," Risitos snarled.

"Wait," Ramón interrupted. "I like it. No chance for an ambush, meng."

Ramón Savajé was beginning to believe the Cataños actually had Dr. Galán and that they were willing to trade her for money.

Carlos continued. "I'll call Juan on this cell phone," he said, patting the phone in his front shirt pocket, "and he will pull up beside you with the woman. *After,* you take the money out of the trunk, *amigo.* Pablo and I will take the money and walk inside the terminal while you put the woman in your car."

"You are fouckem crazy, bro. Absolutely completely fouckem crazy if you think we are going to do the deal at the fouckem airport in front of the whole goddamned city, meng," Risitos said.

"I'm not crazy, Risitos. Just careful, bro. I know how much the woman is worth, meng, and I know you will not part with six mil so easily."

Carlos eyed Ramón through the open car window. The inside of the vehicle was smoky and dark.

"Deal?" he asked. "The money for the bitch, meng. No hassle. Okay?"

Ramón stared back with a leer.

"Ramón?" Risitos asked.

Finally his face opened into a smile

"This is too good to be true, *bro,*" Ramón whispered. "I think this fouckem idiot has the woman. Tell him it's a deal but get him to come with us."

"But Ramón, they will get away with the money."

"It's an investment, Risitos. It's just fouckeem money, bro. Don't sweat the small shit, meng."

"Okay."

Risitos looked back at Carlos.

"It's a deal, meng," he shouted over the sound of a Latin beat. "Let's go," he said, opening the car door.

Carlos stepped back with a worried expression on his face as Risitos held the door open. He looked down at Risitos's disfigured face.

"I'm not going with you, meng. You think I'm fouckeem stupid?" he asked

"Then how we gonna do the deal, meng?" Risitos asked.

"Like this, bro," he said, pulling a pistol from the small of his back.

Two men on opposite sides of the alley opened up from the rooftop shooting directly down on the hood of the car with M-16s. The full metal jacket destroyed the engine. At the same time several *sicarios* jumped from the rooftops of the buildings lining the alley. An army of thugs opened up on the exposed gunmen on motorcycles.

At the sight of Carlos's pistol Risitos grabbed for his gun.

"*No! Risitos,*" Carlos yelled, pointing a pistol at his head. "I have a better deal for you."

Machine guns were aimed at the Savajés from every direction.

Suddenly *Mogrey*, the *sicario* at the trunk of the car went for his gun. Several men opened up on him, grinding him up like raw meat. Then a gunman opened up on the passenger side front door. The machine pistol hammered at the bulletproof glass until only the plastic remained. When the rattling of the nine-millimeter stopped, a knife man sliced open the plastic and a gunner stepped up to take his place. He emptied a clip inside the front seat, chewing up the driver. Blood and gore splattered the inside of the Mercedes. As automatic weapons rattled up and down alleyway, Risitos leered at Carlos. In seconds, Gaviria's men had chopped up the exposed thugs on the motorbikes. Those that could sped away.

"*Carlos, you little fouckem turd!*" Risitos yelled, spitting saliva with each word. "*I gonna keel you for this!*" he growled. "*I will fouckem keel you.*"

"I don't think so, *essay,*" Carlos laughed. "Dead meng don't keel people, bro."

Sicarios on each side of the vehicle jerked the Savajés out of the car and threw them to the ground. With his face twisted to the side Ramón began to offer huge bribes to any gunman who would work for him. He continued to offer huge sums of money until Gaviria stepped out of the shadows.

"Ramón, I have something for you," he mumbled. He tossed a bag of cocaine on the ground near his face. "Enjoy."

The trafficker glared up at Gaviria with one eye knowing his time was short.

"*Rot in hell you son of fouckeem whore!*" he shouted.

Ramón groaned when a thug with a syringe jammed him in the buttock. He was out cold before Gaviria could walk around to the other side of the car.

"*Hola, muerto.*"

"*Como estas, maricon?*" Risitos growled.

Gaviria tossed a hefty bag of cocaine next to Risitos and said something the burly killer couldn't understand him. The gunman standing on his head was smashing his cheek and ear in the dirt. Risitos flinched as the needle buried up in his flesh and he continued to curse the Cataños, the Gavirias, and the Ballesteros with the vilest insults he could think of until he passed out.

* * *

The river was dark and empty as Petty Officer Jeff Ryeback eased off the throttle and let the SOC boat fall off step. He maintained enough way on for steerage and idled quietly toward the riverbank a half mile to the west. To his starboard lay Barranquilla and the port district ablaze with lights. Ships lined the wharf for more than a mile down river. The intensity of the lights rendered his night vision goggles virtually useless. For the last few miles he had relied upon GPS and a thermal imager to ensure he didn't run the boat into a floating log.

"Make landfall over there," Evans ordered, pointing out a landing site on the bank of the river.

Ryeback strained his eyes to see the location. It was pitch dark and the bank was thickly jungled. He let the boat idle ahead until he could see a break in the foliage. He was slightly down stream so he turned up river and slowly motored against the current with a constant bearing and decreasing range until he made landfall. When the boat touched the riverbank the bowman jumped off and held fast with the bowline.

"Maintain station about a half-mile up river," Evans whispered. "I'll call you off and on to keep you apprised."

Evans didn't have a solid plan because he didn't have any real intelligence to go on. "Aye-aye, sir," the gangly petty officer replied.

Evans, Savarese, Swan, and Decker climbed out of the boat dressed in civilian cloths and clambered up the muddy river bank in the same location Masure and Spear had entered the water on their ill-fated diving operation. Fishing gear in hand, Evans and Savarese walked cautiously toward the *Don Blás*. Swan and Decker followed at a distance carrying their operation gear. Keeping to the shadows and foliage they worked their way to the edge of the port district near the bow of the *Don Blás* and there in the bushes they set up an observation site. Using all the high tech surveillance equipment at their disposal they watched and listened until they had located every sentry post.

"This is not going to be easy," Savarese whispered. "Too many lights."

"We're gonna need the boat to get aboard from the riverside," Evans mumbled.

"Not a good plan, Boss," Swan said. "The guy on deck will spot us coming a hundred yards out."

"Got any ideas?" Evans asked.

"We could take out one or two of the pier lights," Decker suggested.

"How are we going to do that, pecker-wood?" Savarese reproved. "Climb the damn pole and unscrew the light bulbs?"

"No, shoot 'em out," Decker said seriously.

"*Shit!*" Savarese hissed. "You bust one of those lights and thirty LBGs will swarming over this place like piss ants," he argued. LBG was his slang for little brown guys.

"Give me a minute to think and I'll come up with something," Evans said.

For several minutes he studied the ship trying to figure out a way to board the vessel without drawing attention to his team.

"Well?" Savarese asked.

"I'm still thinking goddamnit," Evans hushed, frustrated by the problem.

"We could kill the guard on the bow," Savarese suggested.

"And what if they're not on that ship, Boomer? We can't just go around killing people. That'd make us no better than the damn narcos," Evans snapped.

"Maybe we could just walk aboard," Decker suggested.

"There's a watch at the head of the gangway. He'll know all of ship's company, shit-for-brains," Savarese argued.

"If we could just get to that camel at the stern of the ship we could climb her without being seen," Swan proposed.

"How in the hell are we going to do that, *one-eye*. The whole area is lit up like a football field. We'd be in plain view of the watch on that other ship," he said, referring to the *Don Blasón*.

"Boomer's right, Boss. There ain't no way to get aboard without shooting one of the guards," Swan opined.

Evans was still pondering over what to do when a convoy barreled down the road toward them. Two cars with a van in the middle circled around and stopped near the gangway of the *Don Blasón*. Several men jumped out and swarmed the area like army ants.

"Hey, Cap'n. Look at this shit," Swan said, as he handed Evans his binoculars.

Evans focused the field glasses. "Carlos Cataño," he mumbled. "The last time we saw that greasy little bastard he was in Bolivia. I wonder what he's up to?"

"About five foot six and no good," Savarese said.

Cataño walked to the van, said something to the guy in the passenger seat, and pointed in their direction. The gunman jumped out and jogged down the apron toward them then up the gangway of the *Don Blás*.

Evans watched Carlos as he directed several of his henchmen to take up security positions around the van. He opened the side door and two of his *sicarios* dragged a prisoner out of the van. The condemned was wearing a hood over his head and his hands were bound behind his back. Evans's heart raced, thinking it was Master Chief Masure or one of the other missing SEALs.

"Bingo," Savarese whispered.

Then the thugs pulled two more figures out of the van and led the trio to the gangway of the *Don Blasón*. The first captive tripped on the bottom step. One of the *sicarios* slapped the man in the back of the head. Blindly and bound, the man kicked at his attacker and yelled a spate of obscenities. "We're missing two,"

Savarese whispered.

"No," Evans said. "That's not our guys. They're too short for Masure and his crew."

"Sam," Evans whispered, as he tapped Decker on the shoulder.

Decker put down the shotgun microphone and removed his earphones. "Sir?"

"Can you hear anything?" he asked.

"Yeah. They're Colombian and the burly one sure knows how to cuss."

"And now for the bad news, Boss," Swan said. "Both ships are making ready to get underway."

Evans scanned the vessels with Swan's binoculars. Men were rushing about the weather decks preparing to get underway.

"Now what are we going to do?" Decker asked.

"Boomer, call Ryeback and tell him to pick us up."

"Roger that," Savarese replied, as he reached for the radio handset. "Boss?"

"Yeah, Fred."

"Which ship are we gonna board? They're both getting underway."

"Hell I don't know. That one," Evans growled, pointing at the *Don Blás*.

* * *

Outside the steel prison a tugboat took up the strain on a towline causing the vessel to tremble and rock slightly to one side. Masure felt a shudder run through the ship. He rolled out of his bunk and flipped on the light.

"What's was that, Master Chief," Carroll groaned.

"The ship is getting underway," he muttered.

The small compartment where they were sleeping was sweltering in the tropic heat of Colombia and it smelled of sweat and human waste. The privy bucket in the corner was almost full.

Another more forceful shudder ran through the ship.

"What happening?" Spear asked, awakened by the movement.

"The ship is getting underway, sir," Masure replied, with an exhausted exhale. The heat and lack of food and water had sapped his energy.

They hadn't eaten for four days and hunger was gnawing at their backbones.

Masure glanced at his watch. "Two a.m." he said.

"Man am I hungry," Peters sniveled. He rolled over in his rack.

With no portholes and a quarter inch steel hatch for a door, it was impossible to tell the time of day. Their captors had simply forced them in the compartment, bolted the hatch, and abandoned them, leaving them with their personal possessions. Masure and Spear were still wearing their swimming trunks.

"We gotta get out of this place," Simons sang. "If it's the last thing we ever do." Then he turned serious. "Let's bang on the door until someone comes."

"Heat exhaustion," Carroll commented.

"No," Simons said. "Food depravation. If anyone opens that door I'll kill him and raid the galley. C'mon Master Chief. Let's bang on the door," Simons pleaded.

"If you got the energy to bang on that steel hatch, dickwad, go for it," Masure replied.

As Masure climbed in his bunk, Simons crawled out of his. He picked up a large bolt lying in the corner of the compartment and began hammering on the bulkhead. He beat on it with varying degrees of intensity for more than five minutes.

"Simons, stop pounding on the wall," Peters yelled. "There ain't nobody comin'."

"That's bulkhead, knucklehead," Carroll sassed.

"Master Chief, Simons is driving me bat shit," Carroll complained.

Simons kept banging on the hatch until Masure made him stop.

"*Knock it off*, Simons. You made your point. Now get back in your rack and conserve your energy," Masure ordered.

"Aye-aye, Master Chief."

Simons flipped off the light and felt his way back to his bunk. For half an hour the men lay in complete darkness dozing and listening to the ship clang and bang with activity. Then they felt her shudder and vibrate as her screws cut the water.

"We're definitely underway now," Masure remarked. "Destination unknown."

"North," Spear said, matter of factly.

"How do you know that, sir?" Simons asked, curious as to how the young officer knew which way they were sailing.

"Two hundred miles north of Barranquilla is deep water, very deep water. That's were they are going to sink the sub," Spear reasoned.

"And how do you figure that, Lieutenant?" Masure demanded, exercised by the corollary thought that flashed through his mind.

"No sub, no evidence, no problem, Master Chief. That simple," Spear replied.

For several seconds the men were silent, staring into the blackness that surrounded them.

"And no bodies," Simons concluded, echoing Masure's deepest fear.

"I'm not going down without a fight," Carroll bragged. "These bastards are gonna have to shoot me."

"That's exactly what they plan to do, shit for brains," Peters cut.

"Save your energy, men. Our chance will come," Masure coached
278

optimistically. He reflected for a moment then asked, "How long to deep water, L.T.?"

"Fifteen, twenty hours at best," Spear replied.

Okay, thought Masure. *How would Commander Evans get out of this one? He'd think of something creative. What kind of weapons can we make?*

* * *

Evans shadowed the *Don Blás* on her starboard quarter as she headed north toward the Caribbean. He waited until the tug cleared the ship before slowly closing the distance to the freighter. At two hundred yards he scanned the deck with a thermal imager and decided to board the vessel before she reached the sea. The river was flat and smooth, which would make for easier boarding that the open water of the Caribbean.

"Ryeback, give Savarese the helm," he ordered.

"Aye-aye, sir."

Ryeback stepped back and Boomer took the wheel.

"Listen, Ryeback," Evans said. "We're going to board her just forward of the stern on the starboard side. First me, then Swan, then Decker, then Savarese. You've got to coxswain the boat away from the ship without attracting attention. As soon as Boomer has his hand on the caving ladder ease away quietly and drift back on the same angle he uses as an approach. Got it?"

"Yes, sir. I've learned a lot since you put me through training."

"Good. If you're lucky and don't get killed in another three decade you'll have as much experience as Master Chief Savarese. Listen, if you hear any shooting just after we board, look for us in the wake of the ship," Evans continued.

"Got you covered, sir. Alpha Platoon is the best in SEAL Team Two at shipboarding," Ryeback bragged. "That's why we got this mission," he said, referring to their assignment to train the secret Colombian unit.

"Outstanding, then you know the drill," Evans said, patting the petty officer on the back. "Follow the ship at about four hundred yards until we reach open water. Then go back to your base and pray to God that we got the right one."

"Aye, sir."

Evans was following his instincts as well as the information Maria Christina had provided him. The little voice inside his head kept whispering, *They are on the Don Blás. That's the one Stick would have chosen for a target.*

"Now would be a good time, Commander," Savarese suggested. "The clouds are about to cover the moon."

"Let's do it," Evans ordered. He worked his way to the foredeck and joined Swan and Decker with the climbing gear.

Savarese brought the boat slowly up to speed and ran down the outside wake of the freighter closing the range at fifteen knots. When he was ten yards from the ship's hull he throttled down smoothly to minimize the noise of the boat's engines. For a moment Ryeback thought he was going to bump the hull but years of experience proved their worth. The boat settled just under the curve of the ship paralleling her course and speed precisely.

Swan reached up with Alpha Platoon's painter pole and hooked a caving ladder to the railing. While Swan and Decker held the bow of the boat steady with the bottom of the ladder, Evans scaled it like a monkey. In one fluid motion he slid on deck and took cover behind a large bollard post. Seconds later, Swan head peered over the deck. Evans motioned him aboard and covered him with a silenced MP-5 borrowed from the SEAL platoon. Then Decker appeared and slithered quietly under the railing.

When Boomer climbed aboard he tossed the caving ladder overboard and joined Evans behind the bollard.

Decker used the metascope he had hanging around his neck to scan the deck. The tiny night scope turned night to day with an eerie greenish glow.

"Deck's clear, skipper," he reported.

"Aye," Evans whispered. "So far so good," he said to himself.

Evans watched a sailor up on the bridge wing at the O-4 level taking bearings. He knew that all hands would be busy navigating the ship in the confines of the river and that their attention would be focused on ship's work. High up on the bridge wings the lights of the pilothouse blinded the crew to the dark deck below.

"Let's go," he whispered.

With weapons pointing in all four directions they inched their way forward to the superstructure and hid in the clutter of ship's equipment. Using night scopes, imagers, and binoculars they studied the lay of the deck and scurried from cover to cover to the foredeck. Two deck seamen walked right by them, unaware they were just inches away from death.

Using their electronic ability to see in the dark, the SEALs carefully worked their way forward between the large cargo containers that were chained to the steel deck. On the forecastle, Evans selected a secluded hatch that was out of sight of the pilothouse and opened it. He peeked down into the cargo hold, and seeing that it was clear, motioned for the men to follow him.

Inside, the light was dim and the ship smelled of roasted coffee beans. Evans led the patrol forward between rows of semi-truck-sized cargo containers. When he reached the bow he located a line locker large enough for a base of operations and motioned the men inside. With the hatch partially open, Decker took up vigil of the passageway outside the space. Evans plopped down on a bale of rags and leaned back to rest his weary body. They had been on the move for days and he was feeling like a SEAL trainee in the middle of hell week.

Savarese whispered, "What's the plan, Boss?"

For a few seconds Evans was silent. He closed his eyes and took several deep breaths. Then he said, "We still don't know if they're aboard this vessel, right?"

"Right," Savarese answered. He strained to see Evans's face partially illuminated by the dim light coming in through the crack in the hatch.

"So what are we missing, Boomer?" Evans asked.

"Intel, Boss," Swan interjected.

"Exactly. And what do deck seamen do when a ship gets underway?" Evans continued.

Savarese grinned. "Make ready for sea?"

A light had just gone off in his head. He knew exactly what Evans was thinking.

"There you go again grinning like a possum eating crap," Evans said. "You have to start camouflaging your teeth."

"Sooner or later someone is going to come down here to check the gripes," Decker said.

"You got it. And we're going to have a little chat with him," Swan said.

"Listen guys," Evans whispered. "We got enough fire power to sink this garbage scow. But we don't know what we're up against and we don't know were Masure and the boys are located, or even if they're on board this vessel. What I want to do is snatch the crew one at a time, very quietly, like a spider. We'll set a trap and wait for them to walk into a web of our making. Then we'll bring 'em here, interrogate 'em, and truss 'em up like flies. If it takes us all damn day to clear the decks, so be it."

"What if someone spots us?" Decker asked.

"If he's got a gun we'll kill him and take the vessel by force," Evans replied.

"Sounds like a plan," Swan said.

"I'm game," Decker whispered.

"The first step is to memorize the forward compartments and the cargo hold. So let's go do it," Evans said, getting up off the bale of rags.

For a half-hour the SEALs cautiously patrolled around the cargo hold memorizing the area like the killing ground of an ambush site. As they maneuvered, one protecting the other with overwatch, they removed bulbs from several of the lights fixtures reducing the light level inside the hold. They checked hatches and compartments and took note the dark places to take cover in a hurry.

As Evans predicted, when the ship began to roll in the waves of the Caribbean Sea, a sleepy sailor entered the hold and began checking the gripes on the cargo containers. They were stacked two high in long rows that ran fore and aft. Each container had gripes that ran down to the deck on the diagonals. The containers were designed for a crane to lift out of the hold and lower onto the back of semi-trucks. Each was heavy enough to sink the ship if it broke loose in heavy weather. The sailor diligently worked his way forward from container to container physically checking each chain for tautness.

Near the bow he found the one Savarese had loosened. As he worked to release the chock-bar, Boomer crept up behind him. He was struggling to take up a link of chain when the big SEAL placed a paw over his mouth and lifted him up off the deck. The frightened sailor nearly urinated in his pants. He was an older man in his late forties and he was worn beyond his days by years of backbreaking work as a merchant seaman. Swan grabbed his legs and the two SEALs carried him to the line locker like a roll of carpet.

Evans used a soft sell to interrogate the sailor. The first question he asked was the name of the ship's captain. He was surprised when the Colombian answered without reservation.

"How many men aboard this vessel?" Evans asked.

The sailor shrugged his shoulders and gave the Commander a stupid look.

Evans knew a ship the size of the *Don Blás* carried a crew of about ten men, so he asked, "More than twenty?"

The sailor's eyes grew in size when Evans balled up his fist and glared at him with a mean face.

"*Sí, Señor. Mas o menos - more or less.*"

"Are any gringos aboard?"

"*Sí, Señor,*" he answered, with fear written all over his face.

With penetrating eyes Evans glared at the sailor. "*Cuantos - how many?*" he growled like a junkyard dog.

"*Cinco,*" the lowly sailor blurted.

Evans breathed a little easier knowing that all five men were aboard the ship. From the interrogation he gleaned the intelligence he needed to plan the ship's takedown. He scratched a sketch of the vessel on the deck of the line locker and had the sailor draw in the location of every item of importance on the vessel. At ten in the morning another sailor entered the hold looking for his missing mate and received similar treatment. Evans cross-referenced the information to ensure the first man was telling him the truth then he waited for his next victim. By four in the afternoon he had more than half the crew bound, gagged, and bolted in a small out of the way compartment adjacent to the chain locker.

From the sailors Evans learned that the *Don Blás* carried a regular crew of a dozen sailors augmented by ten *sicarios* assigned to guard five Americans. Only a few members of the crew had knowledge of the submarine fastened to the ship's belly and none of them were in the Seal's makeshift brig in the bow of the ship. Evans was missing a key piece of intelligence when he planned the takedown of the *Don Blás*.

Chapter 33

The steel hatch groaned opened and a man armed with a MAC-10 stood outside the compartment. A half-dozen armed *sicarios* lined the passageway backing him up.

"*Un hombre venga aqui!*" he ordered, pointing his weapon at the famished SEALs.

They were lying in their racks stacked like cadavers in a morgue.

"What does he want? Carroll asked.

"He wants one of us to go with him," Spear answered. "I'll do it."

"No, L.T." Masure whispered. "Make him come to us. Then we jump him."

Masure was hoping for an opportunity to grab a weapon and force a gun battle he knew he could win. The gunman pointed the weapon at Spear and motioned with the barrel.

"*Un hombre venga aqui!*" he ordered.

Spear shook his head no and the gunman smiled. He stepped to the side of the open hatch and cut loose with a two-second burst from the machine pistol. Lead fragments ricocheted off the deck and careened all around the steel compartment like BB's inside a matchbox.

"*Goddamnit I'm hit!*" Masure yelled.

One of the bullets had ricocheted off the deck and penetrated the bottom of his bunk. It cut into the flesh of his buttock and buried up a half inch under the skin.

"*Anyone else hit?*" Spear shouted.

"I'm okay," Peters yelled.

"Me too," Carroll shouted.

"I'm alright," Simons reported.

"How badly are you hit, Master?" Spear asked.

"Not bad. *Goddamnit to hell!* Flesh wound," he groaned, feeling lump in his buttock.

"*Ahora! Un hombre venga aqui. Immediatamente!*" the gunman bellowed.

Spear crawled out of his rack and staggered to the hatch, light-headed from lack of food and water. As he stepped out of the compartment he made a move to grab the man's gun. The *sicarios* behind the hatch cold cocked him in the back of the head, sending him to the deck with a thud. They laughed at his feeble attempt at heroics.

"*Otro hombre mas,*" the leader growled.

Masure slipped out of his bunk and limped toward the doorway looking for an opportunity. But before he stepped through the hatch one of the *sicarios* stuck a pistol to the back of Spear's head and grinned.

"Make my day, you stupid fuckeem gringo," the gunman said, trying to sound like Dirty Harry.

Masure stepped out into the passageway and without resistance let them force him to his knees where they tied his hands behind his back.

When all the SEALs where bound the gunmen led them deeper into the bowels of the ship. They crossed through engineering to a location just behind the cargo hold and opened a small compartment near the centerline of the ship. Once all of the men were inside they sealed the hatch. The small compartment contained a submarine-type hatch bolted to the bottom of the hull just to the right of the keel. One of the gunmen opened it and motioned for Spear to climb down the ladder.

"I can't climb down that ladder with my hands tied behind my back," he complained.

The leader of the mercenaries shrugged and nodded at his men. Two gunmen grabbed Spear from behind, forced his legs into the hole, and shoved him down the hatch. Spear fell five feet and landed with a thump on the deck of the submarine. When he got to his feet his head was above the hatch. One of the *sicario* tried to kick him in the face. Masure seized the moment and shoved the thug with his shoulder just in time to prevent him from soccer kicking his officer. When he regained his balance, he planted a front snap kick in the man's gut and spun around to face the other *sicarios*. With his hands tied behind his back he was unable to parry the blow that sent him to the deck. His act of courage resulted in a brutal beating. They kicked and stomped him repeatedly then dumped him head first down the hatch. He would have broken his neck on the steel deck of the submarine if Lieutenant Spear hadn't of broken his fall with a body block.

One by one the *sicarios* forced the SEALs into the submarine and bolted the hatch. In the cramped confines of the sub the SEALs struggled to untie themselves in total darkness. Confusion and fear reigned as they cussed and struggled with their restrains. Simons was the first to work himself loose by rubbing his ropes on a sharp-edged piece of metal. Once free, he felt his way from man to man untying them.

"*Everyone feel around for a battle lantern!*" Masure ordered, guessing that there would be a battery-powered light somewhere inside the submarine.

For ten minutes they groped about in total darkness before Carroll flipped a switch that illuminated their dire predicament.

"Boss, we are in a world of shit," Carroll exclaimed, looking at the controls in the submarine.

"It ain't over till it's over," Masure muttered, with more bravado than he felt.

"Right, Master," Spear concurred. "Let's figure out how to fly this boat."

Simons looked at the air pressure gages and said, "No one's going to fly this boat, sir. The air tanks are empty and the ballast tanks are flooded."

"We'll sink like a rock if they release us," Peters said.

"You mean when they release us," Carroll added.

"I said, it ain't over until it's over, *damnit,*" Masure snarled, searching for an answer. Both he and Spear saw a major flaw in the construction of the sub at the same time.

* * *

The *Don Blasón* came to an all-stop and coasted for fifteen minutes before the vessel was traveling slow enough to release the submarine. The men inside the steel coffin heard the locking mechanism scrapping on the hull and they felt the sub fall free. Without its lifesaving bubble of air to float upon it sank quickly gaining speed with depth. They knew what was coming. Their minds raced crazily in sheer terror.

I'm going to die. Oh God, this can't be happening to me. This is a nightmare. I can't die. I'm too young. Oh God I'm sorry for all the bad things I've done. Please give me another chance. Please.

Designed for shallow water, at two hundred feet the hull began to groan and creak in agony under stresses that exceeded its limits. Risitos thought he heard a voice call out his name. He looked at Ramón and Lucho. Their eyes were filled with terror, their mouths open with fear. Mucus was running from Ramón cocaine inflamed nose. Lucho was babbling prayers and crossing himself.

"Risitos," the voice repeated from somewhere outside in the deep dark ocean. It echoed hollowly, metallically, through his mind, its syllables rolling at him like the waves of the sea.

"*But I don't want to die!*" he screamed, fighting against the voice and the noise of the creaking hull.

"Risitos", the voice said. "Soon there will be a brief moment of excruciating agony and you will be no more. The body you inhabit will be crushed and the fish will eat your flesh. You will not see. You will not feel. You will not taste. You will be no more."

"*I don't want to die! I don't want to die!*" he wailed, saliva projecting from his exposed teeth.

Risitos felt Ramón and Lucho screaming but he couldn't hear them. His mind was in overwhelm.

I'm going to die, he thought.

He took out his bag of cocaine and began vacuuming up the white powder, snorting and coughing, taking in as much of the narcotic as he could. At three hundred feet, water tight seals began to rupture and jets of cold seawater began to spray at them from all direction. Encumbered by the spray, Risitos began eating the white powder right out of the bag, sucking it up across his teeth.

At five hundred feet the sub nosed over and began a bow first descent into the abyss. Inside the Savajés struggled to hang on to the shifting deck, to cling to their last seconds of life. Absolute terror, enhanced by the chemical fire of cocaine, reverberated through Ramón's skulls. But not Risitos. He was smiling his permanent smile, waiting for that moment of exquisite pain. He intended to enjoy the last moment of agony his body would know. Then the hull buckled like a beer can underneath the wheels of a tandem truck, crushing the life out of their bodies in one gushing implosion.

* * *

Evans felt the ship come to all-stop. He gave the men a puzzled look, checked his weapon, and got up off the bale of rags he was resting on. "Let's go do it."

"Yeah," Savarese growled, as he counted the number of magazines he had in his ammunition pouch. "I'm hungry."

"Me too," Decker agreed.

They patrolled back through the crowded cargo hole and climbed up on a short mezzanine deck that crossed athwart ships. At the back bulkhead Savarese opened a small hatch and peeked inside. Seeing the way was clear they entered and patrolled down a narrow passageway that ran above the engineering spaces. Beneath the main superstructure they entered the berthing area and located the compartment where they expected to find Masure and the other SEALs. With Savarese and Decker standing guard, Evans and Swan checked the empty compartment. Swan spotted the full privy bucket and pointed to it without speaking. Evans picked up a spent projectile off the deck. Then he saw blood on the deck.

"This doesn't look good. I hope we're not too late."

"Let's go kick ass, Commander," Swan said.

With Savarese at point they moved out down the passageway toward the galley. When he reached the berthing compartment that the ship's crew had told them was being used by the *sicarios*, they stacked on the door. Savarese opened it wide and Evans rushed in with Decker and Swan right on his heels. They caught three gunmen playing cards. One of them saw the SEALs and made a move for his gun. Swan double tapped him in the chest before he could bring his weapon to bear. The sound of the projectiles striking the man's ribs was louder than the receiver of the cycling MP-5. The young *sicario* clawed at his chest in disbelief as if trying to remove fragments of hot metal. With his companions staring in shock, he slumped to the deck and died frothing blood from his open mouth. The other two gunmen held their hands in the air and begged for their lives.

"*No fuego! Por favor! No fuego!*"

"*Donde estan los Norte Americanos?*" Evans demanded.

When neither of the *sicarios* answered he planted a front snap kick in the nearest man's crotch doubling him up like a rag doll. Evans hammered him in the back of the head with his rifle butt. He looked at the other youth with fierce eyes and slowly raised the can on the MP-5 to crotch level.

Looking down at the man's privates he said, "I will kill you slowly if you don't answer my question. Where are the Americans?"

"In the submarine, *señor*. They are in the submarine," the youth blurted in fear for his manhood.

Evans was confused. "*Don't fuck with me!*" He shoved the can of his MP-5 into the kid's chest thrusting him back into the bulkhead. Then he aimed the weapon at his head.

With eyes wild with fear the young killer pleaded for his life. "They are in the submarine, *señor*," he cried, certain that Evans was going to shoot him in the face.

"What submarine?" Evans growled, confused by the information.

When the sicario explained that there was a sub attached to the bottom of the ship, a light went on inside Evans's head. He had heard rumors that a big South American cartel was using a North Korean submarine to infiltrate dope into the U.S. but he hadn't seen any evidence that the rumors were true. It dawned on him why the Ballesteros were so profitable. They were the biggest traffickers in all of South America and the smartest.

"Sterilize this compartment," he ordered. "This little asshole is going to take us to a submarine."

Evans and Savarese stood guard as Swan and Decker tied up the unconscious *sicario*. They were wrapping the dead man up in a sheet when a young Colombian killer barged in the compartment, followed by several of his companions. He took two steps into the room before he saw Swan and Decker stooping over the body of his associate. For an instant he tried to make sense of the bizarre scene. Then he saw Evans, weapon in hand. As he turned to run, Savarese bashed him in the side of the head with his rifle butt. Surprised, the second gunman took one step back, mouth open. Before he could bring his weapon to bear, Evans hit him with two rounds in the head, knocking him back against the bulkhead. In a death spasm he pulled the trigger on his MAC-10. Ricochets pinged off the deck and steel bulkheads. Savarese rushed out through the doorway and fired at the third gunman who was bolting down the passageway. Frightened out of his senses, the youth ducked around a corner just as Savarese squeezed the trigger. 9mm projectiles pinged off the steel near his head.

"*Damnit, I missed him!*" Savarese yelled.

With the sound of the MAC-10 going off the element of surprise was gone.

"*They know we're here*," Evans yelled. "Let's hit 'em before they have a chance to regroup."

With Savarese shoving the young Colombian down the passageway in front of them, and Decker covering rear security, the SEALs moved out in the opposite direction from the *sicario* that had escaped. At the first athwart ships passageway they crossed to the port side of the ship and doubled back. When they reached the galley they stacked on the door with Decker taking up rear security. Evans put his ear to the door and listened for a few seconds.

"There are several of them in there," he whispered. "Let's take 'em."

On Evans's signal Savarese bulldozed their prisoner through the door and the SEALs rushed in behind him, spitting off in four directions. They surprised three *sicarios* on the other side of the galley talking in rapid fire Spanish trying to figure out what to do. One of them was the man who had gotten away. Out of instinct they engaged the SEALs. Hot lead ricocheted off the steel deck and bulkheads, flying in all direction. The SEALs, trained for such firefights, carefully aimed their weapons and shot to kill. The gun battle only lasted a few seconds but the results were deadly. The three gunmen lay in a heap, bleeding from numerous sucking chest and head wounds. One of them gurgled and gasped for breath racked by the white-hot agony buried in his chest.

"*Anyone hit?*" Evans bellowed.

"Yeah," Decker groaned. "I caught one in the thigh."

"I'm hit, Boss," Swan gasped, trying to get his breath.

He was leaning against a galley table holding his side. As he stumbled to the knees, blood oozed between his fingers.

Evans yanked tablecloths off a galley table and began ripping it into strips.

"Keep a sharp watch on that little asshole," he said to Savarese.

"You bet." Boomer shoved the Colombian to a more defensible position where he could cover both sides of the galley.

"Decker?"

"Yes, sir."

"Crawl over here by Swan and dress out your wound," he said, tossing several table napkins and strips of cloth on the deck near Swan.

"Yes, sir," Decker grunted.

Evans began working on Swan. "This is not so bad, Fred," he exclaimed, inspecting the wound. "The bullet hit the rib but it missed the lung and the liver."

"It just knocked the breath out of me, sir. I'll be okay in a minute," he groaned.

"Keep pressure on it," he said, placing Swan's hand on the layers of cloth he had put over the wound.

He quickly inspected Decker's field expedient dressing. "Good job. Keep an eye on Fred, okay?"

"We'll be alright, Commander," Decker insisted. "You guys go kill the rest of the bastards."

With both men complaining, Evans dragged them to a defensive position and checked their weapons to ensure they were ready for action.

"We'll be back as soon as we finish taking down the ship. Let's go, Boomer."

Evans and Savarese headed for the bowels of the ship with the young *sicario* out in front of them like a shield. He led them down to engineering and forward to the submarine compartment. Just as the thug opened the hatch, the *sicario* leader released the boat. Evans felt the sub scrap the bottom of the ship as it drifted free. Bring his weapon to bear, he shot the gunman in the head, dashed to the locking mechanism and yanked it back into positions. But it was too late. The sub was gone. He looked at Savarese with eyes that betrayed his emotions.

"*Let's go!*" he yelled.

As he turned Savarese cold-cocked the young *sicario* who had led them to the compartment knocking him unconscious. He bolted the door behind them and followed Evans as he raced up through the ship toward the pilothouse. When they ran onto the bridge, the captain and the helmsman threw up their hands and stared at them in shock. The look on the SEALs' faces was enough to frighten the captain out of his wits.

"*The submarine! The submarine!*" Evans yelled, pointing his MP-5 at the captain's face.

Evans's eyes were ablaze and his body was pumping adrenaline. The captain pretended not to understand, so Evans shoved the can of his MP-5 into the man's mouth, knocking him into the bulkhead and folding his teeth back. The surprised mariner grabbed his mouth with both hands. As blood and saliva spewed between his fingers, Evans scanned the sea all around the ship. In the distance he saw the *Don Blasón* and behind them near the stern of the ship, several objects bobbing up and down in the water.

"*Look!*" he shouted, pointing aft with his weapon. "*What's that?*"

"*Water breathers, Captain!*" Savarese smiled. "*Water breathers!* I'll go toss 'em a line."

Savarese ran down from the bridge wing and back to the stern of the ship.

"*Hey, pretty boy! How fast can you swim?*" he yelled at Masure.

Masure spotted Savarese standing on the stern of the ship. At first he couldn't believe his eyes.

"*Well I'll be damned!* C'mon guys. Let's catch that garbage scow before a shark starts to chew on my ass."

Masure swam to the leeward side of the vessel and yelled up at Savarese. "What took you long, big guy?" he complained.

Savarese tossed down a line.

"We had to dispose of the trash," Savarese replied.

Masure scaled the hawser like a monkey, fearful sharks were on the blood trail he was leaving in the water. Savarese helped him climb aboard.

"How did you guys get out of that sub?" he asked.

"You're not going to believe this, Boomer. That damn thing was made in North Korea," Masure explained.

"So?"

"Would you believe the hatch opened inward?" he exclaimed.

"No way."

Then he remembered that the hatch on the bottom of the ship opened up into the compartment and the hatch to the compartment opened inward toward the sub.

"Ahhh. That's why that compartment is so small. It's a safety lock to keep the ship from sinking if the bottom hatch fails," he muttered.

In order to mate the two vessels, the hatches had been reversed from those of a deep water submarine. Savarese chuckled as he visualized the SEALs holding their breath as the sea flooded the boat. Before it sank too deeply they had opened the hatch, flooded the boat and swum free.

"How long were you planning on treading water out here, little buddy?" Savarese chuckled.

"As long as it took, Boomer. Say, do we own this ship?" Masure asked, looking around the empty deck.

"You bet we do?"

When everyone was aboard Savarese led the way up to the pilothouse. Evans began issuing orders without so much as a howdy.

"Lieutenant."

"Yes, sir," Spear answered.

"I'll maintain control of the bridge. Take your men and follow Master Chief Savarese. Boomer, escorted them below decks *and arm them!* Then I want you to conduct a compartment by compartment search of this vessel. Assemble all prisoners here on the bridge."

"Yes, sir," Savarese replied. He gave Evans a backhanded Aussie salute and waved for the men to follow him below decks.

"I'm hungry," he growled as he walked away shaking his head.

* * *

When the *Flash* cruised up alongside four hours later, Evans and company were in complete control of the ship. He left Swan and Decker on the *Don Blás* and boarded the sleek hydrofoil. In less than a half an hour Gomez caught the *Don Blasón* steaming at full speed for Colombian waters. He blew by her at fifty knots and fired one broadside with his minigun against her steel hull. The projectiles stripped the paint off and made a terrible racket, but they didn't do any serious damage to the freighter. The action was a warning and it made the point. The *sicarios* on board the vessel threw down their weapons and held up their hands.

Evans, Gomez, and six men board the *Don Blasón* without resistance. They dashed to the bridge and once in control, fanned out in two, four-man groups to clear the ship. Evans and Savarese came upon Carlos Cataño burning records in the captain's quarters. When he saw Evans working his way down the passageway with an assault rife in his hand, he threw down his pistol, darted out through the ship's galley, and ran as fast as he could for the bowels of the vessel. Running around corners and down ladders, he headed for the sub compartment where he had rigged the ship with explosives. Wanting the man alive, the SEALs gave chase. Carlos was halfway to the fuse, pumped up on adrenaline and out of breath, when he hurled himself down a ladder, slipped, and fell eight feet to the steel deck below. When Evans found him he was semiconscious and dying.

* * *

Ray Keith was seated on a bench in Riberalta, Bolivia, watching the world go by down the muddy clay road when he spotted an old ford truck puttering down mainstreet toward him. He spat out a gob of tobacco juice and wiped his beard. The rain had stopped for a brief respite and the natives were restless. Motorbikes squirted by loaded down with three and four people. The kids on the back waved at him and he waved back. Three men seated near him were playing their trumpets off key practicing for a local festival. He watched as the truck bounced along from pothole to rutted mire, its springs and suspension worn out from overuse. As it got closer he recognized it. It was from Trinidad. It was missing the front bumper and the bed in back had been modified to carry prisoners. As it came near a chicken pecking in the road barely got out of the way. It squawked and darted into the path of a motorbike overloaded with people. Neither driver paid any attention to the bird. It survived the mean streets of Riberalta by providence. Keith strained his neck to see who was driving. Three of the sheriff's goons were in front smoking and joking. As the ancient vehicle putted on down the road toward Trinidad he saw *Viscoso* and *Resbaloso* chained in the back like scruffy dogs.

* * *

I've always reached too high. Now I can see the tragic side of blind ambition. Oh God, I feel the hole in my soul, Carol Galán thought.

For a moment she thought of suicide.

I can feel them closing in on me, like these four walls. I've seen their tracks. Closer and closer. But today it doesn't matter. Why Carol? Because it's brought your to your knees. That's why. You say you won't do it and then you do. You even walk away from your own reflection because you don't want to see what's written in your own eyes.

"I'm afraid of what I'll see, she mumbled.

And all I have to do to end this madness is destroy this tiny little magic pebble, this small lump of chemicals. And myself. Only I know the secret.

For a moment she saw herself flying over the cliff holding the drug in the palm of her hand. In a daze she put on her poncho, grabbed her backpack, and sneaked off into the jungle. It was raining again, but she didn't care. The jungle was alive with the sound of water dripping down through the canopy, cleansing the earth and renewing life.

She walked to her viewpoint and stared out at the abyss. The dark clouds that had drenched the rain forest for days were missing for the first time in weeks. Below her, the rivers were swollen and the savannah was inundated.

In the real world, children cry at night. Hunger and survival are the world they're born into, a junkie's world. In the real world, junkies kill for a fix. Because it's the real world they want to escape. I wanted so much to help them and in doing so help the children that depend upon them. But I have trapped myself in a web of my own making and I can't escape. But if I step over the edge of this cliff, no one will ever know this thing I've come to know. It's so bizarre no one will ever know, if I'm dead. Even Rodrigo doesn't know his secret.

In her mind's eye she saw the shaman conjuring up the spirits from the coca plant he had named after his wife Rosa. She was buried beneath it. Before harvesting the leaves, he chanted around the plant shaking his magic bag of potions, a concoction of plant, bone, and insect matter. Paying respect to his dead wife and the earth goddess that cared for her, he mumbled and sang his ancient prayers. Carol could almost see the moat around the plant filled with a secret liquid that wilted the leaves in the tropical sun. That was the key. C_{31} was made from the plant called Rosa, a special plant Rodrigo cherished. Something in the tonic entered the leaves, wilting them before he picked them. Carol knew it was an honor that Rodrigo had given her the Rosa leaves. They were special to him. They were the leaves he chewed on ceremonial occasions.

Rodrigo prays to the narco god to keep us in the real world. But I don't want to stay in the real world. They're going to find me and they'll make me tell. Then there will be a new drug to poison and ravage the minds of those who are trying to escape the real world. If I can't quit, neither can the weak of spirit. When they find me they will find Rodrigo and they will kill him and his family.

Carol took a small green elliptical shaped leaf out of her pocket and offered it to the jungle. She held it out over the edge of the cliff and dropped it, symbolically let herself go with it. But the tiny leaf of the Rosa coca bush refused to fall. A rising gust of wind picked it up and carried it back up the cliff face. When it was ten feet above her it drifted out of the wind stream and fell at her feet, defying her.

It is a sad irony that mankind misuses the gifts of nature. We turn harmless life-giving chemicals like ammonium nitrate into explosives and blow up little children in the name of Yahweh and Allah and Vishnu.

She picked up the Rosa leaf and felt its smooth surface.

We reduce the natural medicines of nature to a scourge. The alkaloid extracted from this tiny little leaf is the only known naturally occurring anesthesia on Earth. Yet from this blessing we manufacture a terrible magic. The tyrannies unleashed by this little leaf fills prisons with the poor and the ignorant, kills police, corrupts governments, fuels wars, ravages brains, and destroys souls. Those that turn to cocaine seek the euphoric sense of power and success that alludes them in the real world. In the real world you can hear hungry children cry at night. In the real world the weak of spirit can't bear to see less than the sum of what they are. Seeking the euphoria of the soul, they find themselves adrift in oblivion, reaching for something beyond their senses. Yet mankind has survived the ages, conquered other more terrible agonies, defeated the microbial forces that have plagued us since the beginning of time. And we have done so using a much greater magic than that produced by erythroxylon coca.

"The power of the human brain. The power to understand. Will power," she said out loud.

I have to cleanse my mind. I have to end this solitude. You are not going over this cliff, Carol. Not now. Not ever. You are not going to lose your desire to live nor your will to fight for a better world.

She thought of a picture she had seen in Derek Evans's office. It was a cartoon of a crane swallowing a frog. She smiled as she pictured the frog headfirst half in the crane's mouth, half out. In cartoon fashion the frog was reaching down the crane's long neck to pinch off the bird's throat with a huge hand preventing it from swallowing the tenacious amphibian. Below the cartoon was a caption that read: *Never give up!*

"Okay. Commander stuck-on-yourself know-it-all Derek Evans. You want to see me? Well you're going to see me. A new me. I'm going to find you," she muttered.

She left the viewpoint with renewed determination.

Carol hiked to the waterfall and looked out over the river for Slippery and Slimy. Their delivery was overdue by several days. She was about to climb down the cliff face to check her cache site when she heard something move behind her. Turning to look, she screamed. Leering at her was a slim Hispanic male with Indian-black hair tied tightly back tango-dancer style. Carol reached down for her pistol.

"Don't do that, Dr. Galán," he hissed, in a voice she could barely hear over the sound of the thundering waterfall. He waved the barrel of his pistol at her as if shaking his finger at a naughty child. "I have been looking for you for a very long time," he said.

"Who are you?"

"*Don Conrado Cataño Gaviria* at you service, *señorita*."

"What do you want?" Carol demanded.

"I would very much like to see your laboratory. Dr. Galán," he said gallantly.

Carol turned to run with every intention of leaping over the waterfall, but two men blocked the path not ten feet away. When she turned back to face Gaviria, he was amused.

"I'm not going to give you the formula if that's what you're thinking," she said defiantly.

"Oh, yes you will," Gaviria insisted. "And *you will* tell me everything about your little project Mandrake."

"*I'll kill myself first!*"

"No. No you will not. I have very special plans for you, *Doctora*."

Gaviria took a step closer and stared into her eyes expecting to see fear. But what he saw was a slight smile, a little twinkle of hope. Then he saw the mouths of his two henchmen gaping open and their eyes riveted behind him. He slowly turned around to look down the barrel of Evans's 1911 Colt .45.

With Latino bravado he sneered. "Evans. How did you find this place? I got the boatmen."

"I've been watching you, asshole," Evans answered, without blinking his eyes, his pistol aimed squarely at Gaviria's head.

"This, *amigo*, I anticipated," Gaviria smirked, with too much confidence. "Me following you, you following me. My men following your men." He looked back up the trail behind Evans. Two of his men were hidden in the foliage. "And I have more men than you do, *amigo*. There are five of us and only one of you. Let's make a deal. You walk away and I pay you, say, eight hundred grand. It's not a million but you don't have to die trying to get it."

"You forget how to count, *amigo*?" Evans said, derisively. "There are two of us."

Gaviria glanced around the jungle.

"Oh, you mean this woman?" he sneered sarcastically. "This bitch?" he asked, incredulously pointing behind him with his thumb. "You will bet you life on this woman?"

"I taught her how to shoot and most of your men too," Evans said. "Now drop your weapon or I'll take off *your* head."

Gaviria's face was without emotion as he slowly extended his arms out to his sides, pistol still in hand, and slowly turned around to face Carol. Using his eyes, he ordered his men to make a move for the bushes.

"Evans, I don't believe you're the kind of man who would shoot me in the back," he said.

"Bet your life on it, *traficante*," Evans growled. "You'll be the first to die."

"Nine hundred. All you have to do is take a walk, Evans."

"No deal."

"Okay. A million. That's my final offer."

"Not a chance."

Gaviria lifted his chin ever so slightly and the men behind Carol lunged off the trail in opposite directions. He waited for the report of the first round before making his lightning fast cheetah move. Six quick shots reverberated through the jungle in sets of two. *Bang-band! Bang-bang! Bang-bang!* Followed by a burst of automatic weapons fire, as the third gunmen in front of Evans died, finger on his trigger. Gaviria was the second to die, splattered in the side of the head by two rounds that exploded his skull. He fell on the wet earth at Carol's feet.

Evans saw it all in slow motion. As he engaged the third *sicario*, he saw Carol Galán's pistol slide smoothly out of its holster and rise to eye level, pointing in his direction. Falling backwards, he yelled, "*No!*" fearing for Savarese, who was hidden up the trail.

He felt the disturbance in the air as her projectiles whizzed by his face. Before he hit the ground a bullet ripped into the side of his leg.

Carol Galán collapsed on her knees and began sobbing, staring at her pistol. After all her practice she had missed.

Rolling to cover, Evans pumped two rounds into a tree trunk, changed magazines, and fired two more. Then he sighted in and waited until a young *sicario* exposed himself to take another shot. Evans squeezed his trigger gently. He caught the youth between the eyes, exploding his head like a melon. Pounded back by the force of the heavy bullet, the body crashed into the foliage and began to spasm. Seeing the gruesome scene, his partner sprinted through the jungle, zigzagging as he ran. Evans heard the sound of shots echo through the jungle and then a booming voice called out from up the trail.

"*You okay, Boss*?" Savarese yelled.

"*Yeah! Hold your position! There may be more of them!*" Evans shouted.

Evans staggered to his feet and limped to where Carol knelt sobbing on the ground. He took her into his arms and held her.

"I'm sorry," she said. "I tried so hard to learn how to do it. I just couldn't shoot a human being."

"It's okay," he said, brushing her hair out of her face. "Everything is going to be alright."

He held her for a few moments, scanning the jungle around them for more *sicarios*.

When she regained her composure she said, "You're hurt. Let me see."

"It's only flesh wound, thanks to you. You made 'em miss."

"Let me see," she demanded.

As skilled as a medical doctor, she dressed his wound using a medical kit she removed from her backpack.

"Will you go with me?" he asked softly.

"Yes. But first I have something I must do," she said, in a distant voice.

She took the plastic Ziploc bag out of her backpack. Evans knew what she was holding in her hand. He waited and watched the jungle around them as she walked to the river's edge. For a few seconds she hesitated, staring at the lustrous grey pebble, wavering at life's edge. Then she looked back at Evans for strength. She could see he was in pain. Blood was staining the bandages she had placed over his wounds. But he didn't let it show on his face. It was in his eyes. Without speaking he communicated his thoughts. Carol stared at the narcotic, not wanting to let it go. Something deep inside told her she had to go over the falls with the drug, to end it once and for all. Still under the influence of the chemical, she heard the water thundering over the edge, and birds singing in the trees, and a frog. It was croaking with all the energy in its tiny body. Like flipping the pages of a book, the image of the poster in Evans's office popped into her head.

"Never give up, said the frog," she murmured. "*Ribbit. Never give up!*"

She poured the pea-sized chunk of matter in the water and watched the raging current carry it over the falls.

"There may be more of them out here," he cautioned, anxiously scanning the jungle around them. "We'd better be movin' along."

She acknowledged the caution with a nod of her head and walked back to where he way lying on the ground.

She helped him to his feet and said, "I'm not worried. I'm not alone anymore and I know what I want out of life." She looked him directly in the eyes and spoke with an accent that sounded like Fred Swan's desert twang, "Besides, you can handle 'em, Boss."

He looked deep into her eyes and replied, "We can handle 'em."

As they walked down the trail Evans yelled, "*Boomer?*"

"*Yeah, Boss.*"

"*Check your fire! We're comin' at you!*"

"*Roger that!*"

Epilogue

Derek Evans picked up the telephone on the second ring. "Sock ink," he grunted, referring the corporate nickname for Special Operations Consultants, Incorporated.

"Commander Evans?" asked a sexy voice on the other end of the line.

"Retired," he corrected, citing his current status.

"Did you have fun in the jungle, Derek?"

"I certainly did, Alysin. And I'm still waiting for my paycheck," he grumbled.

"That's not my department, Commander. But I might be able to help push things along if you answer a few question for me."

"Ahhh, shit," Evans growled, displeased by the suggestion. "Shoot."

"We should talk in person. Why don't you come to D.C.? We could have dinner and share a bottle of wine while we chat," Harris proposed, in her most seductive voice.

"No can do."

"That's too bad," Harris said, disappointed by the rejection. "Now that you are millionaire you really must take some time to smell the flowers."

For a few seconds silence reigned.

"What do you want, Alysin?"

"So, what gives with the rumor of the third party?" Harris asked, in her most evasive English.

"You're the expert," Evans said sarcastically. "You tell me."

"What's your source?"

"I don't have a source," Evans admitted.

"Evans, I know how you operate. You have a source."

"No Alysin. I don't," Evans replied emphatically.

"If you'd came to work with me, we'd have lots of them."

"Not a chance."

She changed the subject.

"Tell me, what happened to *Señor Gaviria*? He was one of my best sources, you know."

"He got shot," Evans answered, flatly.

"Was he dealing with the Russians?" Harris asked.

"I don't know."

"You were the last to speak with him. What did he have to say?"

"Something like; A million. That's my final offer."

"Evidently he should have offered you two million. He was next in line to take over the cattle and coffee business, you know."

"He was playing *you* and the Savajés like a fiddle."

The accusation annoyed her.

"And how do you know this, *Commander Extraordinaire?*" she asked, in a derisive tone. "How do you know that I wasn't playing him like a fiddle?"

"And me too, huh?" Evans asked.

"I would never do that," she said smartly. "And Carlos Cataño? Tell me, what exactly happened to Mr. Cataño?"

"He fell down and bumped his head," Evans replied.

"What happened to the Savajés?"

"They disappeared," Evans said, coldly.

"Let's see. Gaviria got shot. Two of the Cataños got shot. One fell and bumped his head. And the Savajés disappear. The body count rises everywhere you go," Harris accused, sarcastically.

"*Coincidence!*" Evans growled, displeased by the accusation.

An image of the *Flash* speeding up alongside the *Don Blazón* invaded his thoughts. By the time they had boarded her, the submarine, and with it all the evidence against the Ballesteros combine, was gone. Before he died, Carlos had told Evans about Gaviria's plan to take over the organization. With Don Ballesteros as president of the country and the cartel in possession of weapons of mass destruction, they were planning to control the drug trade from South America.

"Don't get me wrong," she added. "I'm not grieving for the dopers. I just want to know what they said before you killed them."

"I'll tell you what, Alysin. I'll write it down and send it to you verbatim. *After I get my paycheck!*"

"Alright. So I've offended you again. One more question," Harris said.

"Take your best shot, maneater."

"How did you know Aguiillar was dirty?" she asked.

"He talks in his sleep," Evans answered.

"I didn't know you slept with men," she quipped, with mock surprise.

"*Give me a break!*" Evans wailed.

After a few moments of silence she said, "You were right, Evans. There was a third party to the exchange. Karpenko is up to his old trick. But I neutralized him, for the moment," she bragged.

Major General Dimitri Karpenko was a rogue spetznaz general who was selling weapons of mass destruction on the black market. In days gone by Harris and Evans had teamed up in Southeast Asia to prevent the sale of nuclear weapons to the Khmer Rouge.

"Do you want one of my old medals, Alysin? I'll send you one in a lead lined box."

"No. I just wanted to let you know that not everyone in the Company is asleep at the wheel."

"I know that, Alysin. I don't have a beef with the Company. It's the whole damn government I'm pissed off at." For a few moments there was silence on the line. Evans changed the subject. "By the way, thanks for helping me out with the charges against Lieutenant Duran," he said sincerely.

"That's the most civil sentence you've uttered to me in more than two years. Tom told me it was a real nice wedding."

"Yes it was," Evans agreed.

Duran had insisted on wearing his naval uniform. It was his last opportunity before resigning from the United States Navy.

"Odds are Lieutenant Duran will be the son-in-law of the next president of Colombia," she said.

"You campaigning for him?" Evans asked.

"No. But I could influence a small contract to train his secret service."

"Screw you, Alysin."

"That's an interesting proposition seeing as how I just offered you dinner and a bottle of wine," she said, with fake disappointment.

"I'm tired of being used, Alysin," Evans grumbled

"*God!* I wouldn't say a million bucks is being used, *Derek Evans, Commander Extraordinaire!* And I'm the reason you got the contract," Harris sassed, incensed by the statement.

"I spent a half mil looking for Carol Galán and I haven't seen a damn dime yet, not even the fifty kay I demanded up front," Evans snarled, raising his voice.

"You'll probably have to come to D.C. and fill out a little paperwork. I could help you out."

"I'm busy," he said.

"The secret service contract? A chance to be on the inside of the new administration," she said, sounding like a game show host. "Going. Going."

"Okay. Okay, Alysin," Evans agreed. "Set it up. If you can."

"I can. Meet Tom Roth at the *Nueva Granada* in Bogotá next Tuesday. Chow," she said pleasantly.

The dial tone assaulted Evans's ear.

"Goddamn *man-eater*," he grumbled under his breath.

He hung up the phone and slumped back in his chair. Jack Duran had already arranged a meeting with his new father-in-law to discuss a training contract and

Evans had the credentials to back it up. SOC Inc. had been training Ballesteros's henchmen for over two years. Training the Colombian Secret Service would be a piece of cake. The last thing he wanted was Tom Roth screwing things up. He picked up the phone and dialed a long distance number in Arizona.

"Swan here," said the voice on the other end of the line.

"Fred."

"Yeah, Boss."

"You all healed up?" Evans asked.

"Yes, sir."

"You know that gig I was telling you about down in Colombia?"

"The secret service thing?" Swan asked.

"Yeah. We got to move a little sooner than I expected. You and Boomer meet me at the *Nueva Granada* Hotel in Bogotá on Friday."

"Roger that. We'll be there," Swan replied.

"See you in Bogotá. *Luego*," Evans growled, as he hung up the phone.